Muriel Zagha grew up in Paris where ~~studied English~~ ~~at the École Normale Supérieure. She cam~~ Britain at the age of 21, as a French lectrice at Cambridge University, and loved living here so much that she forgot to go home. After completing a PhD on Henry James, she escaped from academia into London's fashion world. She now works as a freelance journalist and broadcaster.

She lives in London with her English husband and their son.

Muriel Zagha

FINDING MONSIEUR RIGHT

EBURY
PRESS

3 5 7 9 10 8 6 4

Published in 2010 by Ebury Press, an imprint of Ebury Publishing
A Random House Group Company

The Random House Group Limited Reg. No. 954009

Addresses for companies within the Random House Group can be found at
www.randomhouse.co.uk

A CIP catalogue record for this book is available from the British Library

The Random House Group Limited supports The Forest Stewardship
Council (FSC), the leading international forest certification organisation. All
our titles that are printed on Greenpeace approved FSC certified paper carry
the FSC logo. Our paper procurement policy can be found at
www.rbooks.co.uk/environment

Typeset in Adobe Caslon by Palimpsest Book Production Limited,
Grangemouth, Stirlingshire

Printed in the UK by Cox & Wyman, Reading, Berkshire

ISBN 9780091933357

To buy books by your favourite authors and register for offers visit
www.rbooks.co.uk

Acknowledgements
Thanks to my agent, Teresa Chris, for her enthusiasm
and caustic wit, and to my editor, Gillian Green, and
the team at Ebury Publishing for all their hard work
and shrewd advice.

To Robert and Hector, and to Emma and Suzanne,
my own 'coven'.

Prologue

Now there was absolutely no reason to panic. Everything was fine. Just so long as Daisy kept her eyes shut a little while longer. Chances were it was just a dream. But perhaps she should open them a tiny bit, just to be sure. Nice and slow, here we go . . . Yup, just as she thought. She was actually standing on the roof of the Paris Opera House in a ball gown, looking down at a swimming sea of lights. Daisy looked up at the cold April stars. It was like being on the moon. And this roof was so damned slippery. She could barely keep her balance. It was probably a blessing that she had lost her shoes in the earlier bun fight with that French, er, witch. Heels wouldn't have been much help up here.

So, to recap: this was *not* a dream. Just a bit of a situation, that was all. Daisy willed herself to take a deep breath and leaned hard against the door. But it was no good, the door was shut. The French witch had actually locked her out. Daisy felt tears of rage welling up. And as for that lying toad, she thought, wait till I get my hands on him – I'll strangle him! On reflection, it was probably best not to kick and punch the air or she might lose her footing. She crouched down – not the easiest thing to do in a deconstructed crinoline and boned bustier – leaned against the door and took another deep breath.

Looking down at the glittering boulevards radiating from the Place de l'Opéra, Daisy allowed herself a minute of wistful admiration. How beautiful Paris was! She had always known that the City of Lights was just the place for her. Daisy Keen, fashion queen, in Paris: it was written in the stars! And look where she had ended up, having somehow managed to get everything wrong about this place and the people who lived in it. She *was* a prize April Fool, Daisy thought sadly. And now Isabelle's life would be ruined too. It was a disaster.

And to think that the swap had seemed like such a brilliant idea to begin with, a year ago . . .

Faster, faster, or they'd never get there in time, Isabelle thought, as the scooter swerved and swayed through the streets behind the Place des Victoires. She held on more tightly and looked round to see if the others were following. At first she thought they'd got lost, but then, sure enough, she was able to count one, two, three, yes, all eight black-clad figures zigzagging behind her on matching black scooters through the lines of late-night taxis and buses. Now they were all motoring up the Avenue de l'Opéra, the illuminated opera house in their sights like a giant cake, with its ornate façade, green domed roof and glinting statues. Out of the corner of her eye Isabelle could see some of the others were catching up with them. Nervous as she was, Isabelle managed a little smile. She was proud of her friends.

One last swerve around the square and they all ground to a halt before the steps of the opera house. They leaped off and dashed towards the central door. Isabelle could see they were expected. The door flew open and they ran up the great staircase in their black catsuits like a squad of avengers, Isabelle in their midst in her red silk ball gown. There wasn't a minute to lose.

One Year Earlier

1 Isabelle

The closest Isabelle and Daisy had come to meeting was in the initial correspondence they'd exchanged to agree the terms of their house swap.

FLAT EXCHANGE. Serious, reliable French girl looking to exchange flat in Paris Left Bank against similar accommodation (preferably quiet) in London for one year, starting early July. Contact isabelle.papillon@lenet.fr

From: **dizzydaze@interweb.com**
To: **isabelle.papillon@lenet.fr**
Salut Isabelle!

Je suis une fille anglaise avec un grand maison à Londres. Et je voudrais tellement échanger avec toi! Cela serait fantastique! Je partage avec mes deux 'housemates' (ils louent une partie du maison), Chrissie et Jules, ils sont très sympa. Il y a un grand jardin. Là où j'habite, c'est comme une petite village dans Londres, très mignonne. Moi, j'adore Paris, c'est mon rêve depuis toujours de vivre là. Certainement tu vas avoir beaucoup d'applications mais s'il te plaît, il faut me choisir! Tu ne regretteras pas!!

Lots of love,
Daisy xxxxxxxx

After Isabelle had replied in slightly more formal English – 'Dear Miss Keen,' 'Yours faithfully' – and explained that she was an academic and would be doing some research in London, further emailing revealed that Daisy worked in fashion. That would explain the loud pink background and curlicued font of her emails, both highly incorrect in Isabelle's opinion. She preferred the neat legibility of Palatino font and plain black and white in what was, after all, business correspondence. *Enfin*, Daisy wasn't French and Isabelle should make allowances for that.

While she was still making her mind up, as they lay in bed in his flat one Sunday morning, Isabelle's boyfriend Clothaire suggested that she might prefer to swap with an academic like herself.

'If this girl works in fashion, chances are she's a weirdo or a bimbo,' he said, stroking her hair while looking through *Le Monde Diplomatique*. 'She won't be anything like you. Doesn't that worry you?'

In truth Clothaire had never been particularly keen on Isabelle's scheme and had done his best to discourage her. London was fine for a weekend but why stay longer? Her boyfriend, Isabelle reflected affectionately, was a creature of habit. Away from the Saint-Germain-des-Prés book-shops where he liked to browse, his favourite walks in the Luxembourg Gardens, the cinemas of Montparnasse and the café where he had his lunch (*salade landaise* and a glass of Brouilly) every day between lectures, he would probably start gasping like a fish out of water.

'But I won't have to live *with* her,' Isabelle objected in

her precise, flutelike tone. 'In fact I have no reason ever to meet her. It's a business arrangement.'

Looking slightly cross, Clothaire put down his paper and picked up his bowl of *café au lait* from their breakfast tray.

'So, you're really going to do it?'

'It's important for my research, you know that. I need to consult the English-language sources properly. And I think I should go now, before we get married and have children. I probably won't get the chance again after that.'

This was not actually Isabelle's own thinking on the question, but a version of what Agathe had said. Agathe was her best friend and she always advised Isabelle on important decisions. Agathe liked Clothaire – she had, in fact, introduced him to Isabelle four years ago. Isabelle was pretty lucky to have netted such a catch, Agathe often said, to tease her. On the other hand she had consistently encouraged Isabelle to go to London. It would be good for Clothaire to miss her a little, Agathe said. And he could so easily pop over for the weekend on the Eurostar whenever he felt like it.

Now Clothaire was sulking behind his newspaper.

'It's only one year,' Isabelle said soothingly. 'And it's not very far away.'

'Just don't turn English, that's all,' Clothaire said huffily. Isabelle smiled at him and threw her arms around his neck. What a ridiculous idea! She was a twenty-two-year-old Parisian, not a naive little provincial. She was used to big cities. How could London possibly change her?

* * *

Three months later, in June, Isabelle looked again despairingly at her brand-new *A to Z*, then her gaze travelled up and down the rows of red-brick, gabled Edwardian houses. The deserted street looked eerie in the morning sunshine, like the setting of one of the anxiety dreams she'd always had before an exam or an important lecture. *Zut, zut et zut*, she thought irritably. This must be the right street, but the numbers stopped at 45. There was no 80 Cavendish Gardens. How could this be? Isabelle reached into her satchel, got out the clear plastic file where she kept all her travel documents and looked again at the printout of Daisy's most recent email. 'Keep going until you see a house with a yellow door. *Et voilà!*' it concluded triumphantly. Isabelle had walked up and down the street twice now, trailing her small suitcase on wheels behind her, and seen doors in almost every other colour except yellow. Although she was dressed appropriately for the time of year (dark indigo jeans, smart belt in navy leather, crisp pale-blue shirt and grey sweater loosely tied around her shoulders), she was beginning to feel hot and sweaty with irritation.

She frowned and pursed her lips. What to do? She had followed Daisy's directions with scrupulous attention. Yet things were not turning out as planned – always a source of intense frustration. London seemed to be conspiring against her. Since her arrival that morning she had travelled endlessly on the crowded and unfamiliar Underground, twice getting on the wrong branch because Daisy's instructions were not specific enough. Then there had been a very long walk from the station, right turn after left turn after right down identical streets that went on stretching and criss-crossing like a maze. And still no yellow door. To cap it all her mobile did not work in this strange country, so she couldn't call Daisy's housemates and ask for directions. The boy called Jules was supposed to be in this morning, waiting for Isabelle in order to give her a key.

Isabelle looked down, about to reach for her suitcase, and gave a little start. There was a white cat at her feet, sniffing the grosgrain bow of her navy court shoe. Seeing the cat suddenly turn tail and strut around the corner, Isabelle instinctively took a few steps to follow her. Now what was this street called? There was no sign, nor could she make anything out in the *A to Z* about the spot where she appeared to be standing at the moment. It was a tangle of overlapping names in tiny letters. Perhaps it had been a mistake to buy a map in such a small size, but Isabelle liked to have everything compact and neat. She walked on for a bit, vaguely following the cat's stops and starts. Having started at 121, the numbers were now decreasing. The cat eventually stopped in front of a house and when Isabelle caught up with her, she saw the number 80 painted above a yellow door. It was ajar.

Could this be the right house? Isabelle rang the bell gingerly. Nothing happened. The cat had positioned herself near the opening. As Isabelle was making up her mind to ring the bell again, the door was flung wide open. A girl her own age, wearing large dark-rimmed spectacles, stood on the threshold. She was dressed in short black trousers, a black T-shirt inscribed with the word 'Rampage!' in lurid red letters above a skull and bones and clumpy motorcycle boots. Her black hair was cut in a vaguely medieval bob, with a long fringe, and her face was very white. She seemed enormously tall.

'Excuse me,' said Isabelle, blushing a little. 'I, *heu*, *enfin* . . .' No, not a single word of English seemed to come. *L'horreur totale!* Her mind was a complete blank. She knew she should have gone on a refresher course before travelling.

'I see you found Raven. Well done,' said the girl without smiling. She picked up the white cat and stood cradling her, and looking at Isabelle, who had recovered some of her composure.

'Can you tell me if this is the house of Daisy Keen?'

'Well, that depends. Are you the frog?'

'I'm sorry, the fr–?'

'Frog, the frog. You know, *'allo-'allo!*'

Isabelle stared at her. The English were a curious people. She produced Daisy's email, pointing at the address on it. The girl pushed her glasses down her nose and peered at it, then turned her expressionless dark eyes on Isabelle.

'Well, what do you know. There's nothing for it, I'm afraid. You're going to have to come in.'

As Isabelle followed her inside with some hesitation, the girl said, 'The street numbers are quirky and the road kinks when you don't expect it. But you managed to find us. Clever you. I'm Jules, by the way. You must be *la belle Isabelle*.'

'Oh, you speak French?' Strictly speaking, Isabelle had

hoped to improve her English while in London but this would make things so much easier, especially on the first day.

The girl called Jules looked at her sternly through her fringe. 'I most certainly do not. What an idea!'

She looked down at Isabelle's suitcase. 'Where's the rest of your stuff?'

'This is all my luggage.'

'Really? Blimey. You could teach Daze a thing or two.' She picked up Isabelle's suitcase and led the way, clumping up the stairs in her boots.

Slowly digesting the fact that Jules was not a boy but a girl, Isabelle began to follow her up the stairs. 'Chrissie is on the ground floor,' said Jules. 'I'm on the first floor and you're at the top in Daze's quarters.' As they reached the second floor, Jules pushed open a door on the right.

'This is it. The bathroom is across the landing. All right, then.' And she clumped her way down the stairs. Raven the cat had also disappeared.

Isabelle took her first look at Daisy's bedroom and reeled backwards. There appeared to be no floor space at all inside the room. Instead there was an ankle-deep carpet of tangled clothes. And shoes: a sea of shoes in every colour of the rainbow. Over the facing wall, which was painted shocking pink, hung a great many hats and handbags. Isabelle wondered where Daisy kept her books. All she could see were hundreds of fashion magazines, piled perilously high and looking like they might tumble down at any moment. Isabelle blinked. She thought briefly of her own plain white bedroom in Paris, with its one Matisse poster, as spare as a monk's cell.

At least this room also contained a bed, she saw with some relief. She waded across to it and sat down, making a space between piles of clothes. A pair of red high-heeled shoes lay on a pillow like the keys to the town being presented to a foreign dignitary. Oh, this was too much! How was she supposed to move into this unacceptable room?

Having washed her hands, tightened her ponytail and straightened her sweater around her shoulders, Isabelle went in search of Jules and found her in the basement kitchen, sitting at a round pine table. The room was painted pale yellow and contained a big cream-coloured fridge and an old-fashioned dresser loaded with a great deal of crockery, including several teapots in different shapes and sizes. Around the table stood several mismatched chairs. Beyond Jules was the sink (which appeared to be full of unwashed dishes, Isabelle noted disapprovingly), above which a window looked into the sunlit garden. Jules was reading a book that was propped up against a teapot, and eating a biscuit. She looked up briefly.

'All right? All moved in and everything?'

'Yes, *heu*, no. When Daisy left . . . she was late for her train?'

'What do you mean?'

'She did not have time to pack her clothes.'

'Oh no, she packed loads. Always does, can't do it any other way.'

Isabelle thought of her own precise method for packing from a list, ruthlessly eliminating everything apart from a few tried and trusted outfits plucked out of a small wardrobe in which all the items matched. She had an alarming mental image of a deranged Daisy shoving armfuls of clothes into every room of her own flat, filling the bathroom with them, perhaps even the fridge . . .

'Do you want some tea or something?'

Isabelle thanked her hostess automatically and sat down, wondering how to broach the question of the room again. She looked up as Jules pushed an enormous cup shaped like a tankard in her direction. It was adorned with a pink capital D.

'That's Daze's mug. I suppose you might as well use it while you're here.'

Rather than the delicate golden brown liquid Isabelle would have recognised as tea, the mug contained an alien-looking opaque grey-beige beverage. She sipped once, then put the thing down hurriedly.

'Please . . .' she said in as firm a tone as she could muster, but before she could continue there was the sound of somebody clattering down the stairs.

'Chrissie's home,' Jules said. 'Hooray.'

Isabelle turned towards the door, curious after all to see the other girl who lived in the house.

But the person who walked in was a very good-looking boy with longish straight blond hair. He was wearing a tight white T-shirt and, extremely oddly in Isabelle's eyes, a sarong. She remembered that the British sometimes wore kilts, like Prince Charles for example, but did not know what to make of this outlandish outfit. On Chrissie's feet were bright yellow flip-flops. He walked straight to Isabelle with both arms outstretched.

'Hi *darling*! I'm Chrissie!'

'Hello. It's nice to meet you,' Isabelle murmured politely.

But Chrissie had somehow got hold of her hands and was pulling her to her feet. For one wild moment she thought he was going to make her dance around the kitchen. Instead he clasped her in his arms for a minute, then pulled away and kissed the air on either side of her face.

'Mwah, mwah! There we are. Just like the French. Now let's have a look at you.' He stared at her for a moment and then, rather woundingly, burst out laughing. 'Oh, my goodness! Aren't you just the *sweetest* little French person! Jules, will you look at the *exquisite* way she's wearing her jaunty little *jersey*!'

Isabelle blushed to the roots of her hair. Jules kept her eyes on her book, but she smiled a little.

'Wait, wait, wait, there's *more*,' he continued, looking down at her belt. 'Is this . . . *Hermès*?'

'Erm, yes,' said Isabelle evenly. 'It was my mother's.'

Chrissie let out a high-pitched squeal. Isabelle flinched a little. He then said in a low, respectful voice: 'It's *vintage*.'

There was a short pause.

'It's just like me, I'm going for a whole Beckham story today. I *know* what you're going to say,' he said, suddenly holding up a hand an inch away from Isabelle's face. 'But the thing is you see it's *so* yesterday that it feels quite *fresh* again, positively zingy. It's *iconic*. It *works*.'

Isabelle, who did not follow football, hardly understood a word of this. He'd said something about a story. Some novel he was reading, or was planning to read?

'My *dear*, you look a bit shaken and stirred,' Chrissie said, not unkindly. 'Was darling Daze's room a bit much for you? I *try* and *try* to get her to change her ways but she just *will not* do capsule. We have an attic here, you know. I'll help you put her things in boxes and we'll store them away. She won't mind.'

'Probably won't notice they've gone,' Jules added tonelessly.

'But first, a lovely cuppa!'

Isabelle was grateful for Chrissie's offer of help and would actually have preferred him to get on with it right away. But it was very difficult to interrupt his rapid flow of speech, particularly as her English felt a bit rusty.

'You see, Daisy called me one day to say she'd bought this absolutely *vast* house and would I like to move in with her. I said, darling, it would be an *honour*! The thing is it was so *timely*, because I'd just got out of a difficult relationship. The whole Mick the Shit frightmare,' he added tersely for Jules' benefit. 'I'd been sleeping on people's floors, practically under *bridges*, for days. But now I have this *lovely* ginormous room where I sleep and entertain and next to it is my studio where I do my work. It's divine, you can see the whole garden.'

A studio . . . that meant *atelier*. That was interesting. 'Are you an artist?' asked Isabelle.

'*Yes*, darling, I *am*,' Chrissie replied earnestly. 'How very perceptive of you to see that.'

'Chrissie is a milliner,' said Jules, addressing Isabelle. Then, seeing that she still looked blank: 'He makes hats,' she explained.

'Hats, tiaras, headdresses, whatever I can turn my hand to. Come into my boudoir and I'll show you, darling, I can *tell* you're interested. Now, let's see . . .'

In truth Isabelle was not at all interested now she'd discovered that Chrissie busied himself, like Daisy, with such a frivolous and useless thing as fashion. What a waste of time.

'Can you please help me with my room?' she interjected desperately while she had the chance. 'I would like to unpack my suitcase.'

Chrissie looked a little deflated. 'Yes, certainly, certainly.'

Thankfully, Chrissie packed as fast as he talked and it wasn't long before Daisy's room was cleared out. Then he left Isabelle blissfully alone in her new domain: an extremely spacious room that could probably have contained the whole of her Paris apartment. There were three big arched windows through which she could see the garden's tree tops against a blue sky. It was a soothing view. She decided to move Daisy's dressing table in front of the central window. It was just the right size for her laptop and would make an ideal desk. On it she placed the framed photo of herself sitting with Clothaire and Agathe on the beach in the Ile de Ré last summer. The wardrobe now contained her carefully laundered jeans and navy trousers, a couple of straight knee-length skirts, shirts in pastel shades, three jumpers (grey, navy and camel), the understated cotton cardigan from Agnès b (grey with pretty mother-of-pearl poppers) that was a gift from Agathe, a belted mac and a little black dress.

First thing tomorrow, she'd go to the library and get her ticket, then spend the whole day there searching the catalogue. From now on it would be work, work, work.

2 Daisy

Daisy lay in bed, hugging herself and smiling. She was in love. Every morning she woke up with a surge of excitement, suddenly remembering where she was. All of Paris was downstairs waiting for her to come out and play. For the first few days she had simply wandered in a happy trance from shop to shop, her mind permanently lit up like a Christmas tree with the names of all the Parisian designers, occasionally refuelling with an espresso before starting again on her fashion pilgrimage. She would manoeuvre herself into Isabelle's tiny bathroom, tucked in a corner next to the diminutive kitchen, and shower carefully (there wasn't much elbow room), listening to the sounds of the Paris traffic below. It then took her hours to get ready. What to wear? Her 1930s tea gown and silver peep-toe sandals maybe? Just the thing for going around the flea markets. Or perhaps, if she fancied tackling the chic Bon Marché department store, something more straightforward – emerald silk cigarette pants, jewelled mules, a Pucci shirt and her big white Jackie O sunglasses. Then there was make-up. Powder, blusher, varying shades of red lipstick and *always* some carefully applied black liquid eyeliner to give herself the cat's eyes of a Rive Gauche siren.

This particular morning, a week into the house swap, Daisy woke up feeling as excited as usual but also, she realised, really quite hungry. She went into Isabelle's kitchen to investigate. The tiny fridge was completely empty apart from a bottle of Evian. Daisy pondered this for a moment, then was struck by inspiration. The greeting letter left by Isabelle had mentioned there was an open-air market on the boulevard every Saturday: she would get some lovely food there!

In keeping with this plan, her sartorial inspiration was on the rustic side – gypsy-style white blouse, long flouncy Liberty skirt, high-heeled red clogs, a red bandana worn as a headscarf and, pulling the look together, Isabelle's wicker shopping basket, discovered in the kitchen.

Walking past the bakery on Isabelle's street, Daisy decided to buy some bread. As she walked into the shop, its owner, a plump middle-aged woman with a huge white-blonde chignon and pink pinafore, practically sang out her greeting: '*Bonjour, Mademoiselle!*'

'Erm, *bonjour*,' Daisy replied happily. '*Une baguette, s'il vous plaît.*'

Since her arrival she had felt permanently like the heroine in a Hollywood musical and half-expected the crowds on the street to break into a choreographed song and dance. And indeed, wouldn't it be lovely, she thought dreamily as she was handed the warm bread wrapped in a sheet of paper and picked up her change, if a lush musical score began to swell in the background as the *boulangère*, gracefully leaping over the counter (admittedly a bit hard to imagine, but never mind) and landing next to Daisy, then took her by the hand and led her in some sort of pas de deux around the shop. Daisy walked out, carefully placing the baguette in her basket. Now she had entered the stretch of the boulevard occupied by the market. A crowd of people were slowly making their way through the stalls. Daisy joined them, gazing at tall symmetrical pyramids of tomatoes, courgettes and apricots as she went past. How beautiful. How long did it take to build those? This was more fun than the weekly trips with Jules to their local supermarket in London, with Daisy trying to keep her friend's fixation on baked beans and chocolate Hob-Nobs in check. It would be so excellent if this (actually rather yummy-looking) fruit-and-veg guy started to juggle a few peaches while this young mother, in her fab sleeveless linen dress, began to tap a funky beat on the handle of her baby's pushchair. More would start to do the same, juggle-juggle, tap-tap-tap, until eventually the whole market erupted into song. Tra-la-la-la-la-la-la . . . Then the fruit-and-veg guy would lift her high up, she'd stretch out her hands and launch into her big number, '*Paris, je t'aime! Paris, je t'adore!*'

'*Non mais! Pouvez pas faire attention, non?*'

Oh no. She had walked slap bang into a man carrying a tray of melons and they had all rolled off everywhere. He looked very cross.

'*Oh, pardon!* Let me help.' Daisy fumbled around, vainly trying to locate the melons between the feet of the moving shoppers. The man was more efficient and managed to retrieve a few.

'*Idiote!*' he threw at Daisy before moving on with his tray. That wasn't very nice! She hadn't done it on purpose.

'*C'est pour aujourd'hui ou pour demain?*' said another voice, which also sounded cross. Daisy looked up. A stallholder was staring at her expectantly. And there were people behind her, huffing and puffing. She seemed to have accidentally come to the head of the queue and she was holding everyone up.

'Er, *des cerises, s'il vous plaît. Et quatre nectarines.*'

Daisy made her way back to the flat, having also purchased a goat's cheese and some olives from a friendlier stall. She was exhausted. It was actually quite hard work being a typical Parisian. After lunch, she should really give some thought to her writing. Daisy had been commissioned by *Sparkle*, an up-and-coming Internet fashion magazine, to write a blog reflecting the experiences of a London style expert in Paris. The deal had come together just as she was about to leave for France, which was good news in terms of her finances. It would supplement the little bit of money her parents had given her, the rent she got from Chrissie and Jules and whatever she could earn by doing a bit of freelance styling or window-dressing. After a stint working as in-house PR for a designer, she had impulsively decided that she needed a change from the London fashion scene without really thinking too much about practicalities. In truth Daisy generally went through life trusting that 'something would turn up', and it usually did.

She walked up the five flights of stairs that led to the flat, her stomach rumbling. As she let herself into the flat, she got a shock. The door was shut, not locked, yet she was sure she had locked it on her way out. A burglar? Daisy pushed the door open, calling out a cautious 'Hello?' Another voice, a girl's, answered *'C'est Daisy?'* A burglar wouldn't know her name, Daisy reasoned. She walked resolutely into the book-filled living room that was also Isabelle's study. An unknown girl, who had been sitting at Isabelle's desk, stood up when she saw Daisy and held out her hand.

'Hello,' she said in fluent English, 'you must be Daisy. My name is Agathe. I'm a friend of Isabelle's. Her best friend.'

Agathe was, Daisy saw, very beautiful, with large hazel eyes and long golden-blonde hair, tied back in a ponytail, which shone like glass. In jeans and a white shirt, she looked incredibly smart. She gave a little shrug and smiled.

'You must be wondering why I'm here!'

'Well . . .'

'I left something here that belongs to me, and I have a duplicate of Isabelle's keys, for emergencies. So I came and picked up my stuff. That's all.'

'Oh, that's OK. But . . .'

'I love what you're wearing!' Agathe exclaimed.

'Oh, thank you.'

'It's very original. Very *folklorique*.'

'What's that?'

'It means traditional, from the provinces. You know, like in Brittany, for example, the women wear black dresses and tall white coifs and the men play old instruments,' Agathe said, gracefully miming the turning of a handle, 'and sing songs in *patois*.'

'What's *patois*?'

'It's local dialect.'

There was a pause, then Agathe, her eyes narrowed, enquired about what was pinned to Daisy's peasant top.

'Oh, that! It's my heart-shaped brooch. It's complete tat

but I love it. It's the way it winks in that 3-D sort of way, like those really kitsch postcards. You see?'

She did a little shimmy to demonstrate. Agathe, who was wearing a small string of pearls, nodded, her face neutral.

'A boyfriend gave it to me years ago as a joke,' Daisy explained.

'He is no longer your boyfriend?'

'Oh, no! As a matter of fact since then he's turned out to be completely gay. Fashion, you know! I'm single at the moment.'

Agathe smiled sympathetically. 'Well, I'm going to a party tonight. Would you like to come?'

'Oh, *yes*! Thank you, that would be lovely.'

'A lot of Isabelle's friends will be there. They are all very curious to meet you.'

Agathe left, promising to call later to arrange a time. Left alone, Daisy first jumped up and down with excitement, then her face took on a more serious expression. She sat down, rummaged for her mobile and texted Chrissie: 'FASHION POLICE EMERGENCY SOS.' He ought to be awake by now.

Sure enough her phone beeped almost immediately: '*ICI LE* FASHION POLICE. HOW CAN I ENHANCE YOUR FABULOUSNESS?'

'PARTY TONIGHT IN PARIS. WHAT 2 WEAR?'

'OH DARLING IT'S A CODE SHRIEK. WHOSE PARTY? IS IT DESIGNER?'

'JUST A FRIEND OF ISABELLE'S,' Daisy texted back. Then she had an inspiration: 'ASK HER FOR TIPS?'

'OH MY DEAREST DARLING NO,' came the reply.

'WHY NOT?'

'ISABELLE V. SWEET BUT NO FASHION GURU. ACTUALLY SPURNS ONE'S HATS. MOST MORTIFYING.'

How like Chrissie to take everything so personally and blow it out of proportion. So what if Isabelle was not a hat person? She was probably mad for shoes instead.

'OK, SO YOU ADVISE.'

'GO KICKASS BOND GIRL PUSSY GALORE.'

'?'

'LEATHER CATSUIT.'

'TOO SWEATY. V. HOT IN PARIS!'

'HOW BROWN ARE U SWEETIE?'

'NOT BAD, FAKE TAN STILL DOING ITS THING.'

'THEN IS NO BRAINER. FULL-ON KITSCHY DALLAS VIBE. HALTER-NECK, WHITE RA-RA SKIRT, METALLIC BRONZE COWBOY BOOTS. TRÈS CHIC.'

'BRILLIANT, THANKS.'

'BIG HAIR.'

'OF COURSE. ALL WELL AT YOUR END?'

'PERFECT HEAVEN. MUST DASH. JULES AND I HAVING A BITCH AT MTV CRIBS. MWAH!'

So her first *Sparkle* blog could be about party wear. Excellent: she would be having fun and doing important research at the same time. Her Parisian life was falling into place.

3 Isabelle

'Oh, I know! I could be a grave digger,' Jules said, holding up her spoon.

'Mmm, *yes*, I can totally see that. Though really I suppose you'd have to start as an apprentice. It's a proper *trade*, isn't it? Besides, wouldn't you have to be a *sexton* or something?'

'You know I couldn't do that – I'm a pagan.'

'Naturally, darling. But *oh*, it would be *gorgeous*, imagine, swanning around among all those beautiful stones and crypts, so *very* Buffy the Vampire Slayer.'

'Well, perhaps.' Jules smiled a little, her mouth full of Weetabix.

Over communal breakfast on Saturday morning, Chrissie was helping Jules decide on her next career move. As usual for this time of day they were both *en déshabillé*, Jules in her purple velvet dressing gown and Chrissie in his fluffy white bathrobe. Jules' long fringe was held back with a plastic hairclip, presumably to allow her to see what she was eating. Cereal as usual. That appeared to be all she ate. Chrissie, who was picking at a half of grapefruit, had a green mud mask on. Raven the cat sat on the dresser cleaning behind her ears. Isabelle, also sitting at the kitchen table, took no part in the ridiculous conversation, which she privately thought was in bad taste. She remained utterly silent, alternately taking a sip of black coffee and a small bite of toasted baguette, while going through the notes she had made during yesterday's library session.

Jules was currently 'between jobs'. Before that she had worked in a pub, in a video store and in a clothes shop, but none of these suited her. She was looking for something cooler and more atmospheric. This was all to do with Jules being something called a goth, a bit of information Chrissie had volunteered. It was *vital* that goths wear black at all times, he had said, or they might spontaneously *combust*. This didn't particularly impress Isabelle, who found Jules' usual get-up – the clumpy motorcycle boots, sinister clothes (usually including strange outgrowths made of net and lace) and dramatic make-up that made her look like a raccoon – disconcerting and, above all, dreadfully unfeminine. Hideous black nail polish, too, Isabelle noticed out of the corner of her eye. *Quelle horreur!*

'As a matter of fact,' Jules said in her usual monotone, 'I've been offered a really plum job.'

'Darling, that's wonderful! Where?'

'A fetish shop in Soho.'

Forgetting that she hadn't been paying any attention, Isabelle looked up, astonished. 'You mean . . . a sex shop?'

Jules stared at her impassively. 'Exactly. That's what I like about it. It sounds like the perfect place to meet Mr Right.'

Chrissie gave a snort of laughter. Jules stood up, picked up her empty bowl and mug and walked slowly towards the sink. It was never exactly easy, Isabelle thought, to decide whether her new housemate was being serious or not. It was a question of semiotics. Perhaps there was an article in it. She finished her coffee and tapped her notes into a neat little pile.

'All dressed up and ready to go, darling,' Chrissie commented. 'Are we off to the *library* again?'

Isabelle nodded. She had been in London over a month and had managed to get into a good rhythm. Every morning she joined the small crowd of enthusiasts waiting for the doors of the British Library to open, then she walked to her preferred seat with a lot of overhead space and close to the catalogues. On arrival Isabelle checked the other regulars off an imaginary list. The Wolfman, so nicknamed by her because of his Dickensian bushy side-whiskers and very hairy hands. The Extremely Skinny Woman with the Enormous Beehive and Beads, who seemed to pile her hair up higher and wear more necklaces every day and muttered little mantras – 'Yeah yeah, sure sure' – like the lyrics of a Beatles song. Isabelle usually sat almost opposite 'Miss Marple', a severe-looking old lady in a stiff tweed suit adorned with a cameo brooch. The mysterious Meredith Quince had probably looked something like this, Isabelle thought wonderingly whenever she saw her.

'It's beautiful out,' Jules said tonelessly from the sink where she was washing up.

Isabelle glanced at her watch and noticed with mild irritation that she was already running a little late. 'I'd better go,' she said.

'Honeybunch,' Chrissie said, looking at her gravely through his green mask, 'has it escaped your notice that today is *Saturday*?'

'Yes, but it's all right. The library is open all morning.'

'I *see*,' Chrissie said severely. He stood up. 'I for one am going back to bed. *Somebody* in this house has to look through Italian *Vogue* properly. See you later, chickens.' Isabelle listened to him bounding up the stairs and then, looking up, was surprised to see Jules standing at her elbow.

Jules stared at her own feet for a moment, then spoke very fast without looking at her: 'I think it might be nice to go to the coast. To Brighton, for example. Do you want to come?'

Isabelle was taken by surprise. She didn't know Jules had been planning to go away for the weekend. 'Oh, you have reservations on the train? You've booked a hotel?'

Jules looked at her oddly. 'Er, no . . . I was just going to get in the car and go. Just for the day.'

Get in the car and go? Just like that? But Brighton was so far away! It simply was not feasible. Isabelle panicked. 'But normally, I work on Saturdays. And tomorrow . . .'

'Well, yes, tomorrow is another day. We may be dead by then for all we know.'

They looked at each other. Jules pushed her spectacles up her nose. Though expressionless, her face was still free of make-up so that she looked less frightening than usual. Isabelle thought for a while. It was a very beautiful day, crisp and sunny, and she loved the seaside. Perhaps she could, just this once, not go to the library. Besides, there were often good second-hand bookshops in seaside towns. So that in fact the trip would be a way of pursuing her research, not a holiday at all.

'The thing is,' Jules added, 'we should leave as soon as possible because of traffic. I'll see you outside in twenty minutes, all right?'

'*Heu*, yes, all right.'

Isabelle had only seen Jules' car, a battered maroon Mini, from the outside. Climbing into the passenger seat for the first time, she noticed that the seats were upholstered in leopard print. It looked suspiciously like Jules had done the job herself with a stapler. Jules got in, wearing a T-shirt that read 'Evil likes candy too'. The plastic clip was still in her hair, presumably to allow for safer driving. She started the car and they drove out of the street in silence. After a while she said, 'That Frenchman who leaves extraordinary messages on our machine, is he your significant other?'

'Clothaire is my boyfriend, yes.'

'Presumably he's more at ease in his own language.'

That sort of comment, Isabelle thought, was really uncalled for. 'His English is not so bad as that. He is not a modern linguist.'

'Ah, but is he a cunning one, that is the question,' Jules muttered – incomprehensibly.

'He is a very brilliant economist.'

Jules nodded. Then, after a short pause, she asked, 'Is he coming to see you?'

'Yes, in a few weeks. He is very busy in Paris.'

Isabelle did miss Clothaire, especially his conclusive opinions about things and people: '*Nul*,' he would pronounce, or, more rarely, '*Pas mal*.' Then you knew where you stood.

Jules, perhaps judging that Isabelle did not wish to be drawn any more on that subject, moved on: 'You know, I still don't really understand what your book is about.'

'My thesis.'

'Whatever. Was it about some woman who'd forgotten something?'

'Er, no. The title is: "The Forgotten Modernist: Strategies of Obfuscation and Deceit".'

'Yikes.'

'It's about Meredith Quince, an author from the 1930s.'

'OK. So what do you like so much about her?'

'She's completely unknown.'

'And that's a good thing?'

'Yes, because . . . Some of my friends, for example, are working on very famous authors like Jane Austen, and then you have to read everything that was written about them before you.'

'But with this woman, you can make it all up?'

'Well, I can find some things,' Isabelle said, bristling slightly. 'It's research.'

'So what did she write?'

'A wonderful experimental work called *The Splodge*.'

'Cool. What's it about?'

'I don't know. I haven't read it.'

'What?'

Isabelle took a deep breath. She'd had this conversation several times before, not least with her supervisor, Professeur Sureau, the renowned specialist of early twentieth-century Anglo-Saxon literature.

'Actually, it was never published. And nobody knows where the manuscript is.'

Jules nodded to herself. 'So . . . you're writing a book about a book you've never read.'

'No, I mean . . . She also wrote other books. I've read those.'

'And what are they?'

'Well, in fact they are, er . . . detective novels. You know, like Agatha Christie.'

That was when Professeur Sureau had seemed about to fall over backwards frothing at the mouth. His faculty was a conservative one and, on the face of it, Quince's novels, which included *Death of a Lady Ventriloquist*, *Murder in Kid Gloves* and *Pink Gin Six Feet Under*, all featuring the same amateur sleuth, a young aristocrat called Lady Violet Culpeper, lacked academic credibility. Jules reacted differently. She seemed unusually animated.

'Really. Are they spooky?'

Isabelle was stumped. Surely Jules could see that this wasn't the point. The point was, of course, *The Splodge*, Quince's lost work, which, according to a footnote in Quince's literary agent's memoirs, she had written in 1932. She ploughed on: 'In reality I am interested in the other book, the missing one. I'm trying to work out what it was like by reading the others.'

Isabelle's theory was this: the failure of *The Splodge* had haunted Quince for the rest of her writing career. In her later, successful novels she had managed to import and conceal some elements of her spurned experiment. The Lady Violet books did have plenty of flashy surface sensationalism. This was unfortunate, and Isabelle fully recognised it. In *Death Under the Mistletoe*, for example, Lady Violet had to pass herself off as a chimney-sweep urchin, then narrowly escaped being crushed under a booby-trapped Christmas tree and finally unmasked the murderer over cocktails at the Savoy. (Jules, who'd been slumping in her seat, visibly perked up at this.) But the books were really about something quite other: shifting structure, ambiguous narrative voices, a Cubist aesthetics that created an alternative, prismatic sense of space and time. (Jules had fallen completely silent. No wonder, as that was the clever bit, the one that had won over Professeur Sureau.) Quince's potboilers contained all the traces of some mind-blowing literary experimentation at work. These hinted tantalisingly at what *The Splodge* might be like.

'No doubt something that Virginia Woolf or James Joyce would have been proud to call their own,' Isabelle concluded, her cheeks pink with excitement. Speaking any amount of English still felt like singing a difficult song.

'Crikey,' Jules said tersely, staring at the road.

They drove in silence for quite a while.

Later, as they walked down the pier side by side, Isabelle thought they must present an unlikely sight as she, in her white shirt, cream linen trousers and pastel plimsolls, struggled to keep up with Jules, who clumped slowly on in her chunky-heeled boots, her upper body completely motionless, her full-length black leather coat swinging in the breeze. She had pulled this unlikely summer garment out of the boot when they parked the car and put it on without comment. It was like taking Frankenstein's creature for a walk, Isabelle thought, and all the more incongruous for the carefree and rather cheesy pop tunes that were being played by an unseen tannoy. She and Jules bought ice creams with an unexpected stick of chocolate and sat on a bench, next to two giggling old ladies. Isabelle breathed in the tang of the sea air.

'You're not missing the library?'

Isabelle looked at Jules and smiled. 'No. It's lovely to be here.'

'Yes, the sea makes you feel free, somehow.'

'The library also makes me feel free.'

'Oh, yeah?'

'It's difficult to explain.'

'Go on.'

'When I'm sitting in the reading room, I feel like . . . a passenger in a very big spaceship travelling through the galaxies. And there's this black tower filled with precious old books, behind glass. It's so beautiful. I eat my lunch sitting at the foot of it. It is like being part of a big mission – gathering all the books, the sum of all culture, and carrying it to another planet.' Isabelle went pink again. 'You must think it's stupid.'

'Actually I think it's quite cool. Dusty old tomes full of secret lore. It must be lots of fun.'

They had finished their ice creams. The two ladies, who appeared to be very old friends, were talking about a dance they had both been to during the war. That was where one of them had met a boy called Ernie, who was just '. . . lovely,' she sighed. Her friend poked her in the ribs with her handbag. They fell about laughing, then relapsed into contented silence.

'By the way,' Isabelle began, 'do you know if there are second-hand bookshops here?'

'Yes, tons. Hey, shall we go and look for *The Clot*?'

'*The Splodge*.'

'That's what I mean.'

'Well, no,' Isabelle said calmly. 'It was never published, remember? But there may be other interesting things.'

Isabelle was surprised and rather touched to discover, as they explored the bookshops of North Lanes, that in her impassive way, Jules was keen to help. She even managed, triumphantly, to root out a dog-eared copy of *The Renegade Emerald* by Meredith Quince.

'Thank you,' Isabelle said.

'Is this one you haven't got? A rare one?'

'I have got it already.'

'Oh.' Jules made as if to return the book to its shelf.

Isabelle had a sudden impulse. 'No, I will buy it anyway.'

At the cash till, Isabelle handed the book, in its brown paper bag, to Jules. 'For you.'

'But you don't have to give me a present. I don't need a present.'

Isabelle laughed a little. Everything seemed to embarrass the British.

'Please take it. It's . . .' What was it Jules had said? 'It's spooky. I hope you will like it.'

On the way back to London, the atmosphere in the car was more relaxed, at least until Jules reached over and put on a CD. It was very loud electric-guitar music of the kind Isabelle hated. 'What is this?' Isabelle asked after a while.

Jules cleared her throat, then said: 'It's a band called The Coven.'

The sound was absolutely terrible: a huge relentless metallic banging mixed with a low, screechy sort of singing. Isabelle sat in polite silence for a few minutes. Eventually she cracked. 'I'm sorry but it sounds like that horrible film ... *L'Exorciste*?'

'*The Exorcist*,' Jules said. Then she grinned broadly, something Isabelle had never seen her do before. 'Cheers. The guys will be so thrilled.'

'What guys?'

'The guys in the band.' Jules cleared her throat again. 'It's my band. That's me playing bass.'

'Oh.' Isabelle made a considerable effort to listen more closely. 'Ah, yes.' It must be Jules making that repetitive dull thudding sound. 'What is the name of this song?'

'"Eviscerate Me".' She paused, then smiled at Isabelle. 'It's a love song.'

4 Daisy

'HI DAZE. SO HOW WAS PARTEE?'

'OK,' Daisy punched in after some deliberation.

'I SENSE A TRAGIC HANGOVER. DID U GET OFF UR TROLLEY AND STREAK AGAIN U DIRTY GIRL?'

Daisy smiled. It was really like having Chrissie in the room with her.

'HOW DARE U? HORRID GIT,' she sent back affectionately.

It would take a very long text message to convey to Chrissie to what extent last night really hadn't been *that* kind of party. There was a lot of champagne, but inexplicably – and, in Daisy's opinion, unnaturally – nobody appeared to get drunk. Actually, there had been *one* drunk person, a girl who had passed out in one of the bedrooms. People had talked about this in whispers as of a great and freakish novelty. Daisy had been taken, along with Agathe and some other guests, to stare at the drunken girl's prone figure on the bed. They had all stood in a group, softly exclaiming and laughing behind cupped hands. Daisy had been on the point of blurting out that she and Jules had once fallen asleep face down in the garden in their nighties after eating a whole lot of hash brownies, but a small voice in her head had whispered that it was best not to.

'BUT U HAD FUN?'

Well yes, she had, at least some of the time. Agathe had picked her up from Isabelle's flat. It had been exciting to watch her new friend navigate with awesome confidence through the terrifying traffic whirling around the Arc de Triomphe. They had stopped at a large and glamorous café on one of the avenues to collect three boys, who at first seemed so alike – dark-haired, languid and slouchy – that Daisy assumed they must be brothers. They all stood to be introduced to her and kissed her on both cheeks with such practised ease and lightness of touch that she – seasoned air-kissing fashionista that she was! – felt like a clumsy bumpkin. They introduced themselves in turn, in almost identical low drawls. *'Bonsoir. Octave.' 'Bonsoir. Bertrand.' 'Bonsoir. Stanislas.'*

Later, walking into the party, Daisy had felt glad to be part of a group. It would have been damned intimidating otherwise. Octave, Bertrand and Stanislas melted into another room full of people and she followed Agathe into a bedroom where they dropped off their bags and checked their faces. Agathe, whose long hair was down, looked lovely in a black dress with tiny white polka dots. Daisy recognised the shape from the iconic picture of Marilyn Monroe standing over the subway grating, but on Agathe's narrow and delicate figure it looked subtle rather than outrageously sexy.

Her friend smiled at Daisy in the mirror. '*Bon, on y va?*'
'Er, *d'accord.*'

The dimly lit apartment seemed enormous, and Daisy
followed Agathe through endless stretches of corridor all
crowded with lounging boys and girls engaged in earnest
conversation until they emerged into the brighter kitchen.
'*Salut,*' said Agathe repeatedly, offering her cheek to various
kissers. Someone proffered two glasses of champagne. In
the trawl through one of the main rooms, where clusters
of guests sat on sofas and on the floor talking, Daisy was
introduced to dozens of people. Soon a pattern began to
emerge.

'*Alors, voilà, je vous présente Daisy,*' Agathe would say,
stepping to one side, then adding, '*qui vient de Londres.*'
The boys would kiss Daisy (she was trying to get the hang
of that, observing Agathe's graceful way of remaining
disengaged), then gaze at her with half-smiling, warm,
silent interest. The girls also kissed her, with a cooler
'*Bonsoir. Sophie,*' or '*Bonsoir. Elise,*' gave her the once-over,
then looked away. That might have been because they all
appeared to wear slightly unadventurous outfits – a lot of
black and a lot of short skirts with demure shirts or little
cardigans – although Daisy had to concede that they all
looked rather good. Chrissie and the readers of her blog
would be interested to hear that big hair was not much in
evidence among them. Or fake tan, for that matter. Ditto
metallic cowboy boots. Daisy was musing on this when
someone – Octave, was it? – materialised in front of her.

'You want to dance?'

Daisy smiled and nodded. The track was some kind of

trancy hip-hop song with an incomprehensible rap in French. Despite that, Daisy noticed with alarm that everyone was dancing in pairs, the boys twirling the girls around. It must be that *ceroc* thing which the French were born knowing how to do. She stopped and turned to Octave. 'I can't dance like that.'

'But yes, you can. *Laisse-toi faire*,' he said, putting an arm around her waist. After two glasses of champagne, it was rather nice to be embraced and gently thrown around this way and that. Octave was very patient, stopping to retrieve her when she whirled too far away from him to catch his outstretched hand and repeating certain complicated steps so that Daisy would know what to do the following time. It was fun once you began to get the hang of it.

'DID U PULL?'
'NOPE.'
'BUT THERE WAS THIS FRENCH BOY, WASN'T THERE?'
Chrissie was truly amazing: his antennae worked just as well from across the Channel!
'WELL, KIND OF . . .'

The track ended and Octave kissed her hand, cheekily but charmingly. They sat down together on a sofa and watched the others. Daisy's eyes became more accustomed to the atmospheric lighting. The room was huge and bathed in a dark golden glow.

'Agathe is such an amazing dancer,' Daisy said wistfully,

as her new friend glided past them effortlessly, one hand in her partner's and the other casually holding up a *lit* cigarette. How in hell did she do that?

'Yes, she's not bad,' said Octave, his eyes on Agathe's receding silhouette. 'You're very good too,' he added gallantly.

Daisy spent the rest of the evening with Octave as her guide. He appeared to know everybody and Daisy was able to satisfy her curiosity about the people who attracted her attention. The haughty-looking girl in the red miniskirt, with her dark hair twisted into a loose chignon, was their hostess, Claire. The apartment was her parents', but she still lived in it along with her sister Amélie – that slightly pudgy younger girl who was dancing with Stanislas.

'So are these people all Isabelle's friends?' Daisy asked later, as they stood side by side in the vast hallway. On a table were ranged row upon row of smart little gold paper cups, each filled a single ball of fruit sorbet: violet blackcurrant, orange mango, dark-red raspberry, snow-white lemon. It was very stylish and Daisy, transfixed with admiration, had dithered for a while as to which one she should have. Finally, she had taken Octave's advice, and was now happily eating delicious pale-green apple sorbet.

'Most of her friends are here, yes. In fact that is Clothaire, her boyfriend, who has just come in. He is the one talking to Claire. It is bizarre to see him without Isabelle, you know. Because normally they are always together.'

Daisy, who had been greedily scraping the bottom of

her cup, looked up. That sounded so sweet! Isabelle was lucky to be in such a romantic set-up.

'I think perhaps I should say hello to him.'

'Come on and I'll introduce you.'

They walked together across the room just as Clothaire was emerging from the group he'd been greeting.

'*Bonsoir, cher ami*,' said Octave as the two boys shook hands. 'I have brought you a nice surprise: Daisy, Clothaire; Clothaire, Daisy.'

Clothaire said hello to Daisy, then, raising his eyebrows, addressed himself to Octave: '*Ah d'accord, je vois!*'

Undeterred, Daisy gave him a friendly smile. 'Hi! It's so lovely to meet you! I feel like I sort of know you! Because of Isabelle,' she added, a little unnerved by his silence.

'But you do not know Isabelle, I think,' Clothaire said, looking over Daisy's shoulder. He smiled at someone behind her.

'No. But living in her place makes me feel that I know her a little bit. So have you been to my house yet?'

'Sorry?' Clothaire extracted a packet of cigarettes from his jacket and made the briefest of gestures with it towards Daisy. She shook her head and he pulled one out for himself.

'I mean, have you been to stay with Isabelle in London?'

'Not yet. I will go soon, I hope.' Clothaire lit his cigarette and blew out a long jet of smoke. 'Do you like Paris?'

'Oh yes! What I really *love* is . . .'

The dark-haired, haughty-looking Claire had reappeared and put her arm through Clothaire's to get his attention. She whispered something to him and laughed.

'Excuse me,' he said distantly, and walked off.

Daisy was left feeling oddly let down. For some reason she had expected Isabelle's boyfriend to be just a tiny bit curious about what she was like. Perhaps Clothaire was shy, she told herself. It wouldn't be surprising, if he was such a romantic. And he must miss Isabelle a lot. At that point Octave, who had wandered into a nearby group, returned to her side, and they went out for a bit of air on the balcony. Claire's apartment took up a whole corner of the top floor and the view, over the tree-lined Avenue de l'Observatoire and the Luxembourg Gardens, was mysterious and lovely.

'You are not cold, I hope?'

'No, I'm fine. I like the breeze.'

'*Tout va bien, Octave?*' said Bertrand, stepping onto the balcony to join them.

'You need any help?' Stanislas – he was the tallest – was there, too.

Octave did not look very pleased to see them. His two friends moved to either side of Daisy, elbowing Octave out of the way.

'Octave, you are monopolising the *petite Anglaise*,' said Stanislas, wagging his finger at his friend.

'It's too much: you exaggerate,' said Bertrand.

'Actually, I'm taking Daisy home now,' said Octave crossly.

'*Oh non, mon vieux*. We will all go together, yes?' said Bertrand, putting an arm around Daisy's shoulders.

She looked at them all and laughed. She could see Agathe inside, signalling to her. 'Agathe is giving me a lift, actually,' she said primly.

* * *

'So, did you have a good time?' Agathe asked Daisy as they zoomed down the deserted Boulevard Saint-Michel towards Isabelle's studio flat on Rue de la Harpe.

'Yes, I did, thank you,' Daisy replied a little sleepily. 'Octave and his friends are really sweet, aren't they?'

'Sometimes they are.' Agathe looked across at Daisy and smiled. Then she bit her lower lip and said, 'There is something I must tell you, Daisy, and I hope you won't be angry with me. You see, in fact it was my idea to ask Octave to be nice to you. Because I was worried you might . . . *faire tapisserie*, er, be a wallflower all evening. That would have been really awful!'

Daisy had been dozing but at this her eyes opened again. Her face felt quite hot for some reason.

'But you don't mind?'

'No, of course I don't mind,' Daisy said quickly. It was a bit of a shock to find that Octave had not actually been interested in talking to her. Then she remembered her tricky conversation with Clothaire and the cool, dismissive glances from the other girls at the party. So they had all hated her! Oh well.

Agathe pulled up to the corner of Boulevard Saint-Germain, let Daisy out and promised to call her soon, then drove off in the direction of Sèvres-Babylone, where she lived.

'HAVE YOU MADE ANY FRIENDS YET?'

Well, she had at least made one, Daisy thought, her spirits lifting a little. Because, of course, Agathe had meant well, trying to protect her. That had been nice. Though perhaps it would have been even nicer not to know about it.

'AGATHE ROCKS,' she texted back. 'AND I HAVE LOADS OF FABULOUS STUFF FOR MY BLOG. OVER AND OUT.'

5 Isabelle

'Would you be looking for anything in particular?' a voice said suddenly. Isabelle turned around. It was the lady who ran the bookshop. Isabelle had been browsing around Bloomsbury on her way home from the library and had been drawn inside this particular store because it claimed to be 'the biggest crime bookshop in the world'. Barely noticing the woman with grey hair who sat behind a counter reading, she went straight to the P–Q aisle to check what they had by Meredith Quince. Ellery Queen . . . Quince usually came next, but instead there was an empty space, followed by dozens of copies of Ian Rankin's novels.

'I was looking for Meredith Quince, but . . .' Isabelle gestured towards the shelf.

The lady nodded sympathetically. 'She always sells out very quickly. She's become very fashionable again, you see.'

Isabelle winced. Fashionable indeed! Surely a literary pioneer like Meredith Quince transcended such superficial labels!

'Ah? I did not know.'

'May I ask where you're from?'

'France.'

'Oh really? How nice. Has Quince been translated into French?'

'Yes, but a long time ago, in the 1950s. The translations are very old-fashioned and full of mistakes.'

'How interesting.'

'Anyway, thank you,' said Isabelle, turning to leave.

'Do you know,' the lady said, 'I'm sure the Quince Society would love to know about those French translations. They might even commission new ones.'

Isabelle stared at her in confusion. 'The Quince Society?'

'Don't you know about it? Oh, but you must join! I'm a member, I can introduce you.'

As Fern, the bookshop lady, explained, the Quince Society had been set up some thirty years ago by a small band of enthusiasts and had grown steadily since – to a slightly larger band of slightly older enthusiasts. The members met about once a month for dinners and readings at a house in Hampstead. Sometimes they went on pilgrimages, to visit some of the novels' locations. Unfortunately, Isabelle had *just* missed the latest meeting on Friday, but Fern would love to invite her to the next one.

'I'll pop you on the list,' Fern said, giving Isabelle the address of the society's headquarters in Hampstead. 'Just turn up. We're very informal.'

'Thank you very much.'

'So tell me, which one is your favourite?' Fern asked breathlessly, clasping her hands to her bosom. She was wearing a long baggy brown dress and a necklace of chunky orange and silver beads. Her hair was a helmet of pale-grey wisps. Isabelle reflected that most of the women who had taught her English at school had looked a bit like that. She was about to say that she didn't actually care for detective novels as such but Fern stopped her. 'No, no, don't tell me! Save it for the meeting!'

Sitting on the train on her way home, Isabelle turned the card from Fern's bookshop around and around between her fingers and looked pensively out of the window. The Quince Society had no academic credentials. How could a meeting with ordinary thriller fans be of any use to her work?

As she let herself into the house she heard music coming from Chrissie's room. Jules was out. On Monday she had started her new job at the fetish shop. Pushing her glasses to the top of her nose, Jules had remarked at breakfast that the customers might be perverts but they were remarkably polite perverts. They said 'please' and 'thank you' and called you 'madam'. Not for nothing was the shop called the House of Discipline, she had concluded in her deadpan way.

Once in her room, Isabelle changed into her black one-piece swimsuit, threw a crisp white shirt on top and slipped on some sandals. The weather was beautiful and she wanted to sit in the garden to work on her library notes. She collected a large glass of ice-cold orange juice and a cushion from the kitchen and walked to the wooden bench in the shade of the magnolia. She made herself comfortable, sighed contentedly and turned to her notes. This, she remembered, was exactly what she had pictured after receiving Daisy's first email: herself at work, sitting in a quiet garden, on her own, completely focused. No distractions, no interrup–

'HELP! HELP! HEEEEEEEELLLPPP!'

Isabelle started horribly. Chrissie was standing at the kitchen door, clutching at his hair. She ran towards him. 'What happened? What is wrong?'

Chrissie fell into her arms, whimpering. 'Oh, Isabelle, what shall I *do*?'

'About what?' Isabelle asked anxiously.

'It's a *disaster*. My life is *finished*.'

Isabelle took a step back and looked carefully at her housemate. No bleeding, no bruising. His hands, she noticed, were covered in sequins and glue. Chrissie sank down on the step, rocking backwards and forwards and running his fingers through his hair – thus coating it with glue. Isabelle opened her mouth to point this out, then thought better of it. No need to add to his worries. She sat down next to him.

'Chrissie, please stop wailing,' she said coldly, 'and tell me what is going on.'

'It's . . . Savage,' he said brokenly.

'What's savage?'

Chrissie looked at Isabelle with swimming eyes. 'No, darling, it's a *person*,' he said patiently, as though talking to a simpleton. 'Savage is a *genius* designer. Daisy used to do her PR and I'm doing the hats for her September show. Which is an *amazing* chance for me. But oooooooh,' he said, whimpering again, 'she's going to have my *guts* for *garters*.'

'Come on,' Isabelle said, helping him to his feet. 'Show me what the problem is. It cannot be so terrible as that.'

As they entered Chrissie's room Isabelle noticed with

satisfaction that she had become almost immune to the decorative scheme. On her first visit, soon after moving in, she had only been conscious of a mass of overwhelming, swirling colours looming at her. She remembered taking in two television sets, a square orange one and a round white one (it later transpired that Chrissie often liked to watch two different programmes at once), a row of lava lamps on the mantelpiece and, in the corner, a large bed covered in fake white fur, over which hung a multicoloured portrait of Chrissie done (not very well, by a boyfriend) in the style of Andy Warhol's Marilyn series.

Since that first visit, and after repeated exposure, Isabelle had become quite capable of standing in the room without hyperventilating, even when Chrissie's giant powered disco ball was revolving at full speed, as was the case today.

They walked into the sunlit studio. Chrissie's working table, which ran the whole length of the room, was lined with tall jars of multicoloured beads, sequins and feathers. Before them lay a narrow strip of felt embroidered with a single and rather forlorn-looking bead – a work in progress that did not look encouraging. The unhappy hatmaker collapsed onto an orange inflatable sofa. Isabelle sat down next to him cautiously. Previous experience had demonstrated that too sudden an impact might send the other person flying out of their seat. After a little questioning, Isabelle got some idea of Chrissie's situation. He had done the odd hat for Savage before, usually a complicated showstopper for the final exit, and he had agreed to work on this collection on the same basis. Now, however, Savage had suddenly decreed that she wanted not one but eight hats for every one of the ten looks she was planning.

'Why eight?'

'We don't know yet. It's all to do with a revolutionary fashion concept she's devised and she won't tell us what it is.'

'So that's eighty hats. And when is the show?'

'Mid-September,' Chrissie whimpered.

'It's only the end of June now,' Isabelle said reasonably.

'Yes, but Savage wants me to deliver *all* the hats to her in four weeks. *Ev-e-ry last one.*'

'Why?'

'She likes to lock herself up for the last couple of weeks to give the collection a last review and tweak everything. It's part of her *process.*'

'I see.'

'And each hat I create takes me up to three or four weeks to get *right*. That's *my* process.'

'Yes, you have a problem,' Isabelle admitted. She thought for a moment. 'Well, she cannot change the conditions like that. It is not fair. What does your contract say?'

'*Dar-ling*,' Chrissie said patiently, 'I don't have a *contract*. The arrangement is that I do *as she says*. I'm so lucky to be given this break. Working with her could make my name.'

'I understand.' It was like having a neurotic but well-respected supervisor for your research.

'The thing is that she's *not human*! The first time I worked with her she had a *major* freakout a week before the show and decided she *hated* the collection. She destroyed *everything*, all our work, and started all over again, working nights as well. We were all *terrified* but *she* was quite chirpy about it.'

Isabelle looked at Chrissie sympathetically. This Savage *did* sound like a tricky proposition.

'Maybe . . . you could hire some people to help you?'

'I can't afford to. The *only* money I'm getting for this is for the materials. There's *nothing* else.'

Isabelle was profoundly shocked. 'You mean you don't get paid for the work you do?'

'*Noooo*! Savage doesn't pay *anyone*. She's skint herself, and anyway she doesn't need to. She's the *hottest* designer around, you know.'

It was unbelievable, Isabelle thought, that some crazy fashion person should command that kind of respect and devotion. After all she was hardly Mozart or Michelangelo. Suddenly Chrissie stopped swaying and clutching his head. He inhaled deeply and took Isabelle's hand between his own lightly sequinned ones.

'Isabelle, will you do me a *huge* favour?'

'Yes, of course,' Isabelle replied automatically. Perhaps he wanted a tankard of beige tea or a biscuit.

'Will you please, *please*, help me with this?'

'Help you . . . make the hats?'

'Yes! You *are* French, aren't you? You must have *heaps* of flair. *Yes*, I see it all!' He squeezed her arm, cheering up visibly. 'Oh, it will be *fun*! Please say yes!'

'The last time I made anything I was six years old,' Isabelle said carefully. 'We cut flowers out of felt and glued them to linen bags. It was a present for Mother's Day. My one looked a bit strange.'

'That's *perfect*! You know the basics already!' Restored to his usual sunny self, Chrissie bounced out of the sofa, sending Isabelle reeling sideways. 'Shall we start?'

'I do not think . . .' Isabelle began, but Chrissie was already marching her towards the jars of feathers.

Much later, there was a knock at the door. It was Jules, back from band practice with The Coven. Since it was not in her nature to show surprise, she merely stood looking into the room in silence, taking in the unexpected sight. Chrissie and Isabelle sat side by side at the work table with their backs to the door and were so absorbed that they didn't look around. They both wore hats: a small black sequinned headdress in the shape of cat's ears tipped at a rakish angle for Chrissie and a high cone of pale-blue tulle dotted with pink rosebuds for Isabelle, who, for some reason, was wearing a swimsuit. A clothing line had been hung across the room and sketches were pegged neatly all the way along it. Chrissie, humming a little, was selecting pheasant feathers of varying lengths and arranging them into a spray. Isabelle was carefully cutting shapes out of a sheet of gold PVC.

'Hello,' said Jules after a few minutes.

'Oh, hey, Ju-Ju!' Chrissie called out, spinning around happily to face her. He pointed to Isabelle's head. 'What do you think of this baby? I'm calling it "Horn of Plenty". Isn't it just *perfect* heaven?'

'It's insane,' Jules said impassively.

'I know. And this one,' he continued, briefly tipping off the cat's ears, 'is "On the Tiles". *Très chic* if I say so myself. Allow me to introduce my new assistant and production manager, Isabelle.'

At the sound of her name Isabelle seemed to snap out of a sort of trance. She looked around at Jules and blinked. 'I'm only staying for a few minutes,' she said quickly. 'I left my notes in the . . .' She looked through the glass wall and seemed surprised to see that it was dark outside. '*Heu* . . . what is the time?'

Jules smiled almost imperceptibly. 'Ten o'clock. I don't imagine anyone's had any supper?'

In the kitchen, as they all ate cheese on toast prepared by Jules, Isabelle began, with great enthusiasm, to sketch out a detailed work schedule for the collection. Her love of organisation had kicked in as soon as she had grasped the urgency of Chrissie's plight. She had convinced him to work methodically (a revolutionary concept for him), starting with the most intricate pieces and leaving simple feather headbands for last. Isabelle was also adamant that she must continue visiting the library in the mornings.

'So I'll see you tomorrow at half past one and we can start with that asymmetric Harlequin bicorn,' she concluded brightly.

Jules opened her mouth wide, then pushed it closed again by placing a hand under her chin – to suggest that her jaw had fallen into her lap and was being repositioned.

'Well, Isabelle,' she said, 'I dare say you've been Chrissie-ed. Not to worry. It happens to us all in the end.'

6 Daisy

Daisy might have noticed her admirer's presence earlier if she hadn't been so absorbed in her window display. She had made it an all-white composition, to create a soothing, cooling fashion oasis for the Parisian passers-by who were dragging themselves through the *canicule* – the heatwave. Besides, it would look so graphic framed by the black shopfront with the name, Organdi & Néoprène, painted in red copperplate letters. Daisy put the finishing touch to her display, shaking pieces of scrunched-up newspaper and broken china out of a flour sack and onto the floor – for that distressed, post-apocalyptic feel – then she took a step back to admire her work. The window contained two abstract evocations of the female form made of tubular steel. One of them wore wide trousers with a mini-train for each leg, a bleach-free paper top by Savage and the briefest of satin capes, beautifully shredded. On the other, Daisy had gone for a full-length crinoline by a seminal young Hungarian designer and a cropped jacket made of kangaroo leather. Both dummies wore identical white wigs, stiffened with glue to look like the hair stood on end.

Now, Daisy wondered critically, was it all a bit too telegraphed, too boring, too déjà vu?

'Anouk! *Tu es là?* Come and tell me what you think!' she called into the shop.

Uncompromising fashion expert Anouk was the inspiration behind Organdi & Néoprène. She only sold hand-picked individual pieces from international designers, the more out-there, the better. Daisy was a huge fan and it was an honour to dress the windows of the shop. Her next blog for *Sparkle* was shaping up as a profile of Anouk.

It had been a relief to meet a Parisian who took fashion seriously. Agathe and her elegant friends showed no interest in trends. Sometimes Daisy even got the feeling that they thought it was all *funny* or something.

'*J'arrive!*' said Anouk, climbing into the window to join Daisy. She was tiny, completely ageless (though Daisy would have put her at fifty-something) and – Daisy knew from having seen her many times at shows in London, where she came to buy from the collections – never deviated from the same look: a black pinafore dress over black cigarette pants, ballerina slippers, her short orange hair carefully marcel-waved, her mouth painted into a dark maroon Cupid's bow. She took in Daisy's work at a glance and clapped her hands in delight. '*J'adore! C'est simple, élégant . . . Merci, ma petite Daisy.*' Anouk turned around to look into the street and tapped Daisy's shoulder. 'But you have a visitor, I think.'

Daisy looked around: it was Octave, carrying a motor-cycle helmet under his arm. For once he was on his own. He and Daisy had bumped into each other at parties but he was always escorted by Bertrand and Stanislas. He removed the cigarette that dangled from the corner of his mouth, and bowed deeply. Daisy giggled and gave him a little wave, then climbed back down into the shop and went outside to say hello.

'Hi, Octave, how are you?'

'*Salut*, Daisy. I cannot believe my eyes. What are these incredible things?'

'Fabulous clothes by fabulous designers,' Daisy sighed happily, looking back at her work.

'But . . .' Octave gestured helplessly towards the crinoline. 'Who would wear this? And why?'

Daisy looked at him worriedly. 'Oh. You don't think it works as a look?'

'"As a look?" Oh my God!' Octave burst out laughing. 'It's very . . . original,' he concluded diplomatically before changing the subject. Did Daisy have a minute for a coffee? She did. She went back in to say a quick goodbye to Anouk, who whispered, '*Très mignon*,' and gave her a conspiratorial thumbs-up.

As they sat in the shade on the terrace of a small café in Rue Montorgueil, Daisy had a good look at Octave, deciding that although he *was* attractive – slim, with broad shoulders, very white teeth and smooth, lightly tanned skin – he was definitely *far* too suave for her. Look at his hair, for example: sleek brown wings that screamed 'mummy's boy'! As for what he was wearing – a really boring blue-and-white striped shirt, indigo 501s and shiny black brogues (not a stitch of Helmut Lang in sight), Daisy told herself firmly not to go there.

All the same, Octave had bags of Gallic nonchalance. Lolling back in his chair, he was talking presently of his high-flying job as an executive something-or-other in telly.

'Octave,' Daisy interjected when he paused to take a sip of his *express*, 'can I ask you something? You remember the last time we met?'

Octave narrowed his eyes, obviously scanning through myriad memories of recent parties. '*Heu, voyons* . . . that was at the party in Auteuil, no?' he smiled at her. 'You were wearing a very short dress, I think.'

'Yes,' Daisy said, blushing. 'Octave, why were you hiding in that wardrobe?'

'Was I?'

'Yes, remember? I saw you, Bertrand and Stanislas come out of the wardrobe in Marie-Laure's bedroom. You were each carrying a bottle of champagne. I waved but you walked straight past me. You seemed in a hurry to get away.'

'You're right: we were. We didn't mean to be rude to you.'

Daisy raised her eyebrows. 'Well? Explain yourself.'

Octave looked briefly embarrassed. Then he took a long, deliberate drag on his cigarette, blew the smoke out and looked at Daisy directly. He leant forward and took her hand. 'Listen to me, Daisy, this is important. Can I trust you? I mean, one hundred per cent?'

'Er, yes, of course.' It was all getting rather exciting.

'Right.' Octave put out his cigarette resolutely. 'Have you ever heard of the *Confrèrie des Pique-Assiettes*?'

An *assiette* was a plate, Daisy knew. And then something about taking a peek? She didn't have a clue about the first word. 'What is it? A restaurant?' That sounded likely. After all, there *was* a restaurant in Paris called the Beef on the Roof, or something.

'Well, in a way, at least sometimes,' said Octave with a smile. 'It's really a group of people.'

'Oh. Who?' she found herself whispering. Octave was being so damned mysterious. 'Are you one of them?'

Octave nodded and squeezed her hand. It felt quite nice. Even though he wasn't her type.

'Who else?' Daisy got a mental picture of Octave at all the parties where she had run into him. That was it: he was never without his two friends. 'Bertrand and Stanislas?'

Another nod, and a more lingering squeeze.

'What does the whatsit peek-assiette mean?'

'The *Confrèrie* – it means brotherhood. And a *pique-assiette* is . . . an uninvited guest, like a stowaway. A sort of secret agent, really.' Octave gave a self-satisfied smile. 'It's extremely cool to be one.'

'So what do you do exactly?'

'We turn up at parties to which we have not, strictly speaking, been invited.'

'Oh, I see,' Daisy said primly, taking her hand away. 'A *pique-assiette* is what we call a freeloader. We get lots of them in London during Fashion Week.'

'A freeloader?'

'Mmm, yeah. Or a ligger. You and your mates are the Brotherhood of Liggers.'

'That doesn't sound very complimentary,' said Octave defensively, before launching into a long glorification of the *pique-assiette* lifestyle. The true *pique-assiette* was not interested in free food and drink. Not generally, he added, remembering that Daisy had witnessed his recent champagne peccadillo. No, the *pique-assiettes* were really heroes, adventurers, the dilettante aristocrats of the night!

'Now that party in Auteuil, that was quite a coup for us. Private parties in a beautiful *hôtel particulier* are worth a lot more points.'

'Points?'

'Yes, we have a scoring system. It makes it more fun. A party like that is worth a lot because to get in you really need a *carton*, a proper invitation.'

'And how did you get one?'

'We didn't.'

Daisy stared at Octave. She remembered clearly that she and Agathe had been asked to produce their *cartons* at the door before being let in. Even though the party was given by Agathe's cousin, a girl called Marie-Laure.

'Wait a minute. I can understand the whole ligging thing when it's just random launches and things but aren't these people your friends?'

Octave waved this aside. 'It is not important. There was a bit of a misunderstanding and now Marie-Laure is sulking, that's all. It is all very silly.'

Daisy digested this. 'So did you go to her party to try and make up with her?'

Octave smiled delightedly and pulled his chair closer to Daisy's. 'Yes! That's perfect – I mean, that's exactly it.'

'But the champagne you stole? Didn't she mind?'

'Oh, it wasn't what I'd call stealing. Nobody missed it.' He cleared his throat. 'You see, sometimes we allow ourselves a little trophy.'

'How did you get in?'

'Climbed up the gutter and through a window at the back of the house.'

'You're joking.'

'But, no, absolutely not. In fact . . .' He looked at Daisy for a moment and then shook his head. 'No, it is a bad idea.'

'What? What?'

Octave now moved around the table to sit right next to her, his face quite close. He had dimples. He also smelled very, very good. Typical suave Frenchman. Not her type at all.

'Would you like to come out with us tonight? It's only a private view in an art gallery, but it should be an interesting one. And afterwards there's the opening of a restaurant-club-lounge, *très hype*.'

'*Très hype*, you say?'

'Yes,' Octave whispered, leaning a bit closer still. Daisy held his gaze smilingly, then very slowly pulled away from him. She was beginning to have fun. So, would she come tonight? Yes, she would.

For some reason it took Daisy even longer than usual to dress. *Obviously* that had nothing to do with Octave. It was always more difficult to dress when it was very hot. Luckily, tonight's expedition would not require any abseiling or crawling through bushes, so Daisy could wear something quite skimpy, *obviously* the most practical option. That short punky number – a red slip dress adorned with dozens of zips – would do very well. She added a pair of patent red trainers and tied her hair into a high ponytail to stay as cool as possible. As she walked past the hallway mirror on her way out, she noticed that, as usual, a few locks of hair were already straying from the elastic band. Agathe's hair, on the other hand, was always disciplined and flawless. How did she do it?

Octave, looking rather good in slim black trousers and a navy-blue shirt, was waiting for her downstairs, leaning against his black scooter. As he put his hand on the small of her back to kiss her, she felt slightly weak at the knees.

'I like your dress,' he said approvingly. 'All those zips. It is very encouraging.'

Then he pointed at her heart brooch quizzically. Daisy explained.

'Yes, it is kitsch,' he said with a smile. 'But it does not matter because you are wearing Cristalle.'

Daisy was impressed. A straight man who could identify her favourite Chanel perfume! Gallantly, Octave insisted on putting Daisy's helmet on for her. She climbed on behind him, gripped him tightly around his waist and they zoomed towards Saint-Germain-des-Prés, where they were meeting the other two *pique-assiettes* in a café opposite their first port of call.

Stanislas and Bertrand greeted Daisy ceremoniously, though not without their customary hint of irony.

As Daisy drank a cooling *citron pressé*, Stanislas explained their plan of attack: 'First of all in a case like this – where you don't have an invitation – what you must do is take up an observation post and watch the entrance.'

Daisy looked across the street. A burly man in black stood at the door of the gallery. Inside, the white space was still empty apart from a couple of black-clad young women talking on their mobile phones.

'*Les attachées de presse* – the PR girls,' Bertrand said, nodding in their direction.

'It's a good thing these girls don't usually stay in their jobs for too long,' interjected Stanislas. 'Or they would soon recognise us.'

'And it's also a good thing PRs are not too bright,' added Bertrand. Octave kicked him hard under the table. 'Apart from you, Daisy, of course,' Bertrand said quickly. He looked so uncomfortable that Daisy had to laugh.

'You know, you really shouldn't underestimate us,' Daisy said mischievously, with a sidelong glance at Octave, who smiled back. 'When I'm on the door for a show in London,' she continued, eyeing them all severely, 'I'm very polite but also ruthless. I can *always* tell when somebody's trying to blag their way in. It *never* works with me.' Daisy refrained from admitting that she always let her own friends in, saying instead: 'What makes you think these girls won't be just as tough?'

Stanislas was briefly disconcerted, then rallied round: 'Obviously you have to apply the right methods. First you have to watch and then decide on the best thing to do.'

Octave moved a little closer to Daisy and lay his arm on the back of her chair. Her heart did a little dance in her chest.

'So, for example,' Octave said, 'do people show their

invitation or is it just a guest list? Do they ask for ID? All that stuff.'

'Sometimes,' Bertrand said excitedly, 'people just walk straight in. It is absolutely wonderful.'

'So you take your time,' Stanislas continued. 'You stay cool. You think it through.'

Daisy was beginning to see who was the puppy in the pack, and who was the mastermind. But what about Octave? What was he?

'Actually I think tonight we are in luck,' Octave said nonchalantly. 'Look.'

Daisy looked across the street, where people were beginning to arrive. There were no signs of invitations being produced or a list being checked.

'Excellent,' said Stanislas, straightening his tie. 'Let's split into pairs. The best plan is that I go in first with Daisy, then if all goes well, you two follow us.'

'I don't think so, *mon vieux*,' Octave replied sardonically. 'Daisy is *my* guest. It was my idea to invite her and she's clearly brought us good luck. *Venez, ma chère*,' he said, getting up and offering Daisy his arm.

As they approached the door, Octave whispered: 'Let me do the talking. Just follow me.'

'OK. I can't wait to see you in action.'

'*Bonsoir*,' Octave said to the man on the door. '*Je suis François Polisson, journaliste à Zurban. Nous venons pour le vernissage.*'

Superstitiously, Daisy thought that she must be sending involuntary signals (RED ALERT, RED ALERT: WE ARE BIG FAT LIGGERS) to the door person. Maybe she shouldn't have worn her brooch: a flashing red thing was bound to send some kind of subliminal message. But he waved them in without so much as a searching look.

Once inside, as they clicked their champagne flutes while feigning interest in the art, Daisy asked, 'So, François Polisson? Who's he?'

'Me, sometimes . . . It's just an easy name to remember. *Zurban* is a big magazine and they have a lot of staff.'

Later Daisy was able to admire the calm efficiency with which Bertrand and Stanislas hoovered up most of the canapés displayed on the buffet. It was all Octave could do to salvage a few for her.

Once restored, Bertrand and Stanislas went their separate ways and, ignoring the art, started checking out the girls in the gallery.

'I feel sad for them,' said Octave, while reaching towards a passing tray for two more glasses of champagne. 'This really seems to be the only way for them to get out and meet girls.'

'I don't know . . . You seem to know quite a lot of girls!'

'Agathe, Isabelle *et compagnie*? Ah yes, but they are *our* girls. In fact most of them are related to at least one of us. It's nice to get out of your milieu sometimes. You meet some exciting people.'

They smiled at each other while Daisy reflected that she, for example, had only ever been out with stylists, photographers or show producers. The whole fashion thing got a bit wearing after a while and it was a welcome change to flirt with a cute Frenchman who wasn't in the least bit fashiony. Not that she was, of course, flirting.

Getting into the 'restaurant-club-lounge, *très hype*' proved not much more difficult, thanks to Daisy's improvisational skills. The place – simply called Le Trend – was in a small street off the Champs-Elysées. As before, Daisy and the *Pique-Assiettes* stood at some distance to reconnoitre the lie of the land.

Having watched several people go in, Stanislas was pessimistic.

'*Merde alors*. They all had a special pass. The PRs must have posted them out. My contact did not tip me off about this.'

'*Attendez-moi*,' Daisy said, suddenly detaching herself from her friends. The *Pique-Assiettes* watched her walk towards a group of girls who were standing further down the street, evidently looking for taxis. Daisy spoke to them for a moment. The girls rummaged in their bags and fished out . . . four passes for Le Trend.

Daisy returned, a little flushed with triumph. 'They were really nice about it! They arrived early and they're going on to something else.'

'I am pleased to welcome a new honorary sister into the brotherhood,' Stanislas said with a smile.

It turned out to be a really good launch and once inside Daisy and the *Pique-Assiettes* spent many happy hours dancing – Daisy was beginning to realise just how much the French loved disco – before re-emerging from the cavernous basement of Le Trend in the small hours of the morning. The sky was blue: it was going to be another beautiful day. Daisy held on to Octave and let her head rest on his shoulder as they cruised home on his scooter.

Ahead of them, Bertrand and Stanislas raised a hand in farewell as they branched out on their own scooters in the direction of the apartment the three *Pique-Assiettes* shared, not far from Boulevard Malesherbes.

As Octave walked Daisy to the door of Isabelle's building, she thought of inviting him up for breakfast. Why the hell not? As she was making her mind up, Octave curled a stray lock of her hair between his fingers and stretched it gently above her mouth.

'It would suit you well, a moustache, I think,' he pronounced gravely.

'Oh, yes, definitely,' Daisy replied. 'People are always telling me to grow one.'

Now! Now he was going to kiss her!

Octave gently stroked her hair back into place. 'So . . . did you have fun, going out with us?'

'It was great.'

'*Alors, à bientôt.*'

'*A bientôt.*'

That was it. No snogging. Just that damned no-contact air-kissing rigmarole. That was much better, of course, Daisy told herself as she walked sulkily up the stairs. Octave just wasn't her type. *Merde alors.*

7 Isabelle

English pubs, Isabelle decided, must be an acquired taste. Where *were* those cosy establishments she had read about in *Marie-Claire Maison*, featuring log fires, beamed ceilings and delicious food? Probably not in Camden, by the look of things. So far, apart from a very old man snoring over his pint at the far end of the bar, she and Chrissie were the only customers in the Dungeon.

The large and very cold room where they sat was painted entirely black. A blackboard advertised the Dungeon's Blood-Curdling Selection of Home-Made Sandwiches and the Grim Reaper's Three-Course Sunday Lunch, but at this time of the evening (much to Isabelle's scandalised astonishment) the kitchen was closed. In desperation she was sharing Chrissie's prawn cocktail-flavoured crisps, a strange and alien food. It was a very low point in terms of gastronomy.

Jules' band The Coven were playing at the Dungeon tonight and they were now 'backstage' (in the storeroom where the pub's brooms and other cleaning equipment lived), getting ready for their performance.

'Well, I *must* say, darling, this is *very* welcome. Very welcome *indeed*. I had been simply *gagging* to go out for a drink,' Chrissie said expansively.

'Yes, I suppose we have been working hard.' Isabelle

pulled out a small notebook. In her neat handwriting she had been keeping a careful account of which hats had been made and which remained to be completed. She smiled, pleased at the steady progress she and Chrissie had been making. 'So tomorrow we do the sequinned turbans. And then we have finished.'

'K-k-kool and the gang.'

Isabelle put the notebook away and looked towards the door. 'Do you really think anybody is coming?'

'Oh, fear not, darling,' Chrissie answered. 'The Coven have a following. I've seen it. It's *quite* scary. Look for yourself.'

Isabelle followed the direction of his gaze. Tonight's audience was beginning to arrive. At first it was hard for Isabelle to see any details: it was like a black tidal wave. After a while, though, she began to see that like all uniforms, *le style goth* actually made it easier to notice people's faces. And what faces they were. There was, apparently, such a thing as *black* lipstick, and goths couldn't get enough of it, particularly applied to faces so white they were almost blue, and festooned with piercings. Isabelle was beginning to see that Jules' usual style of dressing – black jeans and T-shirts – was actually quite restrained. Other female goths did not shy away from delirious fancy dress: a hooded jet-fringed velvet cape thrown over a red rubber corset dress, for example, or a kimono-sleeved purple gown accessorised with a coffin-shaped handbag. And then there was the hair. Some people liked to crimp theirs so that it stood on end. Others preferred to tease their locks through tentacle-like rubber tubes, having first shaved off their eyebrows for good measure.

Within twenty minutes of the first arrivals, the atmosphere in the Dungeon had been completely transformed. The management had put on some suitably mournful-sounding rock music, and there were goths chatting away in every nook and cranny. Isabelle noticed that they all appeared to be drinking the same thing and, surprisingly, it wasn't beer.

'Absinthe, darling.'

The pub had become rather noisy.

'What did you say? Who's absent?'

'No, that's the goth drink *du jour*. They all love it.'

'Absinthe?' said Isabelle, reacting as though a unicorn had suddenly entered the room. 'But no, that's impossible. That doesn't exist any more. It's banned. It's very dangerous! In the nineteenth century in France many poets and artists destroyed themselves with absinthe. They went blind or mad, or died.'

'Is that so, darling? How *sad*.' Chrissie paused to nibble on a crisp. 'But then I should imagine that only *adds* to the attraction for our little friends.' He lowered his voice sepulchrally. 'The seductive embrace of *death*! How *terribly* thrilling! Though, actually,' he added, amused by Isabelle's horrified expression, 'I think you're right. The old kind is *totally* illegal. This is just some boring aniseed drink.'

A group of Coven fans had already secured their places at the foot of the stage in the next room. Gradually, everybody else went in, Isabelle and Chrissie along with the rest. The lights went down and cheers rose from the crowd.

From behind a black curtain, four silhouettes emerged.

The first one, upper body motionless, slowly clumped to the far left of the stage: it was Jules.

'Oh, Isabelle, doesn't she look *fab*? I feel like a proud father.'

Actually, Jules did look rather spectacular, tall and slim in her floor-length leather coat and laced-up ankle boots of Victorian inspiration. She had exceptionally left off her spectacles, the better to show off the elaborate stage make-up Chrissie had done for her – an extravaganza of eyeliner and false eyelashes that, combined with her dark bob, made her look like a 1920s movie star. Then the drummer, a redhead in drainpipe PVC trousers and a sleeveless T-shirt with tattooed 'bracelets' on her arms, came to sit behind her kit.

'That's Ivy,' said Chrissie helpfully, 'and here's Belladonna.'

A plump girl with poker-straight jet-black hair took her place behind the synthesiser.

'And that's Legend.'

The lead guitarist came on last, wearing such enormously high platform boots that she could have been on stilts, and with her hair in a very high ponytail. The crowd began to chant rhythmically, calling out something that Isabelle couldn't make out.

'It's the singer's name: Karloff,'

'His name is Carlos?'

'No, even better than that,' Chrissie spoke close to her ear. 'Karloff, as in Boris. He's a bit of a *character*.'

The drummer raised her drumsticks and then brought them down with a deafening thud. Isabelle felt like she had been punched in the stomach. Belladonna produced some eerie chords on her keyboards. Jules and Legend began to 'play'. It was the same discordant metallic din Isabelle remembered from the Brighton trip. Was it 'Eviscerate Me'? Possibly. She couldn't be absolutely sure. She covered her ears, hoping the surrounding fans were too busy to notice and resent her lack of appreciation. The crowd began to roar and stamp their feet. Then Isabelle noticed a motion behind the backdrop, like a trapped insect trying to get out.

'*Brace* yourself, darling. Karloff will be with us any minute now.'

Right on cue, Karloff emerged on stage in the manner of a cannonball. Isabelle was full of admiration for the practised manner in which Jules, with razor-sharp timing, took a couple of steps sideways to avoid collision. Karloff ran straight at the wall then let out a piercing scream perfectly in tune with the music. The crowd went berserk and howled with delight. Karloff's upper body was cocooned in bizarre black swaddling clothes that appeared to pin his arms to his sides.

Isabelle turned to Chrissie. 'I don't understand. What is he wearing?'

'Oh, *that*! Why it's Karloff's black straitjacket, of course! It's his *trademark*, you know. Something to do with Victorian insane asylums. He really *digs* that vibe.'

Bent double, Karloff had been running from one end of the stage to the other. Now he was gyrating in a central position, the sleeves of his straitjacket flying out like wings. In the course of the next song, he emerged from it, revealing a black shirt, baggy black combat trousers and jet bead necklaces. His black eye make-up made him look like a demented panda.

As the gig progressed, Isabelle tried to think of other things to distract herself from the noise. If only she had had enough foresight to bring her earplugs. She looked around at the crowd. Some of the men were dressed up as Romantic poets, with frilly white shirts and cloaks, and even carried silver-tipped walking sticks.

She looked again at the stage. Something had changed. Although Karloff still stood centre stage, he was turned not towards the audience but towards Jules, who was also facing him. Thud, thud, thud, thud, went Jules on her bass. Meanwhile she looked . . . different, animated and even . . . rapt. And she was . . . staring at Karloff! Isabelle looked at the band's frontman more closely. He was 'singing' (a nameless wailing) and 'dancing' (stumbling around like a bear in his big boots) in time to Jules' guitar. Isabelle's brain began to click rapidly. She looked from Karloff to Jules and back again. They were glaring at each other out of identically black-rimmed eyes, their bodies swaying, Karloff's voice coming in to respond to Jules' rhythm. There was a strain of energy between them, like a powerful invisible chain constantly being yanked. Yes, of course! There was no doubt about it. Having reached the obvious conclusion, Isabelle's brain slowed down again and she smiled. How very intriguing.

She turned to Chrissie, who bent down so she could semi-shout in his ear. 'Are Jules and Karloff very close friends?'

Chrissie looked put-out for a moment. 'I *imagine* so, sweetie. Yes, they must get on OK.'

'Just "get on OK"?'

Chrissie followed Isabelle's gaze and looked at the stage. Hugging the microphone, Karloff was writhing on the floor at Jules' feet like an overexcited puppy.

'Well . . .' Chrissie stopped talking, transfixed by what he saw. He gripped Isabelle's arm. 'My God, she's actually *pouting*. Isabelle! Do you *realise* what this *means*?'

Silently, they nodded at each other and burst out laughing. They spent the rest of The Coven's performance giggling at every sign of Jules' and Karloff's infatuation with each other.

At the end of the performance Chrissie and Isabelle went home early, leaving the band to their adoring fans. The milliner had agreed to give up late nights until he had completed the collection. This was a win-win plan, he thought, because early nights would also do wonders for his skin. When they arrived at the house, the answering machine in the hallway was flashing. Chrissie went downstairs to make himself a cup of Horlicks and Isabelle pressed PLAY MESSAGES.

'*Oui*. Hallo, good he-ve-ning.' It was Clothaire, speaking in a very loud voice as usual when attempting a foreign language. 'I want to live a massage for Ma-de-moi-selle I-sa-belle Pa-pil-lon,' he boomed almost menacingly. 'Can she – Ma-de-moi-selle Pa-pil-lon – call me when she gets the massage. *Voilà. Ah, mais est-ce que ça marche?* Is it working? *Heu*, tell her that this is Clothaire. Clo-thaire. I am living the massage.' Then there was an exasperated

'*Ah, ces machines infernales!*' and the line went dead. Isabelle smiled. Clothaire loathed technology of any kind. She looked at the time. It would be after midnight in Paris and Clothaire was always peevish when she disturbed his sleep. Best to call him in the morning. She erased the message. There was no point in leaving it for Jules to find. In fairness, now that she and Isabelle were on more friendly terms, Jules no longer mimicked Clothaire's voice and manner (at least not openly), but why put temptation in her way? Besides, after tonight, the tables had turned. Now it would be Isabelle's turn to tease Jules about her love life.

8 Daisy

Daisy and Agathe were shopping. 'How French women shop for clothes' was to be the topic of Daisy's next *Sparkle* blog and she was very keen to learn from her friend. That was the thing about the French: they did everything differently.

First, apparently, there was a correct way to walk into a shop. You *didn't* smile at the *vendeur* or *vendeuse* and say a bright '*Bonjour!*' You *did*, however, brush off their own greeting and repel any offer of help with a chilly '*Merci*,' sometimes accompanied by the briefest of smiles. Then you turned your back on them.

Looking through the rails, you *didn't* express enthusiasm or admiration. What you *did* do was flick through the clothes disdainfully, occasionally pulling something out and quickly rejecting it as tragically hideous and unworthy of you. 'Agathe somewhat Terminator, except prettier,' Daisy jotted down excitedly on her pad. 'Seems in trance. Probably wouldn't notice if earthquake or even end of world. Shop assistant suggests another colour, A. laughs crushingly. V. efficient but a bit scary.' What was fascinating was that, although Agathe didn't particularly appear to be enjoying herself – she looked like she was taking some kind of exam – Daisy had to admit that her friend had a very good eye for what suited her.

After three hours, Agathe had acquired two jersey tops, one black, one olive green, both with exquisitely flattering necklines, and a chocolate-brown pleated silk skirt which made her legs look at their most coltish and graceful. Daisy meanwhile had bought a huge lime-green velvet corsage, a frilly purple wraparound shirt, a lot of bangles, a baby-blue suede jacket and some raffia wedge sandals adorned with plastic fruit.

'But all these things, they do not go together,' objected Agathe as they reviewed their purchases over a Perrier.

'Well, no . . . but I always find a use for everything in the end! I promise you that, one day, I'll be rummaging in my wardrobe, half-ready to go out and saying, "Oh, if only I had a . . . purple wraparound shirt! A frilly one!" And then I'll find it and it'll be such a nice surprise because, of course, I'll have forgotten all about it by then. It's my way of planning for every eventuality.'

Agathe laughed and gave a delicate mock-shudder. 'I could never do this.'

'But it's so great to have a lot of fun clothes!'

'Perhaps. I like beautiful, well-cut things. But of course for you it is different. You are English.' She gave Daisy an affectionate smile.

This statement had become a familiar way for Agathe to agree to disagree with Daisy. There had, for example, been the recent occasion when Agathe had invited a few friends around for dinner and Daisy had got there early to help her. In fact Agathe was so organised that Daisy had had very little to do, except for one thing. To round off her menu of *taboulé au melon et jambon de parme* and *saumon en papillote*, Agathe had made a chocolate cake. 'It needs a little decoration,' she had said musingly. 'What do you think?'

Daisy had looked at the cake – a perfect cube dusted with cocoa powder – and said, 'Yeah, perhaps it looks a little boring like that.' Then inspiration had struck. 'You know what, I have some Smarties in my bag. We could dot them all over, it would look brilliant.'

'Hmmmmm . . .' said Agathe, on a rising note. It was a sort of half-miaow that sounded approving but, Daisy now knew from previous experiences, probably wasn't. Come to think of it, that sound had been Agathe's response whenever Daisy held up one of her finds in the course of their shopping trip.

'Don't you like Smarties?' Daisy said, thinking that jelly babies might do the trick instead.

'I used to, when I was a very small girl,' said Agathe, turning to open a cupboard. 'No . . . I was thinking more of something . . . like that.' She unwrapped an edible gold leaf and dropped it cunningly on top of the cake, so that the whole thing suddenly looked like a work of art.

'Oh, Agathe! That looks so stunning!'

'Well, it's very simple. It's the sort of thing I like to make for my guests. But of course for you it is different. You are English.'

And there had been other occasions. Many others, in fact . . . But that was exactly why it was so great to be friends with Agathe! She didn't mean to sound critical: she was just *so* French. It was a mutually enriching cultural exchange.

'Well, I'm really pleased with the things I bought. And I can't wait to wear them,' Daisy concluded happily.

'What do you want to do now?' Agathe was also very good at moving on from difficult topics of conversation. 'We could go to the Paris-Plage.'

'What's that?'

'A beach on the banks of the Seine.'

'Really? Does it have sand?'

'Of course, and also palm trees. It is very agreeable. We could go and drop these things off in my flat and I will lend you a bikini.'

About an hour later Agathe and Daisy sat in blue canvas deckchairs under blue canvas parasols, gazing at the shimmering river through their sunglasses. All along the *quai*, potted palm trees alternated with chic blue banners that looked like sails. Daisy marvelled at the energy the French invested in the pursuit of pleasure. It must have taken ages to put all this together and it would be gone in a few weeks. They had thought of *everything*. There were cafés and grass patches where you could have a picnic. Over there you could play boules on a *boulodrome*. And there was even a siesta area, where people lay serenely like basking seals. It was surreal. One minute you were walking through ordinary Paris streets full of urban people going about their business, the next you found yourself transported to Saint-Tropez. The place was thronged with stylish beach bunnies in Dior swimwear and redolent of coconut sun oil. But actually, thought Daisy, it was *better* than Saint-Tropez: it was Paris-on-the-Sea. Looking around, you knew exactly where you were. You could see the Louvre and the Ile

Saint-Louis. There were graffiti artists at work under the bridge, and skateboarders at play. On the Pont Saint-Louis a group of musicians wearing striped jerseys were playing 1930s accordion music. Daisy's musical-comedy fantasy was shaping up again.

Then Agathe's mobile phone rang, playing a short burst of dramatic music which she had told Daisy was Wagner's 'Ride of the Valkyries'.

'*Allo?* . . . *Près du petit café. Et vous êtes où? Ah oui!* Look, Daisy, over there!'

Agathe began to wave. A group of familiar-looking people were making their way towards the spot where she and Daisy were sitting. Daisy recognised Agathe's friend Claire (the haughty, dark-haired girl who'd hosted that first party) with her teenage sister Amélie, looking painfully diffident in a baggy dress that had clearly been selected in an attempt to cover up her puppy fat. Behind them came Isabelle's boyfriend Clothaire and, closing the ranks, Bertrand, Stanislas and Octave.

'*Salut*,' said Claire, briefly kissing Daisy and giving her the once-over. 'Isn't that your bikini from Princesse Tam-Tam, Agathe?'

'Yes, it is,' Daisy replied. 'We suddenly decided to come here and Agathe let me borrow it. It's pretty, isn't it?'

Claire continued to look at Agathe. 'It is just that it looks so different on Daisy.'

'Ah, but Daisy is much more . . .' Stanislas paused, thinking hard. 'She is *pulpeuse*.'

'What's "*pulpeuse*"?'

'It means you are, *heu* . . .' Bertrand smiled and used his hands expressively to sketch an hourglass figure in the air. 'Like this. *Bien roulée, quoi.*'

Daisy was about to ask what *that* meant but thought better of it. Clothaire was staring ahead, looking bored. Octave, who was wearing shades, had turned away from the glare of the sun to check the messages on his mobile phone.

'Yes, well, she's much larger than Agathe,' Claire concluded drily, taking off her jeans and stepping out of them in a chic one-piece black swimsuit. There was a pause, during which the boys went off towards the blue-and-white stripy tents to get changed.

'Actually, I am jealous of Daisy's shape,' Agathe said as Claire and her sister, now both in their swimsuits, sat down next to them. 'It must be such fun to have really big breasts!'

'They're not really that big,' said Daisy, pulling at her triangle top in an effort to cover some of her cleavage. 'It's because your swimsuit is a little snug for me.'

'Hmmmmm,' Claire said from behind her shades. She lay on her stomach and began to flick through *Marie Claire*.

There was another pause. The four boys returned in their swimming trunks. They all got down to serious sunbathing. Noticing that Amélie was reading a French translation of the last Harry Potter book, Daisy began to chat to her about it. Luckily she knew all there was to know about Harry Potter, having been forced by Jules, practically at gunpoint, to read all the novels. Amélie was shy initially but was soon asking Daisy, in a soft wistful voice, if she'd gone to a school like Hogwarts.

'Not really. It wasn't a boarding school. But we did have uniforms.'

'Oh, that's wonderful! I would love an English uniform. Of what colour?'

'It was hideous, really. Brown with orange piping. I hated mine with a passion.'

'Did you really play a game like Quidditch? Without the flying, obviously.' Amélie was trying hard to be grown-up.

'Well, yes and no . . . Hockey. And also netball. I used to *love* the bit where you spin on one leg . . .' Daisy said, demonstrating and checking out of the corner of her eye to see if Octave was looking. He wasn't.

'And then did you go to Cambridge?' asked Stanislas, looking up at Daisy. 'I spent a summer there once. It is quite a beautiful place.'

'Oh, no!' Daisy shook her head, laughing.

'So you went to Oxford? That is also good, I think.'

'*No!* Nothing like that! I went to university in Bangor. I wanted to do media studies, though I wasn't *quite* sure what that meant, but I thought it sounded cool. But actually I got bored with it, so one day I was in Harvey Nichols – a really great department store in London – and I just got a job there, which was excellent fun for a while. And then there was this girl I knew who was going for a job in fashion PR and *then* she was like, "Oh, I'm suddenly going to Thailand to travel," so *she* went to Thailand and I went to the interview instead. *Voilà.*'

Everyone looked astonished at this, except round-faced fifteen-year-old Amélie, who looked dazzled.

'You English!' Agathe said, looking at Daisy with a brilliant smile. 'You are so eccentric!'

There was a short silence.

'I suppose,' Clothaire said from behind his copy of *Le Monde Diplomatique*, 'this proves that the British really are an empirical people. Nothing has changed since the eighteenth century.'

'Are we going to have the discussion about Newton's apple again?' said Stanislas. 'Because I need coffee for that.'

Daisy looked at Amélie and they exchanged a puzzled shrug.

'*Enfin*, Clothaire,' said Agathe, lazily stretching a slim brown arm to lower Clothaire's newspaper, 'do not be so rude, please. Not everyone can be as Cartesian as you. You are the most rational man in Paris, everyone knows it.'

Clothaire smiled at her and went back to his reading. Daisy flicked through the pages of French *Vogue* for a moment, then turned to look at the three *Pique-Assiettes*, who had found a spot next to Claire. Octave was lying on his back with shades on, sunbathing and listening to his iPod. Fine, Daisy thought a little peevishly, if he chooses to ignore me, *tant pis*! Bertrand and Stanislas, meanwhile, were sitting up and, typically, watching the girls go by. Occasionally, Daisy noticed, one of them would look harder at a passer-by, nod enthusiastically and say something to the other under his breath. This went on for a while, then Bertrand reached for a small notebook and began to write in it.

'Not a bad score this week,' he told Stanislas in French. 'But of course you will not be surprised to know who is still in the lead.'

'What are you doing, Bertrand?' Daisy had walked around to where the *Pique-Assiettes* were sitting. 'May I see?'

Giggling nervously, Bertrand threw the notebook at Stanislas, who caught it deftly in his raised hand and passed it to Octave. Meanwhile Bertrand had stood up to face Daisy. 'It is nothing. Just a boring game.'

Now Daisy really was intrigued. 'You know what I think?' she asked with a laugh. 'I think you give girls marks out of ten!'

At this Octave raised himself on his elbows and looked at Daisy over the top of his shades, smiling slightly. 'Ah, so that is what you think of us, Daisy? That we are just stupid machos?'

'Well, I don't know. Are you?'

Octave got up and, gently moving Bertrand out of the way, came to stand close to Daisy. 'I have an idea. A very good idea,' he said slowly.

'Oh yes?' Daisy said, holding his gaze.

'Yes. Would you like an ice cream?'

'Oh, can *I* have one?' Amélie cried.

'Are you going to Berthillon?' asked Clothaire without lowering his newspaper. 'Get me a scoop of the bitter cocoa sorbet. Not the ordinary chocolate, I don't like that. The bitter cocoa.'

'Banana and strawberry for me, please,' said Amélie.

'Hmm, Amélie, hello? Remember what the dietician said about sugary things?' Claire interrupted.

'Ah yes,' Amélie said, in a crestfallen little voice.

'Nothing for me,' said Agathe. 'I've got my Evian.'

'I have an apple,' said Claire.

Bertrand opened his mouth but Octave stared him down. 'If only Daisy and I are going, we cannot carry ice creams for everyone. Clothaire, *mon pote*, you can get your own when you are ready. I am not the replacement for Isabelle.'

Clothaire looked up furiously. '*I* can't do everything! I am *trying* to do some reading!'

'Yes, we are very impressed. Well, you can stop reading when you want your ice cream and walk over the bridge. Frankly, you need the exercise,' Octave added, smiling at Amélie, who smiled back shyly.

During this exchange, Daisy had got dressed and begun to walk towards the stairs. After hastily throwing on his jeans and shirt and slipping his bare feet into Italian loafers, Octave caught up with her. He took hold of her hand and she didn't take it away.

'What did you mean just now when you said you were not the replacement for Isabelle?'

'Clothaire exaggerates sometimes. He can be a real pain in the ass. Isabelle is sweet. And she likes things to be simple. It is simpler to say yes to Clothaire than to have an argument.'

They now stood in a long queue outside a minuscule ice-cream parlour.

'But Clothaire *is* very romantic, isn't he?'

Octave raised his eyebrows. 'Clothaire, romantic? Not really. Completely *tyrannique*, in fact.'

Daisy was beginning to see Isabelle's relationship with Clothaire in a different light. 'So you think that he doesn't appreciate Isabelle?'

'Well, he appreciates some things. He likes to have a pretty girlfriend. She dresses with elegance and she is a good cook. And she is very intelligent, so when they get married and have dinners, she will be a good hostess.'

Daisy was shocked. 'That sounds dreadful! *Why* is she with him?'

'Good question. Clothaire is quite an interesting guy, but he is so pompous. I think Isabelle is too good for him. But women are strange sometimes.' Octave smiled at Daisy. 'You never know what they are thinking.'

They walked back slowly, eating their ice cream, and stopped on the bridge for a while to look at the river.

'It's so hot!' Daisy said, fanning herself ineffectually with her purse.

'If you like,' Octave said casually, 'I could blow on the back of your neck. Like this.'

He lifted her hair up and Daisy felt his cool breath on her skin.

'Is that better?'

'Mmm.'

'Shall we go back now?'

'OK.'

They walked down to the beach hand in hand. But instead of turning towards Agathe and the others, Octave led Daisy further down the promenade.

'If you are still too hot, I have just remembered that they have this water thing. Like a kind of fountain. You'll see.'

They came upon some amazing giant sprays. Daisy was impressed. The French really did things in style! You waited your turn, then stood in a strategic position and waited for a misty jet of water to start out of the wall. Children, she saw, loved to run right under the water jet and get wet through, while most adults simply cooled their arms or legs. That's what she would do. She stood at the right distance and waited. The water started. Daisy wet her hands and ran them over her neck and throat. Oh hurrah, how refreshing! She waited patiently and after a brief interval there was another gush of water. As she kicked off her shoes to cool her feet she suddenly felt Octave's arms around her as he walked her right into the spray, pinned her against the wall and kissed her with surprising force.

9 Isabelle

On a rainy September afternoon, Isabelle, wearing her belted mac and carrying Jules' enormous black umbrella, emerged from Hampstead tube station. After consulting her *A to Z* one more time, she opened the umbrella and set off confidently in the general direction of the Heath, in search of the squiggly little turns that would lead her to Lucy Goussay's house. Miss Goussay was the president of the Quince Society and Isabelle was on her way to her first meeting. As she came up to the house, at the far end of a leafy street, she noticed a very muddy Land Rover parked in front of it. How strange. It was hard to imagine an old lady driving such a car. Isabelle checked her watch to make sure that she was neither early nor late, but right on time. Then, walking quickly up the few steps leading to the door while shaking the rain out of her umbrella and closing it – the catch was rather stiff – she suddenly ran into someone who was, just at that moment, coming out of the house. She dropped the umbrella and the other person picked it up.

'Oh gosh, I'm so sorry,' he said vaguely. 'I'm afraid I didn't see you. Are you all right?'

'Yes, of course. It is nothing.'

The stranger, who was wearing tortoiseshell glasses and a brown felt hat over floppy blond hair, also had on one of those green English outdoor coats whose name, Isabelle knew, sounded a bit like Babar – but wasn't.

'I'm afraid I'm in a bit of a rush,' he said. 'But you're sure you're quite all right?'

Isabelle nodded. Curiously, she saw, he appeared to have three playing cards tucked into the band of his hat. She couldn't quite tell which they were, although she thought she could see hearts, and also diamonds and clubs.

'Well, goodbye,' he said, 'I really have to run.' He looked at Isabelle in an unfocused sort of way. 'I hope you have fun at the meeting. They're all right, really. You'll see.'

He handed her the furled umbrella, then headed down the steps towards the Land Rover. Isabelle followed him with her eyes. He was wearing jeans tucked into muddy wellington boots. What a curious person, she thought. Was he, perhaps, a member of the Society? If so, why was he running away just as the meeting was about to begin? It was odd. Keen not to be late, Isabelle put the stranger out of her mind and rang the doorbell. After a moment, she heard excited chatter inside, and the door was opened by a lady of a certain age wearing dark tinted glasses. Her shortish hair was of a vibrant shade of purple not usually found in nature.

'Yes?'

'Good afternoon,' Isabelle said politely. 'I'm here for the meeting of the Quince Society. My name is Isabelle Papillon.'

'Oh, how marvellous! You're the French scholar! Do come in!'

The purple-haired lady seized Isabelle's arm and pulled

her inside. Another, stouter lady, with grey curls and the air of a timid sheep, stood in the hallway. One of them must be her hostess, Miss Goussay, Isabelle thought, as she found herself efficiently divested of coat and umbrella, but which one?

'Hello, my dear,' said the sheep lady, 'and welcome! I'm Wendy.'

'And *I* am Maud,' said the purple-haired lady in a tone that brooked no contradiction. 'Come and meet the rest of the gang.'

They shepherded Isabelle into a room in which a group of people were crowded around a large parcel wrapped in brown paper. Everyone looked up as Isabelle walked in.

'This is Miss Peppy-on,' said the lady called Maud. 'You know Fern Goody, I think, from the bookshop.' (Fern gave Isabelle an enthusiastic little wave and mouthed the word 'hello'.) 'And next to her is Peter Holland.' (A man with a grey beard who had the look of a geography teacher.) 'This is Selina Dexter.' (A short rotund lady with a pudding-bowl haircut who was wearing a sort of floor-length poncho.) 'And her sister Roberta.' (Similar shape and hairstyle but wearing a green jersey trouser suit and engaged in knitting something complicated involving many different kinds of wool.) 'Herbert and Emily Merryweather.' (A beaming couple who bore a strong resemblance to elderly squirrels.) 'Wendy and me, you've met, of course. And this is Lucy, our president.'

Lucy was a thin, wiry lady with piercing blue eyes and a cloud of fuzzy grey hair that looked alive with static electricity. This was due, Isabelle saw with some dismay, to its entirely natural state. Miss Goussay had obviously decided a long time ago not to waste any more time on hairdressers, conditioner, blow-drying or any such nonsense and to let her hair do its own thing. Isabelle thought briefly of her own mother's delicately highlighted chignon. Lucy Goussay detached herself from the brown paper parcel and came towards Isabelle.

'Miss Peppy-on,' she said in a voice like a bark, but otherwise behaving in the manner of an excitable twelve-year-old schoolgirl. 'Or may I call you Isabelle?' She pronounced it in the English way, so that it sounded almost like one syllable – Izbl. 'So glad you could make it. Nice to have a young face about the place for a change. And a *French* gel, too. Ha. Makes me feel quite cosmopolitan. Leave your things anywhere. Oh, so you have. Have a seat. Now, then. Oh yes, I know. You do eat normal food, don't you?'

'Yes,' Isabelle said, a little disconcerted, and noticing her hostess's unorthodox outfit: baggy leggings, a rather startling jumper featuring a picture of a dog (with brown beads for the eyes and nose), legwarmers and what looked like tap-dancing shoes.

'I always check with foreigners. More prudent, don't you agree? Never know what might happen otherwise. Ha. Now, then, where were we? Ah yes, drinks. We're all on Wendy's elderflower cordial. Makes it herself, you know. Rather strong stuff. Will it do for you?'

As Isabelle, sipping her elderflower cordial was finally allowed to get her bearings and settle in, Maud said curtly, 'Well, Lucy, shall we unwrap it? We're all dying to see it.'

Sheeplike Wendy turned to Isabelle. 'You see, we've had the most marvellous stroke of luck, Miss Peppy-on.' At which point, perhaps not being a very confident person, Wendy turned bright red and stopped speaking.

Her friend Maud took over. 'This is a portrait of Meredith Quince, a gift to the Society from the author's family.'

'Oh, that's great!' Isabelle said excitedly. 'I would love to know what she looked like.'

'Herbert, you're nearest. Would you be so kind?' Lucy said, handing the elderly squirrel a pair of scissors. Overcome with the momentousness of this task, Herbert began attacking the string with small timid nips, while the others looked on encouragingly. It took about half a minute of this for Maud to become exasperated.

'Give those to me, Herbert, or we'll be here all day.'

A few swift gestures and the painting lay unwrapped. Maud and Wendy propped it up on the sofa and they all gazed at it.

'Painted when she was in her thirties, chap said,' said Lucy.

The picture showed an extremely angular woman with elongated limbs and dark-blond hair worn in fat curls held back with combs. She had on a blue square-necked dress patterned with small sprigs and sat in a green armchair in front of half-open French windows. All around her were walls lined with books. On a writing desk set behind her stood a couple of volumes and an old-fashioned inkpot. On the other side, next to Meredith's unnaturally long legs, which were crossed at the ankle, there was a small round table. On it, a pair of white gloves lay next to a teacup and saucer.

Selina clasped her hands enthusiastically. 'Oh, how lovely! It's Minton! I knew it. We have a very similar service in our collection, don't we, Bobbie?'

'The perspective isn't very good, is it?' Wendy said cautiously. 'It's all a bit skew-whiff.'

'Oh, Wendy, don't be so silly. It was all the rage in those days. They were all Cubists and what have you.'

'Oh, I see. Of course you're right.'

'She does look distinguished, doesn't she?' Maud went on.

'Yes, a very intriguing lady,' said Peter. 'Is she smiling?'

'A little, I think,' said Wendy. 'Anyway, she looks very nice.'

'The colours are rather good. I wonder when it was painted exactly. Is it dated?'

Peter peered into the corners of the painting, then looked at the back of the frame. 'No, Lucy. I don't see a thing.'

Isabelle could contain herself no longer. 'I think it was painted around 1947 to 1948,' she declared in her flutelike tones.

'Do you, Izbl? And why?'

'That hairstyle of hers does remind me of the war years,' Emily, the female squirrel, said timidly.

Isabelle stood up. She felt like Hercule Poirot, having gathered all possible suspects and about to launch into a dramatic reconstruction of the whole case.

'I think you are right about the hair. But I see other *indices*, er . . . clues in the painting.'

'Do you? And what are they?' Maud asked a little testily.

'I think there are visual allusions to the novels Meredith Quince had already published at the time she had this portrait painted. They are like her . . . attributes. This, for example,' she said, pointing to a small branch hanging from the (oddly distorted) ceiling above the subject's head. 'It is a piece of mistletoe, is it not? And yet, the garden we see through the window is in summer.'

'*Death Under the Mistletoe!*' Selina exclaimed.

'Yes, I think so. It was the first novel with Lady Violet as the heroine, published in 1936 . . .'

'Good heavens, those gloves on the table!' Wendy murmured. 'Do you think . . .'

'Yes,' said Isabelle, nodding, 'they might represent *Murder in Kid Gloves*. The piece of lemon zest in the china teacup . . .'

'Stands for *The Lemon Peel Mystery!*' Herbert had also got up to look at the portrait.

'That's my absolute favourite. So cleverly put together. Do you know, I always forget whodunnit, every time,' Roberta said without looking up from her knitting.

'*Murder in Kid Gloves* was published in 1945,' Peter said. 'So that's probably when this was painted.'

Isabelle shook her head. 'I think there's something else. This, here.' She indicated an object near Meredith's foot, almost indistinguishable from the pattern of the green-and-red Persian rug.

'Eh, what? Where?' Lucy said, peering irritably. 'I don't see anything.'

'Oh! I see! It's a cut stone. How clever!' Wendy was doing an excited little dance.

'*The Renegade Emerald*, 1947,' Peter confirmed, stroking his beard thoughtfully.

'What fun!' Fern cried. 'Just like cryptic clues. Do you think it was all her own idea?'

At that moment the telephone rang. Lucy, who wanted to look at the portrait, dispatched Wendy to take the call.

'Yes, I think you're right about the date, *Mademoiselle*,' Peter said courteously. 'It does put the painting somewhere in the late forties.'

'I remember our mother had a dress just like that when we were children,' Selina said. 'Didn't she, Bobbie?'

'Where shall we hang it, Lucy?' asked Maud.

The Society members began to discuss the best possible spot for the painting. The debate became rather heated. When Wendy came back in, she had to make several attempts before she eventually got Lucy's attention. She said something about the telephone call being another lovely surprise. Isabelle did not follow any of this very closely: she was looking avidly at the portrait. Meredith had never courted publicity, and there were no portrait photographs of her that Isabelle knew of. All she had ever come across was a fuzzy group shot of a literary luncheon in the early 1960s. In it Meredith wore a turban and looked away from the camera, so that all you saw of her was what is known in French as a *profil perdu*. As a result, Isabelle had made up her own image of her subject – as a sort of Miss Marple figure. It was exciting and a little bewildering to come face to face with her like this.

'Wendy, are you sure you didn't get the wrong end of the stick?' Lucy was saying. 'It wouldn't be the first time. Just a moment ago, the chap kept saying no when I asked him. Doesn't make any sense.'

'Oh, but it's such wonderful news, isn't it, Lucy?' Roberta trilled.

'I assure you there was no mistake, Lucy,' Wendy said tremulously. 'I *hope* I know how to take a message. He said that he'd just realised he'd been *quite* wrong and had to ring right away on his mobile. He was very clear about it.'

'I wonder what made him change his mind?' said Peter, joining in.

'Ha! Who knows? Woolly-headed, I thought him.'

'But that was when he said no to you,' Maud replied shrewdly. 'Now he's saying yes we all think he's quite clever, don't we?'

'Yes, I expect you're right,' Lucy barked. 'Ha. Well, well. First the portrait and now this. What a day! Huzzah!'

'He was extremely polite,' Wendy resumed more calmly. 'He said you could call him any time to set a date. Now, who would like another elderflower cordial?'

Herbert sidled up to Isabelle, who was still standing before the portrait. She was looking absent-mindedly at the label on the frame peeping out of the brown wrapping. It read 'Portrait of the writer Meredith Quince. Kindly donated by Thomas Quince, Esq.'

'It's not always this exciting, you know, Miss Peppy-on,' he said confidentially. 'You came on a really good day. My favourite Quince novel,' he went on, 'is *Death of a Lady Ventriloquist*. I first read it as a boy and I thought it was a super yarn. I love her evocation of the world of music hall. You can really smell the greasepaint, can't you? It's incredible to think that she hadn't written it when this was painted. But perhaps she was working it out in her mind. How clever she looks!'

'I think *Death of a Lady Ventriloquist* is fascinating,' Isabelle said. This was partly because the novel had been published in 1952, on the unofficial twentieth anniversary of *The Splodge*. Isabelle had been reading and re-reading it very closely for that reason, paying particular attention to ventriloquising as a possible metaphor for Meredith Quince's artistic predicament. On the surface the novel might be about the baffling on-stage murder of a blowsy entertainer whose female dummy spoke in a Cockney accent. But wasn't Quince herself – the thwarted experimentalist turned crime novelist – another lady ventriloquist, who had no choice to survive but to speak in another voice than her own? Isabelle had just emailed a chapter outline about this very point to Professeur Sureau. Herbert was telling her about his favourite scene (the breathless moment when the plucky Lady Violet, posing as a magician's assistant, unmasks the murderer in the nick of time in front of the audience, just as he is calmly preparing to saw her in half), when they were interrupted by Maud calling everyone next door for supper.

The food turned out to be a bit of an ordeal. In particular, there was a most disconcerting salad, which, among other things, contained raisins, potatoes, peanuts, carrots and peas. It had been made by Wendy, and Maud had 'jazzed it up' with cubes of soaplike cheese. Isabelle was reminded of a story that had done the rounds when she was at school. A boy in her class, who had spent a summer in England for linguistic purposes, had returned full of shudder-inducing stories about being made to eat banana and anchovy sandwiches. At the time Isabelle had dismissed this as a tall tale. Now, toying with a portion of minced turkey, tinned pineapple and cottage cheese lasagne made by Fern (who described it gushingly as 'wonderfully slimming'), she wasn't so sure.

'So, Izbl,' said Lucy from the top of the table, 'how did you become interested in Meredith Quince?'

Isabelle gratefully put her fork down and explained that she had read her first Quince novel – *Pink Gin Six Feet Under* or, to give it its French title, *Petit cocktail au cimetière* – purely by chance, having come across it at a friend's seaside house. It had struck her as more interesting than other examples of the crime genre. She had then begun reading Quince systematically in the original English and gradually a hobby had turned into the foundation of her academic research. Unwilling to mention *The Splodge* in front of strangers, Isabelle remained evasive regarding the precise tenor of her thesis, but said enough about her interest in narrative patterns and the sociology of the crime genre to produce a deafening silence around the table.

After a pause, Lucy, her piercing blue eyes somewhat glazed, managed a response: 'I see. Ha. All good fun, all good fun.'

Fern, who was sitting next to Isabelle, added apologetically, 'You see, we at the Society are just what you'd call common or garden fans. We just really enjoy the books.'

Emboldened by Lucy's temporary silence, Wendy joined in: 'We've staged some of the novels as plays, sometimes just the odd scene or two, but it's tremendous fun. We all take turns to play Lady Violet. Or we go on little expeditions, themed walks, you know.'

'Last year we went to all the theatres mentioned in *Death of a Lady Ventriloquist*,' said Herbert, flushing a little. '*I* organised that outing.'

'Yes, yes,' a perkier Lucy interjected. 'But even greater thrills await us. A visit to the author's house. Marvellous!'

'Oh, where is her house?'

'I'm surprised to hear you don't know about *that*, Izbl,' Maud said, a trifle censoriously.

'It's near Kew,' said Fern. 'It's where she lived most of her life after she moved to England. She was born in India, as I'm sure you know.'

'Lucy,' Fern said pleadingly, 'couldn't you call him now and arrange a date? We'd all love to know when we're going.'

'Hear, hear,' cried several members of the Society.

Lucy rolled her eyes in mock-exasperation and trotted off to make the call. While she was gone, the others explained, for Isabelle's benefit, what an exciting development this was. Since its foundation in the early 1970s the Quince Society had been attempting to get into Meredith's house. That was a period when, shortly after her death, Meredith Quince's novels had fallen entirely out of fashion. Meredith's house had passed to her younger brother, and after his death, to his son, Philip. His was not, apparently, an artistic or particularly sympathetic nature and, at any rate, he thought very little of his aunt's oeuvre. As for letting people he saw as mere cranks and nosey-parkers into his new home, he would have none of it.

'But now he has changed his mind?' Isabelle suggested.

'Not him, no,' Peter explained. 'Philip and his wife no longer live in the house. They moved to the country last year, but he didn't let us know, obviously.'

'It was purely by chance that dear Lucy found out,' said Selina. 'She is very, very persistent, you see. She wrote to Philip Quince again, hoping to convince him, and she got a reply from his son. It appears that he now lives in his great-aunt's house.'

'An eccentric bachelor,' Wendy added. 'He's just returned from abroad – Italy!'

'*He* also said no,' said Maud. 'Didn't even bother to explain why. Potty, probably, like his father.'

'Instead,' Peter added, 'he gave us the portrait. Perhaps he felt he owed us some kind of debt.'

'We have been so very loyal!' Wendy said.

Lucy came back in, bouncing with excitement. 'We're all expected for tea next Sunday. Ha! Victory at last.'

Everyone cheered.

'You must come too, of course, my dear Izbl.'

'Yes, thank you,' Isabelle said, nodding absent-mindedly. Something had just occurred to her. Luckily, everyone began to mill around with their coffee and she was free to take another look at the portrait. There was the desk and, on it, the inkpot. But surely Meredith would have typed her novels, wouldn't she? The inkpot cast a dramatic shadow, she noticed, which was odd because the books next to it didn't. Then it was all she could do to keep her coffee from shooting out of her mouth in shock. The black zone at the base of the pot wasn't a shadow at all – it was a splodge.

10 Daisy

'What now?' Daisy said, looking down into the manhole with some trepidation.

'We climb down,' Octave replied airily. 'It's completely safe. We do it all the time. It will be worth it, you'll see.'

A fortnight had gone by since the Paris-Plage clinch, which had ended with Octave and Daisy whizzing back to his flat on his scooter and spending the night there. This was fast work by Daisy's standards but there was something irrepressible about Octave's charm and enthusiasm and she had happily given herself over to what felt like a heady holiday romance. Being Octave's girlfriend was a rather breathless state of affairs: in the course of two weeks they had crashed many parties of all kinds, made love on the floor of various people's bathrooms (and once in a cupboard) and drunk a lot of free champagne. They had also been up on the roofs of Paris a number of times because that was another clandestine activity Octave enjoyed. Now Daisy liked going on adventures as much as the next person. And she and Octave had certainly had some pretty thrilling snogs while leaning precariously against gabled attic windows in the moonlight. But all the same she was beginning to long for a boring, uncomplicated date, one on which she could both wear heels and use her own name.

Tonight, though, was not the night for such a date.

Daisy was going with the *Pique-Assiettes* to a literally underground party in the Catacombs, the network of tunnels that had once served as Paris's cemetery. Apparently, Bertrand had said with puppyish enthusiasm, the tunnels were full of really old skulls and bones. As if that was a *good* thing. Daisy had been a little underwhelmed, but it was certainly something to tell Jules about. It sounded right up her gothic alley.

Daisy adjusted her speleologist's helmet, tucked her torch in her belt and began the descent down the rungs of a narrow steel ladder. Octave followed after a minute, pulling the manhole cover closed after him. Bertrand and Stanislas, who had gone first, were lighting the way with their torches. Daisy was glad she'd taken the *Pique-Assiettes*' advice and worn stout wellies over her skinny-fit designer jeans. It had not been an easy decision in terms of footwear but she had to admit that Stanislas had been right. Some of the passages they were now going through were half-flooded. Daisy and the boys all splashed merrily onwards in a single file.

'According to my map the entrance we used is the closest to the room where the party is,' Stanislas said after a while. 'Let's just stop a second and listen.'

They all stood still. There was a thudding sound of music coming from somewhere.

'*Oh ouais*! It's really close!' said Octave, '*Allez, courage, les gars!*'

They splashed on for a while, then the floor began to dry up and the passages gradually became wider as the music grew louder and louder. Daisy recognised the euphoric thump-thumping of James Brown's 'Sex Machine'.

'Just here,' said Stanislas, shining his torch on an iron door marked *ENTRÉE STRICTEMENT INTERDITE*. Underneath the sign, someone had pasted a green flyer that read: '*Acid Rendez-vous*'. Stanislas produced a pass key and inserted it in the lock.

'*Cinq, quatre, trois, deux, un . . . et hop!*' he said dramatically, pushing the door open.

Daisy was not prepared for what she saw then. Octave had told her of other underground gatherings he'd been to – small, low-key affairs, with thirty guests at the most. You gathered in a room lit only by your torches, opened cans of beer and exchanged a few pleasantries with other *cataphiles* (as catacomb explorers called themselves). Conversation was mainly specialist stuff about new abandoned underground sites someone had gained access to. After an hour or so, people disbanded and disappeared into the night.

This secret party, Daisy saw immediately, was in an entirely different league. The space, lit by hundreds of fairy lights, was absolutely huge, and thronged with a crowd of party people. Psychedelic light projections played on the back wall, periodically spelling the phrase '*Paris nous appartient*': Paris belongs to us. Daisy and the *Pique-Assiettes* removed their helmets and coats and left them together in a pile. '*Whose* party is this?' Daisy asked Octave, putting her arms around his waist. 'It's completely amazing.'

'I know! Crazy, *hein*? It is a group of artists who have taken over this place. They use it as a squat. I don't know their real names. They all use pseudonyms. But Stan met one of them at another party and that is how we found out about tonight.'

At one end of the room, Daisy saw, a large piece of shagpile carpet marked out a glamorous sort of lounge, where dozens of people sat talking on low sofas. At the opposite end was a communal dining area festooned with balloons. Huge cooking pots and piles of plates were laid out on trestle tables covered with white tablecloths. Bertrand immediately went to investigate and came back beaming.

'*Ouais*! They've got couscous! Is anyone hungry?'

'I can't believe it! How did they get all this furniture down here?' Daisy asked in amazement.

'They are incredibly organised,' said Stanislas. 'They even have electricity and a phone line down here. Ah, I see Gaspard,' he said, waving at one of the loungers.

'Stan's contact,' Octave explained. Then he saw something behind Daisy that made him bite his lip. '*Ah, merde!*'

'What is it?'

'Nothing. Just Marie-Laure. What the hell is she doing here?'

'Agathe's cousin? The one you had a little tiff with?'

'A tiff?' Octave asked nervously.

'That argument you told me about.'

'Ah, yes! Yes, that's right.'

'Are you still not speaking?'

'Well, no, not really. I would really prefer to avoid her. But it is too late. She is coming over. What a nightmare.'

'*Ah, tiens*? *Bonsoir*,' Marie-Laure said, joining them. She looked very stylish and leggy in a black poloneck and miniskirt worn with red wellies. '*Salut*, Octave.'

'Ah, Marie-Laure,' Octave said easily. 'How are you? Do

you want a drink? But I see that you have got one already. I will go get something for you, Daisy.' Upon which he scarpered.

Marie-Laure turned to Daisy, who smiled at her.

'Hello, Marie-Laure. It's nice to see you again. I had a lovely time at your party. Is Agathe with you?'

'Oh, no!' Marie-Laure said, laughing a little. 'This kind of party is not chic enough for Agathe. It is far too "underground".'

'No, you're probably right. It's brilliant, though, isn't it? Do you know the people who discovered this place?'

'No, I don't. I came with someone from work. He found out about it on the internet.'

There was a short pause, during which Daisy looked behind her to see if Octave was coming back with her drink.

'You know, I do not think Octave is coming back. Not so long as I am here,' Marie-Laure said, handing Daisy her glass of wine. 'You can have some of this, if you are thirsty. It is quite nice.'

'Thanks very much,' Daisy said, gratefully taking the wine. 'Look,' she then said, putting her hand on Marie-Laure's arm, 'I know you and Octave have had a falling-out. He told me.'

'He told you what happened?'

'Not in detail,' Daisy admitted. Marie-Laure nodded, looking carefully at her face. 'But I really think you guys should make up,' Daisy went on. 'It's always such a shame to ruin a friendship.'

'I agree with you,' said Marie-Laure. She had an unusual

kind of beauty, Daisy thought. On her snow-white face, her slanting eyebrows looked like punctuation marks or Chinese calligraphy. She turned her dark eyes on Daisy. 'So you came here together, you and Octave?'

'Yes. And Bertrand and Stanislas are over there somewhere.'

'Ah, the three musketeers.'

'Exactly! They're so funny together, aren't they? I always think Stan is the brains of the operation. And Bertrand is the baby, following the others around. And Octave . . .'

'Octave,' said Marie-Laure, 'is the *tombeur* of the group.'

'What's a *tombeur*?'

'It means, you know . . . like Don Juan.'

'Yes, I think he's attractive,' Daisy said, turning slightly pink. Octave *was* lovely and they had been having so much fun! He was also incredibly playful in bed, if a bit of a show-off at times. Privately – although she'd found it really entertaining the first couple of times – Daisy was getting a little tired of watching him do headstands in the nude.

'He is attractive, yes. But also completely amoral. For example, he thinks it is OK to take what does not belong to him.'

Daisy was nonplussed for a minute, then remembered those bottles of champagne the *Pique-Assiettes* had snaffled at Marie-Laure's party. They'd probably been seen. Oh dear.

'Octave is . . .'

'A bit of an idiot?' Daisy suggested, laughing indulgently.

'Yes. A cruel idiot.'

Marie-Laure was clearly about to say something else,

but Bertrand suddenly popped up between them, bearing pieces of chocolate cake.

'*Salut, Marie-Laure,*' he said, kissing her lightly. '*Un peu de gâteau?*'

'*Non, merci.*'

Daisy, who was starving, accepted a piece. Bertrand immediately began to eat the second one, silently looking from one girl to the other.

'Daisy, listen,' Marie-Laure said quickly. 'Just be careful, OK? I am going to find my friend now. Bye.'

'Bye.' Daisy was baffled. Bertrand looked at her, his mouth full of cake, and shrugged. Together they went in search of the other two. The music had changed to some kind of French techno and Daisy led the way, pushing through groups of dancing strangers. At last she recognised the back of Octave's head – he was sitting on a sofa with Stanislas, a little way from the DJ and his sound system. They were absorbed in conversation and didn't notice her approaching.

'You have no choice now,' Stanislas was saying in French. 'In fact it's probably too late. You screwed up.'

'I did not screw up,' Octave replied. 'It's not always that easy, you know.'

'I don't know why you waited so long. It's always a mistake with girls. And I don't know why it had to be someone we actually see all the time. Again! It's really against the rules. Anyway, you know what to do.'

They were obviously talking about Marie-Laure! And Stanislas was encouraging Octave to sort things out. How sweet of him!

'Hi,' Daisy said, putting her hands on Octave's shoulders, who jumped a little.

'Ah, the gorgeous Daisy,' Stanislas said. 'How was Marie-Laure?'

'Very nice. I really like her.'

'And so, what did you talk about?'

'Well,' Daisy said, climbing over the back of the sofa and into Octave's arms, 'she warned me that you were a dangerous *tombeur*. Of course, I told her it was nonsense. You know I find you completely unattractive.'

Stanislas gave them a tolerant smile, then got up and left, taking Bertrand with him. Octave stared at Daisy distractedly for a minute. He must be thinking about Marie-Laure. He'd obviously made his mind up to do the right thing. Best not to nag him about it.

'Are you OK?' Daisy said.

'Yes!' he said, snapping back into his usual smiling self. He kissed her. After a while, he spoke again: 'Can we stay at your place tonight?'

'Yes, of course. But I thought you wanted to go back to yours?' On past occasions Octave, who was reasonably tall, had found Isabelle's doll-size shower cubicle a bit of a challenge.

'I've changed my mind.'

The next day, Octave left early to go to the gym. Dreamily, Daisy got ready very slowly, power-dressing with special care. Paris Fashion Week was in full swing and she was meeting Anouk to go to a couple of shows. Afterwards they were having tea at Ladurée, where, if they were in luck, they might catch a glimpse of fashion royalty – Mario Testino, perhaps, or Anna Wintour – sitting incongruously in the midst of *soignées* Parisiennes and their poodles. It was quite a place for fashion moments even out of show season. Daisy had once seen an old lady dressed entirely in shocking pink, hat and gloves included, order a plate of tiny magenta-coloured raspberry and cherry macaroons and feed them discreetly to her basset – who sat quietly beneath the table wearing a small pink coat.

Daisy did not believe in dressing down for the shows: it had to be designer battledress, and preferably by someone only the cognoscenti would be able to identify. She settled on a black high-necked, slim-hipped and belted coat dress by Savage from two seasons ago, worn with long black boots. It was a sample that had never actually gone into production, a unique piece embroidered with intricate braids of stiff black horsehair. Oh yes, it looked *good*. It *did* sort of say 'kiss the whip, slave' but then again that look always went down well in the fashion world. Daisy cocked her head to one side: perhaps she looked a touch too strict? She needed a frivolous touch – her flashing heart-shaped brooch, of course! Daisy reached for it automatically: it usually lived on her bedside table when she wasn't actually wearing it. But now, she saw, it wasn't there. How odd. She hunted around for it for a moment, then checked the time. She should leave right now if she didn't want to be horribly late. Instead, she'd wear that lime-green corsage she'd bought with Agathe. As for the little heart, it couldn't have gone very far.

11 Isabelle

Isabelle was feeling dizzy. Only an hour ago she had been happily ensconced in her research in the now familiar atmosphere of her room in Daisy's house. Now she found herself on the top floor of a dark and derelict warehouse in Whitechapel, apprehensively following Jules, who herself was being led through the alien crowd.

'You're in there, right,' said their guide, a frighteningly trendy girl armed with a clipboard, pointing at a row in a sea of none too clean plastic chairs. 'The two in the middle.'

Isabelle and Jules took possession of their seats. Savage's show was about to begin and the two blocks of grey plastic chairs framing the catwalk were almost full to capacity. Jules had been to a few of these events before and sat unmoved, flicking through the *Sunday Times*. Isabelle, on the other hand, looked about her with the wide eyes of a first-timer. With its peeling walls and concrete floor, the setting did not match Isabelle's mental picture of a fashion show – rows of well-groomed middle-aged women sitting on small velvet chairs among the *boiseries* of a seventeenth-century salon.

Savage, Chrissie had explained, wanted to steer clear of 'the tent', the marquee erected outside the Natural History Museum in Kensington, where London Fashion Week set up temporary home twice a year. That was too soulless and corporate for her, apparently. What she wanted instead was to show in a space that 'felt like home'. Savage must be somewhat *spéciale*, Isabelle thought while surveying the enormous low-lit warehouse littered with mysterious remnants of defunct machinery and smelling vaguely of dust and chemicals.

She turned to Jules. 'It is a bit sinister, this place.'

'Never let it be said of Savage that she doesn't like things edgy.'

'It seems a little bizarre to invite people here for this. Isn't Whitechapel where there was . . . you know . . . Jack the Ripper?'

'Oh yes, absolutely. You can practically feel his presence at your elbow, can't you? It really gives you gooseflesh.' Jules looked around appreciatively. 'This is more of a *Silence of the Lambs* sort of setting, though.'

Isabelle had not seen the film Jules referred to but she got the general idea.

'Have you read the press release, by the way?' Jules said, drawing Isabelle's attention to the photocopied sheet they had found on their seats. Isabelle had nervously folded hers away into her coat pocket on arrival but closer inspection revealed that it was information of sorts on what they were about to see. The text was set out in the style of a blackmailer's letter, with each word looking as though it had been cut out of newspaper:

SAVAGE:

SPRING–SUMMER WOMENSWEAR

ALL TOGETHER NOW!

Isabelle read on:

In her most revolutionary collection to date, Savage waves goodbye to the individual. Collectively produced by Savage and her team, this collection is also designed to be worn collectively.

Savage's clothes are political and non-elitist. They are for everybody to wear at the same time.

All together now!

Knickerbockers come as modules, to fit as many legs as necessary. Asymmetric skirts composed of spiralling press-studded panels may be extended to include all your friends, whole families and neighbourhoods – and ultimately, in Savage's vision, the whole of humankind.

Boundaries dissolve between self and other, ugly and pretty, one and many, soft and rough, safe and risky, yes and no, big and little, good and bad, why and because, hello and goodbye.

Perhaps understandably, Isabelle only took in a fraction of what she read. Dazed by her first exposure to fashionese, she turned helplessly towards Jules.

'You might enjoy the other side better,' Jules said drily.

Isabelle turned the sheet over. It was a list of credits in which she was surprised and delighted to find her own name: 'Headwear by Christopher Seamyngley, with the invaluable assistance of Isabelle Papillon.' That was sweet of Chrissie. But she was also thankful that Professeur Sureau would never get to hear about her unorthodox extra-curricular activities. It had been a bit of a rush to get everything finished in time, and Isabelle could imagine Sureau's face if he'd seen his serious-minded protégée engaged in last night's frantic sewing of sequins (true to form, Savage had demanded some last-minute changes), which had alternated with equally frantic bouts of dancing to Girls Aloud – an indispensable part of Chrissie's creative process.

There followed what seemed like a very long wait – mainly caused by the late arrival of two Very Important Editors, one male, in a floor-length overcoat made of a patchwork of actual teddy bears, and the other female, wearing a lobster on her head. Isabelle stared in disbelief as they settled themselves after much air-kissing, waving and exclaiming. The lights went down. There was an expectant hush.

Then began a most disorientating phantasmagory. Heralded by the sound of howling wolves punctuated by screeching violins and an occasional nerve-shredding clash of cymbals, eight of Savage's models, their faces made up in the style of Japanese geishas, shuffled down the catwalk in two-by-two crocodiles, bathed in a pale-grey light. Closer inspection of their feet revealed that they were perched on extremely high Eastern-style wooden sandals. Above these they wore shimmering white shorts and tank tops which were joined at the hip and waist, forming a single outfit to include them all, and rakish pink and blue asymmetric harlequin bicorns. As they exited, the next crocodile of eight girls was ready to shuffle on, clad in a gigantic black foam rubber dress, each head topped with black sequinned cat's ears tipped sideways. There followed a shared nude-coloured body stocking overlaid with red lurex embroidery, worn with sculptural pheasant feather headdresses. Each outfit was greeted with gasps and frantic applause. Many of the fashion editors, Isabelle was amused to see as she looked across the catwalk, had stopped scribbling on their pads and were weeping freely.

More hallucinatory visions unfurled, punctuated by howls and sounds of clashing brass: girls joined at the hips in columns of metallic taffeta worn with blue tulle conical hats, bathed in electric blue light; girls with their heads emerging from a communal lace ruff over a communal black rubber sleeveless dress, bathed in red light. For the finale, Savage unleashed a sixteen-legged, sixteen-armed gold Aertex catsuit topped with eight futuristic gold hats reminiscent of the headgear worn by cyclists in the Olympic Games. Isabelle felt a rush of genuine joy. It was all *insensé* – insane, as Jules would no doubt put it – and utterly unwearable. It was ridiculous, pretentious and pointless. And yet, much to her surprise, she found that her own eyes, too, were filled with tears.

'There she is. Feast your eyes,' Jules whispered, as a slender silver-haired woman dressed in a black velvet trouser suit appeared at the catwalk's entrance and took a bow. There was a standing ovation but the designer disappeared into the wings immediately. 'Come on,' Jules went on, gathering her coat and bag, 'let's go backstage and get a drink.'

Isabelle's experience of nightclubs was limited to the Club de la Plage, an entirely wholesome establishment on the Ile de Ré, unsullied by the vagaries of fashion. It catered to people of her own set and felt like an extension of Marie-Laure's house or Claire's apartment. Seats of more adventurous and *branché* nightlife had never appealed to Isabelle. And yet, as she and Jules were whisked off behind a velvet rope by the frighteningly trendy girl with the clipboard, now their ally – while members of the press were kept waiting on the other side – Isabelle reflected with astonishment that she had never felt quite so thrilled in her life.

Backstage was utter chaos, a jumble of spaced-out models, near-hysterical dressers and make-up artists, television cameras and androgynous waiters weaving their way through the crowd with trays of glasses. Isabelle sipped pink champagne and stayed close to Jules. The crowd parted and they saw Chrissie sitting in the lap of an enormously tall girl in her underwear, still wearing her gold helmet. They were both giggling helplessly.

Chrissie leapt up and ran towards Isabelle and Jules with open arms:

'*Here* you are, my *daaar*-lings!' He enfolded them both in a group embrace. 'Did you like it? How was it? Did it look all right? Was it OK? Did you enjoy it? Tell me honestly.' He stood back and looked at their faces. 'Isabelle! I do believe you *wept*! Bless you, darling!'

'Er, yes. I didn't expect . . . it was really . . .'

Isabelle's embarrassed congratulations were soon interrupted by the arrival of a small blonde girl with a side ponytail, who plucked anxiously at Chrissie's sleeve. She wore leggings and a knee-length T-shirt printed with an image of a psychopathic-looking Mickey Mouse wielding a chainsaw. This, Chrissie explained, was Posy, Savage's assistant. Posy looked very harassed.

'Hi, how are you?' she said automatically in Isabelle's general direction. 'Chrissie, she's asking for you. Over there. Now!'

Chrissie appeared to sober up instantly and hurried away without argument.

'I thought the show was incredible,' Isabelle said.

'Oh yeah? That's great,' Posy said with a wan smile.

'And how is *she* today?' Jules asked in a low voice.

In answer Posy clutched her ears and performed a vivid pantomime of Munch's *Scream*.

'She must be relieved now the show is over,' Isabelle said.

'Yeah, kinda. This is over so now she's doing her nut about something else. Catch you later. Got to run.'

Without waiting for Chrissie's release by his boss, Isabelle and Jules made their way home, as they both had appointments later in the afternoon. Isabelle was being picked up at three to drive to Meredith Quince's house for tea with the rest of the Society. Before that, at two, Jules was hosting a band meeting to discuss future performance dates and the recording of their next demo.

At the appointed hour, Jules was upstairs, so it was Isabelle who answered the doorbell. A young man dressed in black stood on the threshold. It took Isabelle half a minute to recognise Karloff. His airborne hairstyle was the same but he looked different and more approachable without his straitjacket, as most people would.

'Oh, hi,' he said diffidently. 'Is Jules there?'

'Yes, come in,' Isabelle said, stepping back to let him in.

Jules was just coming down the stairs and stopped dead in her tracks when she saw her bandmate.

'Hello, Kazza,' she said after a moment.

Karloff cleared his throat, then slowly walked like a man in a dream to the bottom of the stairs and stood there looking at his shoes. Jules stared straight ahead at the wall. There was silence.

Isabelle considered tiptoeing away from this tongue-tied tableau. Instead she said brightly, 'So, you are having a meeting about the band?'

Karloff and Jules looked across at her with gratitude and replied at the same time: 'Yeah. Yes, we are. Definitely. Yeah.'

'Are the girls still in the van?' Jules asked in an unusually high voice. She cleared her throat and pushed her glasses to the top of her nose.

'Yeah, about that,' Karloff said, keeping his eyes on Isabelle. 'Thing is, Legend's got a cold.'

'But the others are on their way?'

'No. Ivy had to go in to work today.'

'Bella?' Jules asked severely, holding on to the banister.

'She's got, like, a plumbing emergency.'

'Oh,' said Jules. She slowly walked backwards up one step. 'Do you mean it's just . . . us?'

Karloff nodded several times.

At this delicate juncture the front door opened and Chrissie walked in on the scene. 'Oh hello, Karloff darling. How divinely brooding you look today!'

At this Jules seemed to come out of her trance. She clomped down the stairs and, grabbing Isabelle, led the way into the kitchen. Karloff and Chrissie followed.

In the kitchen Isabelle said mischievously, 'Chrissie

and I should leave you alone, so you can have your meeting. I have some work to do in my room.'

But Jules shot her such a stern look that Isabelle sat down at the table without further teasing. The Coven's bass player proceeded to fill the kettle crossly, muttering to no one in particular, 'I can't believe these girls. I mean, where is their commitment to the band?'

Isabelle and Chrissie swivelled their heads in the direction of Karloff. He stood silent and downcast by the dresser.

'I'm sure they all intended to be here,' Isabelle said reasonably.

'Bloody amateurs. I'm just fed up with the whole thing.'

Jules had now been standing at the sink with her back to everyone for such a long time that Chrissie went over to rescue her.

'I tell you what, honey,' he said, taking the kettle from her hands, then leading her gently to the table, 'why don't you and Karloff make a start? You're both here: bass guitar, vocals. It seems a shame not to get on with it, hmm? Meanwhile *I'll* make some tea.'

Jules sat down slowly opposite Karloff. Isabelle, seated next to him, noticed that he had somehow managed to cross his black-clad legs twice over, tying them into a knot of anxiety.

'Now, Karloff darling,' Chrissie continued breezily, 'you're the front man. *Take charge*, darling. Come on! What's the *buzz*? How's it all hanging?'

Karloff cleared his throat. The two lovelorn goths glanced at one another, then quickly looked away.

'But the thing is, right . . .' Karloff said at length, uncertainly. 'Usually, the others are here as well . . .'

'Is it the first time you two have met on your own?' Chrissie asked without turning around. 'To talk about Coven matters?'

'Well, yeah,' Karloff said, staring at Jules. 'We've never met without the others before.'

'Really, darling? Well, there's a first time for everything,' said Chrissie. 'Shall I be mother?' he went on, dropping tea bags into mugs and taking the milk out of the fridge. 'Sugar, Karloff?'

'Kazza never takes sugar,' Jules replied before she could stop herself. Karloff blushed scarlet at this mark of attentiveness. Jules began to pull her fringe down over her glasses.

Chrissie, looking over at Isabelle with wide eyes and pinched nostrils, distributed mugs of tea and placed a packet of dark chocolate digestives before Jules. 'Open the goodies, will you, darling?' He sat down and rested his elbows on the table and his chin on interlocked fingers. 'Actually, I long to know about the origins of the band. *How* did you guys meet? Tell all.'

'Whitby,' Karloff said enigmatically.

'I don't understand,' Isabelle said in confusion.

Jules turned towards her. 'Whitby in Yorkshire is where Dracula's boat landed in England.'

Isabelle stared at her blankly.

'In the *book*, darling, the novel by Bram Stoker,' Chrissie said between sips of tea.

Jules and Karloff nodded vigorously.

'So Whitby is a place of *pilgrimage*,' Chrissie pursued,

warming to his theme. 'Like a gothic Ibiza. Everyone wears black. Everyone is pale, dark and interesting. The sky is leaden. There is a graveyard with higgledy-piggledy tombstones. It's freezing cold. A great time is had by all.'

'Two years ago,' Karloff said huskily, 'I drove up there with Ivy. We shared a flat at the time. She brought her mate Belladonna. In the car the three of us started talking of this and that and maybe getting a band together. Just messing about, really. Then we got to Whitby, went to a party, got really drunk and forgot all about it.'

Isabelle glanced at Jules. The Coven's bassist was absent-mindedly trying to open the biscuits but her nails found no purchase on the packaging.

Karloff continued: 'Afterwards we crashed at this B & B, then in the morning we all went to this pub called the Elsinore. I had a stinking hangover by then and was in a right grump. Anyway, in the pub, Ivy ran into these two girls that she vaguely knew. She'd met them at a festival in Sweden the summer before.'

'That was me and Legend,' Jules said, taking over.

'Then my hangover just went. Just like that. Magic.'

'Ivy began to talk about starting a band and as we went round the table it became apparent that we could all play something. And the rest is history.' She tugged once more at the biscuits, to no avail. 'Ah, sod this! I mean, am I the only one who gives a flying sod about The Coven?'

'No! No, you're not,' Karloff said in a strangulated voice, 'I give a flying sod.'

Isabelle and Chrissie exchanged a look. The tension in the room had become unendurable.

'We should really leave you . . .' Isabelle said, beginning to stand up, but Jules' hand shot out under the table and closed over Isabelle's wrist in a vicelike grip. Isabelle sat down again while Chrissie opened the packet of Hob-Nobs. Karloff helped himself. He then looked up, met Jules' eyes, panicked and crushed his biscuit into a fistful of crumbs.

'Didn't the sequinned cat's ears look *divine*?' Chrissie asked, tactfully addressing this question to Isabelle.

'Oh yes,' Isabelle replied. 'I felt really proud of all the hats. My favourite was the gold helmet.'

'Quite right. The gold helmet *is* perfect heaven.'

Jules and Karloff drank their tea in silence. After a few minutes, Karloff said in a lifeless voice, 'Right. I think I'm gonna . . . go home. So . . . I'll speak to the girls about setting up another meeting. All right?'

After his departure, Jules went to her room and shut the door. Soon the sound of manic singing and drumming made itself heard.

'Bauhaus, I should think,' Chrissie said, standing with Isabelle in the hallway. 'She usually turns to them at times of crisis. Come into my parlour, darling, we need to talk.' He closed the door behind them and grinned at Isabelle. 'Honestly, did you ever see anything more *excruciating*?'

Isabelle shook her head. 'It is so strange, because on stage they are really not shy.'

'They are *brazen* on stage! I put it down to the magic of *performance*. But offstage they can't look each other in the eye. Poor little lambs. Or black sheep, I should say, in this case. Now, *what* shall we do about it?' He frowned, then snapped his fingers delightedly. 'Wait! Halloween is coming up! Yes, I *know* what we'll do! And the best thing about it is that Jules *owns* the very thing we need.'

There was just enough time for him to outline his brilliant plan before the minibus driven by Maud pulled up outside the house to collect Isabelle.

The members of the Quince Society sat on board in a frenzy of excitement. All the way to Kew, they chattered excitedly at the fabulous prospect of tea in dear Meredith's house. Looking out of the window, Isabelle wondered how much, if anything, Thomas Quince would know about *The Splodge*. He was quite old, according to Lucy – at least thirty – but unfortunately not old enough to have known his great-aunt.

'We're here!' Maud said. 'All passengers off, please.'

The little band of pilgrims filed out of the minibus, stood around for a while exclaiming at the elegance and beauty of Meredith's house, then huddled on the doorstep. Lucy rang the bell assertively. When the door opened, Isabelle was mildly surprised to recognise the stranger with the playing cards in his hat and the muddy Land Rover. They all filed in and Lucy made the introductions.

'And *this* is our most recent recruit, Izbl Peppy-on,' she finally said, her arm around Isabelle's shoulders. 'She's French, you know!'

'Welcome,' Meredith's great-nephew said, smiling at Isabelle with vague affability but showing no sign of having seen her before. He probably did not remember her: it had been such a brief encounter.

The members of the Quince Society were taken upstairs

and ushered into a drawing room, where softly faded chintz sofas and armchairs were arranged around a low table laden with tea things. A fire was blazing in the fireplace.

'Please help yourselves,' Tom Quince said, pushing back his floppy hair. 'There are two big teapots and enough cups, I think. And I made enough scones for a small army.'

These stood in an enticing golden pile at the centre of the table. Everyone sat down. At first the guests were bashful. There was a respectful lull while tea was poured, and jam and clotted cream passed around the table. Then, emboldened by their refreshments, they all began at once to fire questions at their host. Was this all Meredith's original furniture? And what about the pictures on the walls? Which chair did she usually sit in? Did she like China or Indian tea? Did she often visit the botanical gardens? Was that the reason why she wanted to live in Kew? Did Meredith like to knit or embroider? Did she own a television set? Was she fond of animals? Did she keep a dog?

Isabelle sat on a sofa between Fern and Wendy, keeping her own counsel. During the course of her academic training it had been drummed into her that the important thing wasn't a writer's life but their work. I am a narratologist, Isabelle thought primly, and, as such, I do not actually care very much about such fripperies as Meredith's tastes and hobbies. She looked across the table. Lucy, her grey hair bristling and her blue eyes shining, was barking something enthusiastic at Meredith's great-nephew, who listened without a trace of impatience or boredom.

'And what do *you* do, Mr Quince?' asked Maud with

a certain amount of emphasis. She had been trying to interrupt Lucy for a while.

'Are you also a writer, perhaps?' asked Herbert.

'Nothing so exciting. I'm a gardener.'

Isabelle sighed inwardly. It didn't sound very encouraging for her purposes.

'Oh, really? How lovely!' Fern exclaimed. 'Then you must have a spectacular garden!'

'Well, it's quite a lot of fun, you know,' he said vaguely. 'But it needs masses of work. I do have other people's gardens to attend to, so my own garden suffers as a result, naturally. I would show it to you, such as it is, but it's really too dark already.'

'So was it garden design you studied when you lived in Italy?' asked Maud.

He said yes, it was, and turned to answer Selina's questions about Mediterranean flora. Munching on a cucumber sandwich, Isabelle scanned Tom Quince for signs of resemblance to his great-aunt. There didn't seem to be any, apart from general colouring, and even then his hair was actually lighter than hers in the portrait. She took another tiny bite of her sandwich. On the other hand, she thought to herself while examining him, he didn't somehow look quite contemporary. Perhaps it was those tortoiseshell glasses of his: they looked a bit retro. No, it was more than that. The slant of his cheekbones, perhaps, and the firm sinuous line of his mouth. He had the sort of face that in previous eras would naturally have been adorned with a moustache. A faintly military one, she thought, one that curled up at both ends.

At that moment their eyes met. He raised his eyebrows

slightly and gave her a look that was so direct and ironic that she almost swallowed her sandwich whole. Isabelle turned hastily towards Wendy, who sat in meek, contented silence next to her, as though to respond to something she'd said. When she looked across the table again, Meredith's great-nephew had resumed his vague and amiable manner, and was responding to Maud's detailed interrogation about Florentine architecture. Isabelle must have imagined that uncharacteristic glance. He was not, in fact, paying her any particular attention.

After tea, the members of the Quince Society were at long last able to have a look around the house. They started, thrillingly, with Meredith's bedroom.

'Oh,' Fern said, unable to conceal her disappointment.

'Ah yes,' Tom Quince said apologetically. 'I'm afraid it's not "just as she left it". My father turned it into his own study when he took over the house, then stored all kinds of unwanted things in it when they moved out. It does look a little forlorn now. I suppose it might do as a guest bedroom.'

'Perhaps,' Wendy said as loud as she dared, 'you might like to restore it to what it was in her day?'

'Mmm, yes, that is an idea,' he said absent-mindedly.

They looked into the dining room, then went up one more flight of stairs to look at what had been a nursery for Meredith's younger brother.

'Meredith would have visited my grandfather in here and played with him when he was a small boy. Then it became my room, until I left home in my twenties. And now I have reclaimed it. I'm afraid it's rather untidy.'

The room, painted a very dark green, had the look of

an attractive masculine den. Isabelle noticed a lovely etching of formal gardens above the bed and a desk piled high with botanical journals. They all went back down the stairs to the ground floor.

Tom Quince opened a door, saying, 'And this is the library.'

Isabelle was briefly reminded of the games of Cluedo she had played as a child: was she about to come face to face with Colonel Mustard (or Moutarde, as in the French version of the game) wielding the candlestick? Instead, she went in behind Herbert and Emily Merryweather and found herself in the exact setting of Meredith Quince's portrait. There was a chorus of delight from the members of the Quince Society.

This room, in contrast to the others, appeared to be just as Meredith had left it. Isabelle recognised the book-shelves, the writing desk, the round coffee table, the green-and-red Persian rug. Meredith's green armchair had been reupholstered in primrose yellow. Beyond the French windows, the garden was plunged in darkness. Tom Quince was explaining to his rapt audience that this was the room where his great-aunt had done most of her writing, at this very desk. They all gazed at this piece of furniture with reverence. Furtively, Herbert ran his hand over it, no doubt thinking of the genesis of *Death of a Lady Ventriloquist*.

'Which of your great-aunt's books do you like best, Tom?' Selina asked their host.

He ran his hand through his hair, which, after many such questions from the visitors, was beginning to look rather untidy.

'Ah, the books, yes. You're going to think me the most dreadful philistine, but I'm ashamed to say I have never read any of them.'

A polite but scandalised silence greeted this confession.

'It's a feeble excuse, I know, but my parents never encouraged me to take an interest in Meredith's novels. I suppose I've always taken them for granted. I think the original manuscripts are all here somewhere,' he concluded vaguely.

Isabelle's heart did a small somersault.

'Oh, how jolly!' Lucy barked. 'D'you think we could have a peek?'

'I should imagine,' Maud interjected, 'that you keep them locked away in a safe.'

Tom Quince frowned and shook his head. 'N-no, I don't think we have a safe. They're just –' he gestured around the room '– in the house. I'm really not sure where.'

'What do they look like?' Peter asked, stroking his beard excitedly. 'Did she type or write in longhand?'

'Ah, let me see, um, type, I think. I was shown them once when I was younger.'

Isabelle could barely contain herself. Meredith's relative might not have the faintest idea of his great-aunt's literary genius but he lived here, in this house. And somewhere in this house might also be the manuscript of *The Splodge*. She waited until Lucy, Peter and Maud had moved away to examine the bookshelves, then sidled up to him.

'Excuse me . . . Mr Quince?'

'Please call me Tom, Isabelle. That is your name, isn't it?'

'Yes.'

'And the Peppy-on bit?'

'In fact it's Papillon.'

'Papillon? That actually means something, doesn't it? Something to do with fairy tales, isn't it?'

'Er, no.' He wore an open-necked shirt and as Isabelle looked up at him her eye was drawn to a light tuft of interesting golden fur in the hollow of his throat. She blinked, then smiled at him. 'Maybe you're confusing it with Cendrillon – the French name of Cinderella.'

'Of course, yes. How silly of me. Hang on – I think I remember now. Is Papillon something like a whirl?'

'A whirl?'

'Something that carries you off irresistibly,' Tom Quince said.

Isabelle frowned, then her mind cleared. 'Oh, I think you mean *tourbillon*. In fact, *papillon* means "butterfly".'

'Ah, yes, of course. A very nice name.'

'There is something I'd like to ask you about.'

'Oh?'

'It's about your great-aunt.'

'Oh.'

Isabelle looked around. The members of the Society were all chatting happily out of earshot. She had just had an idea.

'Perhaps . . . the people I share a house with are having a little party for Halloween. Would you like to come? Then we could talk properly.'

He smiled vaguely. 'Halloween? Yes. Why not? Should I bring my own pumpkin?'

12 Daisy

'Paris is pulsating to the beat of Fashion Week. Who's in? Who's out? What are the season's most important new trends? And what to wear to be *à la mode* at the shows?' Daisy typed slowly on her laptop, using just two fingers.

So far, her *Sparkle* blogs had flowed out in a frenzy of excitement. This one was much harder going. She stared listlessly out of the window of Isabelle's study and wrapped her fluffy pink dressing gown more closely around her. For the first time since moving to Paris she felt very chilly. Perhaps the notes she'd made at the shows would provide some inspiration. She turned the pages of her pad and typed in whatever seemed vaguely relevant:

> *Patent everything – shiny shiny shiny.*
> *Nude tights in/bare legs out.*
> *Soft pale grey is new black?*

The new black, really? Whatever. It was hard to care at the moment. Daisy paused and looked out of the window. Outside the sky was just that newly fashionable shade of grey. It looked like it was going to rain in a minute. She turned another page and typed in:

Vintage returns with contemporary, slouchy edge.
Airport chic – French pleats and turquoise mascara.
Seven-inch heels on pain of social death – five at a push.
Key look of the season: think Sophia Loren meets Hello Kitty.

Dullsville, all of it. What else? Oh yes:

Best party: launch of Ça pue, non? Revolutionary new perfume that smells like petrol. Brilliant party food – experimental canapés, some delicious, others disgusting, laid on giant Perpex table like snakes and ladders board.

She stared at the paragraph, then highlighted the word 'snakes'. Then she typed:

Snake, snake, Octave is a snake.
A rat.
A complete and utter bastard.
Who'd have thunk it?

Daisy closed her eyes and replayed, for the millionth time, the devastating film of her last encounter with Octave, under the trees of the Luxembourg Gardens. 'Heartbroken' wasn't just a turn of phrase – her heart *was* literally broken. She reached for the box of tissues. After a while her computer went to sleep. It began to rain.

'What heart? Oh, the plastic brooch you always wear?' said Agathe, after taking a small sip of her Perrier. She had been summoned to an emergency meeting by Daisy and they now sat face to face in a noisy café on Place Saint-Sulpice. Agathe looked particularly immaculate and radiant today, in a blue silk shirt that fitted her perfectly, her sleek hair held back with a velvet Alice band. 'Well, that is OK!' she said with an exaggerated sigh. 'Actually, you are lucky, Daisy. Now you can get yourself something pretty instead. I can help you choose.

'They have this rule that it has to be a thing the girl will miss. Like a trophy they can show each other as proof of their conquest. They all do it, but Octave is the most successful, I believe. Can you imagine how many of these trinkets he must have? Hundreds of them, probably, no? He is really awful!'

She started to laugh but, seeing Daisy's expression, stopped herself just in time. She went on: 'In actual fact Marie-Laure told me what happened to her at the time – but in confidence, you know. So I didn't feel that I could tell you about it. It's so important to respect other people's privacy. You understand, don't you? Anyway, judging by your behaviour at the Paris-Plage, you knew what you wanted. That is what everyone thought anyway when we all talked about it afterwards.

'Yes, that little notebook is where they keep score. I think that when they saw you at Claire's party, it was just a question of who was going to get you first. Like betting on a horse. The same thing happened last year when Aurélie's little Swiss-German penpal came to stay. But with her it was just a question of a few kisses at a party. So it was not as humiliating as what has happened to you. And she went home after a few days. But you have to stay and deal with this for the rest of the year. How do you think you will cope?

'Do not take it too personally. There have been so many others. The thing about French men is that they are very proud of being misogynists. They are always talking about *la misogynie* this, *la misogynie* that. They find it hilarious.' Agathe tucked a stray lock of hair behind her ear and smiled slightly. 'And if I were you I would stop plaiting the fringes of your pashmina like that. You are going to damage it.'

'In the Luxembourg Gardens?' Marie-Laure asked incredulously. 'No! Oh, he is completely incorrigible. You know that is also where he told *me* that it was over.'

In desperation Daisy had got Marie-Laure's number from Isabelle's Rolodex. Thank goodness Isabelle was so organised. Daisy now sat on a sofa in Marie-Laure's house, an untouched little fruit tart on the table in front of her. Her tea was turning cold in its cup.

'The funny thing is that it wasn't that long ago, but I can't really remember what he said to me,' Marie-Laure continued, crossing her long legs. 'Probably something from the classics: it was all a terrible mistake; it should never have happened. We were walking. We were holding hands. It was a beautiful day and I was looking around at the other people, and it took me completely by surprise. It was very quick, over in two minutes. You too? Yes, Octave likes to work quickly. He is an expert. And then he put me in a taxi and vanished. *Et hop!* And then he had the nerve to crash my party with his acolytes.

'Of course I should have known that something was wrong. The day after . . . well, that night he spent with me, I couldn't find my favourite earrings, the ones with the coral. They really are swines. *De vrais salauds.* And the worst thing is that I had heard rumours before about Octave and his friends and their little games but I . . .' She inhaled sharply and tossed her head. 'You see, I thought . . . I didn't think it could happen to me!'

She bit her lip and took Daisy's limp hand in hers. 'But you know, Daisy, I ran into Octave the other day with Stanislas and I thought he looked really . . . *embêté*. Pre-occupied, upset. And that's really not his style. Perhaps you have taught him a lesson.

'Actually, you know, it is complicated. It counts a lot for Octave, what his friends think of him. He has a fragile ego, like most men.'

'Daze, you're mad,' Jules said tonelessly on the telephone. 'It's not complicated at all. He just needs a good punch up the bracket.'

13 Isabelle

When Isabelle came downstairs, the preparations for Halloween were in full swing. Belladonna was mixing gallons of Bloody Mary in an enormous punch bowl. Chrissie and Legend were festooning the kitchen walls with garlands of dead leaves they had collected from the garden and sprayed a brilliant black. Flame-haired Ivy stood at the sink, filling surgical rubber gloves with water and fastening them with a knot. Isabelle was mystified but did not feel quite up to quizzing the taciturn drummer. Jules and Karloff sat side by side at the table, without speaking or looking at each other, studiously carving pumpkins into jack-o'-lanterns. Chrissie looked around as Isabelle walked in and gave her a conspiratorial smile. Isabelle smiled back. After dinner, their Brilliant Plan would kick into action – with a little help from the spirits.

Isabelle went back upstairs to make a last-ditch attempt with her boyfriend, who had picked this particular week to come and see her. Clothaire had not taken to Isabelle's eccentric housemates and spent most of his time holed up in her room, reading and sulking. He was attending tonight's party under duress but had refused categorically to wear fancy dress because it was childish, stupid and pointless. Jules and the others, on the other hand, took Halloween very seriously. Jules was going as Cleopatra and Legend as the

Mummy. Karloff, taking the easy option, was going as a Victorian lunatic in a straitjacket, Ivy as Joan of Arc in chainmail, and voluptuous Belladonna as a sexy vampire. Chrissie, who loved dressing up, had considered Dorothy in *The Wizard of Oz* (with Raven the cat cross-dressing as Toto the dog) but had changed his mind after trying on a traumatically unflattering ginger wig with braids. He was now going as cheeky Huckleberry Finn, in cut-off trousers and a straw hat, and Raven, under her own steam, as Catwoman (in a minimalist outfit consisting of a small black satin cape).

Isabelle had not been very keen on dressing up at first, but Chrissie, who could be very perceptive when he put his mind to it, had rescued her by pronouncing that she should come as Audrey Hepburn in *Breakfast at Tiffany's*, more of a concept than an actual costume. Isabelle would wear her own little black dress with a long string of pearls, and borrow Chrissie's cigarette holder.

As she sat at Daisy's dressing table (returned to its original use for tonight) putting her hair up in a restrained version of Holly Golightly's beehive, she tried to sway Clothaire one last time. 'I just think it might be more polite to make a little effort,' she said pleadingly.

'No.'

'You might enjoy it, you know.'

'No.'

It was entirely useless, as she knew from past experience. Clothaire had refused point-blank to visit a fancy-dress shop, so Chrissie had offered him dozens of colourful possibilities drawn from his own wardrobe – since many of his clothes readily doubled as fancy dress. Clothaire had stared coldly and said no. It would be all right, Isabelle told herself, carefully applying lipstick. There would be at least one other guest Clothaire could talk to at dinner: Tom Quince. They would probably get on really well.

Isabelle made her way downstairs, promising to call Clothaire when it was time to eat. By now everyone else was dressed and they stood around in the kitchen, admiring one another's costumes. Standing on a chair, Jules was lighting the candles on the wrought-iron chandelier hanging over the table.

'*Do* be careful, Ju,' Chrissie drawled from beneath his straw hat, 'you're a walking fire hazard in all that lamé.' He looked across at Isabelle and grinned. 'Well, I do declare! If it isn't Miss Holly Golightly!'

The mummified Legend, whose ponytail rose untamed through the bandages at the top of her head like a small geyser of crude oil, shuffled towards Isabelle and gave her the thumbs-up. 'Bloody hell, you look great. You should wear black more often.'

'Everybody should always wear black,' Ivy said gravely, leaning on her sword in front of the dresser, which now bore a whole cortège of grinning jack-o'-lanterns.

The doorbell rang and Isabelle went to answer it. It was Tom Quince in a dinner jacket, carrying a basket under his arm.

'Oh hello, Mr Qu—. I mean Tom.'

'Hi, Isabelle. Now –' he gestured apologetically towards his outfit '– I was absolutely determined to come as something more exciting but it's been a busy week and I ran out of time. And this was hanging in my wardrobe and it was clean. I hope it's OK.'

Isabelle smiled. 'It's fine. You look like . . . James Bond. But with a basket.'

'Well, yes, naturally. He never leaves the house without one.' He handed the basket to her, saying vaguely, 'I thought you might like these.'

Isabelle peered at the contents – several yellow objects she couldn't identify.

'Oh. Thank you very much.'

'You don't know what they are, do you?'

'Well, no. Sorry.' They looked quite exotic. 'Mangoes?'

He shook his head. 'No, quinces.'

As she still looked a little blank, he went on: 'Like my name, you see. Or rather my great-aunt's. It was meant to be a subtle literary joke.'

'Oh! Quince, quinces! Of course. I'm sorry. I had never thought about what her name meant particularly.' She smiled. 'Thank you very much.'

'You look lovely.'

'Thank you,' she said, tucking the basket under her arm. 'The others are in the kitchen downstairs. I'll call Clothaire, my boyfriend. He is very much looking forward to meeting you.' That wasn't exactly true. Clothaire had shown no enthusiasm whatever.

Tom Quince's expression did not change at all. He ran his fingers through his hair. 'Ah, yes. Excellent,' he said after a barely noticeable pause.

Just as Isabelle finished introducing everyone in the candlelit kitchen, Clothaire came in, looking displeased. 'I have been waiting upstairs for an eternity, Isabelle,' he said in French, ignoring everyone else, 'I thought we agreed you would call me when it was time for dinner.'

'I was just about to call you. Dinner is almost ready. This is my boyfriend, Clothaire. Tom Quince, Meredith's great-nephew.'

'Oh, 'ello.'

'Hello.'

They shook hands and Isabelle, pleased with her match, left them to it. She was certain that they would hit it off. Chrissie began to dip a ladle into the large bowl of Bloody Mary, filling glasses to the brim with characteristic insouciance. Several ice hands floated eerily on the surface of the drink – the result of Ivy's earlier activities. Isabelle was impressed. Clothaire, however, took one look at the gothic cocktail, shook his head disdainfully and demanded a Scotch. Meanwhile Belladonna's powerful mix loosened tongues and by the time they began to sit down to eat in the candlelight, everyone was talking at once.

Isabelle had planned to sit next to Meredith's relative at dinner and engage him in conversation about the significance of the ink splodge in the portrait. But Chrissie called her to the stove to help him serve the pumpkin soup and by the time they had finished filling bowls with sweet-smelling orange brew, the seating plan had shifted. Tom Quince had ended up next to Belladonna while Jules, whose goal was presumably to sit as far away from Karloff as possible, had promptly taken the seat on Tom's other side. Only two places remained, one for Isabelle between Clothaire and Karloff and one for Chrissie between Legend and Ivy. Isabelle would have to wait until after dinner to broach the topic of *The Splodge*. They all began to eat.

'This is pretty good, actually,' Legend said from between her bandages, after a few carefully negotiated mouthfuls.

'It's much better than that idea of yours, anyway,' said Belladonna. 'That was just rank.'

'I don't know about that. I still think a boiled calf's head would have made a great centrepiece.'

'So rank.'

'Maybe. Really gothic, though.' Having made her point, Legend tossed her jet-black ponytail.

'I would like to know,' Isabelle piped up, 'how you decide that something is gothic or that it isn't.'

'Anything that has sort of . . . a dark presence is gothic,' said Ivy, her freckled white face framed by her silver chainmail balaclava.

The others nodded in agreement.

'Like a kind of *frisson*?' said Isabelle.

'Ooh yeah,' Ivy said, narrowing her slightly protuberant green eyes. 'Brrrrr . . .

Across the table, Clothaire was quizzing Isabelle's guest about his academic credentials and career choice. 'But I don't understand what you say. Explain me why you want to be a florist. It's a job for a girl, that, no?'

'Some people think so,' Tom Quince said vaguely.

'I once knew a *charming* florist,' Chrissie said, smiling at Meredith's relative. 'He was so *very* fragrant *always*.'

'Good for you,' Tom Quince said, nodding. He looked at Clothaire. 'Not a florist, by the way, a gardener.'

Clothaire snorted.

Tom Quince ate a mouthful of soup, then said, 'Though, as a matter of fact, I did consider becoming a florist. But what I enjoy most is making gardens.'

'It's very powerful stuff you're harnessing, very healing,' his neighbour Belladonna said, looking at him through her eyelashes. 'You must have a really deep connection with telluric forces.'

'Like me, Bella is a pagan,' said Jules, his other neighbour. 'Unlike me, she likes nothing better than dancing naked in the moonlight. I prefer to wear a toga. It's more dignified.'

'I like to commune fully with the earth mother,' said Belladonna, curling a lock of her black hair around her forefinger. 'I'm a white witch, you see.'

Clothaire banged on the table and frightened Raven, who bounded down to the floor with an indignant miaow.

'No, but you are joking with this! You went to a good university. You are an intelligent guy, yes or no? You should do something more interesting.'

Tom Quince calmly shifted his gaze from Belladonna to Clothaire. 'No doubt you're right.'

'Have you quite finished?' asked Jules, who had come to stand behind Clothaire. 'I thought so. I'll take this if you don't mind.' She whisked away his half-empty bowl and placed it on top of a perilously high pile of crockery that she then carried across to the sink.

Isabelle looked across the table to check that Tom Quince was not bored. She needn't have worried. He was laughing with Jules at something Belladonna had just said. Belladonna, incidentally, looked rather good, if (in

Isabelle's opinion) slightly blatant, in a laced-up dress that made the most of her cleavage. Isabelle felt relieved while also experiencing a vague and mysterious annoyance.

Karloff got up the courage to help Jules dish out the next course. Clothaire stared down balefully at the food that was placed before him:

'What is this?'

'Cheese and onion tart. All right?'

'What? *Et alors*? There is no meat? You are joking with me? This is food for the . . . chicks, the women!'

'Actually, *I* think meat stinks,' Ivy said in a slow sing-song voice, as though speaking to a very small child.

'I'm a vegetarian too,' Karloff said mildly. 'Like Ivy. And Bella. And, er . . . Jules. It's *not* food for girls.'

'And so explain me why you are wearing lipstick and mascara?' Clothaire said, leaning back in his chair.

Before Karloff could respond, Isabelle interjected hurriedly, 'The tart is really good, you know. Try a little piece.'

'Pfff, vegetarians! You make me laugh,' Clothaire said, lighting a cigarette. 'Like you there,' he said, gesturing towards Belladonna. 'You are telling me that you are a vegetarian vampire, maybe? Or maybe you drink only the vegetarian blood? *Hein, alors*?'

'It's fancy dress. That means role-play, you know,' Belladonna replied with a frosty smile. 'Besides, you don't have to be a vampire to want to bite certain people's necks,' she added, baring her pointy canines and smiling at Tom Quince.

'You are all stupid or what? Nobody has explained you

that we are omnivore?' Clothaire boomed, grinding his cigarette butt several times into his piece of onion tart.

'That's what the corporations want you to believe,' Ivy said with extreme solemnity. 'Actually, it's all just a big lie.'

'We are all Gaea's children,' Belladonna said. 'We may partake of her vegetable bounty but we mustn't kill other living things. It's terrible karma.'

'I think it's a question of personal taste . . .' Isabelle began.

Clothaire spun around to face her. '*Et l'autre emmerdeuse qui s'y met*! Nobody asked your advice, Isabelle. Just shut up when I'm talking, OK?' he thundered.

Isabelle shut up. Clothaire lit another cigarette, presumably marshalling his thoughts about the proper diet for human beings. Nobody else spoke. After a moment's silence, Isabelle looked around the table in confusion. She suddenly realised that when something like this happened in Paris, another guest – more often than not her dear Agathe – would laugh the whole thing off, scolding Clothaire in an indulgent way so that Isabelle never minded his outbursts. Tonight, on the other hand, the other guests all stared at Clothaire, open-mouthed. All, in fact, except Tom Quince, who was looking straight at Isabelle with an odd expression on his face, almost of anger. She blushed ferociously.

'I have just had *the* most *mar*-vellous idea,' Chrissie said, not a minute too soon. 'Ju-Ju, why don't you go get your Ouija board and we'll have ourselves a little Halloween séance.'

This broke the horrified spell around the table. Jules

went to fetch the alphabet board in her room. While Legend, Karloff and Ivy cleared the table, Isabelle slipped out into the garden. It was a clear moonlit night. Earlier in the day, Jules and Chrissie had made a bonfire of dead leaves on the lawn, and the pile of ashes was still smoking a little. Isabelle walked over to the bench and sat down. A minute or so later she heard the kitchen door open. She didn't turn her head, knowing full well that it was Clothaire, probably with another cigarette.

'Are you all right, Isabelle?'

Isabelle looked up to see Meredith's great-nephew standing beside the bench. She flinched a little and stared straight ahead of her.

'Yes, of course. I'm absolutely fine,' she said primly.

'I thought perhaps . . .'

'What?' she said, and started to shiver.

'How stupid of me. Here, let me.' There was a quick rustling sound, and then Isabelle felt herself enveloped in something warm – his jacket. He sat down next to her.

'Thank you very much,' she said in a much smaller voice than she had intended.

They sat in silence for a while. Tom Quince threw his head back and looked up at the sky. Then he turned towards her and spoke. 'What was it you wanted to ask me, by the way? About Meredith?'

'Oh yes,' Isabelle replied, much relieved by the change of subject. 'The other day at Lucy's house, I was looking at the portrait of Meredith and . . . Did you notice the –'

A cry came from the kitchen door. 'Yoo-hoo! Isabelle?'

And then, in the same voice but one octave lower: 'Tom? Where are you?'

Belladonna was coming across the lawn, holding the hem of her dress in one hand and beckoning with the other. 'Come on, we need everybody to gather for the séance.'

They went back into the house. Most of the guests were sitting around the table, looking at the board and chattering excitedly. Clothaire was leaning against the dresser, away from the rest. When he saw Isabelle, he came forwards, put an arm around her and gave the back of her neck a quick squeeze. She smiled at him and automatically took off Tom Quince's jacket, which she handed back to its owner. They all sat down, except Clothaire who went upstairs to watch television.

The spirits – helped along by Isabelle and, rather less discreetly, by Chrissie – proved to be in great verve. They told Jules that 'S-O-M-E-O-N-E-T-A-L-L-A-N-D-D-A-R-K-S-E-C-R-E-T-L-Y' pined for her and Karloff that his destiny was to be 'L-O-V-E-D-B-Y-T-H-E-Q-U-E-E-N'.

'The Queen?' Karloff wondered aloud.

'Well, not *the* Queen, you know, obviously,' Legend said meditatively. 'She's a bit old for you, apart from anything else.'

'Perhaps it's metaphorical,' Belladonna said. 'The spirits often talk in riddles. Can we ask about *my* love life now?'

'In a minute, Bella darling,' Chrissie said. 'I think we should get to the bottom of this first.'

'Go on, Kazza,' said Ivy.

'All right. Er . . . what Queen do you mean?'

The glass stood still for a moment, then began to move confidently, spelling out: 'T-H-E-Q-U-E-E-N-O-F-D-E-N-I-A-L'.

'What does that mean?'

'Dunno, really.'

'Well, there is one queen in the room,' Legend said, pointing at Chrissie.

'Who, me? Oh, come *off* it, Legend! Karloff darling, you know I find you *maddeningly* gorgeous, but you're really not my type. No, no, that's *not* it, I'm afraid. Let's see . . . the Queen of denial. The *Queen*, you see? *Of. De. Nial*. Mmm . . . It does remind me of something, something that is right under our noses . . . Now what could it be? Any ideas, anyone?'

'I think we should ask about the future of the band,' Jules said severely, adjusting her golden headdress.

Having dispatched such enquiries as briefly and encouragingly as possible, the spirits returned to what they really wanted to talk about: 'T-H-E-Q-U-E-E-N-M-Y-G-O-O-D-N-E-S-S-W-A-K-E-U-P-W-H-A-T-S-W-R-O-N-G-W-I-T-H-U-I-T-S-S-O-O-B-V-I-O-U-S-T-H-I-N-K-U-F-O-O-L-T-H-I-N-K.'

They all looked at one another.

'Wow, this spirit really has a one-track mind,' said Ivy.

'Yeah, it's getting a bit dull,' said Belladonna, glancing at Tom Quince. 'Shall we put on some music? I feel like dancing.'

'There's no full moon tonight, Bella. Don't get overexcited,' Jules said drily.

'Yeah, let's play a game instead,' said Legend. 'How about Eek?'

'What is that?' asked Isabelle.

'Well,' Ivy replied, 'somebody hides, then the others all look for him or her, while saying "eek".'

'On all fours,' Jules interjected.

'That's right. When you find the hidden person, you stop saying "eek" and hide with them. At the end everyone is hiding together and the last one left has lost.'

Isabelle and Chrissie exchanged a smile. The game had distinct possibilities for generating greater intimacy between Jules and Karloff.

'Let's put all the lights out,' Belladonna said, enthusiastically blowing out the candles.

Leaving the darkened kitchen, they went upstairs and congregated in the hallway.

Hearing voices, Clothaire emerged from Chrissie's room. 'What are you doing?'

'Playing a silly game, Clo-Clo darling,' said Chrissie, earning himself a venomous glance from Clothaire. 'Sorry to disturb you.'

'It's a sort of *cache-cache*,' Isabelle explained.

Clothaire drew himself up to his full height. 'OK, and you were just going to ignore me, like I'm not there? Thank you very much, Isabelle. I am capable to play, you know.'

'Of course you can play,' Jules said tonelessly. 'Can't think of anything that would be more fun.'

While Isabelle briefly explained the rules, Chrissie said, 'Now who's going to hide? Perhaps it should be someone who doesn't know the house all that well. Like . . . oh, I don't know, Karl . . .'

'I'll hide,' Tom Quince said quite unexpectedly.

'Great,' said Belladonna.

'Everybody close their eyes and count to a hundred,' said Jules, putting out the light. 'Then start searching, and don't forget to go "eek". No talking.'

As a low chorus of 'eek, eek' rose in the darkness, broken up by a few high-pitched giggles, Isabelle carefully made for the stairs, trying to avoid collision with the other players, who were dispersing like a pack of puppies. Trying to spare her Dior tights by shuffling on hands and feet rather than on her knees, she reached the first floor and sat against the wall. Across the landing was Jules' bedroom. Hopefully there would be nobody in there and she could have a moment of peace and quiet. Inside, it smelled of chocolate incense. 'Eek?' Isabelle whispered as she padded carefully around Jules' bed.

After a moment she realised that the darkness was not absolute in the room. The curtains were slightly parted, letting in a ray of moonlight, which illuminated the floor beneath the window. 'Eek?' said Isabelle, noticing a dark object sticking out from beneath the hem of the curtain: it was half of a shiny black brogue. Cautiously lifting a corner of material, she discovered Tom Quince sitting on Jules' cushioned window seat. Silently, he held a hand out to her and helped her up. They rearranged the curtain and sat side by side for a while.

Eventually, Isabelle turned to her guest. He was staring straight ahead and looked, oddly, rather cross.

'I'm sorry you and Clothaire didn't have more time to talk.'

'That's all right. You and I haven't had time to talk either. About Meredith.'

'No. This has turned out to be more of a children's party than a dinner for grown-ups. I hope you don't mind playing games.'

'Games? No.'

'It's just that . . . you don't *look* like you're enjoying yourself,' Isabelle said worriedly.

'Actually, I was wondering if *you* were, Isabelle. Maybe I'm just being dim.'

'Dim?'

'Obtuse. Other people's relationships are always impossible to understand for an outsider.'

Isabelle turned this over in her mind, then slowly looked up at him. Suddenly, the curtains were parted theatrically:

'Eek-eek to you, my *chickens*!' Chrissie said in a loud stage whisper. 'Room for a little one?' he said, wedging himself in between them.

Before long, Jules and Belladonna joined them and squeezed in, too. When Karloff also turned up, things became rather crowded behind the curtain.

'Perhaps,' Belladonna said, 'we could sit in each other's laps? To save a bit of space?'

'Brilliant idea,' said Chrissie. 'Karloff, honey, why don't you take my place, and I'll sit in Bella's lap . . .'

'No, I meant . . .' Belladonna said, standing up.

'Shush! You'll give us away! Sit back down like a good girl and I'll sit on you. You know I weigh almost nothing.

Now, Karloff, *you*'d better take someone else in your lap. Oh, I know, Isabelle, can you let Jules through? The poor thing is all squashed up against the window.'

Isabelle stood up.

'I'm fine,' Jules said, without moving.

The door creaked open. Hearing it, Chrissie had no choice but to push Isabelle hurriedly into Karloff's lap. They all held their breath. 'Eek?' said a voice in the dark. Then there was a loud bump.

'Ah, bloody hell!' said Legend. 'Who put that there?'

She appeared between the curtains, grinning as she surveyed the hidden group in their various constrained attitudes. 'You look like one of those phone booth challenges.'

At this point there was a metallic clanging sound outside the door.

'That'll be Ivy,' Legend whispered, perching on Tom Quince's knee.

A moment later, Ivy, who was the smallest player, had been hoisted up onto the pile and was lying lengthways across her friends' laps.

'That leaves only Clothaire,' Karloff whispered.

'Yeah,' said Ivy. 'How long shall we leave him to stew?'

'Well, I haven't got any plans for the rest of the night,' said Legend.

'That way he can really think things through in peace,' said Jules. 'Without interruptions from meddling females.'

Isabelle held up her hand to silence them. Coming down the stairs was the slow plodding sound of footsteps, punctuated with Clothaire's exasperated voice going 'Hic! Hic?'

in the quiet house. He sounded so lonely that Isabelle could stand it no longer. She pulled the curtain open and ran to the door.

'Clothaire! We're all here!'

She opened the door and put her arms around his waist.

Jules put the light on, illuminating the rest of the group. They all blinked at one another.

'Mulled wine, anyone, to finish us off?' Chrissie suggested.

Walking down the stairs to the kitchen, Belladonna said to Isabelle in confidential tones, 'I *really* like your friend. He's adorable.'

Isabelle smiled at her. Thank goodness there were some perceptive people who could see through to Clothaire's qualities.

'Thank you. I think so too,' she said.

'Mmm, yes, he is quite attractive in a *surly* kind of way,' said Chrissie, who was right behind them.

'Not her boyfriend,' Belladonna said. 'The other one, Tom. He's so mysterious. Do you think he'd come to our next gig if I asked him?'

'Well, I don't know if it's his kind of . . .' Isabelle began. 'I really don't know him very well.' Not at all, in fact, she thought crossly. She had made no progress at all in her enquiry. At least now the game was over she might get him on one side and question him.

But when they reached the hallway, Tom Quince stopped and turned to Jules and Isabelle. 'It's getting late. I should get home.'

'Oh no, don't go!' Belladonna said pleadingly before Isabelle had a chance to speak.

'I'm afraid I must. Thanks so much for supper,' he said, smiling at Jules, who, astonishingly, smiled back. 'It was very nice to meet you all.'

'Good night, and *do* come again,' said Chrissie, shaking his hand coquettishly. 'Come on, sleepy chickens,' he said, addressing the other guests. 'Mulled wine awaits downstairs.'

'What's that you say? Mulled wine? That sounds completely *dégueulasse*,' said Clothaire, starting up the stairs. 'Me, I am going to bed. *Tu viens,* Isabelle?'

'*Oui, tout de suite,*' she said, looking around at him with a smile. 'In a minute. I'm just saying goodbye to Tom.'

Isabelle frantically tried to think. How to engineer another meeting with him? She opened the door and stood aside to let him pass. 'Er, so . . .' was all she could manage.

'It was very nice to see you again and meet your friends,' he said vaguely. 'Sorry we didn't get a chance to have that talk. Was it something important?'

'Yes! Important to me. For my thesis. Maybe we could talk some other time?'

'I have a lot of work on at the moment, Isabelle. Most of it is outside London. I'm afraid I'm not actually going to be around very much,' Tom Quince said slowly, looking at her in that unfocused way of his.

'Oh.'

'Well, good night,' he said, leaning over to kiss her on the cheek. His eyes, seen properly for the first time, were a dark slate blue.

Before Isabelle could answer, Clothaire's voice came booming down from the top of the house: 'Isabelle!

Non, mais qu'est-ce qu'elle fabrique? Come on, come on! HURRY UP! I'm WAI-TING!'

At the sound of her boyfriend's voice, Isabelle turned away to look over her shoulder. Otherwise she might have noticed Tom Quince's nostrils flaring very slightly. He ran his hand through his ruffled hair and took one step back over the threshold and into the house.

'Actually, Isabelle, it just occurs to me that . . . Those quinces – I take it you don't know how to prepare them?'

'No, I have no idea,' Isabelle said, shrugging and holding her palms out.

He smiled and gave her bare arm a friendly squeeze.

'Oh!' Isabelle said, laughing a little. 'Did you feel that? I got a small electric shock.'

'Did you really?' he said, flexing his fingers. 'OK, how about this: why don't you come and have something to eat at my house, bring a couple of them with you and I'll show you how.' He paused briefly, then added: 'And we can talk about the other thing as well.'

'Oh, that would be great!'

'Tuesday night? Eight o'clock-ish?'

'Yes! Thank you so much.'

Delighted, Isabelle closed the door and smiled to herself. She was one step closer to her prize – she was certain of it.

14 Daisy

Daisy stamped her green ticket in the machine and began to make her way down the aisle of the number 27 bus. It was late morning and there were quite a few passengers – a cocktail of slouching students, old ladies in fur coats and dazzled American tourists – but Daisy spotted a free seat, one of those single ones that come in pairs. The facing seat was empty. It suited her perfectly. She preferred to sit on her own.

The bus started and, right on cue, tears began to roll down her cheeks. Daisy found these days that almost any movement – reaching up, sitting down, running, breathing in, breathing out – triggered the tiresome crying. Public transport was the worst, obviously, what with all the stops and starts. She had become that dreadful stock character of urban life – Tragic Crying Girl. It didn't matter that people gave her strange looks. She didn't care because she couldn't help it. Perhaps one day the tiresome crying would stop, she thought, looking out of the window at the depressing parade of garish fast-food restaurants and cheap clothes shops on the Boulevard Saint-Michel.

These days most of her time, including at night, was spent first in devising ways of running into Octave accidentally on purpose, and afterwards in ringing Agathe, Jules or Marie-Laure so they could talk her out of her plans. Still, it gave her something to think about.

All the way down the boulevard, the small cargo of passengers on the bus ebbed and flowed, unnoticed by Daisy. She was busy picturing herself in an outfit that made her look stunning, but at the same time like she had just grabbed the first thing that came to hand – a denim miniskirt with black leggings and ankle boots, maybe, and her shocking-pink mohair jumper, the one with the cowl neck. And her cream leather Chloe handbag slung nonchalantly over her shoulder. Her hair would be up in a sexy twist and she would be striding along the street on her way to . . . wherever, a very important meeting. She would be completely lost in thought. And then, out of the blue, a black scooter would pull up next to her and she would hear a voice say . . .

'*C'est pas mal quand même, non? Vous ne trouvez pas?*'

Daisy looked up, jolted out of her fantasy. There was now a man in the seat opposite hers. Judging by his expectant expression, he was the one who'd just spoken, and the remark had been addressed to her. She glanced out of the window. The bus had stopped at the lights near the bottom of the boulevard and the Seine was in view.

Daisy said wearily, '*Heu, oui, c'est très joli.*'

To her horror, she could feel tears rising immediately. How predictable and boring. Well, at least that would shut him up and then she'd be allowed to indulge in her pitiful but comforting daydreams. Instead of which he said pleasantly, 'You are American? English?'

Oh, here we go, Daisy thought irritably, how very original. She inhaled, trying to quell her tears. Couldn't he see that she wanted to be left alone?

'I'm English,' she said coldly, without looking at him.

'From London?'

'Yessss,' Daisy said, sighing audibly in an attempt to put an end to the conversation.

And as it turned out her fellow traveller did not ask her any more about herself. Instead, as the bus started again and began crossing the Pont Saint-Michel, Daisy heard him say in quiet wonderment, 'This is a damn fine bus route. Oh, yeah.'

For a split second, Daisy was amused by the incongruous alliance of his textbook Gallic accent and transatlantic style of expression, then she remembered her sad predicament.

'Yeah, you know I have lived here all my life,' the American-inflected Parisian stranger continued, 'but I still get a kick out of how beautiful Paris is. You know what I mean?'

Staring out of the window through her tears, Daisy discerned the movements of passers-by who were also crossing the bridge. Everyone seemed harassed and pinched. They all wore boring clothes. And the Seine and the *quais* looked very drab and wintry today. Daisy closed her eyes. As she strove to recapture her daydream at the point of Octave's appearance on his scooter, she heard: 'Especially I love how this time of year, everything turns just one colour: the sky, the river, the buildings. It's all like this gorgeous beige – grey – gold – I dunno what to call it.'

With an effort, Daisy opened her eyes again and stared at the tree-lined river. She had to admit he had a point about the colours. They were actually more subtle and delicate than she'd realised – chic neutrals.

'Yeah, that sounds boring, I know, but to me, it's not at all. It makes a great background for the life of the city.'

As the bus left the bridge, Daisy glimpsed the thronged stalls of the *bouquinistes* and the glorious mass of Notre-Dame just before they disappeared from view.

'I am in a weird state right now,' he went on confidentially, just as Daisy was beginning to wonder if he was indeed a complete nutter. 'Cos I have just come from a meeting about my next project.'

Looking across in his general direction, Daisy noticed that he was very tanned, with longish dark hair streaked with grey, wolflike green eyes and a lot of rather sexy stubble. In his forties, probably. He wore a black leather biker's jacket over a black poloneck and held a marbled green-and-black portfolio in his arms. What was he? A photographer? A painter? Not particularly wishing to encourage conversation, Daisy turned away and looked out of the window as they drove past that lovely flower market on the Ile de la Cité. It occurred to her that she might come back tomorrow and buy a lavender or two for Isabelle's balcony.

'They make me so mad, you know. They forget to show me proofs or they want me to change a colour. Always something like this! So we shouted at each other like crazy people, banging on the table, and now I have totally lost my voice.'

Well, Daisy thought, if that was the case he wasn't doing too badly. There was apparently no shutting him up.

'Each time I work with this guy – his name is Antoine – it has to be this big macho battle. Sometimes I think maybe it will be better if we actually fight, you know, with fists.

More honest, you know. Now I am totally exhausted. But it was worth it. Because it's going to be a really great book, I think. Maybe the best I have done. *Le top du top.*'

Some kind of writer, then. Well, no self-esteem problems there, Daisy thought, smiling slightly. The bus had taken another turn and the sunlit Rue de Rivoli was unfurling before her eyes. The café terraces were thronged, as usual, with happy loafers nursing a coffee and watching the world go by.

'Then when the book comes out, I'll take Antoine – my publisher – to dinner as usual to celebrate. Like always, we'll get totally drunk on Armagnac and smoke cigars and be best friends again. I like to go somewhere like Hotel Costes for that. It's one of the most beautiful places in Paris. I know the guys who run it, so I always get a great table. I always have the *confit de canard*, really well grilled. I'm from the south-west of France, so it's in my blood.'

While she was listening to him talk, Daisy's tears had dried without her noticing. The bus had driven past the Louvre, crossed the Place du Palais-Royal and was now dancing up the Avenue de l'Opéra towards the opera house, whose green roof and glittering gold statues Daisy could see in the distance. This meant that her stop was coming up. She looked around but her travelling companion was quicker. He stood up, pressed the green button and stayed standing, holding on to the handrail, his portfolio under his arm. So he was getting off here too. While doing up her coat and getting out of her seat, Daisy noticed that he wore dark jeans and, perhaps unsurprisingly given his speech patterns, Texan cowboy boots. Yee-haw, she thought, smiling inwardly. Then, as the doors opened with a whoosh, she felt a pang of conscience. She had been very rude to him.

As the bus departed, leaving them alone at the bus stop, the man smiled at Daisy. 'So, take care now.'

'Goodbye,' Daisy said. 'Look, I'm really sorry. I didn't mean to be unfriendly. I was . . . a bit upset about something.'

'Yeah, I could see that. That's why I kept talking,' he said, making a rapid 'chatterbox' gesture with his fingers and thumb. 'It wasn't too boring, I hope?'

'Oh no!' Daisy said, feeling genuinely touched. 'It was very interesting. Thank you for keeping me company. I'm glad you were going as far as I was.'

He looked at her for a moment, biting his upper lip. Then he grinned, showing very good teeth. 'Well, you know, in fact, I wasn't. I was supposed to get off at Les Halles for a meeting. No, no, it's cool, don't worry,' he said, seeing her expression, 'the earth will not stop turning because of that.'

Daisy looked at her watch. She couldn't possibly be late for Anouk yet again! 'I have to go,' she said, holding out her hand. 'Thank you. *Vous avez été très gentil.*'

'*De rien.* No problem. Hey, wait,' he said, as Daisy began to move away. He tucked his portfolio under his arm, pulled a black felt pen out of his breast pocket and, taking hold of Daisy's hand again, wrote a telephone number on it. 'My name is Raoul. You can call me if you wanna hear the rest of my life story.'

Daisy burst out laughing, something she hadn't done in weeks. 'OK, maybe I will. Bye now!'

'Bye, English girl who did not tell me her name.'

'Sorry. It's Daisy.'

'So long, Daisy. Take it easy.'

Clearly, this Frenchman had watched far too many westerns and the like, Daisy thought as she crossed the avenue. Once on the other side, she looked back. Raoul was still standing at the bus stop. He waved. Daisy waved back and walked briskly towards the Boulevard des Capucines and into the Café de la Paix, where Anouk was waiting for her. When Daisy located her friend's table in the plush red velvet interior, Anouk took one look at her and asked immediately whether she had just had a facial. Daisy shook her head and launched into her tale.

'*Eh oui*,' Anouk said, nodding sagely when Daisy had finished. 'It does happen like that sometimes, just like the cinema. So that's why you look like this, with pink cheeks? And I thought it was just a good exfoliation! So you are going to call this Raoul, yes?'

'Oh, I don't know,' Daisy said, looking at the number on her hand.

'Daisy,' Anouk said earnestly, 'listen to me, *mon petit*. When I was your age, life was completely open, like a book with blank pages. I could go into the Tuileries Gardens, for example, and sit down on a bench and . . . anything could happen. And you know, it did,' she added, smiling reminiscently. 'I don't mean to say that nice things can't happen later in life, so long as you retain a bit of allure, you know. But the truth is they don't happen as easily as when you're young. And also, frankly, having a drink with a good-looking man . . . he is good-looking, yes?'

'Ye-es . . . I think so. A bit rugged.'

'*Rugged*?'

'*He* doesn't look like he exfoliates much,' Daisy said, before describing the sunburn and stubble.

'Oh yes, a real man!' Anouk said delightedly, clasping her hands together. 'But that's perfect!'

'I think he's probably forty or something. A bit old for me, don't you think?'

'What nonsense. Having a drink with a good-looking, rugged forty-year-old man,' Anouk resumed firmly, 'is probably the best way to help you get over Octave. You need a change of . . . climate. And you know why I'm giving you this advice?'

'Why?'

'Because, *mon petit*, it's the first time since your break-up that I mention Octave and it doesn't make you cry.'

Daisy remembered yesterday's text message from Chrissie in response to yet another one of her anguished outpourings. 'GET BACK IN SADDLE ASAP,' he'd said with customary levity, adding after half a minute's pause: 'BUCKING BRONCO WD B BEST.' Daisy smiled, thinking of Raoul's Texan boots. Well then, she thought, yee-haw to you, cowboy.

15 Isabelle

'Oh no, not now, Isabelle,' Clothaire groaned from behind his book, in a martyred tone of voice. 'I'm exhausted.'

Isabelle, who had been covering his chest with delicate kisses and sliding her bare legs caressingly against his underneath the bedclothes, obediently rolled off Clothaire's unresponsive body.

She lay next to him, staring pensively at the ceiling. If not now, when? Clothaire was going home later that morning, after which they would not see each other until Christmas. And it wasn't as though he'd been particularly enthusiastic in his attentions during his stay in London. There had been one, no, two occasions, but generally his mind had seemed to be on entirely other things. He'd spent most of his time reading or going for walks on his own to 'clear his head'. Clear his head of what? Isabelle had hoped for greater passion, but in truth there was nothing very out of the ordinary about this behaviour. Clothaire did sometimes go through these phases, especially when something important was going on at work. Exams had always been a no-sex zone, for example. In fact now Isabelle thought about it, so had the run-up to exams. And also, often, the period that had followed them. And holidays too, because that was when Clothaire needed to recuperate.

Sitting up in bed to put her underwear and T-shirt back

on, Isabelle considered the simple fact that although he talked about it a great deal at dinner parties and had many theories about it, Clothaire just wasn't that focused on sex as an activity. That was because he was such a cerebral and brilliant person. And also because he loved Isabelle for herself, not just her body. And Isabelle, of course, felt exactly the same. That was one of the reasons why she and Clothaire were such a good match – because they communicated on a higher level than just sex.

And now Clothaire was waiting to hear about the possibility of a lecturing job at Sciences Po, the prestigious college where future diplomats and civil servants were trained. Of course, that was it! Well, there was no reason to worry, really. The main thing was not to pressure him.

'I'm going to have a quick bath, OK?' she said, getting out of bed and putting her robe and slippers on.

'Mmm? Yes, OK.'

'Then when you're ready, we'll have time for a bit of breakfast before going to St Pancras Station. And then I think I'll go to the library. I'm looking into the history of ventriloquist acts of the period – the sort of thing Meredith might have seen when she was growing up.'

'Right,' Clothaire said, looking up. 'Did you say you're coming to the station?'

'Yes, of course, silly – to see you off,' Isabelle said, twisting her hair into a ponytail.

'Oh, that's not necessary. You know how much I hate those kinds of environments. I'd rather say goodbye here.'

Isabelle remembered her resolution to keep pressure to a minimum. 'OK, if you prefer.'

Clothaire nodded and went back to his book. Remembering her plans for the evening, she grabbed a couple of Tom's quinces and put them in her satchel. Then she went off to get ready.

As it turned out, Clothaire didn't really want breakfast, either – there was no point, he said, with no decent bread or croissants available. He downed a cup of black coffee standing at the sink, while Isabelle ate a piece of toast at the table with Jules and Chrissie.

'Shall we *all* come to the station with you, Clo-Clo darling?' Chrissie asked teasingly, ignoring Isabelle's pleading eyes. He simply could not help himself.

'Actually, Clothaire is going to the station on his own,' Isabelle said. 'He wants to be in really good time for his train.'

Jules gave her a quick look across her bowl of Weetabix, but remained silent.

There was an entertaining interlude in the hallway when Chrissie, ignoring the Frenchman's protests, forcibly kissed Clothaire on both cheeks. Then it was Clothaire's turn to plant two kisses on a most embarrassed and unwilling Jules, who tried vainly to shake his hand instead. Afterwards Jules and Chrissie withdrew, leaving the French couple to their goodbyes.

'I'm going to miss you,' Isabelle said sadly, throwing her arms around Clothaire's neck.

Showing rather more affection than he had during the past week, Clothaire gave her a long, cool kiss. 'It's not long until Christmas,' he said. 'Agathe and Claire are planning a big party. You will see everyone there.'

'But it's you I want to see,' Isabelle said, standing on tiptoe to kiss his neck.

'You'll see me, too, of course,' he said with a touch of impatience.

'Maybe I could come home for a weekend before then?' she murmured, not for the first time.

'No, no, no, no. I really don't want you to neglect your work,' he added, lightly patting her bottom. 'Sureau will be expecting your next chapter.'

Isabelle nodded, then rubbed her face against his coat. 'Have you got my Christmas present yet?' she asked, more playfully.

Clothaire hesitated for a second. 'Well, no, not quite yet. I have been rather busy, you know.'

'I know, I know,' she said, smoothing down the lapels of his coat. 'Kiss me again.'

Clothaire did so, holding Isabelle with one hand while reaching behind him for the doorknob with the other. He let go of her, picked up his bag and stepped outside.

'I'd better go. I want to have plenty of time to get my newspapers for the train.'

'Have a good trip. I love you.'

'Mmm? Yes, me too, Isabelle, me too.'

Later, sitting on the train on her way to the library, Isabelle felt a little melancholy. Obviously, she diagnosed, she felt that way because Clothaire had gone. And also because his visit had reminded her what an integral part of her life he was. Clothaire might be a little explosive and once in a while unfair in his behaviour towards her, but he was *l'homme de sa vie* – the man of her life. She knew that.

When she went home to Paris in the summer, she would be going back to Clothaire for good, and to reality. Although he hadn't mentioned it in a while, it would probably be the time when they started planning their engagement. They'd have a lovely wedding in Paris, with their families and all their friends in attendance, and Agathe as her chief bridesmaid. By then he'd be settled in his Sciences Po post and on his way to becoming a famous economist. And she'd get a lecturing job at the Sorbonne with Professeur Sureau's support. And then children would come – a boy and a girl. And she and Clothaire would live together happily ever after. Oddly, she felt her chest contract a little at this prospect.

Don't dwell on his reticence this morning, she told herself – not for the first time. He was preoccupied, that was all. Reaching into her satchel for her book, Isabelle's fingers encountered something smooth, rounded and downy – one of the quinces had escaped from its plastic bag. She replaced it carefully with the other one, dug out her copy of *Tender is the Night*, found her place and began to read.

Once at the library, as she stood in line to check in her coat and umbrella, Isabelle found herself looking at the picture on the far wall. It was an ugly but nonetheless fascinating *trompe l'oeil* representing rows of bookshelves. She had noticed it before in passing but, put off by its harsh lines and profoundly hideous colour scheme, had never looked at it very closely. Today she walked right up to it, and then moved slowly from left to right, watching the bookshelves ripple and rise out at her in three dimensions. This optical illusion, she saw, was produced by the play of angles and intersecting lines. Quite cleverly done. It also reminded her of something else. Isabelle narrowed her eyes and bit her lip, trying to place the memory.

When she sat down in her usual seat in the Rare Books Room, the answer suddenly hit her. She had returned the shy nod of greeting from the Wolfman and exchanged smiles with the Woman with the Enormous Beehive and Beads. Looking up, she caught sight of 'Miss Marple' in her customary tweeds, returning from the delivery desk with a pile of books. That was it, of course. The trick picture downstairs reminded her of the painting of Meredith Quince. It was something to do with the portrait's distorted perspective: some of the bookshelves around the novelist looked a little wonky, as though struggling for three-dimensionality, as though they wanted to *open out*. Then Cluedo flashed into her mind and she saw clearly the floor plan on the board and, clearest of all, what had been her favourite part of it when she had played the game as a child: the secret passage.

Isabelle's mouth became quite dry with excitement. Could it be? Well, why not? It was quite an old house. Was it one of those revolving walls camouflaged with fake books? Or just a door? How did you release it? In films it tended to be by pulling on a candlestick. Isabelle shut her eyes and tried to visualise the room. And if there was a door, what was behind it? A secret room perhaps, or some stairs leading . . . where?

And what about Tom Quince – did he know about it or not? Unable to concentrate on her reading, Isabelle leaped to her feet and marched out of the reading room.

She had a drink of water from the fountain, and then paced up and down the landing. On impulse, she dialled Lucy Goussay's number on her mobile phone. It would be very helpful to take another look at the portrait before tonight. But there was nobody home. Well, no matter, in a few hours she would be able to look at the real thing – the actual room in Meredith's house.

The afternoon dragged on interminably. Isabelle forced herself to read and type a few notes but the results were meagre and incoherent. She would have to reserve her music-hall history books and go over them again tomorrow. When the time finally came to collect her things and she handed the attendant the token for her coat, she turned to look again at the *trompe l'oeil* picture. Perhaps she had simply stumbled upon another pregnant Quince metaphor. First, ventriloquism, and now this. What better way of imaging Meredith Quince's literary career: out of sight behind rows of make-believe books – the Lady Violet mysteries – there lay, metaphorically speaking, a secret space where Meredith Quince had put away *The Splodge* for safekeeping, and there the book had waited to be unearthed, triumphantly, by a dedicated scholar – herself, Isabelle Papillon!

Isabelle walked in the rain towards Meredith's house in a sort of trance. She was so lost in her thoughts that she was almost surprised to see, in answer to the bell's summons, Meredith's great-nephew appear in shirtsleeves and braces, a tea towel flung over his shoulder, his hair in its usual tousled state, on what was now, after all, his own doorstep.

'Hello! Come in, come in out of the rain,' he said, pulling

Isabelle inside and kissing her on the cheek. 'Just leave your things up here and come down to the kitchen.'

Isabelle followed him into a room that hadn't been included in the tour given to the Quince Society. Inside, the walls were painted a wonderful shade of dark blue and there were lighted candles everywhere. The centrepiece was a long lustrous oak table, one end of which was laden with rotund pumpkins and a crate full of apples and pears, like a still life symbolising autumnal plenty.

'Are these all from your garden?' Isabelle could see it dimly through the kitchen window. It seemed to go on for miles.

'Mostly, yes. Which reminds me: did you remember to bring the fruit?'

Isabelle rummaged in her satchel and brought out the quinces. Tom took them from her hands and put them down on a chopping board. Following her nose, Isabelle found her eyes drawn to a number of simmering saucepans.

'That smells really wonderful.'

'Well, it's woodpigeon and some chestnuts and cabbage. And we're having celeriac mash. And a sort of cranberry thing to go with it. It's only very simple English cooking, I'm afraid.'

'You went to a lot of trouble . . . just for me.'

Tom smiled, looking down at the fruit. 'No trouble. We have to eat, after all.'

As he walked to the stove, Isabelle found herself looking with interest at the strong and graceful line of her host's neck, shoulders and back. He also had long muscular legs, she noticed, and a rather nice . . .

'Do you like smoked salmon?' he said, turning to face her. Her eyes darted away guiltily.

'Oh yes.'

'Good. We'll start with that, then. Glass of wine?'

'Yes, thank you.'

Tom began to peel and core the fruit with great dexterity. It was essential to bring the conversation around to Meredith Quince as soon as possible. Isabelle cleared her throat. 'Tom?'

'Yes?'

'You know the portrait of Meredith you donated to the Society?'

'Yes. Actually, sorry, I could use some help with this if you don't mind.'

'Oh, yes, of course.'

'Could you pass me that white dish over there, the oval one? Thank you,' Tom said. He then started rubbing butter into this receptacle and transferred the halved fruit into it. 'What were you saying?'

'Did you notice that there is mistletoe in the portrait?'

'Mistletoe, you say? Really?' he said, turning around to gaze at Isabelle. He smiled pensively. 'That is exciting.'

'Yes,' Isabelle said, nodding vigorously. 'I think it's an allusion to the title of one of her books.'

'Ah. I see.'

'And there are others. An emerald, a pair of gloves, a piece of lemon, for example.'

'Interesting.'

'Yes, I think so, too. Especially because . . . Tom, do you know anything about *The Splodge*?'

'The what?'

'*Splodge*. I think she wrote a book with that title. Have you ever seen it, or heard of it?'

'N-no, I don't think so, Isabelle. Sorry to disappoint you.'

'No, no, it's fine,' Isabelle said, waving off his apology. 'I wonder if . . . could I have another look at the library?'

'Certainly, I'll take you in a moment. But first, can I borrow you?'

'Oh, yes,' said Isabelle, stopped dead in her tracks as she headed towards the door. Manners, she told herself. The library would keep. 'Yes, of course.' She joined him in front of the table. 'What can I do to help?'

Tom walked around Isabelle and reached for a jar of sugar and a spoon, then came to stand beside her.

'The thing about the quince, you see,' he said, waving the spoon at her, 'is that it is a rare and precious thing.' He pulled the dish of fruit a little closer to the edge of the table. 'So if you bag a couple – as you have done, thanks to a generous friend – you're on to a good thing.'

'I have never tasted one,' Isabelle admitted sheepishly. 'I don't know what they're like.'

'No? I'm delighted to hear it. It means I can continue to drone on about them for a while longer. You see, quinces aren't fast food. I mean that you can't just pick one and bite into it just like that.'

'You can't?'

'Certainly not. It's a very hard fruit. And tart. But that's only because,' he continued, moving to stand behind Isabelle and placing the spoon in her right hand, 'it needs a little attention. Before you can eat it, I mean.'

'So what do you want me to do?'

Tom's own right hand closed over hers and dipped the spoon in the sugar jar. Meanwhile, though he maintained what Isabelle might have called *une distance respectueuse* behind her, his other hand, she saw, now lay flat and relaxed on the table top, on her other side, close to her waist.

'Well, basically, what I want you to do is sprinkle masses of sugar over the fruit, like this.'

'OK.'

'More.'

'More than this?'

'Yes, I know it seems like a lot but they can take it. You'd be surprised.'

Together, their hands sprinkled more sugar. As Tom reached forwards, the distance between their bodies became fractionally less *respectueuse*.

'Like this?'

'Again. Oh, yes. That's perfect.'

Isabelle let go of the spoon. Her heart was beating extremely fast. Her hand, still covered by her host's, came to rest on the table next to the dish. A delicious silence descended.

Then Tom said softly, 'Allow me.'

He picked up the dish, walked across to the oven and slid the quinces in. Isabelle made herself take a couple of breaths, turned around and nonchalantly perched on the edge of the table. She sipped a bit of her wine.

'So, how long do they take to cook?'

'You bake them for an hour or so. It's best not to rush it.'

Isabelle looked down into her glass of wine until she

knew that Tom had returned and was standing directly in front of her. *Mais allez, vas-y!* What *are* you waiting for, a little voice at the back of her mind asked crossly. Get back to the portrait! Do it now! Isabelle raised her eyes slowly to Tom's chest. 'Won't they be too sweet?'

'What happens is the sugar becomes one with the fruit. By the end you can't tell one –' he moved a little closer '– from the other.'

'Like, um, chemistry?'

'Exactly. Or alchemy.'

They gazed at each other for a while. Isabelle put her wine down and, reaching up, removed Tom's glasses.

'The reason you need so much sugar,' he resumed, his face naked and serious, 'is that it softens the fruit. The flesh melts and becomes . . . succulent and . . . it turns a really beautiful shade of pink.'

Isabelle leaned forwards and rubbed her cheek against Tom's. Encountering his mouth, she nibbled his lower lip experimentally, to see what would happen. The result was extremely interesting. Tom's mouth held hers and they began to kiss. Some years ago Isabelle had written a geography essay about the electrification of the Soviet Union in the 1920s. At the time the whole concept of electrification had seemed to her rather abstract, dry and unrewarding. But now – as she pulled Tom closer and slowly wrapped her legs around his – it no longer did. It was all a question of context, she now understood, as the coil of her hair came undone in his hands. Tom was now caressing her body in a way that made her want more than anything to lie down on the table and fling her arms behind her head. So she did just that. She was aware of her shoes being removed and, rapturously, of her underwear travelling down her legs as though it moved of its own volition. Soon after that her host's warm mouth made its presence felt on the inside of her thigh. '*Oh, oui . . .*' Isabelle whispered under her breath, momentarily forgetting to speak Tom's language. Meanwhile she pulled his head down with both hands, so that, happily, there was no misunderstanding.

16 Daisy

'You are tired?'

'No, I'm OK!' Daisy said. 'But I'm getting pins and needles in my arm.'

Raoul frowned. 'Pins and needles? What is pins and needles? Ah, yeah – *des fourmis*! Sorry. You are very patient. If you can just hold the pose one more minute. It's nearly finished, I swear.'

'Of course!'

'*Et voilà*. I've got you, I think. You want to see?'

'Yes, please!' Daisy said, stepping down from the white cube she had been standing on. Rubbing her arms, she walked across the room to where Raoul was holding up an A3 drawing pad for her inspection.

'Goodness,' Daisy said.

'Oh, come on! Gimme a break! You are not going to say that you don't like it,' Raoul said, looking up at her.

'No, no, I do! I do like it. It's very – *very* – flattering.'

'It's you.'

'Well,' Daisy replied, laughing, 'it's me with bigger eyes, much longer legs and, um, a bit more of other things.'

Raoul looked critically from model to drawing and back, then shook his head. 'Perhaps I exaggerate just a little bit, but it's you, I think. How you look.'

'Oh, all right then, if you say so . . .'

Faintly embarrassed, Daisy began to walk around the studio, examining the pictures on the walls. There were a few exceptions but it was fair to say that, generally speaking, Raoul appeared far more interested in images of women than in those of men. Earlier, when they were in his kitchen, Daisy had noticed that the fridge was covered in transfers of those pouting 1950s American pin-ups. A similar theme could be detected on the walls of the studio.

'That one, that's Barbarella,' Raoul said as Daisy paused in front of a confused-looking and scantily clad blonde floating upside down in a spaceship. 'You know?'

'I think so,' Daisy said, remembering a beauty editorial in *Vogue* a few seasons ago about big, 'bedroom' hair. 'There was this amazing film, wasn't there?'

'With Jane Fonda when she was totally gorgeous. But before that there was a really great *bande dessinée*. It's a total classic.'

Bandes dessinées (B.Ds for short), Daisy now knew, was what the French called comic books. Drawing *bandes dessinées* was how Raoul made his living, he had told Daisy in the course of their first meeting in a bar in Les Halles. He had fifteen books under his belt and a new story in the making, the one he had mentioned on the bus. Daisy's notion of what a *bande dessinée* might actually be like was a little hazy.

'Is it anything like, well, Batman or Spiderman comics, basically?' she had asked tentatively.

Raoul had laughed heartily. 'Spiderman! Ha, ha, ha – stop, you're killing me!' He had taken a swig of his Mexican beer, then said, 'The B.D., it is an art form. In France we call it the ninth art.'

While a perplexed Daisy quietly tried to work out what the other eight arts might be, and most importantly whether fashion counted, Raoul went on: 'In France we are a very literary nation, you know? So a B.D. tells a story, just like a novel, just like a great film. It's more than everything going "pow" and "whizz". The story is crucial. Some guys do just the illustrations and leave the story to a writer. But not me. I am like a total, crazy perfectionist so I write all my own storylines and all the dialogue.'

'And what's your next story?'

'Oh, it's about a girl,' Raoul said, smiling at her warmly across the table. 'My stories are always about a girl.'

'Always the same girl?'

'No, no, different ones. I have lots of heroines.'

'And what happens to this one, your new heroine?'

'She has some cool adventures. It's kind of surreal. Difficult to explain just like that. But listen, tell me: what is it like to live in London? It must be kind of extreme, no?'

'Extreme' was one of Raoul's buzz words. Before getting into the comic book world, he had run a couple of night-clubs in Paris and the South of France and done a lot of motorcycle racing, some of it across China. It had all been 'kind of extreme'.

'It can be, I suppose,' Daisy allowed. 'It's a great city, really diverse and full of energy. And working in fashion, there are moments of tension. Savage – the designer I did public relations for – is very edgy, very avant-garde,' Daisy said, delighted to be using the right French word for once. 'And everyone goes mad at the time of the shows, you know.'

'Is that by her, what you're wearing today?' Raoul asked, gesturing towards Daisy's distressed pink lace tank top.

She nodded eagerly. 'Yes, it is! I love this piece! It's from the first collection I did the press for, when Savage was just starting out. The whole collection was pink, but not at all girly – quite strange and apocalyptic. It was called "Sugar and Spike". She was making a point about women in today's society. *So* inspired,' Daisy said fervently. Seeing Raoul's face break into a wide grin, she checked herself. 'You think it's silly.'

'Not at all,' he said, leaning forwards and fixing her with his laughing green eyes. 'I love that you're so enthusiastic about your job. It's great. And I think fashion is, you know, crucial,' he added more seriously. 'In fact I believe there is nothing more important than making women look beautiful.'

Daisy smiled, basking in the warmth of his interest. On that first date, in case Raoul turned out to be impossible, she had taken the precaution of arranging a meeting with Agathe immediately afterwards in a nearby café. But he wasn't at all. He was easy to talk to, very laid-back and funny, and really seemed to enjoy life. It was also lovely to have made a new friend who had never heard of Octave. Another cool thing about him was that he *actually* smoked Gauloises – as a result, his voice, which was incredibly French, also sounded deeply husky.

A few days later they had gone out for sushi. As they

were settling the bill Raoul suddenly said, thrillingly, 'You know, I'd really like to draw you one day. If you like.'

'Me? That would be brilliant!'

'I like to draw all my friends. And I think you have a really interesting face.'

It was as a result of that conversation that Daisy had found herself standing in Raoul's studio that morning. She had turned up at his flat in Les Halles two hours ago, in time for Sunday brunch. In Raoul's honour, Daisy had gone for a 'frontier' look – black shirt tucked into a long gipsy skirt, short denim jacket, red bandana neckerchief and, of course, metallic cowboy boots. Walking out of the lift, she had been guided to the right door by the sound of music. Daisy smiled as she recognised the song. It made sense that Raoul, who was heavily under American influence, should be a Beach Boys fan.

Raoul had opened the door dressed in jeans and a denim shirt and wearing a pair of his customary Texan boots.

'Hey, Daisy,' he said, kissing her on the cheeks.

'Howdy, partner.'

She followed him down a book-lined corridor and into a large modern apartment, entirely painted white. Most of the furniture looked Italian and was upholstered in white leather. A huge 1950s jukebox stood in a corner, playing the last few notes of 'California Girls'.

'You like my monster?' Raoul said proudly, pointing at the massive multicoloured machine. 'I brought it back from LA.'

'It's fab.'

The jukebox started to play Raoul's next selection, a song by Enrique Iglesias, which was then followed by what turned out to be fun-loving Raoul's default option – insanely upbeat Brazilian music.

After sitting side by side on red diner stools at the Formica counter of his American-style kitchen to eat scrambled eggs with smoked salmon, Daisy and Raoul flopped down on a vast white leather sofa to drink their coffee.

'We'll go into the studio when you're ready. The light is much better there.'

'No one's ever drawn me before,' Daisy said, suddenly feeling nervous. 'What happens exactly? Are my clothes OK?'

'I told you to wear anything you wanted,' Raoul said reassuringly. 'It's real easy. I just need you to stand, I think, not sit, in front of me, just like you are now. And you must try not to move too much.'

In the sun-filled studio Daisy had perched for a good half-hour on a white wooden cube, one arm extended in front of her, pointing with her forefinger at an imaginary object, her other hand resting on her hip. Staring at the opposite wall behind Raoul, she had gradually remembered reading a couple of Tintin and Asterix stories when she was a child. It would be fun to look at stuff like that again.

She now moved away from Barbarella and came to look at another picture of a shapely girl, this one standing in a graveyard in a clinging black dress with a plunging neckline and looking at once alluring and bloodthirsty.

'That's Vampirella,' Raoul said, putting away his pad

and pencils on his desk, 'from a 1970s American comic book. I love her.'

'A friend of mine is in a band in London, and one of the other girls in the band often dresses like that. They're goths.'

'Really? Your friends sound cool.'

'Raoul,' Daisy said impulsively, 'can I see some of your work, please? I'm really interested.'

'You're so sweet. Of course I'll show you some stuff if you want. But I must tell you that it's quite erotic. You don't mind that, right?'

'No! Not at all,' Daisy said firmly, while inwardly undergoing a panic of nuclear intensity. 'Quite erotic'? Good grief. What did that mean exactly? How 'extreme' was Raoul's stuff? She sat down rigidly on the sofa, watching him select a few of his books off the shelves and instinctively gathering her gipsy skirt closer around her legs. Oh, come *on*, get a grip, she told herself, don't be such a prude! You can do this. Look on it as a test, a turning point in your year in Paris. This is your chance to show that you are just as blithe and nonchalant about sex as the French. It's going to be fine.

'*Et voilà*,' he said, handing her the books. 'These are the ones I prefer. You want a Diet Coke or something like that?'

'Yes, please,' Daisy said, relieved to see him leave the room. Right. Now then. She glanced nervously at the cover of the first book. A girl dressed as a pirate stood at the helm of a ship. She wore knee-length breeches and a flouncy white shirt. Her long hair, tied back with a black scarf adorned with skull and crossbones, was floating in the wind. Well, that was absolutely *fine*. The title was *La Flibustière* – The Buccaneer – which was OK, too. Gingerly, Daisy turned the first few pages. The story was set in the eighteenth century. The heroine was called Caroline and she lived in a château by the sea, somewhere near La Rochelle. Raoul really had a great eye for colour, Daisy thought, taking in the exquisite pinks and blues of Caroline's dress. So far, so good. She turned another page and scanned the speech bubbles. It seemed that Caroline's parents had arranged for her to marry somebody she had never met before, as was the practice in those days. How dreadful. But that night, with the help of her maid, Caroline ran away from the château, climbing out of her bedroom window disguised as a boy. Actually, Raoul was right about B.Ds, Daisy thought, turning another page, this was cracking good stuff, as absorbing as any film.

Now the scene had shifted to the harbour in the small hours of the morning and Caroline – who, in all fairness, did not make a very convincing boy – was sailing on a ship on her way to Louisiana. This involved sharing below-deck quarters with a lot of men who adopted her as a sort of urchin mascot, all apparently oblivious to her distracting curves. Now more relaxed, Daisy turned another couple of pages. Oh dear: it looked like Caroline had been summoned to the captain's cabin. He was rather attractive, Daisy noted in passing. Now he would probably find out that she was travelling under false pretences and then she'd be forced to disembark at the next port of call, or something. Although, hang on a minute, he appeared to be sort of . . .

taking her to task about it. Caroline didn't seem to mind too much, though. In fact it looked like she . . . Oh, wow.

This was it, Daisy reminded herself, *this* was the big test. Blithe and nonchalant is how she would remain. She could handle a few saucy drawings and speech bubbles. Nothing to get het up about. Bracing herself slightly, she turned to the next page. Well, yes. Raoul *did* have the most amazing talent for the naked female form. Oh, and also for the naked male form, as it turned out. It was all beautifully drawn and somehow very *real*. Daisy flicked through the next few pages and it became more and more obvious that Raoul, like many of his compatriots, seemed completely unaware of political correctness. Caroline got into all sorts of scrapes. She had to escape again, this time from the captain, who was a little too possessive for her liking. Then, after some adventures in Louisiana – which involved, variously, a plantation owner, his younger brother, a runaway slave, *two* amazingly hunky soldiers and a short stint in a New Orleans brothel – she took to the sea again, this time as a pirate, captaining a crew that seemed entirely made up of very good-looking (and randy) boys. And they lived happily ever after. The End.

Well, it was certainly a change from Tintin's adventures, which, from what Daisy remembered, were not big on graphic depictions of sexual pleasure.

Raoul came back into the room, holding two glasses of Diet Coke. 'So? You like it?' he asked, sitting next to her.

'Oh, it's amazing. I love it.'

'You have a favourite?'

'Actually I've only had time to look at this one,' Daisy

said, composedly putting *La Flibustière* down on the sofa next to her. And frankly, she thought, I had no idea you were so incredibly pervy. Aloud she asked, 'So where do you get your inspiration? For your stories?'

'Yeah, well, it sort of depends,' Raoul said, lighting an unfiltered Gauloise, then removing a fragment of tobacco from his lip. 'I love to do costume stories like this one. Or exotic stuff like this,' he said, picking up another book entitled *La Sultane*, on the cover of which a ravishing girl appeared to be doing the Dance of the Seven Veils.

'Is there a harem in this, by any chance?'

'Yeah, there is,' Raoul said, surprised. 'But I thought you hadn't read it?'

'Just a lucky guess. And your next book, the one you're completing at the moment? You mentioned it was about a girl having surreal adventures.'

'Yeah, in fact it's like a . . . psychedelic fairy tale. You know Lewis Carroll, right? Well, it's based on *Alice au pays des merveilles*.'

'*Alice in Wonderland*? Really?'

'Yeah, but it's very different. My Alice is much, much older – eighteen, nineteen years old – and it's set in the 1960s.'

Daisy considered this for a minute. 'So does she do it with the White Rabbit?' she asked with genuine curiosity. It was amazing how quickly you got used to discussing this stuff.

'Oh sure, but in my version, you know, it's not really a rabbit. It's a *guy* dressed up as a rabbit.'

'Right.'

'She meets him when she's totally tripping on acid.'

'It sounds great,' Daisy said, repressing a small spasm of laughter. 'I look forward to reading it.'

'You're very sweet,' Raoul said with a smile. 'But I also like science fiction,' he went on. 'This one, for instance –' he helding up another book entitled *Planète Femme* '– is about a race of beautiful female aliens who take over the Earth.'

'By killing everybody?'

'No, no. By having sex with everybody,' Raoul said, exhaling a plume of smoke. 'Their weapon is the orgasm.' He caught Daisy's eye and they both burst out laughing. 'I know, I know. It's kind of dumb. But you wanted to know what inspires me. You can borrow those two,' he said, handing her *La Sultane* and *Planète Femme*. 'Keep them as long as you like.'

'Oh thanks, Raoul. That's great.' Daisy looked at her watch. 'I should go,' she said. 'I don't want to be late for my little friend.'

Daisy was meeting Amélie – Claire's younger sister – at the swimming pool. This was part of a project to help Amélie lose her puppy fat. In place of depressing trips to the dietician, Daisy had been taking her swimming or running with her once a week, after which the French teenager went home with her to spend many happy hours trying on all of Daisy's clothes and make-up. This approach was yielding encouraging results. Amélie had lost half a stone and was now – much to her older sister's dismay and Daisy's amusement – dreaming of becoming a fashion stylist.

17 Isabelle

Isabelle and Tom had been sitting in his car outside Daisy's house for quite a while. Isabelle had tried to leave several times but some mysterious law of physics appeared to be preventing her from doing so. As it was, she had somehow manoeuvred herself into his lap and they were kissing deeply, occasionally conversing.

'I should go.'

'Mmm, yes. Absolutely.'

'Thank you for dinner.'

'You've already thanked me.'

'Really? I had a lovely time.'

'So did I.'

'I'm going now.'

'Are you? That's good.'

'Tom, if you do that, I can't get out.'

'Oh, shall I not do it?'

'Mmm. OK, just another minute.'

This went on for quite some time, until Isabelle, by a tremendous effort of will, broke through the invisible barrier that was holding her inside Tom's car. He waited until she had reached her door, then drove off, waving out of the window.

At that moment, without warning, her bubble burst. She felt like she'd just come out of a mad dream. What had she done? Suddenly overcome by a sense of panic, she felt around in her satchel. Where was her blasted key? Eventually she lost patience and rang the bell. Chrissie came to the door in his dressing gown, a sleeping mask embroidered with the words 'The Bitch Is Sleeping' perched on his forehead. He beamed at her. 'Oh, hello, darling! Did you forget your key?'

'No, I don't think so. It's just that . . . I can't find it.'

Isabelle scurried towards the stairs. If she could just get to her room quickly, all would be well.

'By the way, did you pick up a paper while you were out? Or, *even* more brilliantly, some milk?'

She stopped in her tracks. 'No. I . . .'

'You know, you should wear your hair down like this more often: it really suits you,' Chrissie drawled. Then, suddenly, he switched to intense peering mode. He probably hadn't got his contact lenses in yet. '*Hang* on a minute. Aren't these yesterday's clothes? And, darling, if I *may* say . . .' he went on slowly, 'you're looking a little . . . well . . . a little sexed-up and crazy.'

'I don't know wha–' Isabelle began uncertainly. Then she started to cry.

Chrissie was aghast. 'Oh Lord, I'm sorry,' he said, putting his arms around her. 'What's wrong? Tell your Uncle Chrissie.'

Isabelle tried to speak through her tears, but the results were disappointing.

'No. Didn't get a word of that. Right.' He threw his head back. 'Juuules!'

'What?' came the reply from upstairs.

'Get down here. We have a crisis.'

Later on, sitting on the floor of Chrissie's room wrapped in his duvet and equipped with a mug of coffee, Isabelle had regained enough of her composure to speak of the previous night's events.

'On the *kitchen* table?' Chrissie snorted. 'That is so *iconic*. I am *green* with envy.'

'Chrissie,' Jules said tonelessly.

'I don't know what came over me.'

'Now, darling, as for *that*, I think we have a *pretty* good idea . . .'

'Chrissie, shush. Turn it off for a minute.'

'Oh, all right. But I can only take so much provocation.'

'Right,' Jules said to Isabelle. 'So, basically, you've gone and been a bit wanton. Well, you know, we've all been there . . .'

'Especially *me*!' Chrissie said, a delighted smile lighting up his pretty face.

Jules stared him down, then turned back to Isabelle. 'Don't worry, it's not the end of the . . .'

'Darling, I *beg* of you, don't keep us in suspense! *How* was it? Do tell!'

'Chrissie, I'm going to have to muzzle you.'

'It was fantastic,' Isabelle said mournfully.

'And what about his cooking? Or did you not bother with food, you saucy madam?'

'No, we ate afterwards. We were very hungry.' Isabelle paused, then wailed: 'And it was delicious!'

'I knew it. You've set her off again. Just button it, will you?'

'You French are so sophisticated,' Chrissie went on

dreamily. 'With all your gorgeous *affaires* and things. What a perfectly *divine* way to live. And you've got it right, you know. A lover is the *one* accessory one absolutely cannot do without. I must get one too, and *double plus* quick. Two weeks without sex is my *absolute* limit. After that I get all tetchy and start to lose my glow.'

'But Chrissie, I do *not* have affairs!' Isabelle said, taken aback.

'Oh, darling, is this your first time? That's so *adorable*.'

'You mean you've never cheated on Clothaire before?' Jules said, a note of utter disbelief struggling to make itself heard through her usual monotone.

'No, of course not!' Isabelle said indignantly. 'I love Clothaire. And we're going to be married.'

'Oh, I see. You were planning to take lovers *after* you were married?'

'No, Chrissie! I don't know what you're talking about.'

'Honestly, darling, you disappoint me. Not a *trace* of *oh-là-là*. It's enough to make you wonder if you're really French at all.'

'Is Clothaire really hot stuff in bed?' Jules asked, her face impassive.

Isabelle thought for a moment. 'Well . . . You know, with him, it's like . . .'

'A walk in the park?' Jules offered.

'Yes, exactly.'

'And last night?'

Isabelle closed her eyes and said very fast, without a moment's hesitation, 'That was like riding through a thunderstorm on the back of a centaur.'

Chrissie's hands flew to his face and he made a small whimpering sound.

'Blimey,' Jules said, almost inaudibly. Then she added: 'That's quite gothic, actually.'

'Well, well, well. And I thought he looked like butter wouldn't melt in his – Ow! What was that for?'

'Are you going to see him again?' Jules said.

'No. Yes. I don't know. He said he'd call me tonight. Oh, this is terrible. What am I going to do?'

'Honey, if ever there was a no-brainer, *this* is it,' Chrissie said, his eyes twinkling. 'Of course you *must* see him again, for all our sakes. He sounds like a real *find*.'

'Yes,' Jules said coldly, 'that's one way of looking at it. But if Legend were here, she'd say that just because someone can make you come that doesn't make him Jesus. It's worth thinking about that, too.'

'You're right,' Isabelle said. 'I'm going to call Clothaire now and tell him everything.'

'That would, of course, be a brilliant course of action,' Jules said sardonically, 'but it's not at all what I meant. If I were you I would consider the consequences. How do you think Clothaire is likely to react? No offence, but he didn't strike me as particularly easy-going.'

Isabelle was silent.

'Look,' Jules said, 'you're blowing this way out of proportion. What you need is to get some sleep. Then you'll feel like yourself again and you can decide what you want to do.'

Isabelle was beginning to feel better.

'I'll go to bed for a bit,' she said, standing up and

divesting herself of Chrissie's duvet. 'Thanks for being so nice.'

Three hours later, she awoke to find a message from Clothaire on the phone. He was back. He hoped she was making progress with her research and he would call her at the weekend. Yes, her research, Isabelle thought, hurriedly putting on her dressing gown. She had better get to the library to make the best of the afternoon opening hours. Work would clear her head. It always did. Once she had got dressed and tied her hair back in a neat ponytail, Isabelle thought she was definitely back in control. Travelling to the library, she felt stronger, more solidly anchored in reality. As she made her way to her seat in the Rare Books Room, everything was wonderfully normal. She switched on her laptop. And then, as soon as she opened a file and reread her most recent notes, things began to go haywire.

It was as though – just like that, overnight – her experience of research had undergone a dramatic upheaval. Previously, the name of Quince had been almost an abstract concept to her, or at least a purely literary essence, shorthand for her work, her thesis, her academic status as a narratologist. Now, on the other hand, the mere sight of the name on the page, the mere mention of it in her mind, was enough to conjure up vivid images of Tom Quince completely naked, underscored by memories of some of the intoxicating things he'd said, for example when he . . . No, no, stop. Concentrate.

Isabelle shook her head from side to side and squared her shoulders. She was puzzled. This was the very first time that sex had interfered with her intellectual processes. She'd never had that problem with Clothaire, for example. What was happening to her? Last night, it was true, she had been neither sensible nor rational. But then, she thought, remembering the strong pull of his mouth, Tom had been so extremely . . . Flushing a little, Isabelle sat up straighter. She crossed her legs in one direction, then the other. It didn't help at all.

Surely yesterday's aberrant behaviour, that *moment d'égarement*, couldn't have changed her in any lasting way? It couldn't have rewired her brain, her body? Of course it couldn't. *Bon, reprenons.* Isabelle tightened her ponytail and began to type rapidly on her laptop, roughing up a chapter about the pressures exerted by the commercial book market on Meredith's direction as a writer. In particular there was the issue of Meredith's agent Paul Celadon's influence. In his autobiography *My Life as a Bookmark*, Celadon congratulated himself on having discouraged Meredith from pursuing literary experimentation, persuading her instead to exploit her gift for crowd-pleasing 'spine-tinglers'. Isabelle paused. What a clever expression that was. Yes, the spine did indeed tingle – sometimes in other contexts than the enjoyment of crime fiction. Chrissie, who had a word for everything, called it having a ring-a-ding-ding. In spite of herself, Isabelle smiled a little.

Anyway . . . Could it be that Meredith had set out to outplay Celadon by planting experimental clues in the midst of seemingly conventional novels? In so doing she had been pushing hard against the limitations of the crime genre. Ah yes, Isabelle thought, staring at the screen.

Pushing. Hard. Those were such good and evocative words. Not so long ago, she herself had been . . . No, no, no. Stop. Stop right now. She took a deep, calming breath. This was, after all, a library and under *no* circumstances should she allow herself to moan *out loud*.

Last night had been a sort of dream, that was all. In that dream she had completely forgotten about Meredith, the manuscripts and the possible existence of a secret room. But in truth, even now, none of that seemed very real to her. Other things did. For example, how Tom had gathered her into his arms and carried her upstairs to his bedroom; the voluptuous pressure of his naked body against hers; and, flowing between them, the brilliant crackle of energy that had seemed to light up the room. Looking around at the familiar surroundings of the Rare Books Room, those things seemed wholly incredible. Yet they had happened. But most immediately present to her perception was the taste of the baked fruit Tom had brought to her in bed. She had eaten it in his arms, her back resting against his chest, and with every morsel she had crushed with her tongue, an aromatic, almost alcoholic explosion had suffused her mouth.

But, of course, all that was irrelevant, Isabelle told herself firmly. How natural and unselfconscious it had all seemed to her meant nothing, because it had all been a dream, a disturbing but temporary enchantment of the senses. Nothing more. Now she must consider reality – the orderly life that lay mapped out in front of her and her bond with Clothaire, which was unshakeable. She couldn't lose all that. On the tannoy a voice announced that the reading rooms would be closing in thirty minutes. Isabelle saved her work, closed the file and switched off her laptop. She would speak to Tom and explain that it had all been a mistake. He would understand.

18 Daisy

'Oh, I almost forgot,' Clothaire said, addressing himself to Daisy directly, something he usually avoided. 'I have something to ask you.' He had joined their little group – which also included Agathe, Marie-Laure, Claire and her sister Amélie – for a Sunday lunch in Montparnasse and, after holding forth almost single-handedly throughout, speaking over everybody else as usual, was standing up to leave. Daisy looked up at him, surprised.

'It's this university colleague of mine. He lectures in contemporary history, but he's published a few cultural essays. Anyway, he's preparing a new book about the sociology of fashion, or is it the mythology of fashion? Something like that. I thought it was not completely impossible that you could be useful to him,' Clothaire went on, glancing at Daisy and looking utterly unconvinced. 'So I want to know if you will speak with him.'

Daisy was perplexed. 'Me? But . . . I'm not an academic.'

'*No*, to be sure,' Clothaire said with heavy sarcasm. 'He doesn't care about that. He wants to speak to an ordinary person who works in fashion.'

'Who is your colleague?' Claire asked.

'Etienne Deslisses.'

'Deslisses?' said Marie-Laure. 'But he's famous. I didn't know you knew him.'

'Not that famous,' Clothaire said crossly.

'He's not as brilliant as you, perhaps,' Agathe said, 'but he is rather clever. His book on intimacy for example, that was really witty and sharp.'

'Hmmmmm ... I much preferred the one on transgression,' Claire said coldly. 'I thought it was more rigorous, less personal.'

This exchange went into one of Daisy's ears and out of the other.

Then Marie-Laure squeezed her arm and said enthusiastically, 'You shouldn't miss an opportunity of meeting a brilliant intellectual like Deslisses while you're in Paris, Daisy. Personally, I love his work. It is clever, but also poetic. He's a marvellous stylist.'

'Is he really?' Daisy asked, suddenly interested. 'He's a stylist as well as a writer, that's unusual. I suppose he freelances on the side. Who does he work for mostly? Men's magazines? Or women's?'

It was Amélie who eventually broke the silence. 'Not a *fashion* stylist, Daisy,' she said kindly. 'Marie means that he has great literary style, you know, in his writing.'

'Oh, I see,' Daisy said, turning scarlet.

'Daisy, you're so funny,' Agathe said, looking across at Claire, who smiled back. 'If only I could be there like a little mouse when you meet Deslisses, and listen in to your conversation.'

'*I* don't think he's such a great stylist,' Clothaire said jealously. 'He's OK. Nothing so extraordinary.'

'And what is he like, Clothaire?' Marie-Laure asked. 'In person?'

'Oh, I don't know . . . serious, studious, dedicated to his work. The students seem to like him. It's even a ridiculous sort of cult. It's true that he is very productive. He never misses a conference. Personally, I find him boring.'

'You mean he doesn't show enough interest in your own work?' Claire said playfully.

'That's got nothing to do with it. Don't be stupid, Claire.'

Clothaire's friend sounded terrifying, Daisy thought. How to get out of this?

'So what would I have to do?' she asked tremulously.

'Ah, enough with the questions! *I* don't know!' Clothaire said irritably, fastening his coat. 'Go and talk to him about clothes. You can manage that, no?'

'Clothaire, don't be so unpleasant,' Marie-Laure said.

'Sorry,' Clothaire said ungraciously. 'Anyway, I have to go. Daisy, can he call you, yes or no?'

'All right, if you like. But I'm really not . . .'

'Yes, yes, I heard you the first time. You can tell him that yourself. It's not my business any more.'

Etienne Deslisses, who sounded extremely polite and spoke very good English, had rung Daisy the next day and they had arranged to meet a week later in a café on Place de la Sorbonne. In the interests of speedy identification, Daisy mentioned that she would be wearing a bright-pink coat.

When she got to the café, she found almost every table occupied by lone men, all smoking, all drinking coffee and all deeply engrossed in a book. Which was Etienne Deslisses? This one, probably, Daisy thought, noticing a distinguished silver-haired fifty-something who was busy marking his way through a pile of essays. It suddenly crossed her mind that it might have been as well to wear something slightly less frivolous for this meeting. Well, it was too late now and, frankly, if this big-shot intellectual didn't see the point of a bell-sleeved, dip-dyed minidress in tangerine brocade with matching tights and Mary-Jane shoes, that was his problem, not hers. Daisy could only be herself, after all. As she stood irresolutely near the door, wondering whether to make her presence known to him, someone else, at a corner table next to the bar, looked up and waved in her direction. He rose, putting his cigarette out, as Daisy walked over to his table. They shook hands.

'Etienne? Hi, I'm Daisy Keen.'

'Hello. Have a seat. What would you like to drink?'

'*Café crème*, please.'

Etienne Deslisses was years younger than Daisy's mental picture of him. In fact he was probably quite near her own age. He had very dark, almost black eyes and short chestnut hair with a slanting fringe, and was soberly clad in jeans and a navy-blue jumper with a beige tartan scarf, the ends neatly tucked into the loop in that French preppy way. While he ordered, Daisy's eyes fell on the paperback that lay splayed open on the table in front of him. She moved it around to read the title: *Tropic of Cancer*, by somebody called Henry Miller. Some kind of travel guide about visiting hot regions, no doubt. At least they could talk about that to begin with, she thought, relieved.

'So, Etienne, are you planning a holiday?'

'No, not at the moment. Why?'

Daisy nodded in the direction of his book.

'I see what you mean,' Etienne said after a moment. 'It is the most remarkable travel memoir, isn't it? I have read it before in translation but the original is so much better, of course. I imagine you think he's a terrible misogynist,' he added, offering her a cigarette. 'Many women do.'

'Who, me?' Daisy said, startled. 'No, not really.' Better stay neutral on that one. 'I only asked because I would *love* a gorgeous holiday in the sun at this time of year. It's so tempting in this weather to escape to the nearest beach, isn't it?'

'Yes, of course,' Etienne said politely before changing the subject. 'Daisy, I really want to thank you for agreeing to do this. It'll be of enormous help to me with this book. I don't know how much Clothaire has already explained . . .'

'Yes, um . . . Listen, Etienne, I'm really not sure I can help you. I don't even understand what your book is about.'

'It's very simple. It's a study of fashion as semiotics.'

So it was just as she had feared. Daisy stared at the Frenchman helplessly and shrugged. 'I have no idea what that means.'

'Don't worry. Nor do I at this point. But I'm hoping to clarify the concept with your help. It's a question of definition, first of all. On the one hand, there's clothing, which is what human beings devised to protect themselves from the weather. And on the other, there's fashion, which is something quite different. More complicated.'

Biting her lip, Daisy slowly nodded. Actually that didn't sound too incomprehensible.

'If fashion didn't exist, we wouldn't need more than one

outfit each,' Etienne said, tapping a cigarette out of his packet, 'at least in theory. So long as it was well made and kept us warm, that would be enough. But that's not what we do.'

'No-oo! Thank goodness,' Daisy said, her head reeling at the thought. 'That would just be so *boring*.'

'I admit that I am very ignorant about fashion,' Etienne went on earnestly, 'but I have the impression that it is a sort of language, a code even. Would you agree with that?'

'Oh, completely!' Daisy said enthusiastically. She shrugged off her pink coat and draped it on the back of her chair. 'Fashion is *amazingly* complicated. That's why it's so brilliant.'

Etienne reached into his bag and produced a small digital recorder.

'Do you mind if I record this?'

'OK,' Daisy said, her sense of trepidation returning as she eyed the device. Oh please, don't let her make a complete fool of herself. 'What do you want me to say?'

'Let's treat this as a trial session. We'll talk for a while. Do you have an hour or so? Good. Then, if at the end you feel you are not interested, you don't need to do any more. *D'accord*?'

'*D'accord*.'

'Let's start with . . . your coat, for example. What you're wearing now. Why did you decide to wear those particular things today? What do they mean to you? And where did they come from?'

That was unexpectedly easy. Daisy launched into a detailed history of her outfit, warming to her subject by the minute. There were many ramifications, by way of acid colours and contrasting textures being such a big story this season, echoes of Carnaby Street and Twiggy, the refinements of vintage couture, ambient electronic pop and the perfect Technicolor world of musical comedies. Etienne smoked and listened without interrupting, his face quite serious.

'The other thing about my pink coat,' Daisy concluded, her throat a little parched at the end of her long speech, 'is that when I wear it, things tend to happen. People start funny conversations with me in shops. Complete strangers give me things. I've met some really hilarious people that way. It's a lucky coat, for making friends. But when I wear my blue coat, I get stopped constantly by people asking me for directions. Perhaps it makes me look like a traffic warden.'

'Fascinating,' Etienne said, putting his cigarette out. The recorder clicked and blinked. 'You know, I think the disc is full. Would you like another drink?'

'A glass of water would be nice.'

'Yes, you must be exhausted. It was quite a lecture, and without any notes. This is exactly the sort of material I'm looking for. It's amazing how much detail you carry around in your head – you're like a walking encyclopaedia.'

'Oh, thanks,' Daisy said, delighted. 'It's the first time anyone's called me that!'

'So do you think it would it be OK to do this again a few more times?'

'Of course! I'd love to! It was much easier than I thought. I don't mind telling you now that I was scared stiff on my way here. I've never been very good at exams.'

'This is not in any way an exam. In fact if anyone is the

teacher, it's you. And I should have said so earlier but of course I'll pay you for your time.'

'Oh no, don't be silly,' Daisy said, laughing. 'Talking about clothes is my favourite thing to do. I don't need paying.'

She left soon after, having agreed to dispense more of her specialist knowledge on the following Monday, same time, same place. As she walked home, she wondered whether Etienne and his project might perhaps make a good subject for her *Sparkle* blog. It had been an unexpectedly interesting encounter.

A few weeks later, Daisy again stepped on top of the white cube in Raoul's studio.

Raoul studied her for a minute, then his face lit up. 'I think because of how you are dressed today, all in black with the miniskirt and the boots,' he said, 'I would like to try something like *Chapeau melon et bottes de cuir*. You know what I mean?'

Daisy frowned, perplexed. '"Bowler hat and leather boots"? What's that?'

'Oh, sure you know. It's an English TV show, very famous. There's a guy and a girl – they're detectives. He's called John Steed and she's called Madame Peel.'

'Mrs Peel? Oh, you mean *The Avengers*!'

'Yeah, that's it.'

'So, something a bit like this, you mean?' Daisy said, essaying a high-kicking karate chop.

'Oh, I like that a lot,' Raoul said, grinning, 'but you can't hold that pose. You will totally fall over.'

'Yes, you're right. Maybe if I just bend my knees a bit

and hold my arms up like this, sort of criss-crossed, as though I'm about to launch an attack?'

'That looks very cool. But I think it would be even better if we could see the definition in your arms.'

'Oh, I can take the shirt off, actually. I'm wearing a vest underneath.'

Daisy threw her shirt on the sofa and resumed her pose. 'Better?'

'Fantastic. Wow, you have a great tan. You have been in the sun?'

'Yes, in the make-believe sun of fake tan.'

Raoul smiled, working rapidly. He looked up. 'Daisy, just . . . move your right foot a bit to the side, OK?'

'Like this?'

'That's great. No, wait a minute,' Raoul said, rising and walking across to her. 'Can you move that strap just a little, this way?' he said, pointing.

'You do it. I'd rather hold the pose.'

'It'll make a better line.'

His hand straightened her spaghetti strap and, in doing so, trailed lightly across her shoulder, leaving small goose-bumps in its wake. Daisy giggled.

'Sorry. I'm tickling you?'

'Um, no. Yes, a little bit. It's all right.'

'You are being so professional. It's totally amazing,' he said, smiling. He stood where he was for a moment, then rubbed the back of his neck briskly and said: 'OK, so I finish this in a few minutes if you can hold it.' He turned and walked back to the director's chair where his pad lay waiting. 'Then you can rest.'

Daisy made a small noise of assent and held her pose. While Raoul worked, she thought about what had just happened. Was there some sort of physical attraction between them? It was difficult to tell for sure. She certainly found herself drawn to him: Raoul was very attractive in an Indiana Jones kind of way and exuded sexual confidence. But how did *he* feel about *her*? Generally speaking, he always behaved in an entirely platonic and friendly fashion. He had ruffled her hair a couple of times but that was about it. Really he might have been one of her close gay friends who, in some cases, were just as interested in female beauty as Raoul. Well, perhaps not *quite* as interested as Raoul, who was in a completely different league. And he was *definitely* not gay.

But when they were working on a drawing, the atmosphere seemed to become quite charged. He would look at her with a serious, brooding intensity that made her feel a little bashful. Then again, Daisy had seen just that kind of intensity in the eyes of casting directors comparing the model standing in front of them with the photographs in her book. It was probably just that, the external sign of a visual artist's concentration, and nothing more. Anyway, it really didn't matter that much because, in spite of what Anouk or Chrissie might say, she felt it was probably still too soon for her to think of getting involved with anyone again.

'So what do you think? Should I just ask him if he is interested?' she asked Marie-Laure the next day, as they discussed her dilemma over lunch.

'No! It's far too direct,' Marie-Laure said, horrified. 'What if he said no? And anyway, do you like him?'

'Well,' Daisy said with a giggle, 'let's just say that I'm beginning to see the point of the whole "older man" thing. He's just so much more . . . solid than anyone I've ever known. He's done so much. And he's an artist! But I don't even know if he likes me!'

'Couldn't you create an atmosphere, you know . . .'

'But I think that there already *is* an atmosphere. That's the thing.'

Daisy next met Raoul on the following weekend to go to the cinema. It began to dawn on her that she would actually really like him to kiss her, and she found it hard to concentrate on the film, watching out instead for any telltale signs of interest on his part. But Raoul sat next to her throughout with perfect decorum. Afterwards, they went out for something to eat and then went back to his apartment for one of his specialties – a lethally strong mojito.

'You would love Latin America, Daisy,' Raoul said, as his jukebox went into full maracas-shaking Bahia mode. 'The beaches are so unbelievable. And the girls in Brazil wear this amazing swimwear,' he added dreamily. 'It's totally extreme.'

'I can imagine.'

Raoul turned to look at her. 'Are you OK? You're not saying a lot today.'

'I'm fine,' Daisy said, smiling at him, 'I'm just . . . thinking.'

'Just thinking about what? You are missing London, your family?'

'Oh no, nothing like that. I mean I'm looking forward to going home for Christmas, but that's not what's on my mind.'

'So what is on your mind, Daisy?' Raoul said, putting his drink down.

'It's a really silly thing.'

'No, no, you can tell me anything. Come on.'

Oh, sod it, Daisy thought. Sorry, Marie-Laure, I'm going in. 'Well, *sometimes* . . .' she began, her heart thudding, 'sometimes I wonder if perhaps you aren't flirting with me. Just a tiny bit.'

She held her breath and waited. Raoul's green eyes narrowed. He considered her without smiling. 'You believe that? That I flirt with you?'

'Well, I don't know!' Daisy said, rolling her eyes. 'Our cultures are very different, I realise that. We send out different signals. So perhaps I misunderstood –'

'Daisy,' he interrupted, leaning forwards to whisper in her ear, 'our cultures are not so very different. I think you are a very beautiful woman.' Then he added in that Gallic rasp of his: 'And I really desire you.'

Biting the inside of her cheeks to stem a fit of giggles, Daisy stole a glance at him. Yes, he was completely straight-faced. The French were amazing: they simply did not know the meaning of embarrassment. As she attempted to compose herself, Raoul, judging correctly that the ice had been broken, took her hand and placed it quite casually on his crotch. Well, Daisy thought, her eyes widening a little, if you put it like that ... At that precise moment, any remaining doubts evaporated and she felt quite certain that it *was* time for her to get back in the saddle. Raoul might have been reading her mind as he gradually pulled her closer to him until she found herself in pole position, sitting astride him. They kissed. Yes, it was definitely the right time.

'Yee-haw,' she murmured a little later.

'What did you say, sugar?'

'Oh, nothing.'

19 Isabelle

When the downstairs telephone rang that evening, Isabelle stayed where she was, upstairs in her room, and let Chrissie take the call. She needed a minute to rehearse what she was going to say. And perhaps it wasn't Tom after all. But she had no such luck.

'Darling!' Chrissie called up through the stairwell, 'it's His Quincitude for you.'

Isabelle went down to the hallway, where the receiver lay waiting on the table. She stared at it for a moment. It was odd to think that this ordinary-looking object really contained a person's voice. Eventually, she lifted it to her ear.

'Hello, Tom.'

'Hello.'

The amount of caressing warmth he managed to inject into that single word unsettled her. But it was a temptation she had to resist, that was all.

'How was your day?' he said.

'Quite good, thank you. I went to the library.'

'That's great. It's lovely to hear your voice. Are you feeling tired or . . . would you like to come over? I could pick you up in twenty minutes.'

'Tom, I think it would be better if we met another time,' Isabelle said slowly. 'During the day.' Taking advantage of his silence, she continued: 'Last night I think I made a big mistake. It was not your fault at all, but it can't happen again.'

'I see.'

'You know that I'm not available.'

'Yes, I understand what you mean.'

'So I can't behave like this. I have too much at stake, too many plans.'

'Isabelle, you are free to do anything you like. Anything that makes you happy.'

'Yes, I know that. And this is the decision I'm happy with – what I've just told you. I'm sorry if I misled you.'

'Please don't regret anything. I don't.'

'No.'

At least he was not able to see her face. That was something. Now for the really difficult bit.

'And there is another reason for this, which is my work on Meredith. Getting involved with you creates a conflict of interest. It compromises my research.'

'Does it?'

'Yes, of course!'

'Do you say that because we didn't get around to talking about her last night?'

'That was just one example. But generally, even if we had got around to it, I would feel like I was . . . using you. Do you understand what I mean?'

Tom started to laugh. 'You are very welcome to use me in any way you like.'

'Tom, please.'

'Seriously, I wouldn't have minded helping you with your work as well. But no, that's fine. I understand.'

Isabelle took a deep breath. 'But the thing is, Tom . . . This is going to sound terrible after everything I've just said, but I would still like you to help me with my work.'

'Just without any of the other stuff?'

'Exactly. Don't be angry, please.'

'I'm not angry.'

'I'll understand if you say no. I haven't behaved very well.'

'Oh, I'm not sure I did any better, really. Don't worry. I think I understand your difficulty.'

'So would it be OK if we met to talk about Meredith?'

'Yes.'

'May I come to your house?'

'If you think it's safe. Only joking. Of course, do come whenever you like. It'll be strictly business, I promise.'

'It's just that . . . there are a couple of things in the house I'd like to check. I'll explain when I'm there.'

'Excellent. I look forward to it.'

'Are you free this weekend?'

'Free as a bird. Come to lunch on Sunday. One o'clock?'

'That's perfect. Thank you, Tom.'

'And you are welcome to bring someone especially for-bidding from the Quince Society with you. As a chaperone.'

It was a relief to laugh with him again.

'I'm really sorry.'

'So am I. I'll see you on Sunday. Goodbye, Isabelle.'

'Goodbye.'

When Isabelle joined her friends in the kitchen, Jules looked tactfully away but Chrissie said, '*Well*? Darling?'

Isabelle walked straight to the fridge, opened the door

and hid behind it, staring unseeingly at the contents of the shelves. Chrissie waited respectfully, for as long as 12 seconds, then let out a high-pitched squeal: '*Ooooooh!* Darling, have a *heart*! Think of my poor nerves and tell us what happened. *Well?* Are you seeing him tonight? Is he coming here?'

Eventually Isabelle's eyes focused on a pot of yoghurt and she re-emerged with it in her hand. She got a spoon from the drawer and sat down at the table next to Jules.

'It's all been dealt with,' she said calmly. 'We're just going to be friends now. He understands completely.'

'Oh, *darling*,' Chrissie said, stricken. 'What a *terrible* waste of perfectly good sex.'

Silently, Jules pushed her spectacles to the top of her nose.

'I'm just relieved it's over,' Isabelle said, keeping her eyes down and carefully peeling back the yoghurt's lid. 'Now I can forget about it and concentrate on my work.' She ate a small mouthful meditatively, then added: 'And he's agreed to help me with it, which is really kind. I'm going to see him on Sunday to talk about it.'

'Are you now?' Jules said, smiling almost imperceptibly.

'Yes. I'm hoping to get my hands on those manuscripts so I can study them closely.'

'Ha. That's a new name for it,' Chrissie muttered. '*Ow!* Ju, I wish you wouldn't keep doing that. You *know* I bruise easily.'

On Sunday Isabelle presented herself at Tom's house armoured with the reassuring knowledge that she was simply visiting a relative of Meredith Quince with whom she was on friendly terms. She rang the bell and composed her face into an expression of slightly brisk cordiality.

After a short wait, the door was opened by an unknown young woman with a very brown, freckled and vivacious countenance, clad in half-undone and rather muddy dungarees. It had taken Isabelle the whole length of her journey to prepare herself for her reunion with Tom but the unexpected sight of this person on his doorstep was enough to unman her almost completely.

'Yes?' the girl said, raising her eyebrows. She had a quantity of curly brown hair gathered up with a piece of ribbon into an improvised, untidy ponytail. There was a smudge of dirt on her cheek and she was barefoot.

'My name is Isabelle. Tom Quince is expecting me.'

'Oh really? Well, come in, then.'

She opened the door wider and walked back into the hallway, followed by Isabelle. Inside the house the girl called out: 'Tommy? There's somebody here for you!'

There was no response.

'I wonder where he's got to,' the girl said. 'You're not . . . staying for lunch, are you?'

'Um, yes,' Isabelle said, startled. 'I . . .'

'Oh? OK. In that case I think we might as well go into the kitchen and wait for him there. He's probably gone back into the shed for something.'

They went downstairs together.

'We've had such fun all morning, making the best of the dry weather. It was a bit of a mad race to get all those bulbs in but we're a good team, Tommy and I. And now

I'm bushed!' the girl said, before flopping down on the kitchen's tattered velvet sofa.

The table, Isabelle noticed, had in fact been laid for three. The strange girl settled in comfortably, hugging her knees to her chest, while Isabelle, her coat and gloves still on, perched on the edge of a kitchen chair across from her. There was a short silence while they both looked out of the window for signs of Tom's presence in the garden. He was nowhere to be seen. Isabelle turned to smile at the girl as non-committally as she could manage.

'You're . . . French, aren't you?' the girl drawled, stretching a brown foot with bright-pink toenails in Isabelle's direction.

'Yes. My name is Isabelle Papillon,' Isabelle said calmly while thinking: And who the *hell* are *you*? with such helpless, vivid intensity that she worried for a moment that she might have spoken the words aloud.

'I'm Rosie.'

They nodded at each other.

'So . . . how do you know Tommy?'

Isabelle began to speak, but had barely finished a sentence before Rosie burst out laughing and said, 'Oh, I know! You're one of those Quince Society people! How funny!'

'Why is it funny?' Isabelle asked evenly.

'Because that whole cult of Meredith Quince is really *not* Tommy's style. It's so pompous and absurd.'

'Did he tell you that?'

'Well . . . I mean I know they've been hounding him and his parents to get into this house for years. It's creepy.'

'Perhaps it is, but I assure you that he invited me here

himself,' Isabelle said, refraining from adding, 'And not for the first time.'

'Oh yes, of course he did. Sorry,' Rosie said, looking nothing of the kind.

Providentially, Tom chose this difficult moment to come in from the garden.

'Oh, good, you're here, Isabelle,' he said, hanging up his coat and hat. 'Sorry to keep everyone waiting. I was in the middle of washing the outside of the greenhouse and I thought I might as well get it over and done with before lunch. I hope Rosie's been looking after you.'

'Oh yes,' Isabelle said, glancing back at Rosie, who, she noticed, had swiftly taken her hair down, spreading it attractively over her shoulders, as soon as Tom had appeared. Another, perhaps significant fact about the unexpected guest was that there was no sign of a bra under her thin T-shirt.

'Tommy,' Rosie said smilingly, wagging a finger at him, 'you never mentioned that this was going to be a high-brow literary luncheon. Is it because I might not have agreed to stay if you had?'

Tom took the time to pull off his boots, then padded over to kiss Isabelle on the cheek. His face felt cool, perhaps because he'd been outside all that time.

'I've no doubt that you can hold your own, Rosie. Isabelle, may I take your coat?' He laid it carefully on the sofa, then pushed his hair back with both hands. 'Right. And now I'm going to check the meat.'

Soon after, they sat down to eat. As a result of some fairly unsubtle territorial dancing around, Rosie secured the chair next to Tom's while Isabelle sat facing him. She did not find lunch at all easy. It wasn't because of the meal itself. She had learned to expect delectable food from Tom and he certainly didn't let himself down with the magnificent roast beef he delivered, accompanied by what was, to her, a new and exotic delicacy – Yorkshire pudding as airy as a goosedown pillow. What marred the occasion for Isabelle was how swiftly she realised – with a quite unexpected pang – that his initial vagueness of manner had returned, obliterating any trace of intimacy as relentlessly as a curtain of clouds being drawn over the sun.

'Isabelle is in the process of writing a thesis about my great-aunt's novels,' Tom said, pouring Rosie a glass of wine.

'Really? What's it about?'

Isabelle repressed a small sigh. This was not at all how she would have liked to broach the subject of *The Splodge* with him.

'Oh, it's a bit boring and technical, really,' she replied evasively. 'It's about the narrative strategy of her detective novels.'

'That sounds great,' Rosie said, looking deeply unimpressed. She immediately turned to Tom and launched into a long disquisition about the type of bubble polythene best suited to insulating his greenhouse during the winter.

While this was going on, Isabelle experienced the oddest feeling of division of her self. Her conscious mind was firmly congratulating her on how well she was handling herself in the company of Tom Quince. It also stated with pedantic satisfaction that the presence of a third person was a wonderful boon, acting as it did as a sort of censoring device that made it impossible even to allude to certain recent events which had taken place, for some of them, on the very table at which they were now seated.

Meanwhile her body was following a very different course. Almost painfully delighted to see Tom again, it would gladly have leapt over the table that stood between them to be more closely reunited with him. Also, being rather feral in outlook, Isabelle's body did not at all care for Rosie, having instantly categorised her as a first-class *tête à claques* – an irritating person whose face seemed to invite a good hard slap, or several, come to that.

Somewhere between the two, another, more diffident and tender part of her consciousness was following its own meandering line of questioning, chiefly to do with what might be the exact status of the bra-less barefoot Rosie in Tom's life.

'Rosie and I took the same horticulture course a few years ago,' Tom said, as he stood up to clear their plates.

'And then we met up again in Florence last year,' Rosie added for Isabelle's benefit. 'Oh, Tommy,' she said, laughing throatily, 'we had such a fantastic time there, didn't we? And as I only live around the corner,' she went on, her eyes gradually returning to Isabelle, 'I often pop over to help with the garden. By this stage it almost feels like my own garden too. Because it's been such a joint project for us, you see.'

'So, are you also a professional gardener?' Isabelle asked, still trying not to think of Tom and Rosie having a fantastic time in Florence.

'At the moment I work in a nursery.'

'Oh? Looking after babies?'

Rosie laughed a little. 'No, after trees and plants, actually. Though I *am* hoping to have babies at some point.'

'Thank you,' Isabelle said as Tom handed her an enticing piece of apple pie. 'Tom, I was wondering . . . I would be very interested to see Meredith's manuscripts. Can you remember where they are?'

'I *think* they might be in a box in the attic,' he said vaguely.

'Really? Could I go and have a look after lunch?'

'By all means.'

'What do you want them for?' Rosie asked. 'Is it something *else* for the Quince Society? I thought Tommy had already made you a gift of that portrait. Surely that's enough.'

'No, it's nothing to do with the Society. It's for me. I'm trying to get an idea of how Meredith composed her stories, of her creative process. The manuscripts might show corrections, successive versions, comments in the margins, all that sort of thing.'

'All that sort of thing is way over my head,' Rosie said, picking up crumbs of pastry with the tip of her finger and licking them off. 'I can't understand why anyone would want to spend all their time poring over dusty old papers. Personally, I much prefer to be out in the fresh air.'

Tom had been looking absent-mindedly in Isabelle's direction. He turned to his neighbour. 'In that case, perhaps you could make us all some coffee while I take

Isabelle up to the attic. You know where everything is, don't you?'

'Yes, but . . .'

'Oh, thank you. You *are* a good guest.'

Isabelle followed Tom up the stairs to the top floor. Her body remembered very clearly that this was where his bedroom was. Her conscious mind concentrated firmly on the proximity of the manuscripts.

'It's through here,' Tom said, opening a narrow door at the far end of the landing. 'I'll go first – hopefully catch some of the cobwebs on my way.'

Isabelle followed up a cramped spiral staircase and emerged after Tom into a vast cluttered attic.

'Hang on, stay where you are. I know there's a light switch somewhere.'

The light came on, illuminating an overwhelming jumble of travel cases, dismantled furniture and empty picture frames, as well as innumerable cardboard boxes.

'Over here, I think, are some of Meredith's papers at least. I remember helping Dad move them out of her room.'

The boxes Tom was referring to sat on top of a bed, whose sunken mattress was punctured by a few curly metal springs. As Tom opened the first box, Isabelle began to kneel on the mattress to look over his shoulder.

'Keep off that thing, Isabelle, it's booby-trapped.' He pulled out a sheaf of papers and handed them to her.

'Oh. These look like . . . bills,' Isabelle said, disappointed.

'Yes, you're right. Not without some historical interest if you were writing about the day-to-day running of a

1930s household, but possibly not of great literary value. Shall we try the other box?'

'Yes, please.'

The other box was full of yellowed newspapers.

'You know, I think these must be Dad's,' Tom said pensively. 'He's always hoarded papers, thinking he would get around to reading them later.'

'Those manuscripts could be anywhere,' Isabelle said, looking around with some discouragement.

'Too true. We would need to search the place methodically but I think it would take longer than we've got today. Let's go down.'

Tom switched off the light and headed back towards the stairs, closely followed by Isabelle. As she began her descent, one of her kitten heels got stuck between two floorboards. She tried to yank herself free, but her foot slid out of the trapped shoe and she became airborne, careering downwards behind Tom who, alerted by her cry of terror, turned around just in time to catch her in his arms and cushion the impact of her body by hitting the wall rather hard with his own.

'I've got you,' he said, sounding a trifle short-winded, as they collapsed on the stairs in a closely conjoined sitting position. Feeling his breath on her mouth, Isabelle wondered in a rush of bewildered longing what it might be like to kiss this man every day of her life – if only such a thing were allowed.

'Thank you,' she said coldly, disengaging herself. 'I'm so sorry. That was really clumsy of me.'

'Actually, you know,' Tom said, slowly taking his hands

off her shoulders, 'nobody's more graceful than you, even when falling down the stairs. If you will allow me to pay you a small and entirely platonic compliment.'

'I hope I didn't hurt you too much.'

Tom straightened his spectacles and ran his hand over his chest. 'No, no, absolutely not. I have far too many ribs anyway – they're all at your service. It was not unlike dodgems, I suppose, except a lot more fun. And you may remember that something similar happened the first time we met – a collision on the stairs. It's obviously going to be a recurring pattern in our friendship.'

'Obviously,' Isabelle said, smiling a little and rubbing her legs.

'Are you hurt?'

'No, I don't think so. Just a bit shaken.'

Tom got up and climbed a few steps to retrieve her shoe. 'It looks OK to me,' he said, testing the heel. 'Shall I put it back on your foot?'

'Oh no, thank you. I can manage on my own.'

He handed her the shoe and stood back silently while she brushed down her clothes and picked a few cobwebs out of her hair. They made their way down to the landing and Tom closed the door behind them.

'I don't know about you, Isabelle, but I could probably do with some coffee now.'

'Yes, that would be nice.'

'I'm afraid Rosie's usually isn't quite up to Continental standards but at least it'll be hot.'

In the kitchen they found Rosie curled up on the sofa, sullenly looking through a mail-order seed catalogue.

She was now wearing a zipped-up red fleece over her dungarees.

'That attic must be full of fascinating treasure,' she said, without looking up. 'Were you throwing furniture around, by the way? I heard a commotion.'

'Oh, that was just us falling down the stairs.'

Rosie raised her eyes and stared. 'Tommy, you do look a mess! Are you all right?'

'I'm fine. It's Isabelle who's in need of solicitude. She almost lost a shoe, you know. I understand that's quite traumatic.'

'Really? But you're OK, aren't you?' Rosie said, coolly looking Isabelle up and down. 'Apart from ripped tights.'

Tom poured two mugs of coffee, added milk and stirred two lumps of sugar into Isabelle's.

'Oh . . . Thanks, but I don't usually have milk or sugar in coffee.'

'I know, but you're in shock. No arguments. Drink it.'

Isabelle obeyed and felt instantly better.

'So the long and short of it is that we have no idea where the manuscripts are.'

'N-no,' Isabelle said slowly, sitting down next to Rosie without really noticing her presence.

'Who cares?' Rosie said. 'They're probably lost anyway. It doesn't matter that much, surely?'

'Well, it matters to Isabelle,' Tom said vaguely, brushing dust out of his floppy hair. 'And I suppose I do feel some kind of family responsibility too. She was my great-aunt.'

'Tom? I don't suppose your father might remember what he did with them?'

'Oh, he won't know. And even if he did, he would pretend not to. He hated Meredith being an author and wants no part of it now. I suppose that's partly why I've never read her books.'

'Tommy, I hate to interrupt this fascinating conversation but the light is going. We should get started if you want to do any more in the garden today.'

'I think I should go home,' Isabelle said, reaching for her coat.

'Why don't you stay and rest for a while? I can run you home later.'

'No, thank you, I'm perfectly fine now. Thanks for lunch – it was lovely. Nice to meet you, Rosie.'

'Nice to meet you, too,' Rosie said, pulling on her wellies with her back to Isabelle.

'Isabelle,' Tom said, walking her back to the front door, 'why don't you come back tomorrow and start on the attic? Unless you have other plans?' Seeing her hesitate, he added, 'It might make a nice change from the British Library.'

'Well . . . I'd love to if you don't mind,' Isabelle said gratefully. 'But wouldn't I be interfering with your work in the garden with, um, Rosie?'

'Leave Rosie to me. Just concentrate on finding the manuscripts. It might also be an idea to wear flat shoes tomorrow, unless of course you're planning even more ambitious acrobatics. In which case I would, of course, be delighted to assist you again.'

20 Daisy

'You look very well, *mon petit*,' Anouk said approvingly when her friend next visited her in her shop. 'I can see that a little change of climate is doing you good.'

The climatic change in question combined periods of intense shagging with frequent bouts of shopping for underwear, which was fun but also very necessary to keep Daisy provided with a reasonable trousseau. Raoul got through a fair few pairs because he loved to rip them apart when undressing her. Such enthusiasm was very welcome after the Octave debacle. Of course there had never really been any doubt in Daisy's mind that Raoul was generally disposed to show an interest in sex. The first time he'd taken her into his bedroom, she had been quite prepared to find a mirror on the ceiling. In actual fact there wasn't one, but the eye-popping Japanese etching of a kimono-clad couple embracing that hung above his bed more than made up for it. As for Raoul's outspoken appreciation of her person, it could sometimes be a little disconcerting, but overall it was hard not to warm to a man who said, among other things, that her pubic hair was like mink to the touch.

Meanwhile Daisy went on meeting Etienne Deslisses on Mondays for an hour or so of fashion talk. The writer seemed pleased with her contributions, and Daisy really enjoyed her unaccustomed role as initiator into a foreign, esoteric culture. What was perhaps nicest about Etienne was that he never made fun of her. He actually seemed to take her seriously. Not many people had done that, in Daisy's experience. For example, when meeting him for the third or fourth time, Daisy had said, 'By the way, Etienne, are you still reading that travel book – what was it . . . *Club Tropicana*?'

Etienne looked at her for a minute, then said, 'You mean *Tropic of Cancer*.'

'Oh, right. Yes.'

'No, I finished it a while ago. At the moment I'm reading a book about delinquency and repression in the nineteenth century. It's something I'm reviewing for a periodical. How about you?'

'Well, I'm reading *Vogue*,' Daisy said with a certain amount of embarrassment. 'But it's French *Vogue*!' she quickly pointed out. 'So it's a good way for me to pick up more vocabulary.'

'Perhaps you could talk me through it today. I have never read *Vogue*.'

'Really? Not even *Vogue Homme*?'

'No. I didn't know there was one.'

This was simply unbelievable, Daisy thought, managing somehow to resist the urge to text Chrissie on the spot.

'Good grief, Etienne! But you *must* familiarise yourself with *Vogue*. *I* started reading it when I was eleven. Think of it as a serious periodical for people who know about fashion. Right. Come and sit next to me. We don't have a moment to lose.'

Daisy patiently walked Etienne through the entire magazine, explaining how it was put together, why it contained so much advertising and what stylistic impact the fact that one of the editors used to be a certain designer's muse necessarily had on editorial content.

'Now let's move on to the main fashion stories,' Daisy said.

'Stories?' Etienne said, intrigued. 'But in what way are these stories? There's no narrative that I can discern. Just pictures of the same model in different outfits.'

'Ah, but *that*, you see, is the story. Here, for example, the story is all about underwear as outerwear. That's quite an old story, which returns from time to time. The whole thing was really invented by Madonna in the early nineties.' (Here Daisy went into a detailed footnote about the singer's association with Jean-Paul Gaultier, the revival of the corset and the significance of conical bras for men.) 'So the person who styled the shoot will have gone looking for pieces that worked within that story, whether they were intentionally designed as outerwear or not. There's always going to be an element of reinvention with really creative stylists. So you might style a pair of tights as a top, you know, or the model might wear a shoe as a hat. That kind of thing.'

Etienne was listening attentively.

'Here, on the other hand,' Daisy went on, moving on to the next series of pictures, 'where they shot the whole thing in Rome, the story is really '*la dolce vita*' as a general idea, hence the scooters and café society vibe, but also specifically as in that famous black-and-white film. I haven't seen it, but I know there's a scene in it where a blonde girl in a black strapless dress wades into this amazing fountain. They've recreated it here, you see, with this Russian model who's the hottest face of the moment.'

Etienne looked at Daisy while lighting a cigarette. 'But how can you possibly recognise the allusion if you haven't seen the film?'

'I still get the reference because it's a story that's been around for quite a while.'

'But other people might not get the reference at all?'

'No, but they'll still get the mood of the clothes. And, of course, the designers' names also speak to people. For some, *that* is the story: big brands, nothing else.'

Looking at Etienne's profile, Daisy thought idly how ironic it was that he should have so little knowledge of the fashion world because as a matter of fact, if he hadn't chosen to become a brilliant intellectual, blowing everyone's mind with his insights, he might have made a pretty stunning male model. His skin was flawless and his bone structure was really very good, with a firm jawline and elegant nose. He had the kind of full mouth that would surely photograph like a dream and also the longest, darkest eyelashes Daisy had ever seen on a man. Impulsively, she half-raised her hand towards his face, then checked herself. What *was* she doing?

'So, to sum up,' she went on instead, 'the story is the general theme or mood of the shoot – an eveningwear story, a floral story, whatever. But it's also made up of loads of other visual stuff. References to all kind of things, even private jokes sometimes, that only insanely trendy fashion insiders will get.'

Etienne looked thoroughly absorbed. Daisy could see that, in his relatively contained way, he was showing signs of profound intellectual excitement.

'Daisy, I've understood something. I now see that a fashion story is a text,' he said seriously. 'A text determined, of course, by its incredibly rich and complex intertextuality.'

'Do you really think so, Etienne?' Daisy said, impressed. 'And what is inter . . . um . . . textuality, by the way?'

'Well, you've explained to me that the meaning of each fashion story, or text, often depends on other references, or intertexts, within fashion but also outside of it. The meaning of the text, or story, emerges from the staging and also, hopefully, from the reading of the clothes. The stylist and the reader both participate in it.'

Daisy nodded. 'That's right. There are all these layers – some obvious, others really obscure. Every outfit has lots of, er, intertexts. And if you don't pick up on any of that stuff, then it just looks like you're wearing lovely pants or whatever.'

'This is wonderful stuff, Daisy. Excuse me a moment,' Etienne said, getting up as his mobile phone rang.

Watching him walk out of the café to take the call, Daisy gave a private little whoop of joy. Here she was, sitting outside the Sorbonne, being hailed as an important fashion expert by a real-life Parisian intellectual! If only Etienne weren't so reserved she would really like to hug him. But that would probably embarrass him. Even after a number of meetings he still greeted her with a polite handshake.

Later, while getting dressed to go out to dinner with

Raoul, Daisy thought to herself that things really *were* picking up in time for the end of the year. The blog was going well, she was managing to keep body and soul together by helping out Anouk in the shop, and she had also acquired a lovely new boyfriend who really appreciated her. Not too bad after only a few months in France.

Later that evening, looking happily around the huge, square dining room, Daisy basked in the satisfaction of finally being able to enjoy her first proper Parisian date. And it was all down to Raoul. Because even if Octave had, by some miracle, brought her here one evening, Daisy had no doubt that the serious glamour of the turn-of-the-century restaurant – with its dazzling expanse of mirrors and ornate polished woodwork, its chandeliers and its crowd of *bon vivant* diners intent on gastronomy and conversation – would have presented him with an irresistible challenge to misbehave.

Now Raoul, Daisy thought, looking across at him with approval, was clearly at ease in the context of a buzzing Parisian brasserie. He looked very dashing in a dark-grey suit, though the fact that he was not wearing a tie conspired with his customary stubble and untidy hair to give him a rebellious, slightly disreputable air. Very attractive indeed. Daisy had been impressed by the confidence with which he had commandeered a corner table that gave them a view of the entire room. He had also chosen to sit next to her on the red velvet banquette rather than opposite. This meant sitting very close together. It was rather romantic.

Walking through the humming room with Raoul close behind her, Daisy had felt that her Parisian musical comedy was on again. The restaurant was never still and seemed to be warming up for a big song-and-dance number. Groups of happy diners constantly poured in through the revolving glass doors. Others were being ferried from the bar to their table. Meanwhile the army of waiting staff carried out its own mysterious, dramatic choreography. Daisy commented on the difference in their outfits, so Raoul explained the hierarchy of dinner-jacketed *maîtres d'hôtel*, white-aproned *chefs de rang* and younger white-clad *commis de salle*. A sudden burst of flame not far from their table made Daisy look around with interest.

'They're flambéing pancakes in orange liqueur,' Raoul said. 'A dessert called *crêpes Suzette*. It's very delicate to do this right. You see how it's the senior guy who does it while the younger waiter watches and learns. It's a ceremony, an art.'

Raoul had considered opening a restaurant of his own after his stint in clubs, but the hours were not congenial to him.

'If you want to do it right, there's only one way. You've got to get up at three in the morning to go to the market at Rungis and get all the best fresh stuff. Every day. Can you imagine that? I mean, I can stay up all night, that's OK.' He smiled at her pointedly.

'All right, no need to boast,' Daisy said, blushing.

'But getting up before dawn? No way, man. That's not for me.'

Now feeling pleasantly warmed up by the restaurant's atmosphere, Daisy removed her pink pashmina and placed it on top of the embroidered vintage clutch bag she had bought last weekend at the Puces de Clignancourt. She was satisfied that her dress – a short black velvet shift – gave her a grown-up French look. But she had been unable to resist wearing her green satin shoes from Anouk's shop. They were a bit mad – with high, clumpy heels and huge satin bows – but realistically, she thought, there was only so much room for understatement in any outfit. A waiter materialised at their table with two menus.

'You want some champagne while we decide?' Raoul asked, his fingers caressing the back of her neck.

Daisy, who never said no to champagne, nodded enthusiastically and opened her menu. Raoul ordered their drinks, then turned his attention to what they would eat.

'You like *fruits de mer*? Oysters and stuff, you know? Maybe we can share a platter?'

'Yes, that's a lovely idea!'

'And after . . . I always have a *steak tartare* here but maybe you don't want everything raw? You'd like fish? The *cassolette de saumon*? The *magret de canard* is great, if you like duck. Or the chicken with morels. Really delicate, but the flavours are just extreme. You like wild mushrooms, yeah? It's such beautiful, classic food. You will love it.'

Tempted by its delicate and extreme flavours, Daisy decided on the chicken with morels. Octave would have found it impossible to sit still with her in this beautiful place for more than about ten minutes, she was certain of it. He'd have devised some elaborate charade to lure her downstairs to the loo for a prolonged snog, trying to unhook her bra through her clothes or some such schoolboy nonsense. That would have seemed a lot more fun to him than simply having a civilised meal in her company. Raoul on the other hand was a proper foodie. He loved fusion and was a complete sushi freak, but he was also incredibly knowledgeable about traditional French cuisine. It would be such a treat, such a privilege to eat out in his company. She was in for a very French experience, there was no doubt about that. Daisy sighed happily and gazed at the other diners, very much looking forward to her gastronomic initiation.

It therefore came as a bit of a surprise to feel Raoul's hand, which had been lying lightly on top of her knee, make its way rapidly up her skirt and into her knickers with the stunning accuracy of a heat-seeking missile. Daisy raised her menu in front of her face like a fan and glared at him. He was staring straight ahead, looking unconcerned.

'*What* are you doing?' Daisy stage-whispered.

'Who, me?' Raoul said, pointing at himself with his free hand with an air of injured innocence. He gave her a wolfish smile. 'Just checking that you're comfortable, that's all.'

'I'm *very* comfortable, Raoul, thank you. Now get *off*! We're in a public place.'

'Yeah, sure we are. It's fun, huh?'

'*Bonsoir. Vous avez choisi?*'

Their waiter, resplendent in formal black and white, stood in front of the table with a notepad. This was too much. Daisy hastily pulled more of the tablecloth over her lap and pressed her starched napkin against her forehead. She made a half-hearted attempt at escape, shifting sideways in her seat. Raoul's fingers followed implacably, and continued their work with absolute dedication and expertise.

Leaning his other elbow on the table and waving his hand for added emphasis, Raoul explained with excruciating deliberation that they would start with a Sancerre and then, possibly, follow this with a Beaujolais – a Moulin-à-Vent, perhaps, or a Juliénas – something reasonably light but *corsé*, with some depth of flavour. Now I *know* I'm in France, Daisy thought wildly, her eyes streaming, as her thighs came closer together to imprison Raoul's hand. But then again, he went on with careful consideration, might something else be preferable to better complement Madame's *suprême de volaille aux morilles*? What did the waiter think? Yes, something with a little more body, perhaps. Now, *voyons* . . . how about a nice Médoc? This went on for quite a while. Meanwhile Daisy's napkin, which she held with both hands, had relaxed much of the stiffness in its folds. At last the waiter departed. Daisy waited as long as possible before clamping one hand on top of Raoul's, pointing her toes hard and allowing her back to arch just a little. Then there was nothing for it but to bury her burning face in her napkin and pass the whole thing off as some sort of coughing fit.

When she had finished dabbing her eyes (thank goodness for waterproof mascara) and replaced her napkin in her lap, Raoul's hand slowly slunk off like a cat burglar in the night. Daisy surreptitiously checked the neighbouring tables. Incredibly, nobody appeared to have called the police. All diners seemed intent on eating, drinking and chattering. Dozens of waiters were weaving their way around the restaurant carrying vertiginous stacks of plates. Looking down at their own table, Daisy noticed that while she had been otherwise engaged a circular metal base had materialised, along with tiny oyster forks, a plate of bread, a small dish of creamy butter and another of pink shallot vinegar. She was particularly delighted to find a very cold glass of champagne in front of her. She picked it up, took a cooling gulp and pressed the glass against her cheek. When she turned to face Raoul, he grinned at her, wholly unrepentant.

'I don't *believe* you!' she whispered, unable to resist smiling back. 'You're a terrible man!'

Slowly, Raoul raised his hand to his mouth and, without taking his eyes from hers, sucked his fingers one by one. Daisy watched him incredulously. It was hard to know what to say.

'Well, really!' she managed eventually, just as the waiter reappeared, carrying a mountainous platter, which he deposited on its metal legs. On a bed of snow-white crushed ice, glistening silver-grey oysters were fanned out next to a bright red curvaceous lobster, its whiskers curling upwards.

That night, asleep in Raoul's arms, Daisy had a strange dream. Afterwards she wondered if it might have been caused by the *fruits de mer*. Perhaps a sudden and unusually high intake of zinc was to blame. In the dream Daisy was walking through the empty streets of Paris at night, desperately looking for something. It was not entirely clear whether this was something she had lost or something she had not yet found. It was dark; her heart was beating fast; nobody else was around to help, but she must get hold of whatever she was looking for. It was vitally important.

In the course of the following months this dream would recur many times, with subtle variations, and not necessarily after a large dish of *fruits de mer*. So perhaps it wasn't the seafood after all.

21 Isabelle

At the Dungeon, The Coven's post-gig post-mortem was not going well.

'Look, you guys,' Legend said gravely. 'It's like we're not communicating on stage. Maybe some of us are losing sight of their commitment to the band. Anything you'd like to say, Ivy?'

Everybody looked at the drummer, whose face now matched the beetroot shade of her hair.

Legend stared at her challengingly, then shrugged. 'OK, fine. Well, if you all want to know, in the car on our way home after the last gig, she told me she'd rather work a checkout in a supermarket all her life because it would be more fulfilling than being in the band.'

Ivy stamped her foot – there was a silvery whisper of tiny cymbals.

'I was just sounding off! You have no idea what it's like being the drummer. I'm sick of being taken for granted when I'm *carrying* the whole band!'

Belladonna made an inarticulate sound of outrage.

Legend snorted. 'One thing's for sure. It *would* help if our drummer didn't play like a dying old man with one arm.'

'You what?'

'You heard.'

Seeing Ivy's green eyes flash with anger and her knuckles tighten purposefully around her drumsticks, Karloff got up to interpose himself between his two bandmates.

'Right,' he said mildly. 'I'm putting my foot down. Stop messing about.'

'I keep saying we should do more meditation as part of band practice,' Belladonna interjected. 'We should all strive to maintain harmony, like a healing sphere of white light.'

'Ivy, mate,' Karloff went on doggedly, 'you're a great drummer and I won't have anyone say any different.'

'Maybe I've lost a bit of my edge, lately,' Ivy said quietly. 'Things have been frantic at the piercing salon.'

'And what about *your* playing, Ledge? Any comments?' Belladonna asked suddenly.

'I don't know, Bella. Do you have any? Go ahead, then. Though, on reflection, I'm not sure you're the best person to do that.'

'Why?'

'Because I have my doubts about your commitment to the scene.'

'How dare you?' Belladonna cried, drawing herself up to her full height. 'You *know* I donate some of my earnings to the Bat Conservation Trust.'

'Oooh yeah, well done,' Legend said, slow-clapping, 'but I'm not talking about that. I can't be the only one who cringes when you put on a Transylvanian accent.'

'You *know* I have Rrromanian ancestrrry.'

'You do not. Your mum and dad are from Milton Keynes.'

'Well, pardon me for actually doing research into all my

past lives. If you bothered to try regression, you too might discover something interesting about yourself. Though, personally, I doubt it.'

'Ledge has a point,' Ivy said, smiling. 'You do live in fantasy land, Bella.'

'See, me, for instance,' Legend went on, 'I dreamed the other night that I eloped with Robert Smith in a golden carriage, but I know it didn't *really* happen.'

'What a cool dream,' Jules said, with a faraway look in her eyes.

'Who is Robert Smith?' Isabelle asked in an undertone.

'The singer of a band called The Cure,' Chrissie whispered back. 'Major-league goth totty. And actually,' he added meaningfully, 'he looks not unlike Karloff.'

'Since we're being so open,' Jules said, turning to Karloff. 'I have a bone to pick with you, Kazza.'

'Yeah?' Karloff said, looking both tickled and nervous.

'I checked out The Coven's website this morning to see how you're getting on with it.'

Karloff swallowed.

'You posted those sepia pictures of us, the ones we took last summer in Highgate Cemetery.'

'*Not* the ones of us striking ridiculous dramatic poses on gravestones?' Belladonna said.

Jules nodded at her. 'That's exactly what he did.'

'But those pictures are kind of nice,' Ivy said.

'I love them too,' Jules admitted. And indeed Isabelle had noticed a few of the photographs in question – including a rather unsettling close-up of a gurning Karloff – on the walls of her bedroom. 'But I thought we were going to post the other ones. The serious ones where we look dead cool and moody.'

'Oh, right,' Karloff said, crestfallen.

'It's too late now, the fans will have got completely the wrong idea.'

'Does it really matter that much, though?' Ivy asked philosophically. 'At the end of the day, we're still goths. We're scary and mean. It comes with the job title. Check your manual.'

'You're one to talk,' Belladonna said sardonically.

'Meaning?'

'Meaning you weren't always so knowledgeable about the scene.'

Ivy glared at her in silence.

'I'm referring,' Belladonna went on inexorably, 'to your closet love of *pink*.'

Furious, Ivy looked around her assembled bandmates. 'When have you ever seen me wear pink? Except perhaps as an accent or in a sarcastic fashion.'

Belladonna pursed her lips, looking at her short black fingernails.

'That's *now*, Ivy. I'm talking about *then*. Back at school.'

There was an uneasy silence during which they all cast their minds back to their early-teenage selves.

'Ivy,' Belladonna said implacably, 'when I met you you'd never even seen a silent movie. You'd never heard of *Nosferatu*, even. Your favourite film was *Pretty Woman*. I had to start your education from scratch.'

'Oh yeah?' Ivy said. '*You* had blonde highlights and stonewash jeans with stretch in them. And on the subject of education, I seem to recall *I* was the one who showed you how to backcomb properly.'

'You're just jealous because you're still a beanpole with no boobs.'

'ENOUGH!' Karloff suddenly yelled, turning his gentle voice to maximum volume. 'Right,' he murmured, acutely embarrassed now that he had everyone's attention. 'I want you all to make up, all right? All this bitching puts me in a right twilight zone.'

'Sorry, Kazza. Sorry, Ivy.'

'That's all right. I'm sorry too. Sorry, Ledge.'

'I started it. Sorry I was such a bitch.'

'And I'll post the good serious pictures on the website when I get home,' he said in a low voice, without looking directly at Jules, who smiled a little.

'*Glorious* drama, isn't it, darling?' Chrissie said as he and Isabelle headed home together, leaving The Coven to have another round of drinks before dismantling and packing up their equipment.

'Do they often argue like that?'

'Oh, *constantly*. I personally think it's how they keep the band together. I mean these people go on tour for weeks sometimes, all cooped up in a *minibus*, playing at sixth-form colleges and *shopping centres*. In the *North*,' he added, lowering his voice to an awed whisper. 'They wouldn't be able to hold it together without the odd bout of vitriolic banter.'

'I thought it was quite sweet, when Karloff said he was going to replace the pictures on the website just to please Jules.'

'Oh, *adorable*. But over-subtle, as ever. I'm beginning to think they'll *never* get it on – just to spite me.'

The next morning, Isabelle went down early to get some breakfast. She walked into the silent kitchen and put the light on. Then she screamed.

'Whoa!' Karloff said, sounding offended. 'There's no need for that. It's just me making some tea, all right?'

'Oh, yes. Sorry. It's just that . . . I didn't see you there, in the dark.'

Karloff, in a black T-shirt and black boxer shorts, his hair a jet-black mess, grinned at her. 'Yeah, I kind of blend into the darkness, don't I?'

'Why didn't you put the light on?'

'Yeah, that's, like, because I've just put my white contact lens in this eye. You see?'

'Aaah, yes!' Isabelle said, reeling back slightly, 'It's very . . . original.'

'I like that dead-eye look. Anyway, the light hurts my eye a bit at first when I put it in, so I like to keep things on the dark side first thing in the morning. More gentle, like.'

'Of course,' Isabelle said, reflecting on his presence and attire, observing the two mugs of tea he was holding, and drawing a conclusion that made her smile.

Karloff turned bright red. 'Anyway, right,' he stammered. 'Thing is, I'd better take these up. Before they get cold.'

'Yes. That's a good idea.'

Isabelle waited for his footsteps to recede up the stairs

then made a beeline for Chrissie's room. Consumed with giggling curiosity, Chrissie and Isabelle nevertheless had to wait a good hour for Karloff to depart before they could interrogate Jules. As she made a dignified entrance into the kitchen, sporting her hairclip, they both whooped with glee.

'*What*?' Jules said icily, draping her purple dressing gown more closely around herself.

'Karloff stayed the *ni-ight*! Karloff stayed the *ni-ight*!'

'Chrissie, please.' Jules dropped two slices of bread into the toaster and came to sit next to Isabelle at the table, looking her usual impassive self. Isabelle and Chrissie stared at her eagerly, trying hard not to laugh.

Eventually, Jules cracked. Her face broke into a smile. 'Yes, he did. He stayed the night.'

'My *darling*! Oh, I'll *cry*.'

'So, how . . . did it happen?' Isabelle asked tentatively.

Jules took her time collecting her toast and buttering it. Then she reached for the jar of Marmite and launched into her tale.

After last night's cathartic argument, Legend and Belladonna had gone off arm in arm to check out a new club night in Brixton. Ivy had offered to stay behind with the others but Karloff, who knew that she had to get up early the next day for a particularly intricate piercing and body modification job, convinced her to go straight home. He and Jules would be perfectly capable of packing the gear into his van.

'Yes, yes, *and* . . . ?' Chrissie said expectantly.

'Well, you know what Kazza's like. A bit clumsy and uncoordinated sometimes.'

'Especially around *you*, darling.'

'Maybe so.'

They had almost finished packing up and Jules, who had her back to Karloff at the time, was unaware that he was bending down with the helpful intention of picking up her bass guitar and placing it in its case. Jules had turned around to reach for her instrument, somehow tripped over the case which was no longer quite where she expected it to be and bumped her head slap bang against Karloff's.

'So *then* you were both completely zonked out and started having trippy zombie sex *right* there and then?' Chrissie said, clasping his hands together.

'*No*,' Jules said with extreme severity. She had, in actual fact, stumbled on to her knees, clutching her head in pain with one hand while groping blindly for the bass with the other. Rather than the guitar, she had encountered the hem of Karloff's straitjacket and held on to it for dear life.

'And then my hair got trapped in the strings of the bass. I blame that wax Bella used to style my hair. It clings to everything like glue.'

Jules had tried vainly to free herself, cursing loudly, until Karloff suggested that the easiest thing might be to slide her head along the length of the fret board until she got to the machine head.

'And where was the machine head, darling?'

'Kazza had it. He'd managed to sort of trap it with his thigh.'

'Yes, yes, I *see*. And what was *he* doing all this time?'

'He was, you know, encouraging me.'

Some of the orange juice he had been drinking came

shooting out of Chrissie's nose. He composed himself and said, grinning, 'This sounds *just* like a position *I've* been in more times than I care to remember. Give or take a detail or two, of course.'

Jules stared at both of her housemates impassively and said slowly, 'It's not that funny.'

'No, no, of course not,' Isabelle said, trying to sober up. 'What happened then?'

Jules stared intently at her toast. 'Well, Kazza disengaged my hair very gently. He's not always clumsy, you see. Then he . . . helped me to my feet. And then . . . oh, you know! We drove here in the van. That's all. I'm going to make more tea,' she said, standing up. 'Does anybody want some?'

Chrissie folded his arms and smiled at her fondly. '*How* like you to keep the really romantic bit all to yourself. I shan't *pry*, Ju-Ju darling. I know when to step off.'

'Thanks,' Jules muttered.

'You see, I don't *need* to pry because I can just *tell* how it went.'

'All right, all right.' Jules switched the kettle on and, smiling almost imperceptibly to herself, looked across at Isabelle. Then her expression suddenly changed and she put her hand to her mouth. 'Oh damn, Isabelle. I'd completely forgotten . . .' She sighed. 'Last night Bella said something that sort of concerns you.'

'Really? What did she say?'

'You shouldn't take it too seriously. She probably imagined the whole thing.'

'What is it?'

Jules sat down again and stirred her tea. 'Well, she said she saw Clothaire in the street.'

'When? Yesterday?' Isabelle said, confused.

'No, after Halloween. When he was staying here with you.'

'Oh yes? Where was he?'

'In Covent Garden. Bella works part-time in a health food shop around there and she was on her lunch break. And, well, there he was.'

'Of course,' Isabelle said reasonably. 'Clothaire went for a few walks on his own when I was working. He wanted to explore London.'

'Um, yeah.'

'But he didn't tell me that he'd run into Bella. Did she speak to him?'

'No, no, she didn't, because . . .' Jules glanced at Chrissie. She pushed her spectacles to the top of her nose and resumed tonelessly: 'Because the thing is that he . . . apparently he was with someone else, some girl. But I said that you probably knew all about that.'

Isabelle thought hard for a minute. Did Clothaire know anyone else in London? It seemed improbable, but not, perhaps, entirely impossible.

'What did she look like?'

'That's what I asked, because of course I thought it was probably just you wearing a hat or something and that Bella had simply not recognised you from a distance.'

Of course, that would be it. Isabelle had actually walked through Covent Garden with Clothaire a couple of times.

'But Bella said it was a tall girl with dark hair. She looked very French, apparently.'

'What does that mean?'

'Well, I think she looked very ... manicured and ... you know, grown-up. Bella said she was wearing a little red coat and high heels.'

'Have you any idea who it might be, darling?' Chrissie said gently.

Isabelle felt quite cold suddenly. She remembered with crystal clarity the beautifully tailored red coat that Marie-Laure had bought from the Bon Marché department store last winter. She had been delighted with this find, because it was 'so couture', and she wore it often. It had been the envy of all her friends. And Marie-Laure was tall, with dark hair. But surely it was impossible. Why would Marie-Laure come to London and not let Isabelle know that she was there?

Isabelle shook her head. 'Yes ... but no. No, no, I'm sure it's not her.'

Jules moved her chair closer to Isabelle's, and gave her shoulder a little squeeze. 'So you *didn't* know about it, then?'

'No.'

Jules sighed a little. 'Also ... Bella thought they were holding hands. I'm really sorry. I should have kept quiet about it.'

'No, no. It was better to tell me.'

'It's just that Bella is such a big mouth that she would eventually have told you herself. She's a menace sometimes.'

'I just don't understand it,' Isabelle said, blinking.

'Darling,' Chrissie said, taking her hand, 'have you ever considered the possibility that Clothaire might *just* conceivably not be a very nice guy?'

22 Daisy

There were no limits, Daisy thought, to the amount of
kudos Parisians attached to their intellectuals. Until recently,
whenever Daisy spoke about fashion, Marie-Laure had
listened in tactful silence, with a good-natured but scep-
tical smile. Since hearing about her friend's ongoing
acquaintance with Etienne Deslisses, however, she had
changed her tune and suddenly begun to express an interest
in going shopping with Daisy.

'I'm looking for a pretty dress, you know, to go out to
dinner, something like that. And I think maybe I would
like to go with you to your friend's little shop. What's it
called again? Truc et Chose? Machin et Bidule?'

'Organdi & Néoprène,' Daisy said, smiling at her friend.
'Well, well, well. I had no idea you were such a Deslisses
groupie.'

'What? Me? Why do you say that? Oh . . . It's just that,
well, it's *Deslisses*, after all, so . . .'

'And the great Deslisses seems to think that I might
actually know a bit about this stuff, so now you believe
it too. I can't wait to tell him about this. He'll be so
flattered.'

'You know, Daisy, I have always thought you had a
wonderful style, really original,' Marie-Laure said loyally.
'I didn't need Deslisses' opinion for that!'

'If you like,' Daisy said mischievously, 'I could ask him to sign his books for you. Something like: "To the fascinating Marie-Laure, from her No. 1 admirer . . ." You only have to ask.'

'OK, OK, very amusing,' Marie-Laure said. After a brief pause, she added: 'It would be great if he could sign one. If you really think he wouldn't mind.'

On the following day, the two friends made their way to Anouk's shop near the Forum des Halles. Marie-Laure had turned up wearing a black poloneck and short skirt, high-heeled black shoes and that sweet little red coat of hers. She did look very good, Daisy admitted to herself, but oh-so-*safe*. It would be great to take her off the beaten track and shake her up a bit, sartorially speaking.

As they walked past the shop window towards the door, Marie-Laure, who had been very brave until then, slowed down and came to a halt, as though hypnotised by the sight of a dummy which had been kitted out (by Daisy herself) in a radically destructured sable brown fur coat with seven asymmetrically positioned sleeves.

'Isn't it fabulous?' Daisy said, following her gaze.

'Ye-es. But . . . well, why?'

'Oh, the extra sleeves, you mean? It's a bold challenge to our preconceptions. You know, the designer's saying: why shouldn't a coat have seven sleeves? Make your own decisions. Don't believe the hype.'

'I see,' Marie-Laure said, taking her eyes off the mutant coat and glancing nervously at her own two arms.

Anouk came to meet them as they walked in. She looked

sharply and approvingly at Marie-Laure's neat, leggy figure. 'So, *mon petit*, what are you looking for?'

'I'm not sure. Perhaps . . . a little black dress?'

'Now, Marie,' Daisy said severely, 'you have about twenty of those already. I think you should live a little more dangerously. How about something like this?' she said, reaching for the rail and pulling out a rustling little red dress.

Marie-Laure stared. 'But this is a joke, no? It's made of . . .'

'Paper. Yes. So?'

'So it's not a real dress. I mean, you can't *wear* it!'

'It is a real dress,' Anouk said. 'The paper is specially treated so it won't tear. Not for a while, anyway. It is just a *little* flammable,' she allowed. 'So it's better to keep away from people who smoke, for example.'

'But the greatest thing about it,' Daisy added enthusiastically, 'is that you can fold it into an envelope.' She demonstrated, placing the dress in the matching A4 envelope that was attached to the same hanger. 'Which is just *so* useful when you're travelling.'

'OK. *Très pratique*. But I don't need travelling clothes.'

'Oooh look, that's such a great piece!' Daisy exclaimed, darting to the other end of the rail and seizing another dress, which she held up in front of herself. This was a column of entirely see-through nude pink mesh strategically embroidered with clear crystals in the shape of a skimpy bra and knickers.

'Ah, yes,' Anouk said. 'A very witty dress.'

'Try it on! Try it on!'

Marie-Laure shook her head. 'No. I can see that it's amazing but.... *c'est beaucoup trop*! It's too much for me. I can't imagine an occasion when I could wear this.'

'You could wear it to . . .' Remembering what Marie-Laure and her family liked to do to unwind, Daisy was struck with an inspiration. 'To go to the opera! It's glamorous enough for that.'

Marie-Laure burst out laughing. 'I can just imagine my parents' reaction! Daisy, come on: it's completely see-through.'

Anouk and Daisy exchanged a look.

'Perhaps it is better if I just have a look around on my own?' Marie-Laure said apologetically.

'Of course.'

While Marie-Laure slowly made her way through the rails, Daisy said, 'Anouk, I can't thank you enough for encouraging me to go out with Raoul.'

'I'm so glad, *ma chérie*. So, is it getting serious?'

'I don't know. I think so. It's very intense.'

'More intense than with . . .'

'Oh, with Octave, you mean? It's completely different. Raoul is older, you know, more experienced. He makes me feel sort of . . . safe.'

'Perhaps if you had met this Octave a little later in life . . .'

'Oh, I don't think so,' Daisy said airily. 'Isn't that right, Marie?'

With furrowed brow, Marie-Laure was examining a white T-shirt.

'Mmm?'

'Octave. He'll never *ever* settle down. He'll just go on tomcatting forever.'

Marie-Laure turned around, holding the T-shirt. 'Maybe you are right, Daisy,' she said absent-mindedly. 'Anouk, how does this work? I think maybe there's been a mistake.'

'Ah yes, that is a really challenging piece,' Anouk said, nodding.

'No, but look! They've forgotten to make a hole for the head.'

'Not forgotten. It's a deliberate statement. If you look closely,' Anouk went on, pointing at the fabric, 'there is a seam here, like a spiral. You see?'

'Yes?'

'If you actually want to *wear* the piece, you cut out your own neck hole along the line.'

'It gives a beautifully irregular result,' Daisy said, enthralled. 'And then you end up with this gorgeous twisty bit of fabric dangling down the side of your neck. She's such a genius!'

Marie-Laure looked astonished. 'So you have to cut it yourself? And then it looks like . . . you cut it yourself? And some people would buy this, but not to wear, just to . . . have? You are joking, yes?'

'*Ah, mais non*,' Anouk said imperturbably. 'This particular designer only makes very few pieces, you see. She's very collectable. In fact I usually sell most of her things on my website even before I get the stock into the shop.'

'I see. And how much is this T-shirt, for example?'

'Six hundred and ninety-five euros.'

'Six *hundred* . . .' Marie-Laure's voice trailed off and she replaced the T-shirt on its shelf.

'The thing about Savage – this particular designer,' Daisy explained kindly, 'is that she sees herself as an artist. She despises money.'

'Ah yes, *évidemment*,' Marie-Laure said. 'I suppose seven hundred euros is still cheaper than a Picasso.'

'So you have not seen Octave at all, Daisy?' Anouk asked in an aside to her friend.

'No. I did miss a few parties as a result but I've been out with Raoul instead, so . . . But actually, I think it would be fine to run into Octave now. I've really moved on, you know.'

'*C'est très bien*. I'm very proud of you.'

'How about you, Marie?'

'What?'

'How is your love life?'

Marie-Laure suddenly looked quite odd, almost guilty. 'Me? I'm not seeing anybody,' she said uncertainly.

Delighted, Daisy laughed. 'I don't believe you! You look like you've got something to hide. Out with it!'

'But no! There is nobody, except . . . Oh well, it's too complicated. I can't talk about it yet.'

'Why? Oh, he's married, isn't he? You are so naughty!'

'No, no, he's not *married*, but . . . Anouk,' Marie-Laure said, pulling something off the rail, 'may I try that, please?'

'Well played, Marie. But I'll get it out of you later, you know. It's not fair you having secrets when I tell you everything about my life!'

After methodically going through all of Anouk's stock,

Marie-Laure homed in on the one item she genuinely liked. This, perhaps unsurprisingly, turned out to be an understated little black dress made of actual fabric, with the conventional number of armholes and a classic sweetheart neckline already in place as part of its design.

'But this isn't at all the strange and exquisite piece I wanted you to have,' Daisy said, disappointed. 'It doesn't even look like designer stuff particularly.'

'Yes, exactly,' Marie-Laure said, glancing again at the fur coat in the window and shuddering slightly.

'And what about that mystery lover of yours? Don't you want to surprise him with something unusual, more exciting? A completely new Marie-Laure?'

'No,' Marie-Laure said, her eyes lowered. 'I know what he likes. It's classic things, things he understands.'

Having said goodbye to Anouk, the two friends headed back in the direction of Marie-Laure's house.

'So are you going home for *les fêtes*, Daisy?'

'For Christmas, yes. I'm taking Raoul with me to Truro.'

'You are? To meet your parents?'

'Yes!' Daisy rolled her eyes. 'It's quite a big deal. I've never taken anyone home for Christmas before.'

'So . . . it is really serious between you,' Marie-Laure said, looking attentively at her friend. 'Has he told you that he loves you?'

'Yes.' Raoul was passionate in every way and often declared his undying love for her.

'Daisy, that's wonderful! And you, do you love him?'

Daisy thought for a minute. 'I suppose I do, yes.' Which

is what she would have told Raoul if he'd asked her. Probably. 'He's very sweet . . .'

Daisy paused. For some reason, she found herself thinking about that strange recurring dream in which she searched yearningly for something – or was it someone? – through the streets of Paris. She considered telling Marie-Laure about it then changed her mind. The dream couldn't have anything to do with her feelings for Raoul.

If Daisy sounded at all hesitant, Marie-Laure did not appear to notice it.

'That makes me really happy,' she said, slipping her arm through her friend's. 'So are you spending New Year's Eve in London?'

'I haven't decided yet.'

'Well, you could always come back to Paris. I have decided to have a party.'

'Oh? But I thought you said you weren't sure you could face it? When did you decide?'

'Just now, I suppose. I've changed my mind. I want to do it.'

'Shall I bring Raoul? He hasn't met anybody yet.'

'Of course, bring him. It will be great to meet him and I . . .' But Marie-Laure stopped, biting her lip.

'What?'

'There will be . . . a surprise.'

'You'll be wearing something adventurous?'

'No, not that,' Marie-Laure said, laughing. 'Another surprise.'

23 Isabelle

Of course there would be a perfectly simple explanation, Isabelle told herself firmly, not for the first time. Belladonna had only met Clothaire once. In all probability, it was somebody else she had seen, not Clothaire at all.

And then there was the question of Clothaire's character. Her boyfriend was really not the type to have . . . an affair, Isabelle concluded with an effort. Clothaire liked his life comfortable and *bien réglée*, as regular as clockwork. And he relied on her, Isabelle, to ensure that it was and remained so. The idea that he would allow his perfect routine to become complicated with lies and overpopulated with mistresses was plainly absurd. As absurd as her own dalliance with . . . but never mind that now.

And anyway, Clothaire himself would no doubt laugh at the whole preposterous story – when Isabelle got around to telling him about it. He had called her last night but she had thought it more prudent not to bring it up. It was far more sensible to wait until they saw each other again in Paris, tomorrow.

The most difficult aspect of the situation had been the temptation to speak to Agathe about it. That had been Isabelle's first impulse. But after thinking it over, she had decided not to confide in her friend. Agathe would certainly be scandalised. But – and this was an odd realisation –

Isabelle was not entirely sure that she could trust her friend to be scandalised on her own behalf. She was, in fact, far more likely to leap to Clothaire's defence. As for Marie-Laure . . . Well, it was obviously impossible to talk to her, because, although Isabelle's suspicions were bound to be unfounded, there was just the tiniest chance . . . *Bon, ça suffit comme ça*, Isabelle thought, shaking her head impatiently. She would put the whole thing out of her mind for now.

There were more important things to think about. Encouraged by Tom Quince, she had been exploring the attic in Meredith's house over the course of the last week or so, and although it now looked considerably cleaner and tidier, she had not found a trace in it of the manuscripts, nor indeed of *The Splodge*. She had, however, rather enjoyed organising the contents of the attic along more rational lines. And it had been gratifying to show Tom the results of her hard work.

'I can't believe this transformation, Isabelle.'

'I like to be systematic.'

'Evidently,' Tom had said, looking at the orderly piles of boxes, now all neatly labelled with a marker pen. 'Actually,' he had added, turning his attention to the opposite end of the attic, 'some of this furniture doesn't look so bad now you can see it properly.'

'Some of it is really pretty. This chest of drawers is lovely. And that bed, the one with the booby-trapped mattress: it's a *lit à baldaquin*, I think.'

'A four-poster?'

'Yes, that's it. It has been taken apart but all the bits are there.'

'You know, I have an idea that this was all Meredith's furniture from her old room. Naturally you checked the posts – in case any of them are hollow?'

At this Isabelle had turned quite breathless with excitement. Together, they had tapped the oak columns hopefully, but in vain. The wood was solid.

'Oh well, it was worth a try,' Tom had said philosophically.

So that was the attic taken care of. Today, Isabelle would turn her attention to the library. Tom, who was doing something garden-related with Rosie outside, had shown Isabelle in and left her to it, promising to come and fetch her in time for some tea.

Isabelle looked around the quiet room, wondering where to begin. Remembering Meredith Quince's portrait, she summoned, not entirely in earnest, the spirit of the author to guide her in her treasure hunt. Meredith might find a way of indicating if Isabelle was getting warmer – by making a discreet tapping sound, perhaps. Briefly, Isabelle wondered about Jules' Ouija board. Perhaps Tom wouldn't mind helping. The presence of a relative could only be an incentive for the writer to manifest herself.

But perhaps she should exhaust more rational possibilities first. It made sense really to start with the desk. Gingerly, Isabelle opened the drawers. They were all empty, except for a bottle of black ink, quite ancient and almost used up. Isabelle picked it up and stared at it: was this a reminder of *The Splodge*, a sign left over by Meredith that Isabelle should persevere in her quest? Well, why not choose to read it that way? She pulled the drawers out of the desk with great care and laid them on the rug. There sometimes *were* such things as secret compartments in desks. Isabelle ran her hand slowly and systematically inside the desk's every recess. She gave a little sigh. Not a *sausage*, darling, as Chrissie might have put it.

Looking up and through the French windows, she was greeted by the sight of Tom and Rosie side by side, cheerfully digging and planting things. It looked like quite hard work, and in the cold weather, too, but at least, unlike her, the pair knew precisely what they were doing. Isabelle let herself drop into the primrose yellow armchair and leaned back, her eyes roving over the walls of bookshelves. This exasperating Rosie person was certainly a fixture in Tom's garden. Really Isabelle wouldn't have been surprised to hear that she intended to settle permanently in the greenhouse.

Anyway, Isabelle thought impatiently, it was time to test her theory about the bookshelves. She considered for a moment. To her right was the wall in which the door stood: beyond it was the hallway. Behind her was the wall pierced with French windows leading into the garden. On the other side of the wall facing her was another sitting room, which had served the Quince family as a television room. This left only one wall behind which a secret room might possibly be concealed, the one to her left. She noted the absence of a candlestick or other very obvious lever but she did not let that put her off. Most likely the key lay in one or several books. Either something happened when you pulled them off the shelf or there was a switch of some sort hidden behind them. There were dozens of books on that wall and she would have to try them all. But first she would tap and test the shelves themselves for clues. Starting at the far end away from the French windows, she began to work her way across the room, knocking on the wall wherever it was exposed above the books and tentatively pulling at the shelves for signs of 'play'. So far, everything appeared to be screwed into place. Of course there was always the possibility that the whole thing, shelves, wall and all, would revolve on some sort of axis.

Remembering a black and white film in which this happened quite suddenly, swallowing the heroine, Isabelle felt a small pang of apprehension. In the film the girl's disappearance was only noted much, much later. That really would not be much fun, even if it meant laying her hands on the manuscripts. It might have been wiser after all to tell Tom about her theory, however fantastic it sounded. That way he would have been on the alert. Otherwise, if she vanished, he might perhaps think that she'd had to leave in a hurry. Too late now, Isabelle thought, resolutely continuing her progress towards the windows.

And then, as she reached the central tower of books, it happened. As she rather mechanically gave one of the top shelves a little pull, she felt the whole thing move slightly. *That was it*, she thought triumphantly, she had been right! The central panel of the bookshelves *was* a doorway, and in just a moment, she would walk through to the other side . . . It was marvellous. Her heart beating fast, Isabelle grabbed the shelves with both hands and pulled with all her might. Then she barely had time to throw herself out of the way as the whole thing came crashing down in a terrifying avalanche of heavy tomes.

Once some of the dust had settled, Isabelle, who had been crouching with her hands over her ears, slowly looked up. Where she had expected to find a doorway, there was only an expanse of solid wall. *Zut de zut*. Meanwhile, she had been wrong to suppose that Tom wouldn't be paying attention to what was going on in the library. He burst into the room, still holding his trowel.

'What happened? Are you all right?'

Isabelle nodded. 'Tom, I'm so sorry. It was completely my fault.'

Rosie came in and stood surveying the scene. 'I *told* you she'd be fine,' she said coolly.

'Did the shelves suddenly collapse?' Tom said.

'No . . . I pulled them down.'

'Oh, for God's sake.'

'Rosie, Isabelle could have had a serious accident.'

'Yeah, she could have,' Rosie said, looking at Isabelle as if to deplore her failure to achieve this desirable result. 'You are *exceptionally* disaster-prone, aren't you?'

'It was because I wanted to know,' Isabelle said in a small voice, looking at Tom, 'if there was another room behind the books.'

'Another room?'

'I thought maybe that was where Meredith had hidden her manuscripts.'

'Oh, *what*?' Rosie said.

'I know it sounds really stupid.'

'It's a very romantic idea, Isabelle,' Tom said, as seriously as he could. 'But I think perhaps you overestimate my great-aunt's capacity for this sort of plotting in real life. I'm sure she would have loved it in a novel.' He looked down at the collapsed shelves. 'Still, at least now we know that these were not *quite* secure.'

'They would have been all right if I hadn't . . . Oh, Tom, let me help you pick everything up.'

'No, look, we can do it later. Right now I think we could all do with some tea.'

They filed down the stairs towards the kitchen.

'So what's your garden like at home, Isabelle?' Rosie suddenly asked. 'I presume it's very French, all chic and perfect with little symmetrical flowerbeds.'

'I don't have a garden.'

'Oh dear. Bad luck.'

'Actually,' Isabelle went on, annoyed with herself for being defensive, 'private gardens are quite rare in Paris.'

'Oh, really?'

'But I can see a tree from my bedroom window, so I can follow the change in the seasons.'

'How nice. What sort of tree is it?'

'Um . . . I don't know.'

'You don't know?' Rosie said with an incredulous laugh. 'You've never wanted to find out?'

'I've never thought about it,' Isabelle said truthfully. 'I suppose I just like the idea of a tree.'

Rosie raised her eyebrows slightly, looking in Tom's direction. Then she tried again: 'So what kind of gardens do you like?'

Isabelle was dismayed. How many different kinds of gardens *were* there? 'I don't know. I think all gardens are pretty.'

'Really? How very odd.'

'Do you approve of *my* garden?' Tom said gently.

Isabelle turned to look at him, noticing once again the beautiful and unusual colour of his eyes. 'I think your garden is lovely.'

'Do you like what I'm doing at the moment? It's a sort of Christmas garden, really, with all the winter plants – yew, ivy –'

'And holly, of course, for colour,' Rosie interjected. 'I'm crazy about this new holly I got for you, Tommy. The one we planted yesterday, with orange berries – Firethorn.'

A thorn of fire, Isabelle thought distractedly, that was quite a surreal image. She drank the last drop of her tea. The room suddenly felt very warm. In a minute she'd go and get herself a glass of water.

'Do you know it, Isabelle?'

Isabelle shook her head, looking with some fascination at Tom's honey-coloured hand, which lay on top of his thigh.

'We still need to train that other big one to the garden wall,' Rosie went on, beginning to stand up. 'We should get on with it as soon as you're ready.'

'Holly is one of those plants that's either male or female,' Tom said without moving, addressing Isabelle. 'Male holly is a bit dull on its own because it doesn't bear fruit, just flowers. But you want one in your landscape so that the female holly will be able to receive pollen and produce some fruit. Ideally you bind the two together, one male and one female holly. That way you get both flowers *and* berries.'

Isabelle nodded, thinking privately that there was something wildly erotic in the way Tom carried himself, even when just sitting like this, immobile and relaxed.

'And we're also putting in some Christmas roses,' Rosie said, sitting down again. 'Aren't we, Tommy?'

'These really are lovely flowers,' Tom explained, 'white tinged with pink. They bloom in the darkest months of the year when everything else is frozen solid. I love hellebores,' he went on, smiling vaguely at Isabelle, 'because they're so wonderfully promiscuous. I just know they'll seed all over the garden.'

Within Isabelle something that had been kept carefully compressed suddenly broke loose and began to erupt.

'What *is* the matter with you?' Rosie asked curiously. 'You've gone all red.'

'I think,' Isabelle said, slowly rising to her feet, 'I should go outside for a breath of air.'

Tom reached out as if to steady her but she waved him away and picked her steps, like a dignified drunk, towards the garden door. By the time she reached it, she had already got fairly pronounced tunnel vision and it took her a minute to locate the doorknob and turn it in the right direction. She stepped into the garden, vaguely aware of rapid footsteps behind her. There was a wooden bench somewhere in the vicinity, she remembered. The tunnel was closing fast. Then her legs gave way and everything went black.

When she came to, she was lying on the bench with her head in Tom's lap.

'Take deep breaths,' he said, fanning her with his hat.

'Tom,' she whispered, looking up at him. 'What . . . ?'

'You fainted, my dear. It was very dramatic. In Victorian times I would have loosened your stays, but you don't appear to be wearing any.'

Isabelle sat up shakily and rubbed her face. 'But this is ridiculous. I have never fainted before.' She thought for a moment, then added: 'Rosie must be having a good laugh.'

'Actually, Rosie went home. She has no patience with people who are unwell.'

Isabelle looked down and sighed. Then, appearing to change the subject, she said sadly, 'I don't know anything about gardens or gardening.'

'Don't worry about that. I've never read any of my great-aunt's books, remember?'

'Yes, of course.' Isabelle straightened up a bit more. 'I'm fine now. Thank you for looking after me. I'd better go home, too.'

Tom suddenly locked eyes with her. 'Stay,' he said, stroking her hair away from her face. 'Stay here with me.'

Isabelle's throat tightened. She must not cry. Instead, she made her hands into fists and hit him on the chest a few times, not very hard.

'I can't. I can't. I can't.'

He held her lightly for the briefest of moments, then let go. 'OK. I'll drive you home.'

In the car Isabelle kept very quiet, her eyes closed and her face turned away. As Tom pulled up outside Daisy's house, she opened her eyes and said politely, 'Thanks so much for driving me. So, I'll see you in January when I'm back. I hope you have a great Christmas.'

'Yes, and you too, Isabelle. I hope all goes well in Paris.'

Isabelle smiled briefly and began to open the door.

'Wait just one second,' Tom said, turning around to reach for something on the back seat. He handed it to her, wrapped in a sheet of newspaper.

'Please take this. A very small Christmas gift.'

Isabelle unwrapped a spray of small creamy-white flowers.

'It's winter honeysuckle. The scent is rather wonderful.'

Isabelle swallowed with difficulty, then said, 'Thank you, Tom.'

She leaned over to kiss him on the cheek, keeping her mind as blank as possible, and was out of the car in seconds.

When she woke up the next morning, the honeysuckle had scented her whole room and later she thought she could smell it in other parts of the house as well and even on herself. When she left for the station, she left the branch behind, donating it to Chrissie. But the memory of the scent followed her all the way home to Paris.

24 Daisy

Generally speaking, Daisy thought, surveying the scene in her parents' sitting room, Christmas could be said to be going well. For one thing, everyone appeared to have liked their presents, especially Raoul, who had been delighted with the pop-up *Kama Sutra* Daisy had given him before coming down to breakfast. Then, Christmas lunch, always a great source of anxiety for her mother (which the presence of a French guest had done nothing to diminish), had been a complete success. The turkey had behaved very properly, cooking according to Delia's instructions. The pudding had flamed beautifully and the custard hadn't been at all lumpy. Now everyone sat in the usual stupor in front of the television, eating chocolate Brazil nuts.

Her parents were being very sweet to Raoul and doing their best to make him feel at home. To Daisy's relief, her mother had not asked her any searching questions about the direction of their relationship, at least not yet. Daisy glanced across at her, napping in the next armchair with her specs halfway down her nose. It was highly probable – in view of Mrs Keen's romantic temperament – that she was at this very moment dreaming about a smart mother-of-the-bride outfit (something in periwinkle blue, with a large hat).

As for Raoul, he was, in many ways, being a model

guest. He ate of everything, hugely. He had sweetly refrained from comment when Daisy's father had brought out a bottle of Australian wine. He had sat in quiet, respectful bewilderment throughout the Queen's speech. He had pulled crackers and even worn a party hat.

There were one or two niggles, however. Like that mildly embarrassing moment this morning when Daisy's mother had walked into her daughter's room to find her lying naked on her duvet while Raoul, also naked on the bed – but mercifully with his back to the door – was engaged in making a sketch of her.

'Oh, whoops, sorry!' Daisy's mother had squeaked, hastily closing the door.

Daisy, who knew her mother well, had thought it best to go on with the day as though nothing had happened. Unfortunately, she had neglected to explain this to Raoul, who took it upon himself to say courteously, in the middle of Christmas dinner, 'I hope we did not shock you earlier, Madame.'

Daisy's mother stared at him wide-eyed and said, 'Oh no, no! Of course not.'

'Why? What happened?' Daisy's father asked jovially, passing the bread sauce around. Daisy's father approved of Raoul because the Frenchman understood sports. Having grown up in the south-west of France, Raoul had played a lot of rugby in his youth and remained a devotee of the *ballon ovale*. The two men had talked at length of various episodes in the last *Tournoi des Cinq Nations*.

Daisy's mother gave a little laugh. 'Nothing, darling. Nothing happened.'

Raoul turned to face Daisy's father and said, smiling wolfishly, 'Yes, it was nothing. Your wife came in while I was drawing Daisy.'

'Ah yes, Daisy told us she'd become a bit of an artist's model in Paris. It sounds like good fun.'

'Daisy has a magnificent body. It is a pleasure to draw her.'

'Ha ha, well, she's our little girl. Naturally we think she's charming.'

'*Raoul.*'

'What, "Raoul"? It's true. You are not ashamed of your body, I hope?'

'*No.* But . . .'

'You know, Madame, I remember the first time I saw Daisy, I thought to myself: Wow, what I would really love is to see this girl totally naked, with all that long hair around her.'

After a short silence, Daisy's mother said in a rather high, quavering voice, 'Raoul, would you like a bit of salad? I made a real French dressing to go with it. I'm not sure it's quite right, but I hope you like it!'

'Yes, thank you, Madame. I think,' Raoul said reflectively, piling leaves on his plate, 'that generally English women are very beautiful.'

'Do you, really? How nice of you to say so.'

'Yes. Daisy is, of course. She is like a rose,' he said, expressively opening his fingers out to suggest a full bloom. 'And you too, Madame, are a very beautiful and fascinating woman.'

'Oh, that's a sweet thing to say. Thank you, Raoul.'

'We do not know each other very well, you and me, but already I feel certain that there is a lot of sensual mystery in you, a lot of wonderful secrets.'

'Secrets? Me?' Daisy's mother giggled, unconsciously checking the top button of her shirt. 'Oh no, not really!'

'You know, Madame, it's funny because when I was a young boy I was very naïve. For example, I believed that in France we are the best for everything – the food, the wine – and that also our women are the most beautiful in the world. But since then I have travelled and met a lot of different people and it has opened my mind.'

'Good for you, Raoul,' Daisy's mother said encouragingly.

'So now I realise, for example, how interesting English women are. Particularly, in this country,' Raoul said, turning to Daisy's father, 'you have the tomboys, the androgynous girls. That is a *really* great English type of girl. You know, with the very flat chest and the short hair like a schoolboy . . .'

'Cheese, anyone? Raoul?'

'It must be wonderful,' Daisy's mother said, smiling brightly, 'to see the world as you do, through an artist's eyes.'

'Oh thank you, Madame, but I am not really an artist, you know. I have not got a classical training. It's just that I have always liked to draw women. I started very early, when I was a young boy, and I got more and more interested.'

'Really? You never get bored of the same subject?' Daisy's father asked, calmly helping himself to a chunk of Stilton. 'You never want to move on to landscapes, for example?'

'Well, to me, a woman is a landscape.'

'Ah?'

'And there are so many different landscapes in the world. You are always discovering some new ones, you know. Different climates, different colours, different, *heu* . . .' Raoul mimed undulating hills, 'geography.'

'Of course, yes.'

'All the time, I am learning amazing, crucial stuff. Like, for example, about the left breast of women.'

'The . . . *left breast?*' Daisy's father repeated blankly.

'Yes, it was a girl who taught me about that. A dancer.'

'Oh, was she a ballerina at the Paris Opera?' Daisy's mother said conversationally. 'How lovely. I'm so fond of the ballet. Do you also enjoy it, Raoul?'

'Yes, yes, of course. Those long legs and long necks . . . gorgeous. But, in fact, this particular dancer, she worked at the Crazy Horse Saloon. You know that place?'

'N-no, I don't believe I do,' Daisy's father said, looking quite interested nonetheless.

'They have the most beautiful artistic nude show there, a light show, with some of the most amazing girls in Paris,' Raoul explained, gesturing. 'This girl I'm talking about, her real name was Karine but she called herself Froufrou des Jarretelles. It was her name for the stage. Like, you know, a *porte-jarretelle*. What is the English word for that, Daisy?'

'A garter belt,' Daisy said, looking across at her mother and smiling apologetically.

'Garter belt, all right! Anyway, Froufrou told me that when they audition a dancer at the Crazy, they always look at her left breast first, because, you see,' Raoul continued, feeling rightly that he now had Daisy's father's undivided attention, 'a woman's left breast is usually less perfectly shaped than her right. So, if the left breast is completely gorgeous,' he said, leaning back in his chair, 'then chances are the rest of the girl's body will be exceptional, really extreme, in fact.'

Daisy's father swallowed, then said slowly, 'Well, I didn't know that.'

'So, you see, inspiration is always there, around me. Especially at this moment of my life,' Raoul added, gallantly kissing Daisy's hand.

'*OK!*' Daisy said, jumping in when she had the chance. 'Now, who wants coffee? No, don't get up, Mum, I think Raoul should make it. He's got a special talent for it, haven't you, Raoul? Come on, into the kitchen. I'll show you where everything is.'

Somehow, Daisy thought, reaching for a Brazil nut and looking across at Raoul, now ensconced on the sofa next to her father and watching *Octopussy* with every sign of enjoyment, they had kept getting drawn into these kinds of wince-inducing conversations since their arrival two days ago. Possibly Daisy's strategy with Raoul – feigning a French-style blasé nonchalance when it came to sex-related topics so as not to come across as an uptight Brit – had worked a little *too* well. He now had completely the wrong idea about her family's mindset and thought her parents as freewheeling and *libérés* as she was! Not, of course, that she really *was*, but Raoul did not know that. Such was life. It was lovely for once to come home with a presentable long-term boyfriend in tow but a certain degree of embarrassment was unavoidable.

Meanwhile Daisy had been troubled again by her weird dream pretty much every night, and even when she had dozed off for a while on the train on the way to Truro. Again she had found herself wandering down deserted Parisian streets in the middle of the night, only to wake up none the wiser with a loudly beating heart.

Daisy had not mentioned the strange dream to Raoul. It would probably bore him: after all, nothing happened in it. Besides, it was so unlike her to have serious, obscure dreams of this kind. From childhood she had typically dreamed of becoming a brilliant and celebrated shoe designer, or perhaps the youngest-ever editor of *Vogue* – that sort of thing.

Oh well, at some point she would discover what she was trying to find in the dream and then the whole thing would evaporate. Dreams were such silly things, anyway. They didn't mean anything.

25 Isabelle

Many times over the last four years, Isabelle had thought about how it would be when Clothaire proposed, and had rehearsed the moment in her mind. She had imagined that he would perhaps choose the context of the pretty tea room on the Rue de Rivoli, the setting for many of their early dates. Her hand would be lying on the table, between her small pot of hot chocolate and her half-eaten Mont-Blanc, and Clothaire would slowly cover it with his own hand, look into her eyes and say . . . Or he would surprise her as they sat reading side by side on a bench next to the fountain in the Luxembourg Gardens, suddenly dropping down on one knee and . . .

Sitting on the train on the way home to Paris, Isabelle had reviewed these familiar scenarios in a new and colder light. Somehow the proposal scenes had become more diffi-cult for her to picture and, ultimately, to believe in. What had changed? Was it those guilt-inducing memories of rolling around with Tom in his bed? Or was it the nagging, unresolved question of Belladonna's sighting of Clothaire with a mystery girl? No, something else had happened. It was dawning on Isabelle that outside of her daydreams Clothaire was not and never had been at all romantic. It was all for the best, really. Marriage was a serious, lifelong commitment, not the stuff of romance and fantasy. The sooner they did set a date and tell everyone of their intentions, the better.

Isabelle imagined herself standing next to Clothaire in formal evening dress at the Bal de l'X, a smart springtime charity ball given by the Ecole Polytechnique, a prestigious military college, at the Paris Opera House, which they had ritually attended with their friends fot the last few years. Perhaps this would be the best time to announce their engagement. They could dispense with the romance of a proposal.

She might as well mention this plan to Clothaire tonight, since he would be there to meet her when she got off the train at the Gare du Nord, after which they were expected at her parents' for dinner. They would spend the night at her flat, which was vacant since Daisy had gone back to England for Christmas. Isabelle wondered briefly how Daisy's love life was going. There had been a fling with Octave, she had heard from her housemates, and Isabelle now regretted not including a word or two of caution about that incorrigible seducer in the list of the practical guidelines she had left for Daisy in her flat. Since then, Jules had mentioned something about Daisy's new boyfriend, an artist who was quite a lot older than her. Tom was a few years older than herself, Isabelle thought irrelevantly, though you'd never notice it. She shook her head impatiently.

Later, when she got to the platform exit and scanned the sea of expectant faces, looking out for her boyfriend's familiar saturnine countenance, she was instead greeted by the sight of her two sisters – nineteen-year-old Camille and sixteen-year-old Aude – beaming and waving at her.

'Isa! *Bienvenue à Paris!*' Aude cried, throwing herself into her older sister's arms and hugging her enthusiastically.

A little older and therefore much closer to the Papillon ideal of the well-brought-up *jeune fille*, Camille smiled at Isabelle above Aude's shoulder, waited patiently for her elder sister to disentangle herself from her younger one, and then stepped forward to kiss Isabelle lightly on both cheeks.

'*Salut*. Good trip?' Camille asked.

'Yes, thanks. *Hé! Dis donc*, you've had your hair cut,' Isabelle observed, ruffling Camille's new sleek bob.

'And you are wearing your hair down. That is quite a change! It suits you.'

'*Mais c'est incroyable!*' Aude exclaimed, holding Isabelle at arm's length. 'She looks just like a *petite Anglaise!*'

Isabelle looked down at her fawn military jacket and brown tartan miniskirt, with its hint of dark gold lurex. They were a gift from Chrissie, samples from Savage's last winter collection. Back in London, he had convinced her that she looked wonderful in the outfit, but now, under the gaze of her more conservatively clad siblings, Isabelle began to have her doubts.

'It's not . . . too much, is it?'

'No, it's really cool!' Aude said longingly. 'I wish I had one just the same.'

'You look great,' Camille confirmed, adding: 'You are perhaps wondering where Clothaire is?'

'Yes. I thought . . .'

'He called us to say that he had a last-minute *empêchement*. He sounded very harassed and said he only had time for one call, so that's why he didn't call you.'

'Of course,' Isabelle said automatically.

'Don't worry. He will meet us at home a bit later. In fact he's probably there already.'

'Of course,' Isabelle said again. She was puzzled.

The three sisters piled into a taxi en route for the parental apartment, and Isabelle, looking out of the window at the glistening darkness of well-remembered Parisian streets, gave kindly, absent-minded answers to Aude's questions about her London life. Once she was reunited with her parents, things became curiouser. Clothaire had apparently just rung Isabelle's mother to excuse himself from dinner and, indeed, from turning up at all that night. There was, he had said vaguely, an urgent *crise* he needed to attend to. Her parents were very put out and would have liked an explanation, which Isabelle was unable to provide. As a result, there was a slight sense of strain to the evening, and Isabelle was particularly grateful to puppyish Aude for her insouciant stream of chatter.

By the time she got to bed in her own flat, Isabelle was too tired to give much thought to what might have happened to change Clothaire's plans. She had also been pleasantly distracted by Daisy's surprise: bunches of flowers in every colour, like cheerful notes of music, had been left in every available container in the flat to welcome her home.

In the morning Clothaire turned up on her doorstep, looking white-faced and tetchy. Such impulsive behaviour was very much out of character and made Isabelle feel on edge. After a perfunctory kiss, he sat her down next to him on the sofa and impatiently parried her attempts at conversation.

'It is really not the moment for chit-chat, Isabelle. I want to speak to you about something important.'

At first Isabelle thought Clothaire was actually going to propose. Then, looking at his expression, she changed her mind. Quite suddenly, she knew with absolute and chilling certainty that he had somehow found out about Tom. But how? Jules was the soul of discretion, but was it just possible that Chrissie had blabbed to Daisy? And that the story had then made its way into the circle of her Paris friends? In any case honesty was the best policy, since they were, after all, planning to spend the rest of their lives together.

'This is not easy for me to say, Isabelle.'

'No,' Isabelle replied in a small voice. 'Clothaire, I'm really sor—'

'No, no, no. Be quiet and listen to me.'

'OK. Go ahead.'

Clothaire glared at her. 'You know, don't you, that I was completely against your going away to London, but did you listen to me? No, of course not.'

Isabelle sighed and nodded a few times. Clothaire lit a cigarette and went on more calmly: 'So you accept that as a fact. Good. I did warn you before you left that your disappearance would create problems. Well, I was right, absolutely right.'

Isabelle took a deep breath, steadying herself in preparation for Clothaire's accusation.

'Let us get one thing clear, Isabelle. You cannot blame me for what happened. The whole thing was your fault. You behaved very selfishly. You deserted me. I was lonely.

And I have certain needs, like all men. So of course I had to turn to someone else. It was the natural thing to do.'

Isabelle blinked and looked up at him.

Clothaire smiled thinly. 'Yes, you see, if you weren't interested in being with me, there was somebody else who was. Someone quite attractive, I might add.'

'Who?'

'It is not important who she is,' Clothaire said, waving his cigarette. 'Anyway . . .'

'Clothaire, it *is* important, if you prefer her to me, don't you think?'

'Let me finish, Isabelle. You have this habit of interrupting my train of thought. It is exasperating. Surely I have mentioned this to you many times before?'

'Yes, you have. Many times.'

'I am very good at evaluating people's characters, as you know. It did not take me very long to discover that this girl was not, in fact, at all what I expected. She is difficult, very difficult – very *capricieuse*. And endlessly demanding and critical – of *me*!' Clothaire shook his head with some severity. 'It was a shock and a disappointment, as I'm sure you appreciate. But I am over it now. So you will be pleased to hear that I have ended things with her. And,' he said taking Isabelle's hands in his, 'I am willing to take you back.'

'*You* are willing to take *me* back?'

'Yes, Isabelle, I am. Provided, of course, that you curtail this absurd stay in London. I want you to come back here, where you belong.'

'I slept with Tom,' Isabelle heard herself say in her flute-like tones, much to her surprise.

'You . . . what? Slept with . . . who, did you say?'

'I slept with Tom Quince.'

'Never heard of him. What are you talking about?'

'Meredith's great-nephew. You met him at the Halloween party.'

'At the Halloween party?' Clothaire said, narrowing his eyes. 'But that is absurd. All the men there were homosexual.'

'Not all, just Chrissie. Karloff and Jules are together now. And as for Tom . . .'

Clothaire's face flushed a dark shade of brick-red. 'You mean the . . . *florist*? That guy? I do not believe it. I mean, you do not even really enjoy . . .'

'It's true.'

Clothaire was completely silenced, a phenomenon Isabelle did not remember ever witnessing before. After a while he said, 'I am very surprised. But I think I will . . . yes, find it in myself to forgive you, in time. When you come back for good, we can put all this behind . . .'

Isabelle got to her feet. She felt very light, as though a great weight had fallen off her shoulders. '*Joyeux Noël*, Clothaire. Give my regards to your parents.'

'But we are going to see them in two days' time. You can tell them yourself.'

'I'm not coming. I'm going to stay here and spend time with my family.'

'My mother will be very surprised by your extraordinary behaviour. You are not yourself, Isabelle.'

'And afterwards I'm going back to London, as planned.'

'What? But I thought I made myself clear: I will only take you back on condition that . . .'

Isabelle walked to her front door and opened it wide. 'Think about it, Clothaire, and try to understand. It's really very simple. Goodbye.'

'Ah, women! They are all mad, all of them,' Clothaire muttered, putting his cigarette out with furious energy before storming out.

He disappeared down the stairs without a backwards glance.

26 Daisy

As she stood outside the doors of the Sorbonne amphi-theatre waiting for the end of Etienne's lecture, Daisy found herself going over last night's version of her now well-established recurring dream. In it, she had been wandering along Boulevard Haussmann outside the big department stores. At this time of year these were still festooned with glamorous Christmas lights – clusters of oversized Chinese lanterns in a delightful shade of hot pink. It was only a couple of weeks ago that, out shopping with Agathe for presents, she had stared up, entranced at their happy glow. At the time it had felt like half of Paris was out on the same cheerful errand, so crowded were the pavements, but in her dream the lanterns swung ghostlike, dark and drab in the night air, and there was no one about.

Daisy took a turn off the empty boulevard and came in sight of the Gare Saint-Lazare, which, equally deserted, looked almost like a cardboard façade behind which lay nothing but thin air. In an instant she was magically transported to the middle of the station's empty waiting hall. This place, Marie-Laure had once told her, had got the nickname of the *salle des pas perdus*, the hall of lost footsteps, because so many people paced up and down it while waiting for their train, or for a friend's arrival – sometimes in vain. Daisy too, pacing alone in the silent hall of lost footsteps, felt that she was waiting anxiously, longingly, for something, expecting something, but what? No trains were announced on the arrivals or departures boards. Perhaps she was too late and had missed . . . whatever it was. It – or was it they? – had left without her, and now she would never find them again. She had woken up in tears, her heart beating wildly, Raoul peacefully asleep beside her.

Raoul never had nightmares. He only dreamed about pleasant or 'extreme' things. Not that this dream was a nightmare, exactly. It made her sad, yes, but in an odd way Daisy now looked forward to its return when she went to sleep because she hoped, night after night, that it would yield up its meaning to her.

Here too, in the busy corridor outside the lecture halls, people were pacing up and down, waiting for the end of a lecture or the start of another. Today, Daisy and Etienne had arranged to meet at the Faculty before going to lunch. Their topic of discussion for the day was to be, at Etienne's request, appearance and authenticity in fashion. Daisy had no real idea of what he meant by that, though he had wondered aloud how fashion-conscious people could possibly stay true to themselves. How like an intellectual to get into a tizz about such things! She was very much looking forward to defending the sincerity of fashionistas everywhere.

'I mean, why should it be,' she told Marie-Laure, who was standing next to her looking nervous, 'that just because you put some thought into getting a good look together you're not expressing your true self? That's just silly! Why shouldn't your true self express itself in a silver lamé boob tube and pop socks? Etienne is so clueless still. It's hilarious.'

She had been about to add: 'I would love to take him home and give him a complete makeover,' but stopped herself just in time. In actual fact Daisy couldn't help feeling that Etienne – perhaps because he was so cerebral, and so reserved – somehow existed on a higher plane than her own. Trying to get him out of his ultra-traditional togs and into edgy fashion would be like . . . toppling an idol from its pedestal. He was . . . untouchable.

'Yes, perhaps you are right,' Marie-Laure replied, straightening her scarf and hair. 'I think it is almost time. They will be out in a minute.'

Agathe, Claire and Amélie sat on a wooden banquette nearby, chatting and showing rather less agitation than Marie-Laure. They had been having coffee together nearby and, on hearing of Daisy's appointment, Marie-Laure had suggested, in a burst of daring, that they all accompany her to be introduced to the great Deslisses. Claire and Agathe had agreed more languidly, although Daisy could tell that they, too, were actually rather curious to see him for themselves. Daisy glanced at her watch. It was time: Etienne's lecture should be drawing to a close. But as she and Marie-Laure turned to look expectantly at the double doors of the lecture hall, another set of doors opened further down the corridor. Another lecture had finished before Etienne's. A dozen students came straggling out and hurried away, followed, a few moments later, by Clothaire.

Looking around, he caught sight of the group of girls, stood stock-still at first – looking oddly uncomfortable and trapped, Daisy observed – and then made up his mind to approach them.

'*Ah, tiens? Salut.* Are you . . . waiting for me?'

'No, not at all,' Claire said. 'What an idea!'

'In fact we have all come to meet the great Deslisses,' Agathe explained with a brilliant smile. 'Daisy's friend.'

Stepping forward to greet Clothaire, Daisy said, 'Hi! How are you? But in fact,' she went on, squeezing Marie-Laure's arm teasingly, 'it was Marie's idea. She's Etienne's number one fan, you see.'

Marie-Laure glanced at Clothaire and blushed. 'Oh, stop it, Daisy! I am not his fan. I admire his work, that is all.'

Clothaire stared back with icy disdain. 'Well, I thought you had better taste. It is ridiculous the fuss everyone makes about that guy.'

Daisy looked from Marie-Laure to Clothaire, uncertain what to say. Clothaire and Isabelle had recently split up, Agathe had said, adding that poor Clothaire was terribly upset. No doubt that was why he was more than usually unpleasant. Although why he should pick on Marie-Laure, Daisy had no idea.

To defuse the tension, she said, 'Happy New Year, by the way. I thought I'd see you at Marie-Laure's bash but I couldn't make it in the end.'

Clothaire looked at her dispassionately and nodded.

'My boyfriend and I ended up at an all-night salsa party. It was right at the other end of town and we couldn't get a taxi.'

Clothaire sighed theatrically and turned slightly away from Daisy and towards Marie-Laure.

'But I'm so sorry I missed your party, Marie,' Daisy went on. 'Oh, and there was going to be a *surprise*, wasn't there? What was it?'

Marie-Laure opened her mouth to reply, but at that point there suddenly arose, from behind the closed doors of the amphitheatre, the thunderous, exhilarating sound of rapturous applause. Clothaire looked spectacularly cross. The ovation went on for quite some time, then the double doors swung open, letting through a throng of enthusiastic students. Quite a few of them, Daisy noticed, nodded guiltily in Clothaire's direction, muttering *'Bonjour, Monsieur,'* as they walked past. Well, what do you know, she thought, academia isn't a million miles away from the fashion world after all. During Fashion Week, there were those dull shows hardly anyone bothered to attend, and then a few magical, white-hot ones that nobody wanted to miss. In catwalk terms Etienne's lectures were clearly front-page and front-row stuff.

Daisy smiled. 'Wow! That was quite something.'

'You did not know that his lectures were so popular?'

'Well, not really. I know you said so, Marie. But he's never acted like a big famous person or anything.'

'No,' Marie-Laure said in awestruck tones, 'I am sure he doesn't. Somebody like Deslisses has no vanity at all because he is completely cerebral. He lives the contemplative life. He is like . . . a monk.'

'Really?' Daisy said, reflecting that this confirmed her own impression. It was true that Etienne seemed to have almost no interest in his own appearance, unlike most men she had known. Nor had he ever volunteered any information about his personal life, while Daisy herself, who did most of the talking when they met, had probably blabbed quite a lot about Raoul. She had never *dared* ask Etienne very much about himself – his reserve was just too intimidating.

'I bet lots of his students fancy him,' Daisy said.

Marie-Laure looked outraged. 'Oh, but somebody like him would never . . . I mean he has so much integrity.'

'Then you're in with a chance . . . Ow!' she said laughingly as Marie-Laure elbowed her in the ribs.

'Well, I am going to go,' Clothaire said, looking exasperated. 'I do not have the time to hang around here all day. *Alors, salut.*'

As he began to move away, Agathe suddenly stood up. 'Wait! I will come with you.' And after conveying to Daisy that she was concerned for Clothaire and sorry to leave so soon with the help of a brief, expressive pantomime, she hurried after him.

The crowd of students was thinning out now, and Daisy could see Etienne emerging slowly out of the amphitheatre, talking earnestly with a small band of students whose ecstatic demeanour and starry eyes reminded Daisy of what Chrissie was like when they were out clubbing together. And no, her eyes did not deceive her: Etienne really had a navy-blue *duffel coat* slung over his shoulder. Daisy was astounded. Had she missed some sort of ironic revival? Spotting her, Etienne excused himself and joined her group.

'Hi, Etienne! These are my friends: Marie-Laure, Claire and Amélie. They wanted to say hello.'

Etienne smiled at each girl in turn, bowing very slightly, then looked at Daisy.

'Goodness, Etienne!' Daisy said, grinning back. 'I had no idea!'

'No idea?'

'Well, all that applause. You're like a big sodding rock star.'

Marie-Laure, who had been standing on one foot like a child, something she always did when she was intimidated, screwed up her courage to speak. 'I think Daisy exaggerates. I mean . . . what you do is so serious . . . so important. You are teaching people how to think, *comment penser le réel, en fait.*'

Etienne shook his head and smiled. 'I would not go that far.'

'But you have taught *me* so much. The limpidity of your analyses. The elegance of your metaphors!' Marie-Laure went on, changing feet.

'Marie has read *all* your books, Etienne. Every single one.'

'Thank you very much. I am honoured.'

'But you see, if Etienne really *were* a rock star,' Daisy said teasingly, 'you could ask him to sign your bra or something. That would be fun, wouldn't it?'

'*Daisy!*'

'I'm only joking.'

Claire, who had not said a word, was beginning to look bored. 'Daisy, we are going to go.' She nodded curtly in

Etienne's direction. 'It is nice to have met you. Bye, Marie.'

'Wait for me. Goodbye.' Marie-Laure shook hands with Etienne ceremoniously, then departed with the other two girls.

'Your friends are charming, Daisy. Shall we go to lunch? Do you like Chinese food?'

'Love it. I love all food.'

'There is a nice little place around the corner where I have luckily never run into any colleagues. Then you can tell me all about appearances and truth.'

'OK. And then *you* can tell me something . . . Does the name Paddington Bear mean anything to you, Etienne?'

'Paddington? Sorry, what . . . a kind of beer? No, not really, in fact.'

'Yep. I thought not.'

27 Isabelle

'That is really, really fly. But I think we need the puttees to break the look down. With the lurex apron? Or maybe the jumpsuit underneath? We need to rough it up a bit.'

'Savage doesn't want it too pretty. Savage hates pretty. Pretty makes her puke.'

'Right. Those puttees and maybe also . . . a tea cosy on her head or something. Perhaps little fish-face could run and fetch it, hmm? Oi, you, what's your name again?'

'Isabelle.'

'Oh, right. Yeah, get that cosy for me, will you, sweetie? Let's make it surreal.'

'Yeah, and Savage wants some per-so-na-li-ty in that coat! OK, darling?' said Savage.

'I know, I know, it's just that her tits are getting in the way.'

'Can't she suck them in or something?'

'That looks lovely, sweetie, but can you just soften the face, hmm? I'm not getting the right vibe for the look.'

Isabelle cleared her throat as she came back into the room. '*Heu* . . . I'm sorry – I looked in the accessories cupboard and I don't think that, er, thing you mentioned is there.'

Savage slowly turned around in her black leather director's chair to stare at Isabelle through the pink lenses of her enormous sunglasses. She looked like a very glamorous and angry rabbit. She then nodded at Paquita, the stylist standing next to her.

Paquita sighed and gave her many bangles a little shake. 'Oh yeah, no, it won't be in the accessories cupboard, sweetie,' she said with a pitying look. 'If I were you, I'd try the *kitchen*, hmm? Chances are you'll find it sitting on the teapot.' Then she burst into prolonged high-pitched laughter and, after a moment, so did Savage. They turned away and focused again on the model standing impassively before them.

Walking into the kitchen, Isabelle found Chrissie leaning against the counter, furtively dipping a chocolate biscuit into a cup of tea.

'Hello, sweetie! Are Dorothy Discipline and her henchwoman on the warpath?'

'Yes. They're not very polite today. Chrissie, they want something called a ti, um . . . cosi. It sounds Italian?'

Chrissie reached across the kitchen counter for something that looked like a knitted ski hat and twirled it around his forefinger. 'Easy-peasy. This is the *objet* in question, darling. I take it it's to be *worn*?' he asked with interest.

'Yes.'

'Goodness, Paquita *is* clever, isn't she? In a league of her *own* – or should that be "world"? Here, sweetie, take it to Savage *this minute*, or she'll *scream* the place down, and we can't have that because Muggins here is feeling a tad *fragile* this morning.'

Isabelle hurried back into the studio, holding the tea cosy aloft.

'Ah, there she is,' Paquita said. 'About time. Oh wow, Savage! I know what we can do! Let's get little fish-fa— I mean you, sweetie, have a go, mmm? Go on, you put it on Greta's head.'

'Me? Oh, I don't know . . .'

'Come on, come on – we want it to look fierce, fierce, fierce.'

'Savage would really like you to try!' Savage said excitedly.

Kneading the tea cosy with both hands, Isabelle walked up to the expressionless model. She was reminded of being taken to the zoo in the Bois de Vincennes with Camille and Aude when they were all quite small and watching a man climb to the top of a ladder in order to wash a giraffe's head. But before she had to raise the question of whether a stepladder (or at the very least one or two volumes of the *Encyclopaedia Britannica*) would be available, the girl bent her knees and lowered her neck, meekly allowing herself to be crowned with the tea cosy.

'Oh goody, it fits,' Paquita said happily. 'Thank goodness she's got such a minute little pinhead. No cellulite there, eh, sweetie? That makes a nice change!'

Unsure what to do next, but painfully aware that some mysterious fashion statement was expected of her, Isabelle tweaked the tea cosy this way and that.

Paquita looked at Savage, who nodded slowly several times.

'Oh, sweetie,' Paquita said expansively. 'It's just *gorge*! Well, that can be our sample for production, I think, yeah? You can work with that, can't you, Chrissie?'

'Definitely,' said Chrissie, who had come to stand behind them in prudent silence.

'Savage wants it embroidered with magic mushrooms and blue caterpillars,' said Savage.

'Oooh,' Paquita wailed, 'that's *so* genius!'

What had happened to bring Isabelle into Savage's orbit was Posy's abrupt departure in the early days of January. After working under Savage for five years, the diminutive PA had moved on to another job without so much as giving notice, and created a vacancy that needed filling as a matter of urgency. Having noticed that Isabelle seemed listless since her return from Paris – she spent most of her time sitting at the kitchen table staring into space – it had occurred to Chrissie that she might like to replace Posy, at least for a short while. A change of scene would help her get over her break-up with that horrid Clot-(of)-Hair, since she claimed *that* was the one and only cause of her abstracted mood.

Thus it had been arranged that Isabelle and Chrissie would meet Savage at an opening in one of the designer's regular hang-outs, a small art gallery in the East End. Surrounded by a clique of oddly dressed people, Chrissie and Isabelle had looked at the exhibit from every angle, but, Isabelle thought with some exasperation, it remained just what it was – dozens of bottles of soy sauce lined up on a none-too-clean tabletop. Although it did not seem polite to say this out loud, since the artist (a very slim and silent young man in a white boiler suit with a challengingly asymmetric haircut) was present, she thought privately that it was no real competition for a single painting by, say, Chardin or Watteau. After an hour of waiting in vain for Savage, Isabelle's patience was exhausted.

'Oh, she'll be here, darling,' Chrissie said serenely.

'But you said she only lives around the corner. Why is she so late?'

'She doesn't operate on the same timescale as us mere *mortals*.'

Isabelle, who had been taught from an early age that *l'exactitude est la politesse des rois* – that punctuality was kinglike courtesy – was scandalised.

'Chrissie, it is incredibly impolite to keep us waiting like this. Stay if you like, but I have had enough. If she wants to meet me, she'll have to make another appointment.'

Chrissie put his beer bottle down and looked at Isabelle with a mixture of admiration and amusement. 'Temper, temper, my little French firecracker! Oh, all right. Come on, I'll walk you to the Tube.'

They set off together down the empty, darkening street. After a few moments, Isabelle discerned an approaching silhouette in the distance. It looked not unlike the Michelin Man.

'Oh *heavens*,' Chrissie whispered, gripping Isabelle's arm and turning her around with military firmness. 'It's her! It's *her*! Let's go back. She'll be *furious* if she sees that we were about to leave.'

Isabelle allowed herself to be frogmarched back to the gallery, outside which they were standing, nonchalantly sipping from bottles of beer, when the distant apparition caught up with them a few minutes later. On closer inspection, the slender designer looked nothing like the Michelin Man. She was wearing a deliriously oversized white silk puffa jacket over slim white trousers and boots. Beneath her sleek silver bob, Isabelle saw, Savage's large, wide dark eyes were rimmed all the way around with a generous amount of purple glitter. As Chrissie made the introductions, Savage's glittery gaze fastened itself on Isabelle with unwavering intensity, taking in her face, her hair, her clothes, her shoes, and returning to her face.

'Hello,' Isabelle said politely. 'It's nice to meet you.'

After a moment's silence, Savage smiled widely. 'Savage loves your lipstick,' she said breathily.

'Thank you,' Isabelle said, a little taken aback. 'Um, it's Chanel.'

'It's a very chic colour, very elegant. You're very chic, very elegant.' She turned to Chrissie and said in a much lower, louder and slightly frenzied voice: 'Savage *likes*!'

'I *knew* you would, darling. Isabelle's great, isn't she? She's *French*, you know.'

'French? French! *French*.' Savage smiled again, with childlike delight.

'Yes *indeedy*. Well, what do you think? Should Isabelle come in with me tomorrow morning? And I'll show her the ropes and what have you?'

'That would be . . . *cool*,' Savage said, looking at Chrissie with intense earnestness.

Smiling ethereally at nobody in particular, she turned on her heel, floated into the gallery and was soon being embraced and feted by the rest of the crowd as though she were the Queen on a state visit. Even the sullen young artist became animated at the sight of her and came over to present his compliments.

'Am I hired?' Isabelle asked, confused. 'But does she know that I do not have a degree in fashion?'

'Oh, honey. Savage is so *not* corporate in her approach. She likes the *look* of you. That's enough.'

Since that day, Isabelle had taken on Posy's duties. These involved answering the phone in Savage's studio, opening all mail and dealing with press enquiries. But in actual fact the better part of Isabelle's time was taken up with other things, like Savage's complicated brews of tea. Today, for example, the designer had requested a cup made of one-quarter peppermint tea, one-quarter nettle and one-half Lapsang Souchong, sweetened with one-eighth of a teaspoon of Japanese rice syrup; the water had to be Volvic. But the recipe kept changing. It was safer to stock every brand of mineral water, the more esoteric the better, just in case Savage wanted her lunchtime cracked bulgur wheat cooked in something Swedish or Sicilian. That was because Savage's food and drink had to be the result of a spontaneous decision, or so her nutritionist said. This usually involved Isabelle taking a long walk (or several) to the health food shop to pick up a particular kind of seaweed.

There had been an awkward scene the other day when she had returned with absolutely the wrong brand of miso: Savage had locked herself away in the bathroom and refused to come out until the right one was produced. This had lost the team half a day's work on the collection. Savage was exhausting: swinging from elation to fury with alarming suddenness, only to break into the odd incoherent pseudo-poetic oracle.

Yet Isabelle was not overly irritated by these antics, perhaps because only a superficial part of her consciousness was actually engaged with the daily drudgery of serving under Savage's regime. Really her mind was on other things – namely the location of Meredith Quince's manuscripts. She had come to the melancholy conclusion that they did not reside in Tom Quince's house. That meant she had no reason for going there again. Or indeed for ever seeing Tom again. And this was melancholy because . . .

Well, because Isabelle now had to begin her search all over again after wasting valuable time – time she might have spent writing more of her thesis. Now that Clothaire was out of her life, she must think about real things, solid things, like her academic career in France, where she would be returning for good in a few months' time. It was pointless to wonder about . . . well, other possibilities, letting her imagination run away with her. Utterly, *utterly* pointless, Isabelle told herself several times a day and as she lay awake at night, staring at the ceiling.

28 Daisy

'It could be *totally* extreme,' Raoul said once again, stroking Daisy's naked back.

'Yes, yes, of course it could,' Daisy said, turning over on her side to lie facing him. 'But . . . tell me again what your idea is, exactly.'

'It's all about rock 'n' roll! These cool 1950s fashions would look great on you.'

'Ye-es, I like that bit,' Daisy conceded. 'But the thing is . . .'

'What, honey?'

'Well, you're not really a fashion illustrator, are you? Your speciality is, you know, er, nudity.'

'But, baby, I have drawn you naked lots of times.'

'Yes, but that was private. This would be . . .'

'I thought you liked my work,' Raoul said, pouting a little.

'I do, Raoul. Of course I do.'

They kissed.

Later, as they pushed a trolley down the aisles of the local Monoprix supermarket together, Daisy asked light-heartedly, 'Can you give me an idea of my character's storyline? Won't it involve sex and stuff?'

Raoul grinned at her wolfishly. 'You think I am an *obsédé sexuel* or something? I am, a little bit, it's true! OK. I'm thinking Cadillacs, drive-ins, bobby socks, cute ponytails.

A lot of *rock acrobatique*,' he said, twisting his wrist around to suggest complicated dance moves. 'Elvis Presley. Hey, you know what, let's get some of those nachos. The really spicy ones.'

As Daisy reached for a couple of packets, she all but crumpled them in her hands, so forcefully was she struck by a terrible suspicion. 'Hang on, did you say *Elvis Presley*?'

'Yeah, baby.'

'You mean . . . Oh, God. Raoul?'

Raoul had parked the trolley to look at the jars of Tex-Mex salsa. 'What, sugar?' he said absent-mindedly.

'If you think I'm going to shag Elvis Presley, you've got another think coming!'

'Just listen to this, honey. Your character, she could be this cute cheerleader – you know, with the pom-poms and the miniskirt – who runs an Elvis the Pelvis fan club at her high school and then . . .'

Daisy stared at him and raised her forefinger. 'And then nothing! It's completely out of the question!'

But a few days later, Raoul tried again. 'Just let me explain, OK? He picks her out of all the cheerleaders because she is the most beautiful. That's cool, no?'

Daisy paused in the careful application of her eyeliner and made a small face at him in the mirror.

'Her first lover is the King! How extreme is that?'

'Way too extreme, actually.'

Raoul laughed, kissed the top of her head and said, 'Ah, but don't forget it will not be you – just a sexy character *inspired* by you. It will be done with taste.'

It probably would, Daisy thought wearily. And yet the

whole idea made her feel uneasy. Did that make her incredibly British and uptight?

Raoul began to pace the room, insouciantly freestyling. 'Later on I am thinking she will meet Marlon Brando and his friends in, you know, the movie where they have the big motorcycles and dress all in black leather?'

Daisy plonked her make-up wand down and looked up at the ceiling.

'OK, stop right there! This is getting completely out of hand. I will *not* be portrayed as someone who sleeps with a lot of famous people. Not even cool vintage ones. What do you take me for? A groupie?'

'Why are you getting so upset, baby? I don't get it.'

'No, I can see that,' Daisy said slowly, looking at his puzzled expression.

'I thought you were cool with all this.'

'Um, yes, so did I,' Daisy said pensively, buttoning her dress.

Raoul fell silent, and dropped the idea, for a little while. But later, as they made their way to Marie-Laure's house on the leafy western fringes of Paris, Daisy was painfully aware that he was puzzling out a way to bring it all up again. She sat fidgeting in the taxi, keeping up a stream of constant chatter in order to silence him. She was beginning to realise how like a child Raoul was in many ways: self-centred, endlessly playful and very, very stubborn.

On arrival, she leaped out of the car and was already ringing the doorbell when Raoul caught up with her. The door was opened, somewhat to Daisy's surprise, by Octave.

'*Bonsoir*, Daisy,' Octave said charmingly, without a trace

of embarrassment. 'It's nice to see you again. *Bonsoir*,' he said again, shaking hands with Raoul.

They followed Octave into the drawing room, where Marie-Laure lay on the sofa wearing glamorous black silk pyjamas and with one leg in plaster. A stunned Daisy dropped her bag on the floor and rushed to her friend's side.

'Marie! What happened to you?'

'I fell down the stairs. But it is not serious – please do not worry.'

'You should have called me! Are you OK?'

'I am fine,' Marie-Laure said, smiling and squeezing Daisy's hand. 'You are so kind. And,' she added quickly, 'Octave has been very helpful. Because, in fact, he was with me when I fell, you know, so he took me to the hospital and then brought me home.'

Daisy glanced at Octave, who grinned at her and said, 'I'd better go to the kitchen to check on things. I'm cooking dinner tonight. *C'est moi le chef!*'

'He means we are having blinis and *tarama* from the *traiteur* and salad out of a bag,' Marie-Laure said, smiling. 'That is what Octave calls cooking.'

'Maybe I can help him,' Raoul said, following in Octave's wake.

Momentarily distracted – what on earth were those two going to talk about in the kitchen? – Daisy turned back to look at her friend.

'Actually, you're looking really well, Marie,' she said. 'You look . . . like something incredibly nice has happened to you.'

Marie-Laure bit her lip, glancing in the direction of the kitchen, before breaking into an irrepressible grin. Daisy smiled back.

'What happened exactly?'

'Oh, I just tripped and fell down the stairs here. I was not looking where I was going.'

'It's lucky that Octave was there.'

'Yes, it was very lucky.'

Daisy reached over to touch one of her friend's earrings. 'Oh, these are lovely! What are they? Coral?'

'Yes.'

'Are they new?'

'No, they are not new. In fact . . . you know what they are?' Marie-Laure shifted a little on the sofa and looked away from Daisy for a moment. 'They are my old earrings, the ones that I . . . lost. Do you remember?'

'The ones that you lost,' Daisy repeated slowly. 'Oh. But you don't mean . . . the ones that Octave . . .'

'Yes. He gave them back to me.'

Daisy was silent for a moment, then smiled and said, 'Was this before or after you fell down the stairs?'

'Before. It was before Christmas. He just turned up here, with a ridiculous amount of flowers,' Marie-Laure said, demonstrating with both arms outstretched. 'And he was so sweet, Daisy. And I think he is really sorry for the way he behaved.'

'So, the surprise I would have got at your New Year's Eve party . . .'

'Was Octave and me.' Marie-Laure became a little agitated and tried to sit up. 'I didn't know how to just . . .

tell you, because I was worried that maybe you would feel . . .'

'Oh, no, no! Don't worry about that. That was, like, in another life.'

'And then when you said you were so happy with Raoul . . .'

'Oh, I am. Yes. Absolutely. Perfectly happy,' Daisy said with many an emphatic nod.

'He seems really nice.'

'He is,' Daisy said, sighing very slightly. Now was not the time to consult Marie-Laure about her pornography dilemma.

'So now we can all go to the ball together in April!' Marie-Laure exclaimed happily. 'You will really enjoy it, Daisy. The Opera House is very beautiful.'

Daisy smiled back, her mind on other things. Octave had been nothing more than a crush, she knew that now. But she had a niggling sense that the same was true of Raoul. Perhaps the problem lay with her. Perhaps she just didn't feel things very deeply.

Meanwhile, Marie-Laure started to laugh. 'You know, it was funny when I fell down. Octave was chasing me all over the house and tickling me. I am very ticklish – he remembers that from when we were little. I was laughing so hard when I fell that I didn't feel any pain. And then he was so good at taking care of me.'

'That's great. Tell me, what do the other *Pique-Assiettes* think?'

'Octave has renounced the *Confrèrie*. For me. They are still his friends of course, but . . .'

'No more competition? No more little book? No more trophies?'

'No. Because,' Marie-Laure ended simply, her face radiant, 'we want to be with each other all the time.'

Later, in the taxi home, as Raoul fell into a snooze with his head on her shoulder, Daisy stared out of the window, smiling wistfully. It had been lovely to see Marie-Laure looking so happy. Of course she and Octave were a great match, one that had been a long time coming but that would probably last. You only had to see them together for five minutes to know that. And now the über-cynical Jules, who had always snorted derisively at the very idea of romance, was in a fantastic relationship with Karloff. Jules had even started talking of the pagan wedding they were hoping to have in the Yorkshire moors at midsummer. It seemed that, one by one, all her friends were being blessed with romantic love. As for the bond between herself and Raoul, perhaps it had only ever been lust? There was nothing wrong with lust, of course. Lust was fun. But it would be nice, for a change, to feel the other thing and be sure . . . Oh well, it didn't matter all that much, really, did it? And what *was* love, anyway? Nobody appeared to know for certain. The important thing was to have a good time. And she and Raoul were having a great time together! He was fast asleep now, bless him. Daisy felt in her coat pocket and removed from it the small object Octave had pressed wordlessly into her hand as they said goodbye. The car stopped at a traffic light and she opened her hand in the red glow. She was glad to have her heart brooch back. She had actually missed it quite a lot.

29 Isabelle

'Don't you think it is a little bit too tight?' Isabelle asked, looking down worriedly at her outfit.

'*Non*sense, darling!' Chrissie said, smoothing his own black all-in-ones complacently over slim hips. 'It's *got* to be as *tight* as *sausage* skin, don't you see? Else it wouldn't be a proper *cat* burglar's outfit, would it, hmm?'

'OK, if you are sure,' Isabelle said, pulling ineffectually at slinky Lycra.

'Karloff, baby!' Chrissie exclaimed, as Karloff emerged diffidently from behind a screen, also clad in a black catsuit. 'Look at *you*! See, that is the *beauty* of Savage's "all together now" concept. One size fits all – give or take an inch or two . . .'

'Right,' Jules said, staring coldly at her housemate. 'Are we all ready?'

Chrissie stalked across the room towards Ivy, whose small serious face peeped out of her black balaclava.

'Gosh, darling, you are *so* petite that the thing is actually *creasing* on you! Let me just, ah, straighten it a little *here*, and *there*, like so. That's *much* better. As for you, Bella, well, you look *edible*, my lovely. Simply curvylicious.'

'Can we go now and get on with it? I've had enough of standing around!'

Chrissie narrowed his eyes. 'In a minute, Legend, darling.

Listen, are you *positive* that you want to wear your leather jerkin over your outfit? You *are*? Well, OK, though the only thing I'd say is that you are *kind* of going against the *grain* of the whole thing, you know, with this sort of *rampant* gothic individualism.'

'Look, mate, I'm not one of your fashion victims, all right?'

'Well, I was just *saying*, you know,' Chrissie went on as they all walked out of the room in a single black-clad file. 'I mean, these samples may not be my own design but they are my *responsibility* as a fashion person. And *besides*,' he said as Isabelle and The Coven trickled down the stairs and out of Savage's East End warehouse, 'I still think that it was a mistake on your part, Ju-Ju, to get me to separate the outfits. We should have kept to the original design – it's so much more *organic*. Then it really would have been all for one and one for all, darlings!'

'Chrissie,' Jules said tonelessly, 'you're delusional. How exactly would you expect us to get over a garden wall all attached to one another? To say nothing about fitting into the van.'

'And anyway, you can, like, stitch the whole thing back after, can't you, mate? They'll never know, right?'

'Oh, it's *kind* of you to worry about that, Karloff, but *actually* it's only Velcro – so clever, no? – so that's no problem.'

'This is just great,' Legend said, climbing into the van next to Jules and Belladonna. 'Cos I've always wanted to do something a little bit illegal.'

'Actually, it is completely illegal, what we are going to do,' Isabelle said reasonably, buckling her seat belt. 'It is *entrée par effraction*, you know, *heu* ... I don't know how to say it in English.'

'Would that be *breaking* and also *entering*, darling?' Chrissie asked breezily.

'Isabelle? Right or left here?' Karloff asked her from the driver's seat.

'I'm not sure,' she replied in a deflated voice. Her feeling that she had become trapped in a mad dream was increasing by the minute.

'Go right,' Jules said decisively. 'Then follow the signs for the West End.'

'Don't worry, Isabelle,' Ivy said kindly. 'We're going to get them for you, simple as that.'

Isabelle smiled at her automatically and bit her lip. Astonishingly, what had started as a bit of a joke around their kitchen table last night was now actually happening. She should have put a stop to it much sooner, say when Chrissie had had the brainwave about the perfect outfit for a burglary, or when Legend had boasted that there was no lock she couldn't pick. It still wasn't too late to stop it all. As she opened her mouth to speak, though, Chrissie, who sat behind her, placed his hands on her shoulders.

'Now darling, you have *got* to buck up. It might be illegal to break into the man's house, but there is *absolutely* no other way of getting those manuscripts for you, is there?'

'I mean, you said so yourself last night,' Legend added. 'That old geezer sounds dead suspicious. It's obvious he's got something to hide.'

With hindsight, Isabelle thought crossly, it might have been preferable to have kept her counsel last night after returning home from the Quince Society meeting. Had it been such a bright idea to tell Chrissie and The Coven about her discovery? Initially, her announcement had been greeted by a chorus of 'What? Who's resurfaced? Paul who?'

And indeed it had taken Isabelle herself a minute or two to work out whom Wendy was referring to when, while handing out large pieces of home-made parsnip cake, the sheeplike lady mentioned that she had caught sight of Paul Celadon outside the British Museum.

Isabelle's ears had pricked up. Paul Celadon? Where had she heard that name before?

'Paul was Meredith's literary agent, you see, Isabelle,' Fern had explained. 'Years and years ago.'

Of course, Isabelle thought: Paul Celadon was the author of *My Life as a Bookmark*! *He* was the one who'd talked Meredith out of further literary experimentation. Isabelle had actually outlined a whole chapter about him before Christmas. But she had never considered that he might be a real person and not just a trope of Meredith's creative landscape. And so much had happened since then that the name had become a distant memory.

'Paul? *Paul*?' Lucy had barked. 'Ha! Must be a hundred years old. Anyway, thought the fellow had gone east.'

'Don't be so silly, Lucy,' Maud had said, snorting. 'People like Paul never die. They just crawl under a rock.'

At this point, the squirrellish Herbert Merryweather had said diffidently, 'So, Miss Peppy-on, you've had no luck hunting down those manuscripts, then, eh? Not even,' he had added in a wistful undertone, '*Death of a Lady Ventriloquist*?'

'No, unfortunately. I have looked everywhere in Meredith's house.'

'Ha, yes!' Lucy had barked. 'Decent of young Quince, I think, to let you have a good shufti. Turned out to be quite a nice chap really, in the end.'

To her horror, Isabelle had felt the ominous prickle of tears. 'Oh yes, he is very nice,' she murmured. 'He's lovely.' Desperately calling upon the ancestral Papillon tradition of self-control, she looked down at her plate and crumbled off a tiny piece of parsnip cake.

Lucy let her sharp blue eyes rest on her for a moment, then looked away and said briskly, 'You two young people hit it off, Izbl?'

Isabelle swallowed and managed to say with reasonable self-possession that Tom had been very helpful with her work.

'Well, p'r'aps you'll meet up again soon? That would be frightfully jolly, eh?'

'No. I don't think that is going to happen,' Isabelle said in a small voice.

'And why not?'

'Well, I could not find the manuscripts, so . . . So that's it. It's finished.'

'Ha? I see.'

Isabelle sighed. This cake of Wendy's was really quite inedible, she decided. Perhaps she could make her excuses and go home now. She put her plate down with a trembling hand.

'Of course *I* didn't give him the slightest sign of recognition!' Wendy went on, flushing a little. 'After all, Paul never was very nice to our dear Meredith.'

'Well, he did sell her books for her with some degree of success,' Peter Holland said.

'There's *more* to life than *money*, my dear Peter!' Wendy said tremulously.

'You know, Izbl,' Maud had said, between sips of her tea. 'Paul is a sly old puss, and he might just know something about the location of Meredith's manuscripts. I wouldn't put it past him.'

'Ha! Wouldn't put anything past him! Well, Izbl? What do you say?'

'I don't know. I . . .'

Isabelle had felt light-headed, her tears forgotten. The dazzling route leading to the manuscripts, including that of *The Splodge*, had just reopened before her eyes. She could see it all: whatever his faults may have been, Paul Celadon would by now have turned into a charming white-haired *grand-père*, touchingly fond of his favourite client's relics – the precious manuscripts. Little did he imagine that an enthusiastic young scholar called Isabelle Papillon shared his affection! Everything was about to fall into place at long last. With great trepidation, Isabelle had watched Lucy locate the old agent's telephone number on an ancient Rolodex and, her hands folded in her lap, had listened avidly to the conversation that followed.

It was immediately apparent that things were not going well: as soon as she had told Paul that a young French gel was interested in speaking to him about Meredith's manuscripts, Lucy had to jerk her head away from the thundering sound of curses issuing from the receiver. A few barked rejoinders followed on her part, but to no avail. Paul

Celadon hung up in the middle of the last one. Her crimson face now making a stark contrast with the white teapot motif of her bright green sweater, Lucy damned and blasted the fellow's impertinence. Maud remarked crisply that it might have been preferable to put Isabelle on the line, since Paul and Lucy had never been the best of friends. Soon all the members of the Society were arguing about what Paul was really like and how best to handle him. During this commotion, Isabelle had discreetly copied down Celadon's number and address, shut herself up in Lucy's study and tried to ring him herself. But she'd barely had time to state her identity before Celadon, who spoke in a thin, reedy and exasperated voice, abruptly ended the conversation, leaving her like Lucy to listen to a toneless hum.

'But what *exactly* did he say, darling?' Chrissie had asked later that night, without looking up from the pages of *Harper's Bazaar*.

'He said he had retired a long time ago and that, anyway, he didn't know anything about the manuscripts. And that he was going on a long trip and would be away from London for the next few months.'

'Too much information,' Ivy said, nodding. 'That's just, like, devious.'

Legend twisted off the top of her beer bottle with her teeth, then grunted in assent. They all stared at her for a moment.

'*Ledge*. How shockingly *uncouth*, darling,' Chrissie said severely.

'Heh, heh, heh. Don't care. Rock 'n' roll.'

'It's very cool,' Jules said in an undertone. 'Like something out of a book.'

'Yeah,' Karloff said slowly, with shining eyes. 'It's like there's these mouldy old tomes full of, like, incredible secrets. Hidden away in, like, this impregnable black tower or something. Guarded by, like, a dragon or something.'

'Well, I really hope they are not mouldy,' Isabelle said, a little anxiously.

'Are they worth a lot, Isabelle?' Belladonna asked languidly, painting another long fingernail dark purple. 'Maybe he's already flogged them on eBay or something.'

'Oh no!' Isabelle said, instinctively horrified, even though she had never heard of eBay. 'I hope he hasn't sold them!'

'Not *very* likely,' Chrissie interjected. 'Don't take this the wrong way, darling, but Meredith Quince is, um, really rather *niche*, you know.'

'There is a Society in her name,' Isabelle said defensively.

'Um, yes, but they're all a bit *crusty*, aren't they?'

Crusty or not, Isabelle had become rather attached to her Quince Society friends. Chrissie would probably be scandalised to hear it, but her recent immersion in the world of cutting-edge fashion had made her appreciate the idiosyncratic dress sense of those who existed entirely outside that world. Roberta and Selina had adopted their pudding-bowl hairstyle because they liked it, not because it was the latest thing seen on some hot Brazilian model. Maud wore her tinted glasses not in an effort to be cool but because she must realise how fantastically intimidating they made her look. And as for Lucy, Isabelle was quite certain that she hadn't got the idea for her multicoloured jumpers and leg warmers from the pages of *Vogue*. Simply, she chose to express her forceful personality through her intrepid choice of knitwear. After two solid weeks of Savage and her crew, this sort of thing had become very restful.

After that, Isabelle reflected as Karloff's van clattered through the West End in the direction of Clerkenwell, one might say that things had got rather out of hand. Chrissie had ordered a Chinese takeaway for everyone and because the food took rather a long time to come, Isabelle had rashly drunk two whole glasses of wine on an empty stomach, thus breaking one of her steadfast rules. This had dangerously eroded her self-control. Later on, as Chrissie, Ivy and Karloff started planning an 'intervention' to reclaim the manuscripts by all means necessary (while Legend and Jules marched tipsily up and down the kitchen, shouting 'Power to the people!' and punching the air), Isabelle, instead of saying something sensible and sobering, had merely laughed helplessly. As a result, here they all were, in the early hours of the morning, climbing out of the van into the dimly lit square where the self-styled 'bookmark' had his domicile.

Initially, much time was spent by The Coven in giggling and shushing each other loudly while Jules and Chrissie discussed how best to break into the agent's house. Isabelle listened with a sense of unreality, telling herself firmly that they would never be able to get in and that the whole mad enterprise would soon collapse of its own accord. Next thing she knew, however, she was perched on top of the brick wall that separated the street from sunken private gardens. Beyond the gardens rose an intimidating row of tall houses. In one of these the elusive Celadon dwelled, withholding knowledge of the manuscripts' whereabouts. It was tantalising – that man knew all about *The Splodge*! She looked down at Jules, Chrissie and Karloff beckoning from the flowerbeds. All she could discern in the dark were her friends' pale faces looking up. While she sat there frozen, Ivy, Belladonna and Legend clambered past her over the wall.

'*Darling!*' Chrissie called out in an exasperated stage whisper. 'Stop *dawdling* and get down here this minute.' In a flash of inspiration he added: 'Quince, darling, think *Quince!*'

Galvanised, Isabelle jumped into the darkness.

'Damn! We didn't think to bring a piece of that sticky stuff,' Jules said crossly, as they all stood looking up at Celadon's dark windows.

'Sticky stuff, darling? *Euw!* Gross! Whatever for?'

'To remove a pane of glass, dummy.'

'Hmm, yeah,' Ivy said pensively. 'Except you'd need a ladder first. Cos he lives upstairs, don't he?'

'I wish we'd brought a torch, too,' Belladonna said, after colliding for the twentieth time with an absent-minded Karloff.

'Can we stop this faffing and go in? You're all doing my head in.'

'All right, Ledge, if you're so clever. What do we do now?'

'Throw gravel at his window.'

'Put that *down*, you loon. Do you want to wake him up?'

'Well, duh. That way we ask him direct. Hello, mate, give us the paperwork, ta, and home to bed.'

While this went on, Isabelle's attention was drawn to a faint creaking sound issuing from the garden wall. A door was being opened from the street side. Before she had time to warn her friends, a beam of white light from an extra-powerful torch hit her in the face. She covered her eyes. That was it: the police! They were all going to jail. She could kiss her academic career goodbye.

'You, there!' said a thin, reedy, exasperated voice. Celadon! Isabelle opened her eyes in shock. 'Stay where you are! Don't you know that you're trespassing on private property?' As Meredith's agent pointed his torch towards the other members of her gang, she was able to make out the nonagenarian's wiry silhouette, framed by the extremely small door through which he had just walked.

'Who are you people?' Celadon demanded severely. 'Are you thieves? Let me assure you that you will get no money from me! I shall call the police and have you all arr—'

'Whoa, hold your horses! There's no need for that kind of talk,' Karloff said, putting his arm around Jules protectively.

'Be not afeard, friend,' Bella added in a beatific voice, holding out her hands. 'We come in peace, to restore good karma.'

'Good *what*? Are you all right, young lady?'

'Look, mate, enough of the yapping. Just let us have the stuff sharpish, all right?'

'*Not now*, Ledge darling,' Chrissie whispered.

'The stuff? The *stuff*?' Paul Celadon stamped his foot in exasperation. 'I'll have you know that I am not a drug dealer. You'll need to look elsewhere for your *stuff*, you disgusting hooligans!'

Isabelle could now see Paul Celadon's birdlike countenance quite clearly: he looked furious and also appeared to be weighing his torch in his hand as a potential blunt instrument.

'*Monsieur* Celadon,' she said, taking a step towards him. 'I am Isabelle Papillon. We spoke on the phone earlier about the manuscripts.'

'What?'

'This is all my fault. I am very sorry. We did not mean to be rude. We only came here to . . .'

'Nick the stuff . . . Ow!'

'Tell you more about my academic research,' Isabelle continued, as Legend rubbed her arm furiously where it had made sudden contact with Isabelle's elbow. 'I assure you that I am a serious scholar. My supervisor Professeur Sureau will be happy to confirm this. I know that meeting like this doesn't look very good, but my intentions are quite honourable. If only I could consult Meredith Quince's manuscripts, I could show the academic world what a great author she was. Please will you help me?'

While Isabelle talked, Celadon cocked his head to one side and nodded along. That was encouraging. She looked at him expectantly.

'My dear young lady, this is all very touching.' Celadon then said, in a tone of infinite sarcasm. 'Believe me, if it were up to me, your chances of getting your hands on Meredith's manuscripts would be . . . *NIL!*' he screamed, his voice rising to a hysterical pitch. 'And since it *IS*, in fact, *UP TO ME, MAY I SUGGEST THAT YOU ALL SKEDADDLE! GET OUT OF MY SIGHT! NOW!'*

Isabelle sighed. For a moment nobody said a word, then, suddenly, there was the sound of Jules clearing her throat. Much to Isabelle's surprise, Jules reached forward and directed Celadon's torch towards her own face.

'Hello,' she said simply.

Celadon seemed utterly transfixed. He opened and closed his mouth a few times, but produced not a sound.

'Well, well, well,' Jules said sternly, pushing her spectacles to the top of her nose. 'And what's happened to our manners? Hmm?'

'Good evening, madam,' Celadon produced eventually, while bowing slightly from the waist. He now spoke in quite a different tone, exceedingly meek and silken. Isabelle, Chrissie and the rest of The Coven stood stock-still, amazed at the transformation.

'Yes, yes, good evening,' Jules replied. 'Well? I'm waiting.'

'I am most terribly sorry for my outburst, dear madam. It was quite unforgivable.'

'I should think so too. You have upset this lady very much,' Jules went on, indicating Isabelle.

'Yes,' Celadon murmured, looking at his feet and shuffling a little.

'You've let all of us down. You've let Meredith Quince down, too. But most of all, I think you'll agree, you've let *yourself* down.'

'Oh yes, I have. I am most dreadfully sorry.'

'So. Do you have the manuscripts, yes or no?'

'Yes, madam, I do. They're upstairs in my study.'

'And you are, of course, willing to let Miss Papillon have them?'

'Yes, certainly. I should be delighted to help you in any way I can, madam,' Celadon said, addressing Isabelle.

'Thank you,' Isabelle murmured automatically.

'Right, then,' Jules said. 'We haven't got all night. Go and fetch the manuscripts. Chop-chop.'

'Yes, madam, of course. I shan't be a moment. Shan't be a moment.'

As Paul Celadon trotted off obediently in the direction of his apartment, everybody looked at Jules.

'What the bloody hell just happened?' Legend asked, speaking for all of them.

'Well,' Jules said tonelessly, 'I said, didn't I, that the customers at the House of Discipline were all very polite?'

Isabelle, feeling rather light-headed, thought that Jules was speaking in riddles.

Then Chrissie burst out laughing, clapping his hands in delight. 'Oh my goodness, *of course*, your *kinky* shop! Darling, I always *knew* that you'd be *excellent* at retail, provided it was the right kind! Tell me, how many of your *super*-naughty trinkets have you sold him?'

'Lots, as it happens. He's one of our best customers. He owns pretty much the entire catalogue.'

'No doubt he'll be back to buy it all again after tonight. I think the old boy really enjoyed himself there.'

'Thank you, Jules,' Isabelle said gratefully. 'You were great.'

'Oh, it was nothing,' Jules said modestly.

'*Not* nothing, darling,' Chrissie said sententiously. 'It goes to show, boys and girls, what I've *always* believed. An *honest* day's work – whether it be spent in furnishing the good people of London with S & M knick-knacks or not is *quite* immaterial – is always, *always* rewarded.'

30 Daisy

It was the cake that did it in the end, and really tipped Daisy over the edge. Coming as it did towards the end of a pretty jaw-dropping evening, the cake made everything quite, quite clear, and she had no alternative but to speak out.

The cake in question had been baked specially to mark Raoul's birthday. Daisy remembered how he'd first begun talking about this important event several weeks ago, discussing various possible ways of celebrating. Should they fly to Rio? Or have a big private party at his favourite club, Les Bains-Douches? Or maybe do both? Then with only three days to spare before the big day, Raoul realised that he had run out of time to plan anything remotely complicated and so decided instead on a simpler, more homely sort of celebration – a dinner party at his flat with Daisy and his closest friends. Afterwards, he would take Daisy to Deauville for the weekend.

Although she had met a few of Raoul's many friends, Daisy had not yet been introduced to his inner circle, the people he referred to as his 'family', and she was curious to see what they were like – a bunch of extrovert machos, as likely as not, and all as obsessed with rugby as he was! The dinner party would also be a welcome distraction from her current state of mind: an overwhelming sense of listlessness that she had never experienced before and was at a loss to understand. This had been accompanied by a considerable increase in the frequency of her recurring dream. It had her wandering the dark, deserted streets of Paris almost every night, looking anxiously for something – or someone – she yearned for very powerfully, but never managed to find. If only she could work out what the dream meant!

When the doorbell rang for the first time on the night of his birthday dinner, Raoul was still shaving, and it was Daisy who answered the door. On the landing, holding a pile of presents wrapped in pink-and-gold paper, a bunch of flowers and a large oven dish covered in foil (for Raoul, who did not believe in wasting time on cooking when he could be enjoying himself, had had the foresight to ask each of his guests to bring a different course), stood two stunning girls. Daisy had a vague impression that she had met them somewhere before.

'*Salut*! You are Daisy, yes?' one of them, a blonde, exclaimed with a big smile. 'I'm Natacha.'

'And I'm Stéphanie. *On a apporté des lasagnes.*'

'Oh, that's great! Thank you,' Daisy said, carrying the dish into the kitchen-diner. The two girls followed and removed their coats. They were both wearing extremely sexy dresses and vertiginous high heels, Daisy noticed. Natacha, the one with blue eyes and a spectacular mane of golden curls, immediately proceeded to set the oven to the right temperature. Meanwhile, Stéphanie, an olive-skinned girl who was wearing a bright-red afro wig and huge gold hoop earrings, opened the fridge which Raoul had packed with magnums of pink champagne. She pulled out a bottle and opened it with a nonchalant swiftness that bespoke many years of practice. Daisy got some glasses from the counter and Stéphanie began to pour the wine.

'So, Daisy,' she said, 'you're Raoul's famous *petite chérie anglaise*!'

'*Santé*!' Natacha said, clinking her glass with Daisy's. 'It's nice to meet you, finally.'

'Thank you,' Daisy said, touched by their friendliness. 'So we haven't met before?' she added, tentatively. 'Because I thought that we had, maybe?'

The doorbell rang again.

'I'll get it, baby,' Raoul called out from his bedroom.

A minute later he came into the kitchen dressed in jeans and a white shirt open to the navel, and forming the central element of a cluster of enthusiastic girls – four more guests had arrived and they were all hugging him, whooping all the while in excited Gallic voices:

'*Ouais! C'est la fête!*'

'*On va s'éclater ce soir!*'

'*C'est trop!*'

'*Wou-hou!*'

Natacha and Stéphanie distributed glasses of champagne and Daisy was introduced to another four glamourpusses: Lola, Vanessa, Karine and Nathalie. All were dressed to the nines and smelled wonderful. It was weird, Daisy thought, looking at the new arrivals, because she had a nagging feeling that she might have seen *them* somewhere before, too. Raoul unwrapped dishes of *taboulé*, *salade au Roquefort*, chilli con carne and *mousse au chocolat* and kissed every cook on the cheek. Lola, who wore a skintight spangly catsuit with thigh-high boots, and Karine, in a draped silver minidress and stilettos, walked over to the jukebox and put some music on. At the first notes of the 'Macarena', delighted squeals rose from every corner of Raoul's living room and all the girls leaped to their feet to form a line, hands on hips, and hop their way through the song's routine.

Raoul took Daisy by the hand. 'Come on, let's go dance.'

'Oh, I don't know the steps,' Daisy said hesitantly.

'Just follow the others,' Raoul said, demonstrating by hopping forwards and backwards in time to the music. '*Sympa, non?* They really know how to party, my friends, right? You're having fun? They're sweet, no? You like them? *Ehhhhh, Macarena!*'

'Oh, yes! They seem really nice,' Daisy said, surveying the scene as the doorbell rang again.

Shortly afterwards, as she sat on the white leather sofa with Mélodie, Juanita and Patricia, all gorgeous sultry creatures in tiny dresses, wondering whether she might also have met *them* somewhere before, it occurred to Daisy to ask herself what was keeping all the male guests. Was there an important rugby game on or something?

Raoul emerged from the kitchen arm in arm with Vanessa, who carried off red satin hotpants and a matching boob tube with the easy confidence of the very slim and beautiful.

'OK, *les filles!*' Raoul called out, holding out a saucepan for Vanessa to bang on with a ladle. 'The food's ready. Come on, let's eat!'

Daisy signalled to him to come over and whispered in

his ear, 'Don't you think we should wait a bit longer for the other guests?'

'What other guests? No, no, baby, everybody's here,' Raoul said, grinning. 'All my best buddies, yeah! Come on, everybody – *feeling hot, hot, hot!*' he sang out, pulling her to her feet and leading a stampede of singing girls into the kitchen. Daisy was staggered: so he had invited *no* men *at all*! Raoul really was outrageous!

The girls all climbed, with much giggling and pouting, onto the high diner stools of Raoul's kitchen counter. Dishes began to circulate and they helped themselves. Daisy, who sat next to Raoul, soon found herself deep in conversation about the Paris fashion scene with Patricia, a friendly model perched on her other side. Across from her, Vanessa and Mélodie were discussing beauty treatments. Next to them, Nathalie, Lola and Juanita were talking about yoga retreat holidays. Natacha was telling Raoul about the songs she was recording for her next album. At the other end of the table, Karine and Stéphanie, both dancers, were talking about their present contracts.

'So you like it at the Moulin Rouge?' Karine was asking, delicately sipping her champagne. 'Are they good guys?'

'Yes, I get on with all the dancers,' Stéphanie replied breathily, chewing a small forkful of lasagne. 'A lot of my friends are in the company. But it doesn't really compare to the Crazy. You are so lucky to work there.'

Daisy pricked up her ears. *The Crazy*? Wasn't that the club Raoul had mentioned to her dad at Christmas, the one where they had the live nude show? Then Karine had to be . . .

'*Eh oui*, it's still Froufrou des Jarretelles,' Karine was saying at that very moment in answer to a question from Vanessa. 'It's quite easy to remember and I guess it suits me, right?' she added with a sexy little shimmy. The other girls applauded, and there were a few cries of '*Ay, ay, caramba!*'

So! Karine used to go out with Raoul, Daisy thought with slight annoyance. Really, he might have warned her that one of his exes was coming tonight! Oh well, she told herself, philosophically, he probably thought that it didn't matter. After all, he was with her, Daisy, now, and if he'd kept on good terms with Karine, then good for him. Which was when Patricia said, 'You know, when *I* was with Raoul, he always used to eat chocolate chip cookies in bed. All those crumbs! They got everywhere. He doesn't still do that, I hope.'

'N-no, I don't . . .' Daisy began to say, startled.

'That's nothing!' Juanita said. 'When *I* was with him he had that thing for wearing leather trousers with no underwear!' She turned to wink at Raoul, who smiled back. 'I kept telling him: where's the mystery in that?'

'Well, I don't do that any more!' Raoul said mock-indignantly. 'No way!'

'With me,' Lola said, blowing a ribbon of smoke from her cigarette, 'it was his love affair with crazy golf. We had to go and play *every* weekend.'

'I still like crazy golf,' Raoul admitted. 'We can play in Deauville, baby,' he added, leaning towards Daisy. 'I'll teach you.'

As Vanessa, and then Stéphanie launched into their own

romantic reminiscences, the truth began to dawn on Daisy. All the members of Raoul's 'family' of 'best buddies' were ex-girlfriends, every single one of them.

'OK, Raoul,' Mélodie said, tapping her knife against her glass to get everybody's attention. 'Are you ready for your special cake?'

'You bet!' Raoul said, squeezing Daisy's hand. He turned to her and said, 'This is going to blow your mind. Lola is, like, a total artist.'

Lola, who had been putting the last touches to her creation in the kitchen, turned and slowly walked, beaming, towards the counter, onto which she now deposited a large pink and white concoction surrounded by a glowing circle of candles. Like a chorus of sirens, the guests launched into a melodious rendition of '*Joyeux Anniversaire*' and Raoul blew all his candles out with gusto.

'Bravo, Raoul! *Ouais! Wouh-ouh!* Feeling hot, hot, hot!' everyone shouted, throwing their napkins into the air.

After that Daisy was able to see the cake in all its glory. Its round base was topped with two perfect mounds of snow-white meringue in the shape of breasts, complete with erect pink sugar nipples. She stared at it, lost for words.

'Oh,' she managed. 'It's . . .'

'Lola, honey,' Raoul said solemnly. 'I mean, wow . . . it's really, really extreme. Thank you. I'm touched.'

Champagne glasses were clinked around and across the table.

'*Hé*, Raoul! It's nice to be *entre nous, hein?*' Juanita said. 'Just our little group.'

'You know what it reminds me of?' Stéphanie said, giggling. '*Planète Femme*! It's just like in your story. Like we have completely taken over the world.'

Raoul roared with amusement. '*Allez, les filles*! But of course nobody could resist a gorgeous alien like you, Stéph!'

Wide-eyed, Daisy looked at Stéphanie. *Now* she remembered where she had seen her before. *Planète Femme*! One reason why, perhaps, she had not immediately recognised her as the leader of Raoul's army of sex-crazed alien invaders was that in real life she did not have bright blue skin. Daisy slowly shifted her gaze to Natacha. Yes. Put *her* in an eighteenth-century costume and what did you get? Caroline in *La Flibustière*, of course! As for Nathalie, that was obvious: she was the sultan's bewitching favourite in *La Sultane*. And on and on it went, all the way down to Vanessa, who had, Daisy now realised, inspired Raoul's central character in his most recent oeuvre, the psychedelic sex romp *Alice '69*, and must therefore be the girl who had immediately preceded Daisy in his life. And next in line was . . . herself, of course.

Daisy remained quiet and subdued during coffee and was so lost in thought that she did not notice Raoul's perplexed glances. Afterwards, when some of the guests started dancing and others remained in the kitchen making tequila slammers, Daisy took advantage of the party atmosphere to go into Raoul's bedroom to collect her coat and bag.

'What's going on, sugar?' Raoul said, coming in and closing the door behind him. 'You are not leaving?'

'Yes, I am. I'm very tired.'

'Oh, baby, don't go! My friends all love you. Don't you want to stay and hang out with them?'

'I think your friends are all very nice. But I really have to go.'

'OK, that's cool,' Raoul said easily. 'So what time do you wanna meet tomorrow?'

'Tomorrow?' Daisy asked vaguely.

'To drive to Deauville. Don't you remember?'

'Ah.' Daisy sat down on Raoul's bed and looked up at him. 'Raoul, listen. I know it's your birthday but I don't think I want to go away this weekend after all.'

'No?' Raoul came to sit next to her, looking concerned. 'What is it, Daisy? You had too much champagne? You don't feel so good? Don't worry, baby, lie down and I will give you my special foot massage.'

'No, I'm OK, thanks. It's just that . . .' Daisy stopped. How best to explain what she was feeling? 'Raoul, are all your stories inspired by ex-girlfriends?'

Raoul grinned. 'Yeah, they are, a little bit.'

'I thought so. You know, you might have warned me that all your guests tonight were your exes.'

'Oh, but that's not how I think of them any more. We're all just really good friends.'

'Well, the thing is,' Daisy said, looking at him seriously, 'I think that's what we are too, you and me: just really good friends.'

Raoul seemed surprised. 'Why do you say that?'

'I mean . . . you know your idea for your next album, with me in it as the 1950s nympho cheerleader?'

'Uh-uh.'

'Tell me, with your other girlfriends, what came first, breaking up or putting them in one of your stories?'

Raoul stared at her in silence.

Daisy shook her head slowly. 'Well, either way it means it's over between us, doesn't it?'

'But, baby,' Raoul protested, taking her hand in his, 'you don't understand: I love you.'

Daisy sighed and looked at him affectionately. 'I know you do, Raoul. But the thing is . . . you love *all* women!'

Raoul opened his mouth to protest, then smiled and nodded. 'Well, er . . . yeah, I guess I do.'

Daisy began to laugh. 'I mean, look at you tonight: you're the only man allowed on Planet Woman! I think it's great that you're happy, but . . . the whole thing is . . . not right for me. I'm sorry.'

'OK,' Raoul said after a minute. 'You are sure?'

'I'm really, really sure. And Raoul, about that cheerleader story: just do what you want, OK?' Daisy said, hugging him. 'I don't want to stand in the way of your creative urges.'

Raoul hugged her back and kissed the top of her head. 'You're very sweet. So long, Daisy. Take care now. *Hasta la vista*, baby. See you later, alligator. After a while . . .'

Oh, really, Raoul! Daisy thought, and bit her lip to keep from laughing.

31 Isabelle

At first Isabelle had experienced a sinking feeling when, having gone feverishly through the reams of Meredith's manuscripts, she had found the novels all present and accounted for – except, that is, for *The Splodge*.

Jules wasted no time in telephoning Paul Celadon in her most severe voice. Celadon apologised, dear madam, but assured her that the missing manuscript was not in his possession. The thing had never actually been published, thank goodness. As far as he knew, there had only ever been one copy and a quick look at it had convinced him, at the time, that it simply would not do. He had advised Meredith to put the worthless piece of drivel in the dustbin. Since then, he had put it entirely out of his mind and, sixty-odd years later, he was very much afraid that he couldn't remember anything about it. He apologised again, wished Jules a very good day, dear madam, sent Isabelle his compliments, reiterating that the manuscripts were hers to keep, and that was that.

The next morning Isabelle instinctively rang up Lucy Goussay, who, on hearing that dear Meredith's manuscripts were available for perusal, let out a yelp of delighted excitement and called an emergency meeting of the Society for that very evening. Such enthusiasm was infectious, and Isabelle was much cheered by it. When she later turned up in Hampstead with the manuscripts, carefully packed into her small suitcase on wheels, she was given a heroine's welcome.

'You really have done us proud, Izbl,' Maud said, peering at her over her dark glasses with something like approval.

'Yes, bravo!' Lucy barked. 'Ha, ha! Frightfully plucky of you to stand up to Paul.'

'My friends helped me,' Isabelle said, thinking it best not to go into too much lurid detail about the House of Discipline.

'I'm so glad I invited you to join us on that day you came to the bookshop,' Fern said, giving Isabelle a warm hug. 'I just knew that you were one of us.'

'You have been a tremendous addition to our little group, *Mademoiselle*,' Peter Holland said, twinkling at her.

'Have a fat-free carob biscuit, dear,' Wendy said, proffering a plate of dark brown discs. 'They're a bit overdone, but very slimming. And will you have a cup of nettle tea?'

'Thank you,' Isabelle said, a little embarrassed at all this attention. 'But really it's you who have all been so kind to me.'

She sat down near Meredith's portrait and watched as Wendy and Fern unwrapped the reams of paper with great care, arranging them on the coffee table in a dainty fanlike effect. Each of the members then settled happily with the manuscript of their favourite novel and silence descended, only broken by the occasional appreciative grunt.

As he started leafing through the pages of *Death of a Lady Ventriloquist*, Herbert Merryweather looked up and gave Isabelle a shy, toothy smile. She smiled back. It was nice to feel that she had done the right thing. Agathe's advice, when Isabelle had called her earlier today, had been not to worry about informing Professeur Sureau of the new development. What Isabelle had mentioned regarding sets of horizontal, vertical and diagonal corrections done in blue ink in Meredith's decisive hand and of varying stylistic significance sounded so promising – best to look into it first and surprise Sureau with a real breakthrough! And as usual her dear Agathe had been right: Isabelle was quite happy to share her discovery with her Quince Society friends first.

'So,' Roberta said to her, while carrying on with her knitting, 'are they all here?'

Isabelle shook her head regretfully. 'No. I mean, all the *published* novels are here, but there was something else I was hoping to find. An interesting stylistic experiment that didn't work out. But unfortunately Mr Celadon didn't have it.'

'Bad luck, Izbl!' Lucy said.

'Oh dear, I hope you're not too disappointed?' Fern asked anxiously.

'Well, a little bit,' Isabelle admitted, looking up wistfully at Meredith's portrait and the ink splodge on the desk. 'Unfortunately, I now think that Meredith may have destroyed it. But it is wonderful to have all this,' she added, looking on the bright side, 'because I will be able to work out her creative process – you know, shifting paradigms of concealment and *trompe l'oeil* – the poetics of Cubist story-telling – all of that.'

'Oh, yes!' Fern said, shrinking a little into the sofa. 'That sounds marvellous.'

'It doesn't matter about the other thing,' Isabelle went on resolutely. 'I am beginning to wonder if my instinct was wrong.'

'Maybe so,' Maud agreed, before adding crisply: 'But it's a little early to throw in the towel, isn't it, Izbl? Tell me, have you tried Philip Quince?'

Isabelle shook her head, flushing. Philip Quince was, of course, Meredith's nephew and Tom's father. Trying to contact him was a frightening notion for all kinds of reasons.

'No, not exactly,' she replied after a moment. 'But everyone seems to think that he has absolutely no interest in her writing.'

'That's quite true,' Peter Holland confirmed, looking up from the pages of *Murder in Kid Gloves*. 'Personally I always found Philip Quince to be a very blunt sort of man. No feeling for the arts, no sensibility.'

There was a pause, during which, unnoticed by Isabelle, who was gazing at the portrait, Maud, Fern, Wendy and Lucy all exchanged meaningful glances.

'Yes!' Wendy said tremulously, clasping her hands to her bosom. 'And there is *nothing* in this world more precious than sensibility, is there, dear Izbl?'

Isabelle looked at her, disconcerted. 'Well, perhaps. I . . .'

'What Wendy *means*,' Maud said sharply, 'is that we thought you might *also* like to show the manuscripts to young whatsisname, Philip's son . . .'

'Tom,' Isabelle murmured.

'Ha! Yes, frightfully good!' Lucy chimed in, her blue eyes shining. 'Quite the decent thing to do.'

'And then, you see, you'd even be in a position to ask him to contact his father,' Fern added, playing with the beads on her necklace.

'But it's entirely up to you, Izbl, of course,' Maud said, pouring herself another cup of tea.

Lucy, Maud and Fern gradually returned to their reading while Wendy took a few nervous bites out of a carob biscuit.

Isabelle turned the suggestion over in her mind. The ladies of the Society had a point. Never mind her supervisor – she really ought to let Tom know that she had got hold of the manuscripts. It was true that he had never bothered to read his great-aunt's novels, but he had let her search all over the house.

'Well, I suppose . . .' Isabelle began hesitantly. The four ladies instantly turned expectant faces in her direction. 'Yes, it would be more polite to let him know and . . .' She stopped as a thought occurred to her. 'I should really give them to him. Because they belong to Meredith's family, don't they?'

'Goodness! How wonderful!' Wendy cried joyously.

'Very jolly!' Lucy yelped. 'Quite the thing!'

Isabelle stood up, resolute. 'May I use your phone, Lucy?'

'No need, Izbl. He's on his way,' Maud said, without missing a beat.

Isabelle sat down again abruptly. 'He . . . Who?'

'Why, young Quince, young Quince, of course!' Lucy barked. 'Gave him a bell after I spoke to you. Invited him round. Returning his invitation, after all, you know. Only proper.'

'That's why I did this bit of impromptu baking, you see,' Wendy interjected. 'He gave us such a lovely tea that day.'

Lucy fixed her blue eyes on Isabelle, who sat still, as though entranced.

'Don't mind, do you, Izbl?'

'No, of course not. I'm just . . .'

Maud looked out of the window. 'There's his car now, I shouldn't wonder,' she said, getting up and striding towards the door, eagerly followed by Wendy.

And then, before Isabelle had had time to worry about how she looked or what she should say, Tom came into the room.

'Ha!' Lucy barked as she bounded forwards to greet him. 'Splendid to see you again.'

In the confusion of greetings that ensued, it took Tom a moment or two to make his way to Isabelle, who remained rooted to the spot next to Meredith's portrait. Then all of a sudden he was there, very close, and she was conscious of his light kiss on her cheek. He said something to her, and it was so lovely to hear his voice that she didn't take in a single word. Now it was her turn to speak, but she couldn't think of anything to say – nothing cogent, at any rate. Briskly shepherded by Lucy and Maud, the others left the room, congregating next door to help themselves to more tea and biscuits. Isabelle and Tom were left alone. He laid his hand on her arm and they sat down next to each other.

'Lucy told me the most exciting story on the phone,' he began, smiling at her. 'I think it's just possible that I may have misunderstood her. Tell me, is it true that you climbed over a garden wall in the middle of the night, all in pursuit of Meredith's manuscripts?'

'Yes, it is true,' Isabelle said, sighing with embarrassment. 'I find it hard to believe myself.'

'Oh, *I* don't. I remember what happened in the library at home when you started looking in earnest. I learned that a determined young scholar won't let anything stand in the way of her desires.'

Briefly their eyes met, and Isabelle smiled.

'Well, here they are at last,' Fern said, coming back in and gesturing towards the manuscripts, which Wendy had gathered into a neat bundle. 'Dear Meredith's manuscripts. Isn't it wonderful?'

The other members followed, munching biscuits, and took their places around the room.

Tom raised his cup of nettle tea and said solemnly, 'On behalf of the estate of Meredith Quince, I would like to thank Isabelle Papillon for rescuing my great-aunt's work. And for doing it in such a dramatic manner. I'm certain that Meredith would have appreciated it.'

'Oh, yes!' Emily Merryweather exclaimed, her nose crinkling with excitement. 'It's just the sort of thing Lady Violet might have done. So very dashing and intrepid.'

'Like in *Pink Gin Six Feet Under*,' Tom said, 'when she captures the Russian spy using a big net on top of a moving train?'

'Oooh, yes,' Selina said cosily. 'Exactly.'

'Or in *Murder in Kid Gloves*,' he went on calmly, 'when she runs back into the burning castle in her opera cloak and manages to get all the children out before the whole thing crumbles.'

Isabelle looked at him, astonished. 'But I thought you'd never . . .'

'Yes, yes – and it was really remiss of me. But you'll be pleased to hear that I have started reading them. I think they're excellent.'

There was a happy murmur of approval in the room.

'And may I ask what made you change your mind at last?' Maud asked with a hint of asperity.

'I wanted to know why Isabelle liked them,' Tom said.

Isabelle blushed deliciously and looked down at the floor.

'Ha! Quite so!' Lucy said.

'So that I now feel that I would very much like to have a look at the manuscripts myself, Isabelle,' Tom said.

Isabelle nodded. 'Of course.'

'I wondered,' he went on quickly, looking at her in that unfocused way of his, 'if the best thing might not be for you to bring them to the house. And then you would, of course, be welcome to come over and work on them whenever you wanted. You could have Meredith's desk,' he added, smiling.

'Imagine writing at her *actual* desk!' Herbert Merryweather exclaimed reverently.

'Good heavens! How exciting!' Roberta said, so moved that she actually put her knitting down for a moment.

Indeed it would, Isabelle thought, be rather exciting.

'And you could explain to Tom about the . . . poetics of . . . you know . . . the thing,' Fern said.

'I'd love to hear all about it,' Tom said. 'Of course I could just take them home myself,' he went on. 'But I think *you* should be the one to do it. As a symbolic gesture,' he added, looking up at his great-aunt's portrait.

Isabelle nodded, smiling.

'Shall we go now, right away?' Tom said.

Why not? Isabelle thought. Knowing that the precious manuscripts were safe and sound in their rightful home, she would finally be able to recuperate after her exhausting catsuited expedition.

As they drove off in Tom's car, the manuscripts stowed away in the boot, she could see, in the rear-view mirror, that the entire Quince Society had gathered on Lucy's porch to wave them away. Wendy seemed very moved. That was sweet of her: she must really care about the fate of the manuscripts. Isabelle leaned back in her seat.

'Happy belated New Year, by the way,' Tom said, after they'd been driving for a few minutes.

'Oh yes, Happy New Year to you, too.'

'Did you have a good time in Paris?'

'Yes, thank you. It was lovely,' Isabelle said drowsily.

Tom nodded, staring ahead at the road.

Isabelle yawned. 'Sorry, Tom, but I'm feeling so sleepy.'

Tom reached over and put the radio on. 'Just relax,' he said gently. 'We'll be there very shortly.'

On arrival Tom unpacked the manuscripts while Isabelle sat like a tired child at the kitchen table.

'It's strange,' she said after a while. 'I feel like I've been travelling for a long time.'

'Well, it's the end of your quest,' Tom replied, walking

over to the fridge. 'Would you like a celebratory snack? Those biscuits were a little odd, I thought.'

'Thank you, no,' Isabelle said, laying her head down on her folded arms. 'I'm too tired to eat or drink anything. I should go home.'

'You could stay the night in the guest bedroom, if you like.'

'I didn't know there was a guest bedroom,' Isabelle said, opening one eye.

'Oh, but there is. Come on, I'll show you.'

They walked upstairs together and Tom stopped on the first floor, outside the door to Meredith's room.

'Oh, this room?' Isabelle said, remembering the forlorn storage space she had glimpsed on her first visit. 'Was there actually a bed in there?'

'There is now,' Tom said, opening the door.

Isabelle went in and looked around in amazement. The room had been cleared of all clutter and wallpapered in a beautiful dusty-pink chinoiserie pattern. Tom had brought down Meredith's chest of drawers and small four-poster bed from the attic. They had been polished and now smelled deliciously of beeswax. There were snowy white sheets on the bed and vases filled with masses of parrot tulips on every surface.

'How perfectly beautiful,' Isabelle murmured.

'Well, I had the furniture, so it seemed silly not to use it. Do you like it?'

'I love it, of course,' Isabelle said, swinging around to face him.

'Then it's yours.'

'Mine? How?'

'I do not intend this room to become some sort of shrine to Meredith. I'm quite sure it's not what she would have wanted. But I didn't like to see it deserted and abandoned. Now it's just another comfortable bedroom in the house, and you can stay in it whenever you like.'

'But, Tom, I don't understand. I mean . . . when we said goodbye before Christmas I wasn't even sure . . .'

'That you would ever come back here?' he said, leaning against the door frame. 'Well, I remember reading that sixteenth-century courtiers used to have the prettiest room in their house always ready in case the Queen decided to drop in on a whim.'

Isabelle looked at him, nonplussed.

'I suppose I was thinking along the same lines,' he said.

'Tom, it's lovely,' she said, blushing

'Do you need a toothbrush?'

'Yes, thank you. That would be great.'

'Anything else?'

'No, not really.'

'Wait here. I'll get you a toothbrush and a towel.'

After saying good night to Tom, Isabelle returned to the bedroom and closed the curtains, singing absent-mindedly to herself. She suddenly felt so exhausted that she undressed where she stood, most uncharacteristically letting her clothes fall to the floor in a heap. Climbing between the cool sheets, her skin tingling with fatigue, she breathed in the delicious smell of lavender. Silently, she thanked Tom for thinking of everything. She burrowed into the pillows to make a perfect nest for her face, stretching out her arms and legs.

She reached to extinguish the bedside lamp. For the first time in weeks her body relaxed completely. She slept.

In the morning she was awakened by birdsong. One phrase, possibly the vestige of a dream, was ringing insistently through her mind like a mantra. The phrase was 'a winning hand' and she could still see it written out in relief calligraphy, beneath the crystal-clear image of the playing cards Tom had worn tucked into the band of his hat that first time. She stretched luxuriously. Why was it that she had never liked taking chances? She had avoided risk like the plague all her life. Now, suddenly, she no longer felt frightened of it. Possibly because she had slept so soundly, she experienced none of the usual mental chaos and anxiety that usually accompanied her early mornings. Her head felt light and clear, and it was occupied by one thought and one thought only. That thought was – how wonderful it would be to see Tom right away, to be near him.

She got out of bed, walked to the window and pulled aside a curtain. It looked beautiful outside. The garden was serene in the pale sunlight. Feeling a little cold, she looked around for something to put on. A folded tartan throw had been thoughtfully left on an armchair in case she needed it in the night. She shook it and draped it around her body in vaguely Indian style. It was a bit short, perhaps, but perfectly decent.

It was just possible that Tom was still asleep. She couldn't remember where she'd left her watch and had no idea of the time. It didn't matter. She padded quietly up the stairs to the top floor. His bedroom door was wide open. He wasn't there. She went downstairs to the kitchen. Tom wasn't there either, although there were signs of recent tea drinking and a few biscuit crumbs on the table. Isabelle felt the side of the teapot. It was still warm. Why not have a quick look at the garden? In her intensely clear-headed state, it did not occur to her to go back upstairs to dress. That would have constituted a titanic amount of effort. It didn't look very cold outside. Looking at the row of muddy wellington boots next to the door, she noticed a pair that looked about her size. Why not just slip them on and go out as she was?

She made her way slowly down the garden path, stopping along the way to feel the bark of a tree trunk or rub some leaves between her fingers. There was something magical about how quiet and warm it was in Tom's garden, Isabelle thought. It was like a balmy microclimate, unconnected to the wintriness that reigned elsewhere. She could see the greenhouse a little further away. And here was the shed, which he had recently painted a lovely shade of blue-grey.

The door was half open. Inside, it was very clean and tidy, with scrubbed floors and walls lined with deep wooden shelves filled with gardening-related paraphernalia, which she was at a loss to identify. Mysteriously, there was a subtle but pervasive scent of apples. At the far end, beneath a window, Tom sat at a table with his back to her, seemingly in the process of potting a plant.

'Hello,' Isabelle said, after gazing at him for a moment.

'Oh, hi,' he said, turning around. 'Did you sleep well?'

Isabelle went in and closed the door behind her. 'I haven't slept so well in months. Have you been up long?'

'Not very.' Tom watched her approach, taking in the boots and the draped tartan. He smiled at her. 'You look like you should be on a horse leading an army – a warrior queen. Holding a spear, or perhaps a crossbow. I think this might be the most charming outfit I've ever seen you wear.'

Standing over Tom and looking into his eyes affected Isabelle like a burst of pure oxygen, clearing her head even further. Without a moment's deliberation, she flung off the tartan throw and let it fall on the floor at their feet.

'Actually, you know,' Tom said thoughtfully, removing first his gloves, then his glasses and putting them both down on the table. 'I take it back. This one's even better.'

He drew her down into his lap and kissed her, his hand running lightly over her breasts, her belly, her thighs. Eventually they pulled apart and looked at each other.

'I was so completely, completely stupid,' Isabelle said. 'Forgive me.'

'Not at all. It's perfectly natural to be scared of powerful emotions at first. They take a bit of getting used to.' Holding her round the waist with one hand, he bent down and pulled her boots off with the other. 'Don't get me wrong. I wouldn't want you to think for a moment that this naked-in-wellies look doesn't turn me on. I am, after all, a gardener. But really there's no need to gild the lily for my sake. And you have very pretty feet.'

'I was scared of you,' Isabelle said, kissing every part of his face with slow deliberation. 'It's so silly. Why weren't *you* scared?'

'I didn't have time to be scared.'

They rose together and dropped onto their knees on top of the blanket.

'I blame myself about what happened before,' Tom said, unbuttoning his shirt at breakneck speed and tearing it off. 'I rushed you too much the first time and frightened you away.'

Isabelle pressed herself against his chest. 'Oh, it wasn't your fault.'

'It was foolish of me. We should have taken it more slowly.'

'No, no, I don't think so,' she replied, rapidly unbuckling his belt and unzipping his trousers. 'I was just confused by what I felt,' she explained, deftly freeing and caressing him. 'I realise that now.'

Tom glanced down briefly at what she was doing. Hearing his sharp intake of breath, Isabelle looked up.

'I'm hurting you?'

'*No*. Quite the opposite.' He kissed her hard, his fingers thrust deep in her hair, then said, 'Correct me if I'm wrong, Isabelle, but does this mean that you did *not* get engaged in Paris?'

Isabelle grinned at him.

'Quite the opposite.' She reclined, pulling him down with her.

As they began again with wondrous ease, Isabelle closed her eyes for a moment. In her mind's eye she could see an arrow shooting through a blue sky, a lovely image of flight. She felt that she and Tom were both shooting through the air together. They were the arrow, the arrow's true aim and the graceful arc it traced before hitting, with a satisfying 'tchuck', the heart of the target – concentric circles in bright Technicolor red, yellow and blue. As her thighs rose to caress his sides, she opened her eyes and bit his shoulder delightedly. A moment later, dislodged by the rhythmic vibrations arising from their activity, a small object fell off one of the shelves, bounced off Tom's moving back and rolled onto the floor. He did not notice it at the time and neither did Isabelle.

Later, as Isabelle leaned on one elbow gazing at Tom, who lay sprawled on his stomach in a most alluring attitude, she noticed the small meteorite on the floor and picked it up. It was something roundish, wrapped in a sheet of thin paper.

'Tom, what is that?'

He shifted on to his side and peered at the object in her hand. 'Oh, I thought I'd felt something. It's an apple that must have fallen off one of the trays. Probably an Egremont Russet. I had a real glut of those in the autumn. A fine variety of apple – nutty. Eat it if you like.'

Isabelle carefully removed the apple's paper wrapping. 'You keep your apples in here?'

'Yes, that's what the trays are for – storing them. The paper is for protection.'

'Oh . . . but it's *lovely*.'

'Yes, isn't it? Give me a bite, will you?'

Together they demolished the apple, then Isabelle picked up the crumpled sheet, intending to wrap the core in it. There was something printed on the paper and she automatically ran her eyes over the words.

'Tom?'

'Mmm?'

'What did you use to wrap your apples?'

'Well, I would normally use newspaper but the recycling van had just been, so Rosie wrapped them in some scrap paper that she found.'

'Scrap paper she found where?' Isabelle said, suddenly scrambling up. 'Is there any more of it?'

'Yes. It's on the trays. I think she used all of it. It was quite a harvest we had.'

Isabelle, her head buzzing, looked at the trays stacked all around the shed, lined with dozens and dozens of carefully wrapped apples. She smoothed the sheet of paper she was holding and passed it to Tom.

'What do you think this is?'

He walked naked to the table to retrieve his glasses and perused the piece of paper for a minute.

'Unusual. Some sort of . . . poem?'

'A poem,' Isabelle repeated, her voice shaking. 'Yes, oh yes! Tom, help me: we need to unwrap all the apples.'

32 Daisy and Isabelle

'Good *grief*, petal! Tit cake in Bimbo World! Now that's what I call going *beyond* the call of duty!' Chrissie said with feeling into his mobile phone.

Meeting Jules' blank but nevertheless perplexed stare across the kitchen table, he burst out laughing. 'I'll explain later, Ju-Ju. *Long* story.'

Jules nodded, pushing her glasses to the top of her nose, and went back to her toast. For the next few minutes Chrissie remained uncharacteristically silent, listening intently, then he said, 'Hold on a minute, sweetface. Ju-Ju?'

'Yeah?'

'Do you still have that full-length purple number you bought in Amsterdam?'

'I do as a matter of fact. I haven't worn it for ages.'

'Well,' Chrissie said, grinning, 'the time has come to give it another airing. Because you *and* I, my dear,' he sang out dramatically, 'are stepping out to breathe an atmosphere that simply *shrieks* with class!'

'Chrissie, what are you going on about?'

'In a *nutshell*, darling – and *you too*, darling,' he said into the phone, 'I've just had the most *enthralling* brain-wave. Listen to me, Ju-Ju: we *shall* go to the ball! Aren't you *thrilled*?'

'What ball?'

Chrissie sighed, rolling his eyes. '"What ball?" she asks,' he said into the phone. 'It's only this *lethally* glamorous ball at the Paris *Opera House*! Black tie and everything! *Thousands* of guests! Apparently there'll be a lot of men in *full* uniform! And then *waltzing*! The whole thing will *wreck* you, Jules, simply.'

'Has Daze made friends with the French royals or something?'

'D'you know, I don't *think* they have them any more, darling,' Chrissie said slowly. 'They chopped their heads off, didn't they? No, this is some sort of big *charidee* do . . . What's that, darling?' he said into the phone. 'Ah, OK. Daze says that it's organised by some big, famous *military* college. Hence the scrummy uniforms.'

'And why are *we* going?' Jules asked, impassively munching her toast.

'*Because*,' Chrissie said patiently, 'Daisy was going to go to this ball with Rrraoul – oh *God*, I'll *never* be able to pronounce his name. Those rrrs – just can't do them to save my life. But *anyway* the *point* is, darling, that Rrrr . . . – dammit, you know who I mean – is *no longer* going as Daisy's escort. I'll explain that too. And now Daze is all in a *bother*, wondering whether she should still go, you see. Well, it seems to *me*, darling,' he went on, speaking into the phone, 'that there is a *risibly* simple solution to your quandary. I'm free as a bird, more's the pity, and Kazza won't mind – it's basically a day trip. So we'll *both* come as your escort! Jules and I!'

As Jules sat pondering this announcement, there was

the sound of footsteps on the stairs and Isabelle came into the kitchen hand in hand with Tom.

'Well, hello,' Jules said with a slight smile.

Chrissie gasped audibly and half turned away. 'Daze, *listen*,' he stage-whispered into the phone, 'I'm going to *have* to call you back. Something *pant-droppingly* incredible's just happened, which I *have* to experience *one hundred per cent* in the *moment*. But *listen*, sort us out for tickets, OK? Speak later. Love you loads!'

He put his phone down and ran round the table to embrace Tom and Isabelle.

'My darlings, my *darlings*!' He air-kissed them both. 'Isabelle, darling, you look like the *cat* that got the *cream* . . . And as for *you*, dear, *well* . . . Now listen to this: Jules and I are going to a *fabulous* ball at the Paris Opera House with Daisy in a couple of weeks. Isn't it amazing?'

'Oh yes,' Isabelle said. 'Actually, we are also going!'

A few days ago Agathe had called and mentioned the ball in passing, implying that, of course, Isabelle would not be coming, to spare poor Clothaire's feelings. Somewhat to her own surprise, Isabelle had found herself disagreeing with her friend.

'For one thing,' she had said to an astonished Agathe, 'I have to be in Paris around that time for a meeting with Professeur Sureau. And for another, never mind Clothaire. I love going to the ball. I look forward to it all year and I am going.'

'Isn't that rather selfish?' Agathe had asked huffily.

Of course her dear Agathe was baffled: she did not know about Clothaire's infidelity or indeed about Marie-Laure's possible involvement with him. Isabelle always favoured discretion in such matters, and she had not wanted to bring any of it up. Anyway, none of it really mattered now that she and Tom had found each other again.

'I'm bringing Tom as my escort,' Isabelle went on happily. 'Then he can meet all of you.'

Now when she pictured herself at the ball it was in Tom's arms, and that felt like the most natural thing in the world.

And so, three weeks later, after whizzing under the Channel on the Eurostar, Isabelle, Tom, Jules and Chrissie all found themselves standing outside the Gare du Nord at noon on a beautiful sunny day.

'We'll see you tonight at six o'clock for drinks, OK?' Isabelle said. 'And then we'll go on to the opera.'

'Right you are, sweetie,' Chrissie said from behind enormous aviator sunglasses. 'Come along, Jules dear. There's some *fiercely* important shopping to be done. We'd better hurry *tout de suite*: we're meeting Daisy at Anouk's place in an hour. Now *where* does one get a taxi around here?'

'Where it says "Taxis", dummy,' Jules said tonelessly. 'You can't see for toffee in those things, can you? Plus they make you look like something out of *The Fly*.'

'They do *not*! They make me look the very height of *le fachonne*. Isabelle?'

'*Très chic*,' Isabelle agreed, laughing.

While Jules and Chrissie headed for their hotel, she and Tom went to her flat, which Daisy had kindly vacated for the night, going to stay with Anouk. Isabelle reflected, as they rode in a taxi through the sunny streets towards the Rue de la Harpe, that she was really looking forward to meeting Daisy at long last. She had a lot to thank her for.

Once at the flat, while Tom showered, she opened her suitcase and pulled out her ball gown and the blue folder containing *The Splodge*, whose pages she and Tom had painstakingly ironed one by one. She hung up the former, shaking out its creases, and laid the latter on her desk in readiness for her meeting with Professeur Sureau on Monday morning. Her supervisor had seen all her chapters to date and wanted to give her some feedback. Little did he suspect that she was bringing him this latest and most dazzling discovery! On hearing that she had at last found *The Splodge*, Agathe had congratulated her and even come around to the idea of Isabelle bringing Tom to the ball as a fitting way to celebrate.

Already a new direction for her thesis was shaping up in Isabelle's mind: something along the lines of 'Suppressed Sensuous Stirrings: Seeking *The Splodge*', perhaps, or how about 'Thoroughly Modernist Meredith: The Reinvention of Love Poetry'?

Though quite different from what Isabelle had imagined, *The Splodge* had turned out to be just as much of a revelation as she had hoped. A long and beautiful poem written in free verse, it told the story of a passionate love affair, and so confessional and enraptured was its tone that it was hard not to conclude that it related to something in Meredith's private life.

'You're quite right,' Tom had said, coming out of his house to join Isabelle in the garden, after getting off the phone with his father. 'I had to push him, but Dad eventually admitted very grudgingly that Meredith had had some sort of "free love" episode in her late teens with somebody he described as "unsuitable" – an artist. The family was horrified and put a stop to it, and the man married somebody else soon afterwards.'

'Poor Meredith,' Isabelle murmured, her eyes full of tears. She remembered the poem's closing lines:

> *Walking through forests dark*
> *Her moon-white gown of silk trailing black ink*
> *In which she wrote of you*
> *On the rim of the sky*
> *And half-unheard the jangling bell*
> *Calls farewell, farewell*
> *Farewell*

'Yes. I imagine that's why she never married,' Tom had said, sitting down next to her on the bench and enfolding her in a warm embrace. 'Instead she invented a brilliant, plucky character, also unmarried, who got to have all kinds of daring adventures.'

Isabelle nodded pensively. Meredith *had* gone on to create some wonderful books, but how she must have mourned her lost love!

'So . . .' Tom had said after a short silence, 'you have a job lined up in Paris.'

'Yes, I do,' she had replied, looking towards the orchard.

Then, after another pause, she added: 'I understand that you have some quite respectable universities here, in England.'

'Quite respectable, yes.'

'Perhaps I could . . .' She had let the sentence trail off and turned to him, smiling.

Tom had looked into her eyes, then said slowly, 'It must be rather nice, don't you think, to be married to the one you love?'

'I can't think of anything nicer,' she had replied, lifting her face to his.

In her Paris flat Isabelle stood stock-still for a moment, smiling at the memory, then she went back into the bedroom and returned to her open suitcase, intending to unpack methodically in her usual way. As she straightened up, holding a pile of neatly folded clothes, she suddenly felt Tom's arms encircling her waist.

'Come to bed,' he said, his lips caressing the back of her neck.

Isabelle dropped the clothes and turned around to face him. He was smiling, his hair and eyelashes still wet from the shower. Her eyes travelled down to the smooth, hard planes of his stomach, his hips and . . . Oh, resistance was futile. She sighed and walked into his embrace.

'But I'm not sure that we have time,' she said, rubbing her face against his chest. 'Not if you want to see a few sights before tonight.'

He laughed, his fingertips sliding tantalisingly between the buttons of her shirt, and whispered something in her ear that made her blood beat much faster.

'It's just that I . . . prepared a very interesting itinerary,' she protested, her voice waxing a little thicker.

'Oh, so have I,' he replied, holding her wrists behind her back and pulling her closer.

Next door the phone rang shrilly.

'*Merde*,' Isabelle groaned.

'Let it ring,' Tom said, his hand closing over her breast.

After a few rings, the answering machine clicked into action and Isabelle jumped to hear Professeur Sureau's voice: 'Good afternoon, *Mademoiselle*. Sureau here. I'm calling to cancel Monday's meeting. Certain information has come to my attention regarding your research and I need to consider it carefully before we speak again. I will call you back when the situation is clearer. Goodbye.'

Her heart pounding, Isabelle ran to pick up the receiver. Too late: Sureau had already hung up. She immediately tried his office at the Faculty, but the phone just rang and rang.

'What do you think?' Anouk asked, smiling. 'I could see you in it as soon as it came in. It's so fabulously feminine, but also radical.'

When Daisy had turned up at her stylish, minimalist flat, Anouk, who had a strong sense of the theatrical, asked her to close her eyes and led her wordlessly into the living room. When Daisy opened them again, she saw that the room was plunged in darkness, apart from the light created by a single industrial spotlight. This threw a star-white glow over the evening gown Anouk had placed on one of the tubular steel dummies from her shop. Daisy gave a small gasp of wonder and slowly walked around the dress, taking in the strapless boned bodice, the half-exposed mini-crinoline, the cascade of fabric that finished in a floor-length train at the back. She reached out to touch it. It was made of organza dyed a heavenly shade of dirty pink and irregularly adorned with silk roses in different, subtly darker pinks.

'It's by this fantastic young French designer I discovered,' Anouk said, pleased with Daisy's reaction. 'He really has a vision. You know, he didn't want the silk flowers to look too perfect, so he took them out into the street and trampled them before sewing them on,' she went on, clasping her hands in rapture. 'He says what he does is anti-couture couture. *Ah, quel talent*! This is just a sample, but I have decided to sponsor his collection. I think he will go far.'

'It's just beautiful,' Daisy said. 'May I . . .'

'Try it on? Of course, *mon petit*,' Anouk said, swiftly taking the dress off the dummy and handing it to Daisy. 'Go to my room – there is a big mirror there. I will bring you a few pairs of shoes as well.'

A few minutes later Anouk, who had been helping her into a pair of delicate silver stilettos, straightened up to take in the full effect.

'*Ah oui, magnifique*,' she said, hugging Daisy. 'The belle of the ball.'

Daisy stood gazing at her reflection, her delight faintly tinged with melancholy.

'And your hair, you wear it up, yes?' Anouk said. 'But you leave it a bit messy, a bit rock 'n' roll. I will do it for you if you like.' Turning away from Daisy to look for hairpins, she added: 'You know, *mon petit*, it's quite OK to go to a party without a boyfriend. I'm sure that you will have a great time with your London friends.'

'Oh, yes!' Daisy said, more brightly than she felt. 'Of course.'

'Have you spoken to Raoul recently?'

'Actually, he did this really sweet thing,' Daisy went on, a smile spreading on her face. 'He dropped off this folder full of drawings he'd done of me. Just left it outside my door as a surprise.'

On opening the folder, which bore the title *The Ballad of Daisy K.*, Daisy had found a series of very pretty 1950s-style pastel cartoons. A stylised evocation of her time in Paris, they showed her sitting outside a café reading a copy of *Vogue*, walking down the street with a tiny poodle on a leash, coming out of the Dior boutique followed by Raoul (thinly disguised as a bellboy) laden with a teetering pile of beribboned boxes. In the last one she stood on tiptoe on top of the Eiffel Tower, arms outstretched like a ballerina.

'Raoul, I think they're fantastic,' she'd said, calling to thank him later that morning. 'I really like all the outfits – very Bardot. But what will your publisher say?'

'Whaddaya mean, sugar?'

'What happened to shagging Elvis?'

Laughing, Raoul had explained that he had changed his mind about that, adding that, in any case, the drawings were not for publication but for her to keep, as a souvenir.

'Ah, *un vrai* gentleman,' Anouk said, nodding.

'Well, I don't know about *that*. You haven't heard the

best bit. So *then* he said, all tender and moody –' Daisy grinned and put on a sexy Gallic growl '– "Ah, I'm gonna need to go to the end of the earth to forget you, baby." And *then* he tells me that he's off to Brazil for a couple of months by the sea! Can you believe it? The rogue! Somehow I don't think he'll have any trouble forgetting me when he's there.'

Anouk giggled indulgently, putting the last diamanté hairgrip in. '*Voilà*! What do you think?'

Daisy smiled at her in the mirror. 'It's *really* lovely. Thanks, Anouk.'

Turning this way and that to make her organza train rustle glamorously, Daisy reflected that it was silly, really, to call any party a ball. The trouble with a ball was that it sounded like something out of a fairy tale. And it was all nonsense, because life was not really like that. And a party, even if it were huge and smart and set in a big gold-and-marble palace-type building, was still basically a party. She had been to *a lot* of parties and she could totally handle herself at this one. Especially with Jules and Chrissie by her side. So there.

'I don't understand,' Isabelle said for the hundredth time to no one in particular. 'What information about my research? It sounds really bad!'

'It's probably just to do with admin,' Jules said. 'Maybe there's a form you forgot to fill in?'

There had, it was true, been many complicated forms to fill in over the last couple of years, Isabelle thought. Had she made some terrible mistake somewhere? But where? Had she unwittingly committed some sort of perjury?

'And now it's Friday night and I will not be able to get hold of him before Monday. It's just terrible,' Isabelle said, her head in her hands.

'*Please* cheer up, darling,' Chrissie said kindly. 'Hey, I *know*: why don't you get *changed*, hmm? You'll feel *so* much better in your lovely frock!'

Isabelle looked unseeingly at her dress, then back at her friends, both resplendent in their evening finery. 'I feel so anxious,' she said eventually. 'I would not be good company. But you should go. Daisy is expecting you.'

'Oh, wait till you see *her* dress, darling! She had it on when we arrived at Anouk's. It's just *glorious*. You will *expire!*'

'She won't mind if we're a bit late,' Jules added more calmly. 'I'll give her a call.'

Isabelle looked across at Tom, who stood leaning against her desk, clad in the jeans and polo neck he'd travelled in and holding a cup of tea.

'I understand how you feel, Isabelle,' he said, 'but I think Chrissie's right.'

'*Do* you, your Quincitude? Thank you *ever* so!'

'Not at all,' Tom said, giving Chrissie a quick smile before returning his attention to Isabelle. 'You're quite sure that we can't reach your supervisor before Monday?'

'Yes, unfortunately.'

'Then I would say that getting dressed up and going out is the thing to do. You'll enjoy seeing your friends again.'

It would, of course, be lovely to see Agathe, Claire,

Amélie, Octave and the rest of the gang, Isabelle thought wistfully. And, of course, Marie-Laure too, in spite of that lingering suspicion. Oh, but did she really care about all this now?

'Oh, I don't know,' she said in a small voice. 'Clothaire will probably be there, so . . .'

'No, no, no, no, *no*, darling!' Chrissie said, energetically wagging a finger. 'The Clot-of-Hair is no longer *allowed* to stop you from having fun. That was *then*, remember. *This*,' he went on, pointing dramatically at Tom, 'is *now*!'

Isabelle smiled at Tom, who smiled back and said quietly, 'Though, of course, if you'd really prefer to stay, you know I'll do my best to keep you amused.'

'Oh come *on*, darling,' Chrissie said, stamping his feet. '*Seize* the flipping day! *Seize* it! For me!'

'Look,' Jules said, crossing her legs and revealing the sturdy Doc Martens boots that had hitherto been concealed by her velvet gown, 'you've been away from home a long time. You need to show that you're back in town. It's a territorial thing – like a cat. Clothaire doesn't own Paris, does he?'

'N-no,' Isabelle admitted.

'And how long have you been going to this do?'

'For the last three years, but it was always . . .'

'With all your friends, I know,' Jules completed with unusual warmth. She squared her shoulders. 'Well, this year you're going with us. We're your friends too. All right?'

Isabelle was beginning to feel better. 'All right.'

'I'll do your hair and make-up for you, sweetie!' Chrissie

said, taking Isabelle's hands in his. 'Trust me, I will *excel* myself!'

Isabelle could not help smiling. 'As long as you don't make me look like Savage's models.'

According to the press release, the make-up for the February show was 'natural, but also conceptual', which did not quite capture the profoundly disconcerting effect of the glossy red-and-white horizontal stripes that had been painted over the girls' faces as they paraded in the designer's fantastical creations: a corset and oversized puff-ball skirt covered in tiny squares of mirror; a house-shaped dress with holes for one arm and one leg only; and, walking the line between the sublime and the ridiculous, an inflatable egg-shaped dress out of which the model's striped face looked out, defiantly glamorous.

'All right, all right,' Chrissie admitted as Isabelle raised her eyebrows sardonically, 'I won't do anything *quite* so radical, and I *promise* that you will look *fabulous*.'

'ONE LAST DAB OF ROUGE AND WE'LL BE ON OUR WAY,' Daisy read on the screen of her mobile phone. Well, today would be nice, she thought, heaving a small sigh. It was typical of Chrissie to be late for everything, even an event where he was supposed to be her escort, or half of it, anyway. The evening had not started well. First the London gang had kept her waiting for half an hour in a bar off the Place de l'Opéra, then Jules had called, arranging to meet inside the venue instead. Outside the Opera House, as Sod's Law would have it, Daisy had run into the last person she wanted to see: Clothaire, wearing a smart dark overcoat over his dinner jacket.

'*Bonsoir*, Daisy,' he had said coolly, performing his usual trick of letting her kiss his cheek without actually touching her face with his own lips in return. After a moment of awkward silence during which she looked around in vain for another familiar face, Clothaire had eventually glanced at his watch and, putting out his cigarette, said irritably, 'Look, I do not want to go in on my own. It looks stupid. Shall we go together?'

Charming as ever, Daisy thought.

'Oh, I would be *honoured*!' she replied sarcastically, taking his arm. So that they had made their entrance into the Opera House together in the midst of a chattering crowd of French people in evening dress, and ascended side by side to the top of the monumental *grand escalier d'honneur* between two rows of solemn Republican guards in uniform.

Seeing Clothaire had automatically reminded Daisy of Etienne – with a bit of a pang, for her meetings with her intellectual friend had now come to an end. They had petered out over the last few weeks until the other day, when Etienne had announced that he had all the material he needed. Daisy had been surprised and not a little disappointed. She had really enjoyed their talks. Etienne had thanked her courteously for all her help and bought her a lovely lunch before saying goodbye. And that had been that. As far as she knew, he was now in the process of writing the thing up. Perhaps she would see it one day in a bookshop and be reminded that she had played a part in bringing it into being.

After everybody had gone into the auditorium to watch the ballet that was part of the evening's entertainment, Daisy remained outside, leaning on the enormous banister overlooking the staircase to await the arrival of her friends. Looking around, she had to admit that the place was stunning – a riot of red velvet, crystal and marble. But she probably would have enjoyed it quite a lot more if she hadn't felt so forlorn and out of things.

'*Ça va*, Daisy?' a small voice asked shyly. It was Claire's sister Amélie, who added: 'You are looking a bit sad.'

'No, no, I'm fine,' Daisy said, smiling brightly at her little friend before hugging her. 'Hi! Are you here with all the others?'

'With Claire and Agathe. Have you seen Isabelle yet? With her new English boyfriend?'

'No, not yet. What do you think he's like?'

'I don't know. Nicer than Clothaire, I hope!'

Daisy smiled knowingly, rolling her eyes. Earlier in the day, over a quick cup of tea at Anouk's, Chrissie had described Isabelle's new flame as 'a scrumptious hunk of loveliness'. As for Jules, she had merely said expressionlessly that he was 'all right', which, given her systematic tendency to understatement, amounted to the same sort of accolade. Daisy sighed deeply. Isabelle was lucky to be in love with her scrumptious hunk of loveliness. Daisy wished them both well, of course, but all the same it did seem just a bit unfair that nobody appeared to want to love *her*.

'Oh, but you *are* sad!' Amélie exclaimed, looking worriedly at Daisy's face. 'What is wrong?'

'I don't know,' Daisy said, bursting into tears. 'Oh, Amélie, I'm sorry.'

'No, no. Come on, let's sit down.'

'It's just . . .' Daisy said, then stopped to blow her nose in the handkerchief Amélie had produced from a small reticule. 'Oh, I don't know. Sometimes I wonder what's wrong with me.'

'But nothing is wrong with you, Daisy. You are really nice.'

'I *know* I'm being silly,' Daisy went on, wiping off fresh tears, 'but after a while it drives you mad to feel that boys never take you seriously. Nobody ever does, you see –' she looked into a mirror opposite their banquette and caught sight of herself in her vaporous dress '– because they think I'm just . . . a bit of fluff. I *know* they do. And maybe I *am*. Oh, never mind.'

'You just haven't met the right person, that is all. But you will, I am sure of it.'

'I just feel like it's all gone a bit . . . flat, you know? Coming to Paris was such a big thing for me, and I got *so* excited about it,' Daisy continued, shaking her head ruefully. 'And, for a while, it did feel like my life was really changing. I even thought . . . I might actually want to live here. But now the year's almost over and I haven't done anything with my time here apart from write a pointless blog for *Sparkle*.'

'Daisy, that is not true,' Amélie said seriously. 'You have really helped me, for example. You know, you are much more my sister than Claire ever has been.'

It was Amélie's first ball and she looked adorable in a

white-and-gold vintage prom dress they had found together on an expedition to the Puces de Clignancourt.

'And the year is not over yet,' Amélie continued, slipping her arm through Daisy's. 'You have the whole summer left. Why don't you come with us to the Ile de Ré? Everybody will be there.'

'Well, maybe,' Daisy said, smiling. 'Come on, I need a bit of fresh air. I think I look a bit . . . blotchy.'

As they approached the nearest set of tall, gleaming French windows, Daisy could see the outlines of a man and a woman standing on the monumental balcony, looking out at the city lights. Champagne glass in hand, they were laughing together and looked the epitome of glamour. The man had his arm around the woman's waist. Daisy sighed – yet another happy couple! She was really beginning to feel like a prize gooseberry! Then the woman's voice rose, clear and confident, and Daisy and Amélie stopped in their tracks.

'Do not worry,' the woman was saying. 'Isabelle is no match for me. She never was. I thought we always agreed about that.'

'Of course,' the man replied. 'But how can you be sure that it will work?'

Daisy and Amélie looked at each other: it was Agathe and Clothaire!

'Isabelle will never *dare* stand up to me,' Agathe went on dismissively. 'She is nothing but a little mouse.'

'I don't know,' Clothaire said uneasily, 'she's changed. She's become quite assertive.'

Agathe laughed. 'We shall see. Surely you agree that it would be a waste for somebody like Isabelle to get the lecturing job at the Sorbonne? I would obviously be much better at it. She might have stumbled upon something interesting by accident, but I am the one who can turn it into a really brilliant piece of work. No, no, Clothaire, Isabelle belongs in a little job in a little provincial school. I think that will suit her much better. And believe me, once I have had my chat with Professeur Sureau tomorrow morning, it will be over for her.'

'But are you ready for Sureau?' Clothaire asked, sounding nervous. 'He is pretty shrewd, you know.'

'Well, he can cross-examine me as much as he likes. I know everything there is to know about Meredith Quince. Remember, I have all of Isabelle's files.'

'Even the preliminary research?'

'Oh yes! I got hold of that as soon as she left for England. Daisy almost caught me that day in the flat, but she did not suspect anything. She is not exactly a bright spark, is she?'

Clothaire gave a short scornful laugh. At this Amélie made a dash forwards, but Daisy held her back.

'Go back to your sister,' she whispered. 'I'll deal with this.'

Amélie hesitated for a moment, then obeyed.

'And as you know, I had no trouble helping myself at regular intervals after that,' Agathe went on complacently. 'Isabelle likes to email her work to herself for safekeeping. Well, it wasn't safe from me – I know her password. And now all I need is the manuscript of *The Splodge*. As soon as she arrives I will slip away and get it from her flat. *That* should convince Sureau, I think.' She threw her arms around Clothaire.

They kissed.

'But her friends in London?' Clothaire said after a moment's silence. 'They might be able to back her up.'

Agathe sneered. 'Oh please, Clothaire. A bunch of senile eccentrics and a *gardener*? Do you really think Sureau would take their evidence seriously? Relax, Clothaire. I promise you: nothing can go wrong.'

Daisy took a step forward.

'Oh yes, it can!' she cried, trembling with shock and anger. 'And I promise you that it will.'

'Hello, Daisy,' Agathe said, unruffled. 'What a very . . . *unusual* dress! How long have you . . . ?'

'Long enough. I know what you're up to. Agathe, how could you? You're supposed to be Isabelle's friend! And *you*!' she went on, turning to look at Clothaire, who shrank a little from her glare. 'You really are the lowest of the low!'

'Do not speak to me like that,' he spat back. 'This is nothing to do with you.'

'*I* will be the judge of that, thank you very much,' Daisy said, standing her ground.

'Clothaire, let me speak to Daisy alone,' Agathe said calmly, gesturing him away. 'I think it is better if I explain myself to her.'

Clothaire slunk off, glowering.

'All right, then. Explain away,' Daisy said.

'Yes, of course. Come with me, we will walk a little. It will be easier for me to find the words.'

Daisy, struggling to keep her emotions in check, followed her back inside.

Looking entirely self-possessed in her elegant black dress,

Agathe looked to right and left, then said, 'Shall we have a drink at the bar, Daisy?'

'I'm not in the mood,' Daisy said shortly. 'Let's just have your explanation.'

'I know what you are thinking,' Agathe said softly, fixing her clear eyes on Daisy's. 'That I am a . . . bitch, yes? And I can understand that. But it is not as it seems. You do not know everything.' So saying, she began to walk off again slowly and Daisy fell into step with her. 'You have never met Isabelle, I think?'

'Well, no,' Daisy admitted. 'But . . .'

'Oh, I am sure that your English friends told you that she is great,' Agathe said, smiling a little.

'Yes, they have, actually!' Daisy snapped back.

They walked through one, then another dazzling salon adorned with gilt mouldings, antique mirrors and crystal chandeliers. The ballet had finished and the guests were gradually coming out of the auditorium, looking for a pre-dinner drink. Daisy could hear an orchestra downstairs playing an annoyingly romantic waltz.

'Daisy, you must understand that Isabelle has a lot of charm. She can be very persuasive.'

'Really? But didn't I hear you say that she was nothing but a little mouse?'

'Well,' Agathe continued, as they made their way through the growing crowd of revellers into yet another magnificent salon, 'I meant that she can make herself appear more interesting than she really is.'

Daisy looked back over her shoulder, wondering whether Chrissie and Jules might have arrived with Isabelle. But she could always catch up with them later. This was important.

'You think badly of me, don't you?' Agathe said, looking shamefaced. 'I admit that Clothaire and I have been having an affair for a long time. I know it was wrong, but I could not help myself!'

'Oh, really?'

'You see, I love him,' Agathe said seriously. 'And I believe we belong together.'

Daisy pondered this. She knew very well how difficult it was to fight romantic impulses. But she musn't let Agathe get to her.

'But you're planning to disgrace Isabelle and ruin her career!' she parried. 'Or couldn't you help that, either?'

Agathe stopped before another set of enormous doors, which were closed. She glanced around and pushed them experimentally. They opened.

'Let us go in here, it will be more quiet,' she said.

'Isabelle's work is *hers*,' Daisy went on earnestly, following her inside. 'You *can't* say it's yours instead. It's like stealing another designer's collection.'

'Ah, Daisy, always thinking of fashion,' Agathe said, smiling at her. 'You see, Professeur Sureau was always talking about how brilliant Isabelle is – it drove me mad. Because actually, Daisy, how do you know that I did not give Isabelle the idea for her thesis in the first place?'

Daisy was silenced. Because, of course, Agathe was right – she did not know this for sure. They were now standing in an empty, less ornate room. The noise from the ball seemed much further away.

'Have you been to the Opera House before, Daisy?' Agathe asked conversationally. Daisy shook her head. 'It really is a remarkable building. Did you know that the ballet school used to be up there, in the rooms under the roof?' she went on, pointing at the ceiling. 'There used to be all these *petits rats*, the little girls training to become ballerinas, in their pink tutus. It was very charming.'

'Agathe, tell me the truth,' Daisy said, a little shaken. '*Did* you give Isabelle the idea for her thesis? Yes or no?'

'Well, we used to talk about Meredith Quince, certainly,' Agathe said, looking down and biting her lip. 'I'm trying to remember exactly how much I said to Isabelle, but, you know, when I read her chapters it all seemed really familiar. So I began to wonder about it, and then it did not seem right that she should get all the credit. What do you think, Daisy?'

'I don't know,' Daisy said, frowning.

'You see?' Agathe said, with a little shrug.

Daisy looked at her, uncertainty dawning. Perhaps she *had* misjudged the situation, and yet . . .

'But why don't you confront Isabelle directly? It seems really mean to go to her supervisor behind her back.'

'As I have said, you do not know what Isabelle is like. You are going to laugh at me but . . . I was afraid.'

'You, afraid?'

'Well, yes,' Agathe said, smiling at Daisy with disarming self-deprecation.

They had now drifted across the empty room and were standing near another, more modest-looking door. Agathe stopped and said conspiratorially, 'You know, Daisy, I think this might be the way upstairs to where the ballet school was. I have always wanted to see those rooms. I'm sure it's not really allowed, but shall we try to find them? Will you come with me? Please?'

'I really don't have time for this,' Daisy said, opening her bag to check her mobile. 'I bet Chrissie and the others have arrived.'

'Oh, come on, this will only take a minute,' Agathe said, putting a hand on Daisy's arm. She took a deep breath and added, 'And then we will go and talk to Isabelle together. I promise!'

Daisy stared at Agathe. Did she really mean this?

'Well, that would be the right thing to do,' she agreed, automatically closing her bag again.

'Thank you! You have changed my mind,' Agathe said, laughing a little and squeezing Daisy's arm. 'I am sure I will be braver if you are with me.'

She opened the door and they stepped out onto the landing of a narrow wooden staircase. Agathe found a light switch, and then, lifting the hem of her dress, began to walk up. She beckoned to Daisy to follow.

'This is exciting, isn't it?' Agathe said with a giggle. They arrived at the top floor. 'Now let me see. This way, I think,' she said, finding another switch and leading Daisy down a corridor. They walked past several sets of French doors beyond which lay mysterious darkened rooms.

'Are these the rooms you meant?' Daisy asked, stopping to peer through the panes. She tried a door: it was locked. 'I don't think we'll be able to see very much. Perhaps we should go back.'

'Yes, perhaps,' Agathe said vaguely. But she kept on walking and Daisy followed her until they got to a steel door bearing a large red sign that read: DANGER − ACCES INTERDIT.

Agathe clasped her hands in excitement. 'Oh, Daisy, look! I believe this is the door to the roof. Can you imagine how beautiful the view must be from there?'

'But the sign says . . .' Daisy began.

'Oh, do not be such a coward,' Agathe said, laughing lightly. 'Look, the key is in the lock.'

She unlocked the door and Daisy felt a gust of fresh night air on her face.

Agathe stuck her head out and gasped, 'Oh! It looks incredible! We are so close to those wonderful statues. We will never get such a chance again.' She turned around and caught hold of Daisy's arm. 'Come on,' she said.

'Well, OK,' Daisy said reluctantly. 'Just a quick look.'

As she stepped outside, Agathe stepped back, snatching Daisy's clutch bag from her hand and throwing it down on the corridor floor. 'You will not need this,' she hissed, as Daisy stared at her in amazement. 'And now, if you will excuse me, Daisy,' she went on, kicking the clutch out of reach, 'I have something important to do. There is a manuscript in Isabelle's flat with my name on it, and I don't want you interfering, OK?' Upon which she gave Daisy an almighty shove, pushing her further out on to the roof. Daisy instinctively fought back, grabbing hold of Agathe's hair and pulling hard.

'*Aïe!*' Agathe yowled. 'Let go!'

For a moment they struggled desperately at the

threshold, panting and shrieking, then Daisy felt one of her stiletto heels give way, breaking with a snap. She stumbled back onto the roof, her arms flailing.

'*Et voilà!*' Agathe yelled triumphantly, slamming the door shut and turning the key in the lock. After getting her balance back, Daisy threw herself against the door and banged on it furiously. But it was no use. Agathe had gone.

Amélie was getting worried. She had looked everywhere for Daisy, in vain. Where had her friend disappeared to? She had just seen Agathe walk past, but had not dared approach her. Agathe had never taken her seriously and would just dismiss her like a child. Who could she possibly turn to?

At first Daisy had been brave, even laughing at her own foolishness. How could she have been so silly as to let Agathe lock her out like that? Her French 'friend' had not been far wrong when she had said that Daisy was not exactly a bright spark. In fact that had to be the understatement of the century!

Then, while waiting for Agathe to come back – surely she *would* come back? – Daisy had tortured herself by replaying the film of her Paris life and dwelling on every instance of her own cluelessness. But at the end of the day, she told herself miserably, what had happened to her – two failed romances, a wholly imaginary friendship with Agathe, and, at this very moment, the fact that she was shivering with cold in a torn, crumpled dress and laddered tights – all that was very small beer indeed. No, what was truly terrible was that by letting Agathe get her out of the way like this, she had ruined poor Isabelle's career for her. Even now Agathe was probably getting her mitts on the manuscript that Isabelle had brought back from London, and tomorrow she would give Professeur Sureau a performance just as sleek and convincing as the one that had got Daisy onto this blasted and very, very cold roof. Meanwhile poor Isabelle must be innocently enjoying herself downstairs, never dreaming that Agathe was lying in wait for her with a fully rigged guillotine, or something to that effect.

Huddling against a cupola, Daisy looked up at the swimming stars and began to weep.

Unsure what to do, Amélie gravitated back towards her sister, who was talking on her mobile phone.

'It's Octave,' Claire whispered to her. 'They'll be here in a minute.'

On impulse Amélie held out her hand. 'I would like to speak to him.'

'OK,' Claire said, perplexed. 'Octave, Amélie wants a word with you. But hurry up,' she added, handing her younger sister the phone. 'I thought you wanted to see the quadrille?'

'Yes, yes, I will see you there.'

'As you wish,' Claire sniffed irritably, before walking away in a rustle of pale-grey chiffon.

'*Allo, Octave?*' Amélie said, as soon as Claire had left.

'*Allo, petite Amélie,*' Octave said kindly. 'So, you are having fun?'

'No, not really! Listen, I need some help. I can't find Daisy anywhere. I am worried that something has happened to her.'

'Don't worry,' Octave said airily. 'Daisy probably made a new conquest at the ball, that is all.'

'Please listen to me, Octave!' Amélie said, close to tears. 'Agathe and Clothaire are up to something. You must warn Isabelle! Tell her to hide the manuscript she brought back from London, because Agathe wants to steal it!'

'Agathe wants to steal . . . what?' Octave adopted a more serious tone. 'Calm down, Amélie, and start again from the beginning.'

Briefly, Amélie recounted the conversation that she and Daisy had overheard.

Octave listened attentively, then said, 'I understand. Don't worry. Marie and I are very near Isabelle's flat now. Bertrand and Stan are with us, and also Gaspard and some of his *cataphile* friends. That's a lot of scooters. We'll pick up Isabelle and her friends and we'll meet you at the entrance in fifteen minutes. Meanwhile, you keep an eye on Agathe and Clothaire, OK?'

'Ah, *chers amis*, here you are at last!' Octave exclaimed half an hour later in his most urbane and charming voice. '*Bonsoir!*'

Agathe and Clothaire had been standing together watching men in uniforms and girls in red-and-black gowns twirl their way through a quadrille of military precision. They turned around to find themselves greeted by Octave, Marie-Laure, Amélie and Stanislas.

'*Ah, bonsoir,*' Clothaire said with his usual scowl.

'What a smart dress, Marie. You always look good in midnight blue,' Agathe said approvingly. 'Is Isabelle with you?'

Marie-Laure nodded, her face set.

Agathe exchanged a significant glance with Clothaire and said, 'Actually, I've just remembered that I left something in my coat downstairs. I'll see you in a minute.'

As she turned to make her way towards the cloakroom, Stanislas took her arm.

'Do stay with us for a minute, Agathe,' he said, with a sardonic smile. 'We have only just arrived.'

'With the London gang,' Octave added, gesturing towards Chrissie, Jules and Tom, who were making their way towards them, preceded by Isabelle in her red dress, looking extremely fierce and determined.

'Oh, God,' Clothaire muttered.

'Check it out, darling: Little Red Riding Hood Goes Kick-Arse!' Chrissie whispered in Jules' ear.

Isabelle walked right up to Agathe, who greeted her with a bright,

'*Salut! Ça va?*'

'*Ça va, merci,*' Isabelle replied coldly. 'Where is Daisy?'

'Hmmmm, I really don't know,' Agathe said insouciantly. 'I imagine she's dancing somewhere.'

'Agathe,' Isabelle said with a dangerous edge to her voice. 'I haven't got time for your little games. You can have Clothaire, I really don't care. You're welcome to the Sorbonne job if you're so desperate for it – I'm now planning to stay in England. But you can't have *The Splodge*. Am I making myself clear?'

'How dare you talk about me like that!' Clothaire cried indignantly.

'Be quiet,' Isabelle said without looking at him.

Clothaire spluttered, then was quiet.

Chrissie gave a delighted little whoop. '*Bravo*, darling! What a diva! Look at her, Tom – I swear she's got more attitude than *Attitude* magazine.'

Agathe looked put out for a minute, then drew herself up to her full height and, ignoring Clothaire's increasingly frantic headshakes, said, 'Well, I might as well tell you that Clothaire and I have been lovers for ages. It started long before he met you and, afterwards, we just continued as before. I knew he'd tire of you eventually.'

'I did love you, Isabelle,' Clothaire protested. 'In a way.'

'Except you only really love *me*,' Agathe said smugly, slipping her arm through his.

'Ah yes? And what about *me*?' cried another, very angry voice. They all turned around. Claire stood there, livid with rage.

'Not now, Claire, please,' Clothaire said, looking trapped.

'And why not now?' Claire asked, glaring at him. 'Tell me, does Agathe know about your little London escapade with me?'

'What – London – escapade?' Agathe asked in an arctic tone of voice. 'Clothaire?'

'Claire!' Marie-Laure cried, scandalised. 'If I'd known that's what you wanted my coat for, I would have said no!'

'It was just for one week,' Clothaire said, exasperated. 'If that.'

'You are forgetting all those months in Paris before that,' Claire said mercilessly.

Agathe turned a withering eye on Clothaire, who was dancing from one foot to the other like a very sullen and uncomfortable bear.

'You are also forgetting,' Claire went on furiously, 'what you told me in London – how possessive Agathe was, and that I was the only woman for you.'

Isabelle looked from Claire to Marie-Laure. Both tall, rangy and dark-haired, they did look superficially alike. Now Isabelle understood: it was Claire whom Bella had seen in London with Clothaire – Claire wearing the red coat she'd borrowed from Marie-Laure!

Stanislas patted an ashen-looking Clothaire on the shoulder and said, laughing, 'Well, good luck, *mon vieux*.'

'I am sure that you will think of a way out of this one,' Octave added, putting his arm round Marie-Laure's shoulders.

'Are you all finished?' Isabelle asked crisply. 'Very well. Now, take me to Daisy *at once*.'

For a minute, Agathe tried to hold her gaze. Then she crumpled. 'She's on the roof, through there and up the stairs,' she said, extracting the key from her bag and handing it to Isabelle.

'I am *loving* this staircase, darling,' Chrissie trilled, standing with Daisy at the top of the *grand escalier d'honneur*. 'Believe me, if I weren't wearing some *very* expensive and virtually irreplaceable bondage trousers from Westwood, I would be *skipping* up and down it like Audrey Hepburn in *Funny Face*!'

Daisy smiled, wrapping her pink pashmina more snugly around herself. Having just eaten a lovely hot dinner with her friends in a vast and stunning hall of mirrors, she was beginning to feel much better.

Just at the point when she had seriously begun to worry that her exile on the roof was never going to end, the door had magically swung open, and a small, slender girl dressed in red, with her hair piled up in a fantastic chignon, had stepped out onto the roof: Isabelle! Behind her, Jules and Chrissie emerged, followed by a tall stranger whom Daisy immediately identified as the scrumptious hunk of loveliness, Tom.

Isabelle had held out her hand to help Daisy to her feet. '*Salut*, Daisy,' she said. 'Are you OK?'

'Oh, hi!' Daisy had replied, shivering. 'Yes, I'm fine. Thank you for rescuing me.'

'Thank you for rescuing *me*!' Isabelle had said, squeezing her hand. 'Come on, I will help you. Be careful not to slip.'

It was now close to midnight and dancing was in full swing all over the Opéra. Having checked out the disco, Daisy, Chrissie, Tom, Isabelle and Jules had returned to the *grand escalier* around which hundreds of people were now waltzing.

'Say *what* you like, darlings,' Chrissie mused, dropping down on a small gilt chair, 'I say *trad* is always best when it comes to a ball.'

'It's funny you should say that,' Jules replied tonelessly, sitting down next to him, 'because I thought you were going to desert us when we looked into the disco just now and they were playing Sister Sledge.'

'Once disco-damaged, *always* disco-damaged, remember? Not a *thing* I can do about it.'

For a moment, the three friends sat together in companionable silence, gazing out at the glittering ballroom filled with swelling music and whirling couples. Looking through the anonymous crowd, Daisy could make out Octave dancing with Marie-Laure and, just a little further, Stanislas with Amélie. And over there, that flash of red was Isabelle's dress, swirling as she waltzed rapturously with Tom.

'Excuse me,' an attractive male voice said, addressing Daisy. 'May I have this dance?'

Daisy looked up to see a tall, dark-haired young man in a black uniform with gold buttons – one of the students from the military-college whatsit, presumably – standing before her with a hopeful smile. She smiled back, shaking her head. 'Oh, thank you. But I can't waltz.'

'I can teach you, if you want,' he said politely.

'That's really sweet of you, but no. The other problem is I don't have any shoes on,' she said, stretching out her stockinged feet.

'I promise I will not step on your toes.'

'Sorry. But thanks!'

After watching him bow regretfully and walk away, Chrissie and Jules turned to stare at Daisy.

'*Darling*,' Chrissie said with great intensity, 'are you *insane*? He was *gorgeous*! Did you see the way he looked at you?'

'*And* he had a sword,' Jules added impassively. 'Like a knight. Which is quite cool.'

'I think I need a break from all that stuff,' Daisy said, taking a sip from her glass of champagne. 'Look where it got me in the end: absolutely nowhere.'

'Daisy, my angel,' Chrissie said, putting his arms around her, 'have your little chastity interlude but the moment you get back to London, we're going to find you a grade-A, drop-dead-gorgeous, *super*-delicious boyfriend, I *promise*.'

'Thanks, Chrissie,' Daisy said, hugging him back.

'Speaking of which . . .' Chrissie said slowly, suddenly looking fascinated. 'Who is *that*?'

Daisy followed the direction of his gaze. All she could see was Bertrand sitting alone on a small gilt sofa, dreamily eating his way through a plate of *petits fours*.

'That's Bertrand, a friend of Octave's. But I thought you'd all come together? You must have met him earlier.'

'Darling, *believe* me, if I had, I would remember those *cheekbones*,' Chrissie said, gazing at Bertrand appreciatively. 'He must have been the one who had his helmet on when they collected us in their *divine* motorcycling leathers. And then he *vanished* mysteriously when we got here.'

'Yes, that makes sense,' Daisy said, nodding. 'Bertrand always makes a beeline for the buffet when he gets to a party.'

Watching Chrissie rise and turn to the mirrored wall to straighten his white tie with quick, practised movements, Daisy said gently, 'Chrissie, wait. Bertrand is completely straight.'

Chrissie looked at her gravely. 'Ah, yes, *of course* he is, darling,' he said, before throwing his head back and giving a peal of silvery laughter.

Daisy grinned back. Her friend's instinct had proved pretty unerring in the past.

'Help me out, Daisy darling. I need something of an opening gambit. What's the French for dream? *La rêve?*'

'It's *le rêve*,' Daisy said automatically. 'Dreams are masculine in French.'

'How *fitting*,' Chrissie said, his eyes on Bertrand. 'And a boat is . . . *le bateau?*'

'Yes,' Daisy confirmed, giggling. 'But "dreamboat" doesn't really translate into French. Try saying "*Bonsoir*" instead.'

'Right. See you later, angels,' Chrissie said, gliding away decisively in Bertrand's direction.

Isabelle and Jules watched him sit down next to the young *Pique-Assiette* and help himself to a *petit four*, all the while talking animatedly. Bertrand's face, Daisy noticed, seemed to light up. Within minutes, the two were laughing together.

'Chrissie never ceases to amaze me,' Daisy said. 'I've really missed you two.'

'Yeah,' Jules said, clearing her throat and pushing her spectacles to the top of her nose.

Daisy smiled. Her friend was, she knew, profoundly moved and wanted to conceal it. They sat in silence, then: 'So, Paris: good times or bad times?' Jules asked tersely.

Daisy closed her eyes: she could see, all jumbled together, her picnics in Isabelle's little flat, the gleaming window of Anouk's shop, the beach on the banks of the Seine thronged with glamorous Parisians, Etienne's face as he listened intently to her fashion musings and the cinema screen at the Catacombs party flashing with the words, 'Paris Belongs to Us'.

'Oh, good times! Absolutely!' she said, opening her eyes again. 'It's been a real adventure. I made some great new friends. And I also learned loads about life.'

'Right. Like what?'

'Maybe . . . that you can't always have everything,' Daisy said slowly. 'And that it's completely OK. Take it as it comes.'

Wordlessly, Jules slipped her arm through Daisy's. Daisy smiled at her, leaning against the back of her chair.

'It's almost over. Soon I'll be coming home. And then I can look back on it all and say: "Goodbye, Paris – it's been nice."'

THE END

WELL, NOT QUITE . . .

Epilogue

Daisy turned away from the wall and stretched drowsily. What time *was* it? It still felt like the middle of the night. She slowly counted fifty sheep, her eyes closed. Then she opened them again and turned to lie on her back, looking at the ceiling. It seemed unfamiliar, much higher than usual. It took her a minute to work out where she was: Anouk's loftlike living room, of course. Now she remembered her friends dropping her off after the ball, and how she had collapsed a few minutes later into the sofa bed Anouk had made up for her.

There followed a few blurry flashbacks of the ball, her rooftop adventure and the end of the evening when, stepping out of the Opéra with Jules, she had wondered aloud where Chrissie had disappeared to. Wordlessly, Jules had shown the three breathless text messages Chrissie had sent her in the course of the last hour:

'SORRY, GIRLS, HAD TO GO. HAVE UN-EXPECTEDLY FALLEN IN LOVE. OH GOD, OH GOD. JU-JU, SEE YOU BACK AT HOTEL FOR DEBRIEFING.'

Then: 'OOPS CHANGE OF PLAN, SWEETIE. CATCH UP WITH YOU TOMORROW INSTEAD.'

And finally: 'NO, SCRAP THAT. PLEASE ASK LOVELY HOTEL TO HOLD ON TO ONE'S

THINGS. WILL COLLECT THEM ASAP BUT ACTUALLY NO NEED FOR ANY CLOTHES WHATSOEVER IN FORESEEABLE FUTURE. MIGHT STAY ON IN PAREE FOR TEENSY BIT. BON VOYAGE TOMORROW, JU-JU! BIG LOVE TO DAZE!'

'Yeah – he bolted with the dreamboat,' Jules had concluded.

It was very unlike Chrissie to be so lackadaisical about his beloved clothes, Daisy thought drowsily, to say nothing about his grooming products. Clearly something unusual had happened – something impulsive and romantic. Well, Bertrand was very sweet. Go, Chrissie.

She stretched. Now what time was it? She hadn't worn her watch last night because it didn't go with her dress. She needed to find her mobile. She turned her head and looked at the floor. She could just about make out her clutch bag where she had dropped it last night, with most of its contents spilling out – a jumble of keys, purse, lipstick and miniature hairspray. No phone, though. Where could it be? Her coat pocket, maybe?

Daisy rolled over, reached for the chair where she had dropped her clothes and located her pink coat. Drowsily, she flopped back down and felt her way inside the first pocket. To her surprise her fingers encountered an unexpected object. She pulled it out – it was a white envelope. Daisy frowned: where had this come from?

She yawned. There was a reading lamp, somewhere – yes, there. She ripped the envelope open and pulled out a single sheet of paper. She brought it close to her face, peering at it through sleepy eyes. It was in French and began, traditionally enough, with the greeting '*Chère Daisy*'.

'*From the very first time I saw you,*' it went on, '*I knew without a shadow of a doubt that I had found the great love of my life.*'

Daisy sat bolt upright in bed. The rest of the letter read:

> *I am sure you have already guessed how I feel about you, although I'm doing everything I can to conceal it. I think about you constantly. I can't eat or sleep. I only live for the times when we meet, for those precious moments when I can gaze at your lovely face.*
>
> *You are the most adorable person I have ever met and I do adore you.*
>
> *I have never felt this sort of passion for anyone else and I know myself well enough to realise that I am unlikely ever to feel it again. There is no one else for me but you.*
>
> *Daisy, I have found it much easier to declare myself for the first time in writing. But now, would you allow me to speak to you about this face to face?*
>
> *Please meet me tomorrow at noon on the Pont des Arts, between the Louvre and the Bibliothèque Mazarine. I very much hope you will be there.*
>
> *If, however, you choose not to come, I promise I won't mention any of this again.*
>
> *Yours,*
>
> *Etienne*

Daisy fell back on her pillows, silently mouthing the words: 'Oh my God'. Though she'd had a certain amount of experience of men, she had never before received a letter of this kind. Now wide awake, she reread it several times with the sort of extreme attention she usually reserved for reports on the new collections.

It was astonishing, yes, but it was there in black and white. Etienne, who had always seemed so cool and distant, so wrapped up in his work. Etienne, whom she had thought of as utterly out of bounds. Serious Etienne with his long lashes and his rare, flashing smiles. Etienne *loved* her. He really did.

And she, what did she feel? Well, she . . . She felt hot and cold, delighted and terrified all at the same time. And now she became aware of a strong rising tide within her, something that had been there a long time. It was on the tip of her tongue like a memory coming up to the surface but that wouldn't reveal itself to her. What was it? What did it mean? Was it possible that she could . . . that she did, in fact, love Etienne? There was only one way to find out for sure. She would, of course, go and meet him later on the bridge. They would talk it over. Oh, what to wear for such an occasion, she wondered, spreading her hair all over the pillow. She would go shopping later this morning and buy something *especially* pretty, something irresistible. Shifting around in the bed to put her feet against the back of the sofa, she began to read Etienne's letter once more, letting every word sink in.

It was then that she noticed the date at the top of the page. February the fourteenth. That was Valentine's Day, of course. The most romantic date of the year, how lovely . . . Hang on a minute! What? No, it *couldn't* be, because on Valentine's Day, Daisy clearly remembered, she had gone out to dinner with Raoul to a mega-trendy new Chinese place. And that had been . . . seven weeks ago!

She sat up again and thought hard. Her pink coat! She hadn't worn it for quite a while. In fact the last time had been . . . yes, Valentine's Day. On that day she had met Etienne in the afternoon before going out with Raoul in the evening. Now she understood! Etienne had decided to tell her that he loved her by means of a handwritten letter. But he had not dared to give her the letter directly, so he had slipped it into her coat pocket, thinking that she would find it when she got home. But she hadn't. She'd never been terribly methodical about emptying her pockets, for one thing. And then, she remembered, there had been a spell of exceptionally warm weather, and she had gone out without a coat for ages.

And meanwhile . . . Oh, meanwhile, Etienne had waited for her in vain on the Pont des Arts, all those weeks ago! And since then . . . well, that bit was even worse, Daisy thought, clutching her forehead. He and Daisy had carried on meeting to talk about his research – and she, of course, had not *known*. Vaguely registering that Etienne was a little withdrawn, she had chattered away and made silly jokes just as she had before. He must have thought her so cruel and unfeeling, so cold-hearted – a real monster. Now she remembered the dark circles she had noticed under his eyes. And there had been occasions when it looked like he hadn't even shaved, when he was usually so immaculately turned out. She had put that down to hard work making him cranky. But it hadn't been crankiness. It had been sadness, perhaps even despair.

She swung her legs around and sat on the edge of the bed in her nightshirt. She would call him. That was the thing to do. She located her mobile in her other coat pocket: it was half past five. Never mind. She searched for his number, her heart thumping. There were four, five, six, seven rings, then an electronic voice informed her in French that the person she was trying to call was not available. The tone sounded and she jumped.

'Oh! Um, hello, Etienne, it's Daisy. Hi! It's very early and I'm very sorry to be disturbing you. Though I'm not really disturbing you, obviously, because you're not picking up. Which is fine. In fact it's *brilliant* that you're asleep. But, um, I wanted to speak to you as soon as possible because . . .'

Because what? I only just got your letter from two months ago because I live in a slightly slower parallel universe?

Daisy dithered, then resumed in a panic: 'Um, er, I think it would be best if we met, actually. I mean, I know you're busy with the book, but . . . Call me as soon as you get this. OK, bye,' she finished breathlessly.

Now she'd have to wait for Etienne to wake up, check his messages and get in touch. There was no other way. Or . . . she could just go and see him. Now, immediately. Why the hell not? No faffing – just put a coat on and go! After all, she knew where he lived. If this wasn't an emergency, what was? Daisy stood up and, for the first time since the age of eight – when she had first started selecting her own clothes from the Next catalogue – did not give any thought to her outfit. She threw on her coat over her nightshirt. Over there was one of the battered pink plimsolls she'd worn yesterday before getting changed for the ball. It took her barely a minute to locate its partner behind the sofa. After tying her pashmina around her neck, she scribbled a note for Anouk, grabbed her clutch bag and went out into the street.

Anouk lived in a tiny street in the Marais. Daisy had hoped to find a taxi outside, but there weren't any, so she headed straight for the Rue de Rivoli, and beyond it, the river. It was still dark and the streets were quiet, but there were already signs that Paris was waking up: dustbin collectors out on patrol in their green lorries and bundles of today's papers being dropped outside news kiosks. Daisy walked on. This must be what it was like to be a homing pigeon. A few minutes after crossing the bridge, she emerged onto the Rue des Ecoles.

One of the very few personal facts she knew about Etienne was that he rented a *chambre de bonne* – a tiny studio flat – which he claimed was the smallest in all of Paris. This was a temporary arrangement while his own apartment was being refurbished.

Daisy turned into the Rue Monge and suddenly, there it was, the Place Cardinal-Lemoine, with all its shops still closed and their iron curtains pulled down. Etienne lived on a street just off the square, the Rue des Boulangers. Hooray: here it was, right in front of her. Having located Etienne's building, Daisy stood outside the *porte cochère*, staring in frustration at the impenetrable panel of letters and numbers that guarded the door. The building could only be accessed by dialling the right electronic door code. Daisy did not know the code and there was no way of guessing it. It was now almost six o'clock. Should she try his phone again? Or come back later? She was beginning to walk away when the door suddenly opened wide, as though in answer to her desire. An old lady emerged with a chic little dog on a leash – a brown terrier wearing a tiny red tartan coat – and held the door open for Daisy, who thanked her and stepped inside.

Only one staircase and no lift. Grateful for the months of training she had had in Isabelle's building, Daisy bounded up the stairs to the top of the house. There were seven doors, but the name of Etienne Deslisses was clearly written above one of the bells. She pinched her cheeks and shook her hair out, and then, before scaring herself by thinking too much about what she was doing, rang the bell. There was silence on the other side. She rang again, twice, and then once more for good luck. This time she heard a bit of a commotion, as Etienne presumably jumped out of his skin prior to falling out of bed.

'*Oui*?' he said behind the door, sounding none too pleased.

'Etienne, it's Daisy.'

A full minute's silence greeted this announcement. Then Daisy heard him moving about – throwing some clothes on, possibly. Eventually the door opened and he stood on the threshold in jeans and a sweatshirt, which he had put on back to front. He'd obviously attempted to smooth down his hair as well, but Daisy could see one untamed bit sticking up at the back of his head. He stared at her.

'It's really you.'

'Yes, it's me! Hi! Can I come in?'

'Of course,' Etienne said, letting her through and closing the door behind her. 'Tell me, is there a fire or something?'

'N-no, no fire,' Daisy said slowly.

The room she walked into was still warm from sleep. The window blind was down. She looked around, taking in a table and two chairs in front of the window, piles of books everywhere and the bed he'd just got out of, its white duvet flung back like the crest of a wave. Daisy put her bag down on the table next to an object of some considerable antiquity – Etienne's typewriter. She rubbed her face, took a deep breath and turned to face him. He was leaning against the door, his arms crossed. She threw herself into it.

'This is going to sound a bit mad but the thing is I got your letter today. Your letter from February. I mean, I've only just read it. I found it this morning.'

Etienne's eyes narrowed as he digested this news.

'I'm so sorry,' Daisy went on. 'It had been in my coat pocket all this time.'

Etienne, silent, continued to lean against the door. Daisy turned away to give him time and discovered that what he'd said was true: his kitchen was even more minuscule than Isabelle's. He *actually* lived in a garret. How utterly fantastic. She continued, ignoring her shaking hands, 'I thought I should tell you right away. Because until an hour ago, I didn't know. I didn't know anything!'

She glanced at him. He was looking pensive, rubbing the back of his hand against his mouth.

'What I mean is that if I'd . . . if I'd found your letter in February, then I . . . I would have been there to meet you on the bridge. That's all I wanted to say, really.'

Etienne let his hand drop slowly to his side. His eyes met Daisy's across the room.

'And so you came here right away, just like that?' he said, taking a few steps from the door.

'Yes!' Daisy said, rolling her eyes. 'Actually, I'm still in my nightie.' She pulled one side of her coat open. 'Ta-da!'

Etienne began to laugh. 'And I thought it was another amazing designer outfit.'

'No. Although,' Daisy said, looking down critically, 'now that you mention it, it might actually work, but with different shoes. Chunky biker's boots, perhaps. And this is really a man's nightshirt, so I think it would need a belt to turn it into daywear. That would be a lot more flattering, like a shirtwaister sort of thing. But I didn't have time to think about any of *that*,' she said hurriedly, remembering her purpose. 'I wanted to see you. I'm sorry I'm so horribly early. And horribly late, of course, as well.'

Etienne nodded, smiling. '*Mieux vaut tard que jamais.*'

'Better late than never? Yes, I think so, too.'

'You want a coffee?'

'That would be lovely.'

She attempted to follow him into the tiny kitchen, but it soon became apparent – after almost bumping into each other several times as Etienne reached for the kettle and realising that he would have to squeeze impossibly close to her to get at the cups and sugar – that there was only room in it for one person. She sat down at the table instead.

'How are you, anyway?' she asked nervously after a few moments' silence.

'Stunned, I think. But fine,' Etienne said, bringing the cups through.

'That's great. Because lately, I thought you seemed a bit . . . down.'

'I was. Very down.'

Etienne poured them both coffee and offered Daisy the sugar bowl. She dropped one lump into her cup and stirred.

'I wish I'd known sooner, you know, about, um . . . Do you have any milk?'

'Ah, no. Sorry.' He got up suddenly. 'I'll go out and get you some.'

My hero, Daisy thought.

'Please, no, it's fine,' she said hurriedly. 'I'm sure everything's still closed. I'll have it black like a French person. It'll be an adventure.'

Etienne sat down again. They each had a sip of coffee, then he said, 'I'm sorry. I'm not normally so . . . You've taken me by surprise, completely. I can't believe you're here.'

'I am here. Really.'

'No, I don't believe you,' he said, his chin resting on his hand. 'It's a dream.'

Daisy reached over and gently pinched his arm. They laughed and the tension relaxed a little. Etienne caught Daisy's hand in his own. Slowly their fingers became entwined.

'Is this new?' he said, indicating the heart brooch on her lapel. 'I haven't seen it before.'

'Oh, I've had it for years. But for a while it sort of . . . went missing. Then I found it again, quite recently.'

Etienne nodded and placed her hand on his own heart. He then brought the palm of her other hand to his lips and kissed it. Daisy was grateful to be sitting down. The room was pitching a little.

'I think we should go out,' Etienne said after another pause. 'For a walk.' He stood up, still holding her hands. 'There are many things I need to say to you. All the things I wanted to say in February. And now it's morning. Look.'

Daisy looked: golden light was peeping out all around the edges of the window blind. She smiled at Etienne. Now they could see each other much better.

'Let's walk to the river,' Etienne said, smiling back.

Outside, the streets were still quiet, and for a while it was almost possible to believe that she and Etienne were alone in the city. They found a little more activity when they emerged onto the riverside. Some *bouquinistes* were already setting up their stalls. A few fitness enthusiasts jogged past them. Etienne and Daisy walked side by side along the Seine, past Notre-Dame and towards the Pont des Arts. At first they were both silent, then Etienne took her hand in his again and began to describe their first encounter in great detail: how Daisy had looked, what she had said.

'I wasn't prepared for you, you know, when you appeared in that pink coat, the one you said was lucky. I wasn't expecting you to be so beautiful. I thought you'd be more of a –'

'A fashion freak extraordinaire?'

'Well, my source was Clothaire. He did say you were *pas mal, physiquement*, but . . . let's say that he has very rigid ideas about how girls should dress.'

'Yes. *Chacun à son goût*.'

'Exactly. And then, you turned out to be so incredibly interesting, far more of an expert than I'd been led to believe. You were a godsend. And . . . by the end of our second meeting I was head over heels in love with you. It's lucky I recorded all our talks so I could play them back later. Because most of the time I was so distracted by your . . . physical presence . . . that I couldn't concentrate at all.'

'Is *that* why you were so quiet most of the time?'

'Yes. By Christmas I knew it was very serious. January was very hard for me. All I could think about was how to tell you, but I knew you had a boyfriend, and you seemed happy. Nor did I want to interrupt your train of thoughts. Our conversations were precious.'

Daisy turned to him, delighted. 'You were really interested in what I had to say?'

'Of course,' he said, surprised. 'Fashion is more than a passion for you – it's your philosophy of life. I couldn't have hoped for a more illuminating source of knowledge.'

They were now on the Quai de Conti. The Pont des Arts was in sight. They climbed the stairs leading up to it, walked to a bench near the middle and sat down.

'I chose this as a meeting place,' Etienne said, 'because the view is beautiful all around, wherever you turn.'

Daisy gazed off into the distance at the tip of the Ile de la Cité – pink houses and a tiny patch of greenery – then turned to him. 'How long did you wait? On that day?'

'For a while. Daisy, it really doesn't matter now.'

'Oh!'

He must have been there for hours, thinking up all kinds

of reasons why she should be late. Any passing girl would have looked like her, but none of them ever was. Daisy could imagine how his mood, exhilarated and hopeful at first, had then gradually descended into the most terrible sense of disappointment and failure. And then he would have gone home on his own. It made her feel cold just to think about it.

'But you could have called me,' she said gently. 'Why didn't you?'

He frowned. 'Because you were supposed to be there, or not be there. It was the way I'd set it up in my mind.'

'And in the letter I didn't find.'

'Yes,' he said, laughing. 'There was a flaw in my plan. I've always been far too inclined to rely on abstract theory.'

'But afterwards, when we met a couple of days later, couldn't you tell that I had no idea that anything was going on?'

'I thought that ignoring it, pretending it had never happened, was your way of –'

'Of letting you down easy? Are you *serious*? You must have thought I was a complete cow!'

'No,' he said, looking at the river. 'I accepted everything that came from you.'

'How could you stand it?'

'Not very well,' he said, turning to look at Daisy. 'But it was worth it in the end.'

Daisy slipped her hand through his arm and put her head on his shoulder. They sat without speaking. Meanwhile she was turning a question over in her mind, about something that still confused her.

'Etienne? You remember my friend Marie-Laure? You met her once at the Sorbonne.'

'Yes, I think so.'

'Well, she told me that in order to be a brilliant big-shot *intello* like you, you had to be completely dedicated to the life of the mind and not care about anything or anybody else. That you had to be like . . . a monk or something.'

Etienne stared at her. 'A monk?'

'That's what she said. And that's also how I felt about you.' She bit her lip and fell silent.

'Ah, so you thought I was above carnality,' Etienne said pensively. '*Très intéressant.*'

Daisy glanced at him sideways, still a little worried. 'But I mean you're *not*, are you? Above it, I mean?'

He held her gaze. 'Daisy, I would love to throw you down on this bench right now. Surely you realise that.'

'Oh. OK,' she said breathlessly. 'I mean, I do realise it.'

He gently squeezed her arm with his. 'You want some breakfast? Shall we go back? We'll get some croissants on the way, if you like.'

'That would be lovely.'

As they stood up and faced each other, some of the original tension returned. After a couple of heartbeats, Etienne drew Daisy's face to his and kissed her mouth. It was a tremendous relief to let herself fall against him and to kiss him back extensively. How amazing, Daisy thought as she reluctantly pulled away to get her breath and gazed into his dark eyes, that you could get this close to someone physically and still find him so enigmatic.

There was a brief pause, then: 'You know what would be terrible?' Etienne said seriously, tracing the outline of her mouth with his thumb.

'N-no. What?' Daisy managed to say.

'If after all that – the letter you didn't find, the misunderstanding, your visit this morning – we turned out not to be compatible. Sexually.'

'Oh, yes,' she whispered against his shoulder, 'that would be terrible.'

'It always comes down to theory *and* practice, doesn't it? I don't know, perhaps we should experiment a little, just to be sure.'

'That's a good idea.'

'Like this, for example,' Etienne said, sliding his hands under her coat and proceeding to kiss her throat with slow, tormenting deliberation, and just hard enough for the bridge they stood on to start pitching at a most languorous pace. Daisy closed her eyes and tilted her head back. She could have sworn that the Pont des Arts had come free from its shackles and was now travelling slowly down the Seine, like a raft in the middle of the ocean.

'So, *not* a monk, then,' she murmured after a moment.

'No, absolutely not,' he said, the expression on his face a bewitching mixture of shyness and desire. 'Still interested?'

'Yes!' Daisy said, clasping her arms around his neck. 'And I would say, based on this highly scientific experiment, that we are *fairly* compatible.'

Through half-closed eyes she watched over his shoulder the approach of two buskers carrying a guitar and a saxophone. Sunburnt and dishevelled, they looked like

Australian surfers on a year out. They hesitated for a moment, looking around, then chose a spot opposite the bench where she and Etienne had been sitting. The one with the guitar put down his open case on the floor and arranged a small pile of CDs next to it. The other musician stood looking out at the river, entranced. Daisy could see his point. It was the most perfect springtime morning. Trimmed with green, the waters of the Seine shimmered gloriously in the sun as the first white riverboats of the day slowly made their way under the bridge.

She pulled back a little to look at Etienne's face and smiled up at him saucily. 'So tell me, *Monsieur*, did your off-the-scale intellect ever allow you to think about me sometimes, in your bed at night?'

'All the time. I didn't sleep that much, so I did a lot of thinking. And when I did manage to fall asleep, if I was lucky, you would be in my dreams.'

'Nice dreams?'

'Oh, very, very nice,' he said, kissing her hair, 'once in a while.'

'I see.'

'Yes. You don't mind?'

Daisy shook her head, smiling. She was listening with one ear to the first tentative jazzy strummings of the guitar, the first exploratory arpeggios of the mellow saxophone.

'But you know, most of the time,' Etienne went on, stroking her face and looking into her eyes, 'I had these terrible anxiety dreams, like nightmares. It was always the same: I looked for you everywhere in the streets at night. Half the time I didn't even know where I was or where I was going. It felt like I would never be able to find you again. Daisy, why are you crying? I hope they're tears of joy.'

Daisy nodded, unable to speak. The tide had now risen fully, that elusive memory was now bobbing on the surface of her consciousness. What had been on the tip of her tongue was Etienne's name – that was all! Her dreams, her dreams! That was what they had meant, from the very beginning! Oh *my*, as Chrissie would no doubt put it. So this was, in fact, it – the real biggie.

'Etienne, I love you!' she exclaimed.

'Oh, *you*,' he said, his mouth on hers. 'Say it again.'

'*Je t'aime.*'

'*Je t'aime aussi.* You're trembling.'

'A little bit. But I'm not cold.'

'I know. Come here.'

The musicians picked up the pace, and launched into a song Daisy had never heard before. By now the sun was deliciously warm and the gilt dome of the Bibliothèque Mazarine sparkled in a Parisian sky of radiant blue. Etienne pulled Daisy close to him and, slowly, they began to dance.

An exclusive interview with Muriel Zagha....

What was the inspiration for Finding Monsieur Right?

It's a piece of fiction loosely inspired by my own experience – I have worked both as an academic and as a fashion PR and am, like Isabelle, a French expat in London.

The idea of the Paris-London flat exchange came to me when I was on holiday in France and kept noticing, as ever, how incredibly different people are on either side of the Channel. I just wondered idly what would happen to these two girls once they were transplanted into each other's world. Then I became pregnant with my son. It was a very happy time and it triggered something: I sat down to write and the whole thing really came to life.

As a French writer writing in English, did you find Daisy harder to write than Isabelle?

No. The writing of the book was powered by the contrast between two temperaments. It was fun to keep switching from one to the other, between Daisy's enthusiastic ditziness and Isabelle's (hopefully comical) serious-mindedness.

Obviously, I have inside knowledge of what it's like to be French, and my educational background is very similar to Isabelle's. Her circle of Parisian friends was inspired by the very specific sliver of people I knew when I was a student – typically, young people from the haute bourgeoisie who like to intellectualize everything!

When it came to the British side of things, I have probably lived here long enough – almost twenty years – to have become somewhat acclimatised, and in any case the idea was always to go against certain stereotypes, in particular the idea that all French girls are raving sex kittens. Here it's Daisy who's the bombshell and Isabelle who's the repressed, buttoned-up one.

And in a similar vein, are you more like Daisy or Isabelle?

They're both my girls and I love them equally, but neither of them is based on me. With a biggish cast, you tend to channel yourself into many different characters. I suspect most of what I'm really like is split between Chrissie the hat maker and Legend the uncouth goth – though I personally draw the line at opening beer bottles with my teeth.

Which would you choose if you could only choose one: fashion or academia?

I am becoming increasingly frivolous in middle age, so probably fashion, but only provided I could be as ground-breaking and revered as Savage!

What do you think the most useful phrase an English woman in Paris should know?

Probably a firm '*Laissez-moi tranquille!*' (Leave me alone!) as French men can be very persistent. French comic writer Pierre Daninos wrote: 'In the street, French men gaze at women; Englishmen walk past them.' It's an entirely different level of exposure for a girl.

And what about as a French woman in England?

'Hello, I'm French.' – a good all-round ice-breaker. Beyond that you find yourself up to your neck in an ocean of complexity and perplexity. The English language is wonderfully subtle: something as simple as an 'Oh, really?' can mean so many different things.

Do you dream in English or French?

Both, mysteriously, depending on the context. My subconscious is bilingual.

Which book are you reading at the moment?

The Allure of Chanel, by travel writer Paul Morand, a fascinating memoir based of conversations he had with the couturière in the 1940s, which suggests overall that fashion revolutions are not achieved by those blessed with a sweet and accommodating disposition.

Who are your favourite authors?

From heavyweight to featherweight: Proust, Jane Austen and PG Wodehouse. Comedy of manners is my favourite thing.

Which classic have you always meant to read and never got round to it?

Too many to mention, but I'd say *Don Quixote*, which I'm afraid I always used to refer to confidently in my essays when I was a student.

What are your top five books of all time?

A terrifying question. I'll go for five favourite books written by women:

Gentlemen Prefer Blondes (1925), by Anita Loos – the hilarious diary of the archetypal gold-digging blonde.

The Secret History (1992), by Donna Tartt – in many ways the perfect novel, combining as it does crime and the college story.

La Princesse de Clèves (1678), by Madame de Lafayette – one of the greatest French novels, this is a tale of forbidden passion set at the royal court.

To Love and Be Wise (1950), by Josephine Tey – an utterly astonishing thriller set in the English countryside.

Cold Comfort Farm (1932), by Stella Gibbons – a fantastic work of pastiche with a wonderfully bossy heroine and the best-ever scene featuring porridge.

Do you have a favourite time of day to write? A favourite place? What's your writing process: are you a planner?

I am, to the extent that I do write a detailed scenario and cast list before I start. Then I write chronologically with an idea of where I'm going. What's wonderful is when things suddenly start to move of their own accord – characters speak their own lines and make decisions that sometimes take me by surprise. The book becomes a real place where I can go, like Dorothy in *The Wizard of Oz*.

I like to write at my own little desk, which I've had since I was fourteen, with the sound of London traffic in the background. The question of a favourite time of day